S

~~NOT RENEWABLE~~

911   SILBER, Joan.

Household words.

~~NOT RENEWABLE~~

HOUSEHOLD WORDS

HOUSEHOLD WORDS

Joan Silber

THE VIKING PRESS NEW YORK

Acknowledgments:
J. B. Lippincott and Harold Ober Associates:
From "The Night Will Never Stay" from
Eleanor Farjeon's Poems for Children by
Eleanor Farjeon. Copyright 1951 by
Eleanor Farjeon. Reprinted by permission.

Portions of this work appeared, in
slightly different form, in *Mulch* (Summer 1976).

First Published in 1980 by The Viking Press
625 Madison Avenue, New York, N.Y. 10022
Published simultaneously in Canada by
Penguin Books Canada Limited

LIBRARY OF CONGRESS CATALOGING IN PUBLICATION DATA
Silber, Joan.
Household words.
I. Title.
PZ4.S571Ho [PS3569.I414] 813'.5'4 79–14742
ISBN 0–670–38037–7

Printed in the United States of America
Set in Trump Mediaeval

For
David Glotzer and
Mark Bregman

HOUSEHOLD WORDS

I

Rhoda was pregnant in 1940. From her mother, a woman with progressive leanings, she got books about birth. Also suggestions for names, bids on behalf of dead uncles. The feminine form for Harold would be Helen. Be active. Drink a pint of milk a day. A quart even. Eat a little meat. But cooked well—no germs. "Talk to your husband," she said to Rhoda.

This last bit of advice, although unnecessary, affected Rhoda pleasurably. Leonard had a way of calling her "kiddo" which was not at all the way actors said it in the movies, where it was a tough word. Rhoda did not, like some of her friends, make the mistake of expecting life to be too much like the movies. Ginger Rogers was not Jewish. Clark Gable had probably never even met a Jew before he went to Hollywood. What she did expect from ordinary occasions was a certain zippiness of speech. "That's a hot one," she used to say when anyone said anything funny. Lenny liked to say, "Let's get this show on the road." They mispronounced words on purpose. "Have some vegetaybles," she would say over dinner. "I don't mind if I diddle-do," he'd say.

She read the books her mother gave her. It was all very matter-of-fact; your baby passed through a series of diagrams like the outlines on a Parcheesi board. The section on congenital heart defects was unnerving, as was the mention of nephritis, hereditary blood disease, mongolism, and miscarriage. On one page she felt smug (for Christ's sake, *every* one knew that), on the next page she felt stranded, a visitor in a foreign country where, watching her p's and q's at every turn, she could unwittingly lapse into a deep and awesome crime. It occurred to Rhoda that she didn't know how to be pregnant. *Everyone makes mistakes.* A ruin as awful as the girl who bled to death under Fatty Arbuckle's soda bottle. A spoilage you could never make up. The fat funny-man gone into hiding, producing films under the name "Will B. Good."

None of her friends would believe she was pregnant. This was largely because she hadn't told anyone, until the start of the fourth month, when she no longer felt, as she said, "weak on her pins." A secondary symptom persisted in the form of clogged sinuses. Having her nose run all the time made her feel oddly loose and wet as though she were crying. Any sad news was sadder, as the water gummed up in her eyes and she wiped her nose with a handkerchief. It was like a corny movie touching you unawares.

Her friends were a bit put out that she hadn't told them, hadn't come to them to complain. "I can't believe it," they said, suspicious. "A skinny malink like you." "Rhoda," they said, "you're such a kidder. Come on."

The three women were drinking coffee in her friend Hinda's dinette at a square table covered with yellow oilcloth. They were sturdy young women with bodies tucked solidly into their blouses. Hinda, sitting next to Rhoda, stroked the flat lap of Rhoda's brown crepe skirt. Rhoda gave her a tight, fishy look, and she withdrew her hand.

"No stomach," Hinda said. "But you're wearing a girdle. Rhody, please, are you kidding?"

"Yuk, yuk," Rhoda said.

"You really are a character," Annie Marantz said. Annie was a wiry woman, barely five feet tall; at thirty, she was only four years older than Rhoda, but she was sinewy all over; she looked as though someone had chewed on her like an orange. "Ah," she said, "you'll be a swell mother. Don't get all nervous." Rhoda did not consider herself the nervous type. "Listen, let me tell you from experience," Annie said, "don't have one too soon after the first."

"You're rushing her," Hinda said, laughing.

Hinda was especially hurt that Rhoda hadn't told her. Rhoda could tell. Hinda had been Rhoda's friend when they were five. Rhoda even as a child had had a startling hardness; she was athletic and boisterous and powerfully light, and she used to pick on Hinda. Hinda, round-faced as a plum, had always forgiven easily enough because she couldn't bear to live without Rhoda's favor.

"Plus," Annie was saying, "I've really got three babies. I mean, Philip makes a third." Philip was Annie's husband.

"Oh, but Leonard's not like that," Hinda volunteered. The women murmured and sighed. Leonard was a great favorite with them. "There's a fineness to him," Hinda said. "Never coarse. A real person. Rare."

"I bet he'll never hit the kid," Annie said. "You wait—you'll have to do it all."

Rhoda felt that the women were speaking in a way that made them sound less intelligent and simpler than their true natures; her news had spurred them on to it. Now Hinda was talking about their childhoods, about something Rhoda had done in the first grade. A boy had come up from behind and pulled her sash and she had given him a bloody nose. Rhoda did not remember any of this; she thought Hinda must be talking about someone else. She did remember that, coming from a home where her mother couldn't stand dawdlers, at school she had been amazed by the slow dreaminess of the other children. The boys kicked at the chairs in front of them and gazed sulkily at their shoes; the girls squirmed in their starched dresses and said their names in tiny piping voices. Rhoda had come back from the first day of school disgusted.

"Hah," Annie said, "wait till you have one like yourself."

"At least the house is plenty big enough," Hinda said. Rhoda's house was actually slightly bigger than either Hinda's or Annie's. All three of them had moved to the area within the past few years, to the small, rather old township, in the vanguard of a population shift out of Newark.

Rhoda was now looking around at Hinda's kitchen, which was green. That is, everything that could be painted—the window frames and the wainscoting—was swabbed with a light mint green, a color born to fade. On the upper walls in the breakfast nook was a wallpaper with pictures of teapots, their spouts tilted in mad gaiety; dashing beneath them was the repeating caption, "Tip me over . . . Pour me out . . ."

Hinda's cat—an ordinary cat, a striped chesty animal which did not move around much—circled Rhoda, stretching its chin over her ankles. Rhoda stamped her foot, and the cat flinched. "It's overfed," Rhoda said, looking at the cat's bulging side, which it was sliding against her skirt. Rhoda hated all fat things. She would chide loose-fleshed old ladies: *you just let yourself go.* Of chubby schoolchildren she asked: *what does your mother feed you?*

"Not a genius among cats," Rhoda said. "Get it away from me."

Hinda picked up the animal and carried it against her bosom out to the porch; the cat, who did not like to be picked up, stiffened his legs in protest. "Ouch," Hinda said.

"Gads," Rhoda said, when Hinda returned to the kitchen. "You've got a red mark on your neck—it's like a welt."

Annie said, "Rhoda, enough with the animal already. Have a heart."

"He's not really a bad cat," Hinda said.

"Well, let's not discuss it." Rhoda smiled, the peacemaker.

———

That evening, when Leonard saw her nod and stare over her dessert, he said, "Feeling tired, kiddo?" He was waiting for her to wince, smile wanly. She was watching the fuzzed outlines of her dish of canned peaches, willing them to come back into focus. They were still more or less unappetizing, with their frayed edges where the pit had been removed. They would go down soft and floppy; their color was like the yolk of an egg. For spite she ate one. "Eat your peaches," she said, chewing. "You like them."

"Yes, ma'am," Leonard said.

The dog, a patient, sighing cocker spaniel, came over and sniffed at their knees, which he was not supposed to do near the table. Leonard gave him a piece of cookie.

"Hinda wants to bring over a batch of her old maternity clothes for me to go through," Rhoda said.

"That's nice of her. She's broader than you though—isn't she?—in the shoulders and all."

"Also, you know what she wears. She wears those moronic ruffles."

Rhoda had not worn ruffles for twenty years; she had not worn ruffles even for her own wedding. She had dressed in a plum-colored traveling outfit and Leonard had worn a business suit; they had opted for street clothes, exactly as though they were going on with the business of their life. She still had the hat somewhere—a triumph of smartness, worn tilted to one side, and trimmed with a small bird, its feathers dyed deep wine and rose. Her brother Andy had told her she looked like Francis of Assisi in it, but he always thought anything fashionable was foolish. Rhoda had never felt less foolish than when she had stood before the hallway mirror (with her mother holding a hand mirror behind her) and set the hat in place with a pin. She remembered—happily—that the tilt of the hat had looked almost military, like the uniform of some exotic foreign army.

Leonard still looked much the way he had looked then. She had never seen him without his mustache. He didn't, like vainer men, touch or stroke his mustache. His only habit of that sort was to smooth the back of his hair where it was thinning, but he did this often when he was thinking before speaking, so it had the look of someone taking his own phrenological reading. He was doing it now.

"It's too bad we can't use Pluto for a middle name if it's a boy," he said.

"*Pluto*?" Rhoda said. "Pluto is a dog's name." Their own dog, on hearing his generic title, lifted his head, expectant. "Not you, Timmy," Rhoda said.

"Walt Disney ruined the name already, I know," Leonard said. "He made a joke out of it. But it was such a tremendous thing when they discovered the planet. I think the newspapers I saved from then are still at my mother's."

Leonard was the most serious of spectators at planetariums; he was interested in all unmapped possibilities—the dark side of the moon, that sort of thing—and he used to quote some raffish professor's poem, "O moon, when will mankind / Ever see thy glorious behind?"

"I'm for normal human names," Rhoda said.

"I guess I am too, actually."

Sometimes in the nights they lay in bed and amused themselves thinking of silly names—Ada Maida Taber or Thrushbottom Snazzlewit Taber—but under all of it they rested secure in the pleasantly prolonged expectation that between them they would choose judiciously. They were competent people, companionable in their adequacy. Rhoda nibbled at the piece of lemon from her tea, and then she took up the lemon from Leonard's cup and chewed that too.

Tonight Leonard cleared the dishes so Rhoda would stop hopping up and down like a rabbit. He was short and tightly built, and when he rolled up his sleeves his forearms looked raw and muscled. Like most men he was awkward at dishwashing, and the sight of him—normally so measured and decisive with his hands—poking at the inside of a glass with a sponge was quite endearing.

During the week Leonard worked full-time as a pharmacist, so that he and Rhoda, who taught school five days a week, were both away from the house a good deal. It always surprised Rhoda that the house did not stay cleaner. Where did it come from, the dirt? Airborne dust motes, afloat in the light of the rooms, descended on their own schedules and settled on all the surfaces by the time Rhoda got home in the late afternoons.

In spring and summer, when the sofa and wing chairs were covered with slipcovers (a giant print of lilacs on a brown ground) and the Venetian blinds let the sun come in in stripes, a little glisten of dust was not so bad. Winter solids were harder to keep up, but also, Rhoda thought, more restful to the eye. She preferred the house then, when it was all beige and brown and maroon—the upholstered shapes, worsted and plush, sitting in their neutral peaceableness on the rug, which was a taupe color, like stockings. The furniture all had Chippendale ball-and-claw feet—an oddly fierce touch, even Rhoda sometimes noticed, for her living room. Leonard liked to ask if the coffee table were going to spring at him. But even the carved feet had, when taken in the proper spirit, a stiff stillness, which was the presiding tone of the house—with its snake plants in their shallow ceramic holders on the Pembroke tables, and on either side of the mantel, figurines and vases in shelves at the windows.

It was an unremarkable house, but as the home of a couple who were only just past "starting out," it was notably filled and complete, and Rhoda always left it in the mornings a bit sadly, as she locked the back door and put the washed milk bottles in their box on the porch. She walked out through the driveway toward the bus stop, and the dog on his run barked his daily outrage at her leaving.

For two years before her marriage and in the four years since coming back from her honeymoon, Rhoda had taught French I to ninth-graders. Her personality altered when she spoke a foreign language. She became crisp, bemused, and prissy, like an older woman who has a grip on her world, or a wise aunt uttering oracular phrases from a severe and mysterious knowledge. *"Jean, soyez gentil,"* she would say to the red-haired kid who laughed too loudly at a girl who kept making mistakes in the *récitation*.

She was known for her control in the classroom, an effect she obtained the first day by announcing, "I never raise my voice," in a low tone full of menace. Troublemakers she sent to the principal's office, the unknown showdown designed to alarm and warn those left behind. She also cracked jokes, an allowance of pleasure in the classroom which amazed her students. It gave them a trust in her. This, coupled with her staunchness, induced even the wilder boys to join in on the little French songs she taught them at Christmastime.

The work made her pleased with herself, striding through the halls in her suits, efficient and fresh. She avoided the other teachers, finding them weaklings, full of complaints and petty office politics. To her students she was encouraging; she dispensed praise to each like a vitamin. They told her she gave them more freedom than the other teachers; in certain other classes they were not allowed to leave to go to the bathroom, whereas she let them go one at a time.

Already the students knew, as they always did, why she was leaving in January, and they'd grown harder to handle, as though her pregnancy were a scandal to them. They were fresh more often: she was like a *déclassée* aristocrat. Everyone knew she'd had sex.

After November the children whose houses had no heating came to school early, and they were social and bothersome, standing by her desk. She had withstood the fatigue of her early months and taught quite capably, but now she was ready to leave. Sick of kids.

One winter morning she walked into her second class and on the blackboard someone had written MRS. TABER HAS BUETIFUL BUNS. *"C'est très intéressant,"* she said. *"J'ai un admirateur."* The class giggled softly. She said in English, "Alain, will you erase this for us? I might get conceited if I have to look at it all day." Laughter broke out wildly among the students. They nodded and gasped and poked each other and twisted in their seats. They made a blurred unanimous sound, like barking dogs. "*Assez!*" she said. In her chair she swiveled slightly to watch the boy moving up and down as he wiped away the sentence. Not for all the tea in China would she have turned her back to them.

Rhoda's idea had been to keep her pregnancy as undramatic as possible. When Hinda suggested that she buy a special calendar to mark off the days, Rhoda laughed at her. "And afterwards I should frame the pages like a diploma?" Hinda seemed obsessed with the minutiae of expectation; she wanted Rhoda to weigh herself on progressive days, even to measure her girth. "Next you'll be counting my varicose veins," Rhoda told her.

Leonard, on the other hand, tended to be airily expansive —mentally extravagant—in his view of the whole project. At night he lay in bed and wondered aloud when consciousness entered the body of a child, whether at conception or at birth, whether spirit meant "breath" as a physical fact or it was just a metaphor. Rhoda found these ruminations as tedious as Hinda's suggestions—she could never participate in his enthusiasm for the intangible (although she was willing to admire him for it). Between the world of her friends and Leonard, she had wedged herself into a groove that seemed purely and comfortably hers—although she had no real attitude of her own about what was really of interest and value in life—so that without constant contact with these contraries, she might have fallen through the crack, in time.

For years she had used her job as a counterweight against too much time spent with people; once she stopped working she found herself helplessly available to phone calls and spontaneous visits. Nor did she like the feeling of waiting for Leonard to get home. He worked till seven at the pharmacy, plus a half-day on Saturday, and three nights a week he worked late.

Once, when the roast was overdone and tasted—as she herself said—like an old gray suède pocketbook, her voice got plaintive and exasperated: the money, the waste. "Baby," he said, "what are you getting so excited about?"

She hated the keyed-up significance now infused in dull things. It reminded her of the spinster who lived downstairs from her mother—she used to come rushing up the steps, wailing breathlessly, "She's leaving him! So he's out of work, so, that's no reason." Rhoda's mother always fell for it—"who? what?"—offering her tea—"sit down and tell." The truth would emerge: the woman was talking about the day's installment of a soap opera on the radio.

In penance for the ruined roast, the next evening Rhoda economized: macaroni and cheese, and a lovely salad. "There's nothing to eat," Leonard said. "A person could starve here."

"There's plenty," she said.

"I like macaroni and cheese," he said, "but with something else in it. Celery or something. Olives. I don't know."

"You remind me of my brother Andy," Rhoda said. "At least he was cheap to feed when there was no money around. His whole life he ate nothing but peanut butter and jelly sandwiches."

"Oh, come on now," Leonard said. "Andy's been here for supper. He inhaled half a chicken, as I remember. He outgrew all that when he got older."

"That's what I mean," she said. "How old are you?"

He nodded, as though he appreciated her retort, but she couldn't shame him out of his discontent. With her job gone, she had lost practice in certain devices. Leonard at the supper table was always low-key and soft-spoken. Rhoda, who saved things from her day to tell him, found that unless she was very funny in the way she recounted something, her words lost importance as she spoke. She was now coming up against the fixed quality of his nature in a way she hadn't since the early days of their dating. He hadn't struck her then as the one she'd marry, but he seemed to go right past her to what he wanted, a higher interpretation of things. She admired him, a unique sensation which robbed her of her usual resources.

They finished their meal calmly enough, and had tea together in the living room. Leonard sat in the maroon horsehair plush chair which made everyone else itch, holding the saucer balanced on his knee and adjusting it without looking at it; he was quite graceful, in a cautious, masculine way. It reminded her of when she'd first seen him. She'd gone down the shore to Atlantic City for the weekend with a group of girlfriends and they had been promenading, for the third time that afternoon, along the boardwalk in the hot sun. Hinda had suddenly broken away and run up to a group of men walking towards them—she knew one of them—and she blocked traffic, exchanging introductions. A breeze had just come up, and the men's wide trousers flared up like sails in the wind; one of them was nearly muzzled by the flaps on his collar. Only one of the men, Rhoda had noticed, didn't seem to look disgraced by the rebellions of his clothing; he was squinting steadily into the wind and he bore the beating of his sleeves about his shoulders with a bemused tolerance.

She'd been quite impressed by his capacity to transcend this particular small indignity. When he opened his eyes more fully, she saw that one of them was green with a yellow cast and one of them was gray; the difference was quite subtle (she felt rather pleased with herself for having noticed it); it gave him the starry, unfocused, earnest look of dogs with the same genetic fluke. She had of course not known that the attention he called up in her would settle in her as something permanent. She had simply found him interesting (but not conclusively so: that had been his idea).

Now he had put down his tea and taken up the newspaper. His face was remarkably motionless when he read; he didn't move his lips and his eyes barely flickered. He looked intent and worried; he squinted into the news, bearing up under its obdurate nightly failure to improve.

He was so patient; he read through all of it, the sports section, the obituaries. A methodical man: in the beginning she'd been sure he wasn't her type or what she had in mind; she had just split up with someone she'd "almost" married and she'd expected to end up next with a perfected form of the same type—boyish, sharp, wisecracking—instead of this stocky, maturely genial person.

Her initial judgments were usually reliable. In her circle of friends she'd been known as sensible to the point of being hardhearted. Once a very handsome boy named Fritz Pearson had given her a big rush, sending her a corsage of gardenias every morning. Their white, heavy petals stayed in the icebox, spotting brown at the edges and scenting the family's butter. She hadn't cared for Fritz, with his seedy eagerness and the way he had money when nobody else did. And she had been right; afterwards he had taken Hinda out and he had tried something—driven into a dark street, put his hand up her skirt or tried to bully her into sex—but in a grim way which had frightened Hinda. "But how did you know?" Hinda said. "He was always so well-behaved." "You don't have to roll in it," Rhoda said, "to know it's dreck." This was a favorite saying of Rhoda's mother.

Leonard had put down his newspaper and was picking the dog hair off the cuffs of his pants in a somewhat irritating way. Rhoda said, by way of conversation, "I'm highly disappointed that I haven't started craving strawberries and pickles these days."

Leonard, looking up from his shins, said, "We couldn't get the strawberries at this time of year anyway. The pickles of course we could always get in the middle of the night from your mother."

Rhoda's mother loved all pickled things. Cucumbers, sliced onions, and oversize green tomatoes: her craving for sour was like a child's attraction to sweets—a wintry love for the chilled vegetables stored in glass containers; in their vinegar, yellowed with garlic, dill seeds bobbed like snow in a paperweight. In the afternoons, on Rhoda's visits, she would be found reading at the table with her fork poised in a jar—a satisfaction almost painful, sharper than the pleasures of the newspaper.

"I was there today," Rhoda said. "At my mother's."

"What does she have to say?"

"Her radio's broken and my father says it's a noisemaker, he'll throw it out the window if she brings home another one. He wouldn't really do that."

"I guess it bothers him," Leonard said. "That's too bad."

Rhoda's mother loved the radio; she was fond of classical music, and she also enjoyed talking back to the commercials. "Are you tired, nervous, rundown?" the announcer would ask. "None of your business," she would tell him. Like many people, she would pick up pet phrases from the comedy shows. When *Amos 'n' Andy* was popular, she went around saying, "I'se regusted." This had a special comic effect due to the overlay of her own European accent. She could never lose the uvular hook of her r's, but her grammar was notably classy, a source of envy to the neighbors, who agreed she spoke like a Yankee; unlike a certain person who made a fool of himself every time he opened his mouth.

Rhoda's father had never learned to speak English properly. This was not from any lack of intelligence, but from a willful disgust at the irrationality of the English language. "Suing machine," he would say, referring to his wife's Singer. "Come on, Pa," Rhoda corrected him. "Everything it knows," he would snarl. Her brothers were called upon to bear witness, but no amount of jeering convinced him. He was not given to extensive conversation in any language and he did not like noise of any sort around him.

"My father," Rhoda said, "is an old fart, if you really want to know."

Leonard said, "He's just a man of few words, that's all. All that tumult makes him uncomfortable. Some people are not outgoing." He said this in a very low, even voice.

At the moment she found Leonard's steely mildness

irking—that superior way he had of always speaking softly (a technique she had borrowed for the classroom). She said, "Why are you always mumbling in your beard like that? You make me feel like a fishwife. You do it on purpose."

"Kiddo," he said softly.

"Be quiet," she yelled horribly. She was making herself ridiculous. She couldn't stop. She liked Leonard—she always liked Leonard—but she saw no reason why he had to be so maturely patient about her father, on whom—she happened to know from personal experience—the exercise of virtue was wasted.

Leonard said, "Rhoda, you're not understanding me." It was unbearable.

"I told you to be quiet," she said. "I don't want to hear any more."

They stayed separate for the rest of the evening. He read in the den while she moved from room to room, performing tasks and looking at magazines. In the night they slept turned away from each other in their twin beds. But towards day her sleep was invaded by a vivid dream, a vision of real danger from the outside world. Her eyes weren't open yet, she was struggling to be awake, and she had escaped what it was: there had been the face of a man in a movie they'd seen, *Confessions of a Nazi Spy;* he had teeth with gold fillings, and he was smiling maniacally. The room around her had the edge of strangeness, the excited light of early morning. "You told them everything," she was saying. "You let them take me."

Her husband said, "It's all right. I'm here."

She remembered something else. "I'm sorry I yelled at you so hard," she said.

"It can't be helped," he said. He was still mad, but quietly. Almost absently, he stroked her hair.

In the morning she was full of little kisses and a sense of horror. All day she was good for nothing. At night she swarmed him, she was lively with little jokes and long stories to bring Lenny around. Her voice was high and sweet, almost lispy to make things funnier.

He laughed as much as he could. He was a decent man who sincerely did not wish to fight, and if he kept grudges, he let them give way slowly inside, unnursed. He could not keep up the high pitch of fun she was now asking for, but he showed his amusement in slow smiles, resigned.

Leonard brought her Empirin from the store, to take instead of aspirin, now that aspirin made her stomach lurch. She was ashamed that when she was nauseous she ate anyway, like a person with a cold who insists on smoking. The Empirins were small and hard as little pebbles. "They're 'sweet pills,'" Leonard joked. "To make you sweet."

Rhoda never took them; instead she found herself free of aches in the following weeks. The weather deepened into winter; her middle, under protective wraps, curved into a buoyant, simple shape. The trees along the suburban streets were stripped and bare (except for the evergreens), very dark against the white sky. Walking through the cold to Annie's house on a Sunday, she watched the outline of the branches. She noticed the trees, now that they lived here: they were one of the things to like. There had been trees in Newark, if you wanted to look at them; some of the outlying wards had been, if never exactly verdant, almost rural in a scrubby way. Her sister-in-law remembered seeing a bunch of cows come down Irvington Avenue, but that must have been a sight even then.

At Annie's house Rhoda rang the doorbell four times, the rhythm of Beethoven's Fifth—dit-dit-dit-dah—the Morse code for V. Everybody did it now. *V for victory*. They shall not flag or fail. Inside she could hear women's voices.

"Surprise, surprise!" they all shouted, a minute too late, as Rhoda stood at the door, arrested by their cries. She had her beaver coat on, half-open, showing a red silk blouse with a collar that tied like a scarf, centered and prim. Hard and lipsticky, she gave them an unaccustomed smile, a little off; she looked both crafty and sheepish. It was her party, and she had known before. "My! My!" she said, as though she were talking to her classes.

They led her into the room, where crepe-paper streamers were twisted on the wall in great sweeping loops. On Annie's rickety mahogany side table there was a bouquet of peach-colored carnations with torn edges, fashioned from Kleenex. They sat her down in the big wing chair, on whose twill surface someone had Scotch-taped the letters MOTHER cut from construction paper. Rhoda sat and picked at the letters, saying, "Look at this!" She faced them then, rubbing from her cheek the marks of lip-rouge. "Well," she said, "what's for lunch?"

Hinda, standing behind Rhoda's chair, put her hands on Rhoda's cheeks and pivoted her face to the left so that she could see the pile of wrapped presents stacked on the carpet. "Open 'em so we can eat," Annie Marantz called out.

Her father, who was given to mulish certainties, had predicted a girl, but no one else could be sure of the future baby's sex, so many of the gifts were yellow: a yellow baby blanket, a crocheted yellow cardigan, a snuggly suit made of pale lemon terry cloth. "Just a little lighter than baby doody," Rhoda said. "Easy to wash." The women laughed, repeating what she had said to the ones in the back. From Hinda there was a white canvas satchel with brown bows and ribbons printed on it, lined with rubberized cloth like a beach-bag, for carrying diapers or bottles. "Gorgeous," Rhoda said.

For lunch Annie served creamed chicken dotted with pimientos, poured from a chafing dish into individual pastry shells. Rhoda sat with the plate on her lap, holding her knees together. Sybil Jawitz was the only one who couldn't taste the chicken because she kept kosher. She ate her nude pastry shell with a fork. "Flaky," she said. Annie offered her slices of American cheese, which she accepted with a bitter and patient smile.

Rhoda's mother came over to congratulate her daughter. "You have wonderful friends," she said.

Mrs. Leshko from down the block, who always wore a cotton housedress with a brooch pinned to the bodice and whose heavy powder gathered on her face like fur, leaned down to kiss the guest of honor. "Eat," she said. "So skinny. But listen, who can tell, in a month you could be big as a house. Twins, maybe."

"Who asked her?" Rhoda's mother said, as Mrs. Leshko backed off towards the buffet table.

Rhoda had stopped eating. "Nobody believes me," she said, "when I say I feel strong as a horse."

"You could run a race, I suppose? Win a little money for your old mother?"

Rhoda held up her fists in sparring position and began dancing back and forth, jabbing the air as she hopped nearer to her mother's face. "Wanna fight, Ma? Put up your dukes, there."

Her mother said, "You look like a mosquito."

"Look," Bev Davis said, passing them, "how light she is on her feet still."

At four o'clock the men arrived: Leonard and two of his friends in baggy flannels, their mufflers tied loosely under their overcoats, nodding slowly at the women from beneath the shadows of their tilted hat brims.

Leonard kissed his wife and let himself be led to the table where the presents were piled. Rustling through the tissue paper he picked things up and put them down. "Nothing for me?" he said. "Now these booties, Rhode, a little small, but if you washed them and blocked them, I could use one as a nose-warmer."

And in fact his nose at that moment looked red and genial from the cold. "Is it true you've come to take me home?" Rhoda said.

II

She went with Hinda to pick out wallpaper for the baby's room. What Rhoda liked was a paper of red-white-and-blue polka dots in a swirling pattern. Running her hand across the paper, Rhoda fingered the white dots printed on the white ground and wondered why a designer had bothered to put them there. Could an infant see them? Hinda said, "The first color a baby sees is red." Rhoda found this information exciting. Facts were beginning to stir her more deeply, like coming attractions for a movie.

Hinda's mother thought it was bad luck to buy anything for the baby before it was born. Rhoda was disgusted at the backwardness of this superstition. "It's very morbid of her," she said.

"You're right," Hinda said.

"Imagine stopping yourself from arranging for things. There's no reason. In general. In the Depression, I admit, you couldn't plan. It wasn't even such a good idea to look ahead."

"That's done and over with," Hinda said. She was somewhat distracted, still looking at the sample-book of wallpapers. "In those days you certainly couldn't get patterns like these. I kind of love this one with the Little Bo-Peeps. I wish you knew already whether it was a boy or a girl."

"Some things," Rhoda said, "you can't plan."

Precisely on the morning of her due date, Rhoda was admitted to the hospital. Shortly after the later, close-spaced contractions began, it became apparent that the baby was too big for delivery without tearing her and she was put to sleep while they cut at her. Later she was told that, coming out of the anesthetic, she had answered, "Yes, I know, my father told me," when the nurse said, "It's a big, beautiful girl."

The baby was unusually well-developed and had a full head of hair, which the nurses, in a moment of leisured playfulness, tied in ribbons. These early signs of advancement pleased Rhoda. When, still dopey, she held the baby, she was aware of the damp, silky quality of its skin, which seemed too thin and soft to hold the nearly boneless mass within, and she wondered that there had been so much struggle to eject this puddle of a body. "You're a little bowl of Jell-O," she said, lifting the baby under its arms. "You can't even stretch your legs." Its bunched face seemed impersonal, the features an abstraction of a face. She felt for the soft spot on its skull, but she couldn't distinguish a more delicate area; the head itself seemed only slightly tighter, less fatty, than the cheeks.

Even the baby's bowel movements, as she watched the nurse peel off its diaper like a Band-Aid, were soggy and clotted, like mashed squash. She wanted to ask if the baby would be more formed by the time they left the hospital together. Already it had corresponded to her expectations by its cheering normalcy. "Healthy," she whispered to it. The baby had heard its first command. Pushing itself from the nurse's pinning hands, it screamed—a loud, wet-faced bawl—it would not stop screaming. Rhoda, looking at the nurse, said, "That's a healthy set of lungs there."

It was Leonard who first suggested to her gently, "You have to stop calling the baby 'it.' It's 'she' or 'her' even before we have a name for her." "You're right, you're right," she said, in a hushed eager voice. "Well, now, there's something I don't hear very often," he said.

The second time she held the baby, her shape seemed dear and familiar. Cozy, and then the feeling rose. The sensation of yielding was almost shameful to her. But it was a private tenderness she could feel without speaking, like the aftermath of sex.

They named the baby Suzanne Helen, after Leonard's father Samuel (Shmuel, really) and a cousin Herschel on her mother's side who'd been short of namesakes because no one remembered much about him. Leonard had wanted the name Sandra, but Rhoda knew that people would shorten it to Sandy, and she hated nicknames. She didn't want her child made light of in that way. "And no calling her Sue or Suzy," she said. To the baby she repeated softly, "Say: *Je m'appelle Suzanne.*"

Suzanne was not colicky, but the ensuing months were the hot ones of early summer, and she was often fretful in the evenings. She cried when Rhoda tried to put her to sleep in her crib. "*Shah,*" Rhoda barked to her in Yiddish, and tiptoed out of the room. She sat with Leonard in the living room, gulping beer out of a green-tinted tumbler; the glass dripped with moisture and slid against her hand. The baby's sobs ebbed and burst forth fresh in an alternating pattern of resignation and outrage. "She'll stop," Rhoda said, and just then the baby did stop, as though to prove her expertise. The night was hot; the beer smacked their tongues with its carbonation and in the sudden hush of relief from the infant's crying and in the taking of adults' refreshment, there was vague ease and calm.

At quarter to four in the morning Rhoda awoke. She could hear the attic fan running with disturbing power above her, rattling the windows in their panes. She pulled the sheet and the light chenille spread from her body and walked to the baby's room. Her bare, flat feet slapped the wood floor of the hallway and stuck slightly to the nursery linoleum. Suzanne was whimpering in her sleep.

Rhoda went to the kitchen, where she took a bottle from the refrigerator and set it in a pan of water on the stove. Not yet inured to the new routine, she still liked the vague energies of this hour, the muted elation of night work. She padded back to the baby's room and lifted her from under her fat, limp arms. The baby took the bottle happily, reaching for it and gripping it with specialized cleverness, her only deftness. "A little snack for you," Rhoda said.

Rhoda saw that the baby was opening her soft, toothless mouth too wide—she was gulping air. "Not like that," she said. Helplessly she watched. Suzanne was plainly hungry; she drank her full portion, then, still captive at the bottle's nipple, stopped sucking and began to cry. "You see," Rhoda said, "I told you." Curled in Rhoda's lap the baby thrust out her legs and fists in a miniature tantrum. "Wah, wah, wah," Rhoda said to her.

Rhoda set the baby on her shoulder and patted the soft, cottony back. Firmly she sang (in a nonsense-Yiddish, dimly traditional): "*Shooby shooby shooby shoe.*" She sang loudly. From teaching school she had the habit of raising her voice when she sang, so that the students, having a line to follow, would join in. The baby's room filled with noise, as the simple chanting bellied out with nasal undertones. She kept time, patting Suzanne's back. Like an entertainer working to raise the troops' morale, she felt her own willfulness battling Suzanne's sadness. Her singing drowned out the crying. At first the baby wailed more loudly, but Rhoda's chorus was solid, with a cantor's sob or a torchsinger's wail to the tune she was inventing. Subdued, held tightly, Suzanne hiccuped softly and was silent.

_____

The morning light hit them, lying in bed, with such moist, unwholesome heat that Rhoda felt real alarm when Leonard said, "It's going to be a scorcher."

"A real stinker for a Sunday," she said. She had planned to sit out in the backyard with Leonard and the baby, but even under the trees it would be stifling. Draped in a towel, back from washing, Leonard stood by the bed and touched her on the forehead. "We could go to the beach," he said.

She took the suggestion as an offering. "I can be ready in two shakes," she said. Dressing, she called out to him, "We could ask Hinda and Stanley if they want to go."

"We could," he said, "but we won't." She said nothing. He wasn't susceptible to persuasion and he couldn't be jollied into something he chose not to do. He had a way of cutting her off that left her with no resource but to be ruefully impressed with him for it. At first she had railed against his rigidity, but once she took it as fact, she felt herself older, no longer a girl. Once she told her mother—boasting—"Boy, have I learned."

This morning she and Leonard were dropping the baby off at Rhoda's mother's apartment, and when her mother came to the downstairs door, she cried, "Ah, there you are," and made a great fuss over rocking Leonard in a hug. In her mother's hallway was the old-fashioned odor of boiled vegetables and spitting fats, the traces of ignorant people cooking away the vitamins. Rhoda's mother had been proselytizing for years about the benefits of modern cookery, but to no avail; in her own apartment was the faint smell of paste wax, rising from the dark tables lit by little lamps.

Rhoda's father was in the kitchen having breakfast; he wore his suspenders over his undershirt and his neck was goatish before his shave. "You look like Pa Kettle," Rhoda said.

Her father said, "Who's he?" What he really wanted was to hold the baby. He smiled when they let him take her in his bare, blue-veined arms—already he had the arms of an old man—and he made smacking, kissy noises; he shook his head closer to her and growled like a dog worrying a bone, in a way that he thought would amuse the child.

"Everybody loves a baby," Rhoda said.

Her mother made them sit down and have coffee before they were up and away in such a hurry. She reminded Rhoda of how, when she was engaged, Leonard used to come to the house every morning to have his coffee before work. Rhoda remembered this well; she had once told him not to come every day for fear they would get tired of each other. She'd thought this was unusually sage of her until Leonard had pointed out that they were going to be seeing each other every day anyway once they were married. It embarrassed her a little to think how dim her maidenly foresight had been.

Rhoda's mother, who had liked Leonard from the first, was speaking very animatedly to him now; they were nodding at each other about something. They were talking (who could guess from looking at them?) about public sanitation. Newark was in the process of deciding whether or not to provide garbage collection at municipal expense (an advance not even contemplated yet in the suburbs). Rhoda's mother—as a Social Democrat—naturally favored any small civic improvements as steps toward long-denied justice, whereas Leonard cared more about the white light of reason bringing enlightened hygiene; he went on about Lady Mary Wortley Montagu in the 1700s having her own children inoculated for smallpox to prove the serum was safe. They kept talking and nodding, deploring the narrow thinking that made people want to let their garbage fester; they were united in their fine passion to elevate the ordinary, until Rhoda began droning, as background music, a blues parody she'd heard once in a revue "Garbage . . . he treated me like . . . garbage."

"I think she's getting restless," Rhoda's mother said to Leonard.

"We're really lucky to have them," Leonard said, as they walked to the car.

"That's true," Rhoda said. "Hinda's mother won't watch her kid for her because she reads all these stories in the paper —*a grandmother was taking care of a little girl and the girl fell into a ditch and drowned.* She's got a million of them."

It always amazed Rhoda that someone as sour as Hinda's mother—with her peasant shudders over natural disasters just around the bend—could have raised someone as placid and easy-natured as Hinda. The only thing Rhoda had ever heard Hinda distress herself over was expenses, which, considering how they'd all grown up, was only sane. They had once taken a poll in Rhoda's high school—"What do you need most for future happiness?"—and 87 percent of the student body had laughed and written down "money."

Rhoda still basically felt that this was a sensible response to an obvious question. Not that she was insensitive to other (admittedly less immediate) things; the ongoing war in Europe was on her mind often now. Both her parents had family trapped in occupied Poland. Rhoda was the only one of the children who had ever seen any of them; on a trip to Europe with a girlfriend years ago she had met a great-uncle who lived in Cracow. He had been very old even then; she still remembered very vividly the clipped intonations of his elegant, citified Yiddish, and the sly, downy face of a younger cousin who was now in England.

Today they were going to the beach and she kept thinking about the helpless English beaches, strafed after nightfall. (They must hate the dark now, ordinary people in those seaside towns.) Having an infant of her own had let certain images eat into her thoughts. Lately she had been haunted by visions of propaganda posters she must have seen in books (since she would have been too young to remember them from the last war), photographs of Hun soldiers with Belgian babies stuck on their bayonets.

What bothered her most now was thinking about things that were left out of the news; scraps of information filtered through about Jews in occupied countries carried off to camps whose locations and conditions were left, as it were, to the imagination. Facts not spoken of were always the worst: wasn't that the meaning of the word *unspeakable?*

She'd read that Axis troops were planting on the Western

Desert a new sort of land mine that blew straight up into fragments, so that soldiers who walked over them got blasted in the groin, and ever since, she'd been gripped by the notion that Leonard, if he went to war, would be sent as a foot soldier. She would have talked about it except that she felt her horrors were idle, compared to the burden on him, and he should have the right to speak of these things or not to speak, as he wanted to. She was also restrained by a parallel and actually somewhat stronger feeling that nothing this extreme and fantastical was likely to happen to either of them.

They had hit heavy traffic and it was hot inside the car, with its chafing, straw-like upholstery. Leonard said, "Feel like a schoolgirl on holiday without the baby?" She was glad not to have Suzanne on her lap, stirring and squirming, but the question surprised her. There was nothing she wanted to be older or younger for. Already she had stopped understanding what people did with themselves when they didn't have children. The smell of the ocean was coming through the car windows, disappearing, then returning, as the sighting of the shoreline along turns in the road began to excite their imaginations.

They parked along the boardwalk and undressed in the car, writhing on the seats to remove their outer clothing, kicking like overturned crabs, and emerging suddenly from out of the car into the sunlight—she wore a white two-piece and he wore blue wool-knit trunks with a white belt and a white stripe down each side—they were peeled down to their brighter selves. Leonard, with his wide shoulders and short arms, looked strong and tidy and compact, she thought. They walked toward the water; the surf made swelling noises and the sand grew hotter under their feet. "Whoo, hah," she said, doing a little dance.

She suddenly frightened herself remembering that in Abyssinia Mussolini's army had poured acid on the desert sands when they were being chased by the Ethiopian soldiers, who went barefoot. It was unbearable to be hopping around on the sand while remembering this, and she began running faster toward the water. Leonard came from behind and overtook her. They ran together for a moment and she felt happier; they both had their mouths open in smiling breathlessness like panting dogs. They stopped when they hit the water line. "Cold on the ankles," Rhoda said. Leonard took her hand and led her out further, until the waves smacked their chests and they were drenched. Rhoda squealed as though she had just taken a turn on a roller coaster. She slipped, and he reached out quickly and held her up—his skin was nicely wet and cold—and she remembered how fast he always was to grab the baby before she fell or touched hot things. She liked the solid feel of him now, and she kissed his shoulder, which was salty. "Roll on, thou deep and dark blue ocean, roll," he sang out. They stayed in the water, bouncing up each time a wave came, until the surf got too rough.

Later they lay with the dark plaid car-blanket spread out beneath them. The sand stuck to the tanning oil on her legs and Rhoda said she felt, with her knees bent, like a chicken breaded for frying. Leonard was flat on his stomach. She reached out and touched his rear end, giving it a light tap with her fingertip. "It bounces back," she said. "If you were a cake I'd say you were done." He rolled over and smiled, dropping his mouth a little, playful like a dolphin. He was squinting his eyes shut now; he looked almost the way he did in certain stages of lovemaking. It startled her slightly to think of this while they were out on the beach. At first the discontinuity of sex had shocked her, the grasping, un-Leonard-like seizures in raw pursuit of a goal. But she had trusted him, and imitating him, she had been drawn into it. By now sex with Leonard— which she certainly enjoyed, and whose sustained continuance in their marriage made her secretly proud—was exempt from ordinary thought, since arousal took away judgment, just as it took away one's breath.

She was tracing with her finger the center line of hair on his chest, which thickened around his navel and above the belt of his suit. "Do you feel rumblings in my belly?" Leonard said.

"This is because I'm hungry." He wanted to go up to the
boardwalk to bring back some food. "You stay." He shook sand
on her as he got up.

Alone, Rhoda sat up and took a look around her at the other
people on the beach, who had amassed into a considerable
crowd by now. The waves were thick with them. Farther from
the water, four or five boys about college age were practicing
gymnastics. One of them stood with his arm outstretched
while another boy sprang on his hands and flipped backwards
over it. The others followed in sequence; the boy was raising
his arm higher to make it harder. They had to stop in between
to avoid kicking passersby. They had wonderful physiques,
especially the long-waisted blond one. Rhoda was attracted,
but in an amused way; it had never been in her nature to
swoon, not even as a young girl. It always seemed a distortion
to her—the languorous craving, the humorless sacrifice to a
single idea. A healthy interest was one thing.

She was thinking now of all the boys she'd gone out with, in
high school and in college and when she'd worked and lived at
home. She'd been popular for her liveliness, and there had been
quite a stream of them, with their slicked-back hair and
self-conscious smiles. "So when is Mr. Right coming?" her
father used to say. Rhoda had assumed she would pick one of
them, but she had waited. She could bide her time, she was
content where she was, all things considered. Florence Pinskow, who had worked with her part-time in Woolworth's
when they were both in school, used to wail dramatically,
"Lyons Avenue is not the world." "What world?" Rhoda used
to say. It had seemed to her the height of willful innocence that
a girl whose parents, in Europe and here, had had their bellyful
of "experience," would ache for a taste of it.

Leonard was walking toward her, veering as he passed the
boys, who were on to cartwheels now. He knelt on the blanket;
he had brought back hot dogs and a doughnut to share. The
doughnut was a little old and musty. "It tastes like a wet dog
smells," Rhoda said, but she finished her portion.

They were cautious about going into the water right after eating. Neither of them really liked to lie in the sun. They had forgotten to bring books to read; Rhoda noticed that it was hard to think of things to say in the heat. She wasn't comfortable not talking; in fact she often wasn't comfortable with Leonard. It was an odd thing and he would catch her at it sometimes, flashing him a delayed smile or wandering in her speech as she tried to construct, without confidence, a conversation.

Rhoda wanted to walk along the boardwalk a little. She liked the thin knocking sound the crowd's feet made on the diagonal gray boards. Leonard took her arm. They wore their shirts over their suits and felt the shaking motion of their thighs, exposed but legitimate here.

"Well, for goodness' sake!" a man in front of them was saying, and Rhoda saw that walking toward them were Liz and Herb Hofferberg. They were a couple on the fringes of Rhoda's and Leonard's acquaintance. Liz was small and darkly pretty, thirteen years younger than her husband. Rhoda had gotten the idea that she was from a family with no money at all and Herb, with a medical practice already established, had been considered a good catch; Rhoda wasn't crazy about Herb.

The summer before, Rhoda and Leonard had spent a weekend at a lake resort with three other couples, including the Hofferbergs. Herb was always making jokes like, "An old husband and a young honey—and who gets tired first?" or "You're as young as you feel—and I'm getting younger, the more I get to feel." The Hofferbergs' room was directly above Rhoda's and Leonard's, and before breakfast they heard the rhythm of the bedsprings squeaking and they smiled at each other uneasily. One evening, as Leonard waited in the hall and Rhoda stood at the mirror putting on her lipstick before going down to dinner, she heard above her the thud of a body hitting the mattress and then Liz giggling. Rhoda was startled and alert, as though to danger—she felt dismayed for Liz's sake, but then who knew? She was ill at ease with the mingling of annoyance and her own slightly shamed arousal. She would have preferred to mind her own business.

Five minutes later, sitting down to supper, she saw the Hofferbergs come into the dining room followed by Bev Davis, who had the room next to theirs. They were all laughing and Bev kept gasping, "Oh, Herb," as though that were the joke. "You won't believe it," Beverly said, between laughs. "This joker." Beverly had been trying to tiptoe discreetly past the Hofferbergs' room, so as not to disturb them since they were obviously busy inside, but then what did she see but their door wide open and Herb Hofferberg, fully clothed, bouncing up and down on the bed, while Liz leaned up against the wardrobe and tittered. The friends at the table screamed with amusement. "Is it my fault," Herb said, cocking his head toward Beverly, "if you people just have dirty minds?"

The Hofferbergs seemed genuinely glad to see them; Liz was grinning and saying, "What a surprise!" in her deep, pleasant voice, and Herb rubbed her shoulder and said, "How're you doing, Rhody?" which was not what she liked to be called.

The Hofferbergs were on their way to have their pictures taken with their heads stuck through a piece of cardboard that had cartoon bodies drawn below. Leonard, in a burst of group spirit, wanted to go with them. "That man is a horse's ass," Rhoda whispered, but Leonard turned his head away and steered her by the elbow to walk with the others. It especially annoyed her because when she had been single she used to feel that she had to put up with unsuitable, irritating groups for the sake of an ongoing social life—and now, married, she wasn't exempted from it either. She wanted Leonard to protect her from time spent with the Hofferbergs, just as she wanted him to protect her from thinking about the war.

She found it strange that Leonard, who was so dignified, found anything to like in Herb, but men were odd in their enthusiasms for each other. Actually, Leonard was more of a snob in private. All his personal possessions were heavy with conservative quality. He had beautiful brushes—silver, monogrammed—and a shaving set from Belgium with badger-hair bristles. He would not let her buy him clothing at sales. But his sense of fun in public was unhampered by taste; he was happy to wear silly hats at parties, ready to contort himself playing charades.

Herb knew the place; half a block down the boardwalk a man in shirtsleeves and a maroon bow tie nodded at them in nervous pleasure. "I think he sells glass fruit-knives on the side," Leonard murmured, and Rhoda laughed. She continued laughing uncontrollably as they poked their faces through the garden scene they had chosen—she and Leonard were daisies, Liz was a rose, and Herb, standing on a stool, was a sly bumblebee. Pilloried, they twisted their necks to look at each other. Leonard's bobbing profile was unspeakably amusing to Rhoda. When the man said, "Hold it!" she was pained, like a child, to stop her wriggling.

The men paid, wrote their addresses to have the prints mailed, and the two couples parted from one another again. Her shoulders began to feel heated through and crisp, and she was worried for Leonard, who was fairer than she. The sky was still dizzyingly white as they made their way back to the car.

They were jostled on the boardwalk by a bum whose shirt was buttoned staidly at the collar but flapped open below, showing the hairs on his chest and belly. He walked with his arms out straight in front, waving them to part a way through the crowd. His face was small and boyish, except for the smudged growth of beard. He whimpered as he passed them. "He's gone," Rhoda said, meaning in the head.

She couldn't help feeling contempt when she saw people who would choose misery, carrying it with them like an unattractive feature they made no attempt to conceal. Her upbringing had been in a different direction, toward staunch-ness and against dramatizing. Leonard gave the man some change.

On the ride home, Rhoda felt richly exhausted, dazed from

the heat, and she let the rocking motion of the car put her to
sleep. When she woke, twilight had fallen and Leonard had put
the radio on. She crooned a loud comic yawn to let him know
she was awake, but he shushed her—he wanted to hear the
news. Churchill and Roosevelt had met secretly on a ship
somewhere off Newfoundland and issued a high-minded decla-
ration; all nations were going to act nobly in such-and-such
ways "after the final destruction of the Nazi tyranny." "It
means Roosevelt's going to get off his behind soon, doesn't it?"
Rhoda said. "Everybody knows it's only a matter of time, but
he's so slow. First we call Hitler names, then we have to get in
the war finally."

Leonard shrugged. The weather report came on (more
temperatures in the nineties) and then the music again, and
they drove ahead in silence. "Will you go, do you think?" she
said. "Into the service, I mean." She had been trying to think
how to phrase this delicately, so as not to let him think that
she expected anything cowardly or shrinking from him, or, on
the other hand, that she was in any way eager to see him go. He
had occasionally evinced pacifist sentiments, but she wasn't
sure how serious they were or whether the current situation
overrode them. He was over thirty and a father and he probably
wouldn't have to go right away unless he wanted to. She
wanted to know if he wanted to.

He wasn't answering, and she wondered if she'd annoyed
him (he sometimes accused her of asking obvious questions
and being dense on purpose). "I'm thinking," he said, catching
her looking at him. Perhaps it was wise to prepare: she couldn't
quite bring herself to the point of expecting this to happen. I
would manage, she thought, I wouldn't sit home and brood. In
his absence, she would, for instance, have gone down the shore
today with Hinda and Stanley, as she'd wanted to in the first
place, yukked it up with Hinda on the beach, kept Leonard's
name out of the conversation so that no one would feel sorry
for her, and avoided more than a polite hello to the Hofferbergs.

This is a little crazy of me, Rhoda thought, it's not true that I want him to go. It was juvenile to be fooling around mentally with notions of her own fortitude. She had been having, she realized, a *fantasy*—frivolous and inaccurate—about how offhandedly brave she was going to be. Her sunburn hurt her slightly, and reminded her how little interest she had in ennobling herself with more tragic emotions.

"I think I don't know what I'd do," Leonard said. He drew his brows together and tilted his head at her and then he smiled weakly in a way that she found somehow beautifully modest and responsible. "I'd figure it out when the time came. I'd have to go, maybe." Rhoda's mind cleared suddenly—he was so sensible, and he saw into the heart of things. At once she was bitter at the thought that anything might take him away from her. It was no time to speak of the risks of combat; she wanted him to think that she was feeling the right thing. All the ride home she bore her panic silently; in this restraint she felt her strength.

They arrived home stiff and sticky with salt, wanting to shower and eat quickly in peace before going to pick up Suzanne. The house looked shaded and cool, as they drove up to it, with its deep lawn and the brick steps leading to the porch; the flagstone walk was in shadow from the chestnut tree. Leonard made sandwiches while Rhoda took off her suit to rinse it in the kitchen sink. "Look at your strap-marks," he said. "Look at your shoulder. Your skin always looks so smooth. Healthy and smooth."

He heard her singing in the bathroom. She had forgotten about the war, and her voice copied the tune as she had heard it on the radio, so that he was startled at the unaccustomed merging of styles—her voice was extra brassy, as though she sang from a microphone to a large audience, and the words had a stagey accent from another part of the country, further west or further south. She was pleasing herself.

III

In December, when America finally entered the war, Rhoda kept telling friends that it was a relief; it meant, at least, that something was happening to stop more Jews from being killed. At home, her own uneasy opinion was that Leonard, as an overage father, shouldn't go unless he had to. Still, when Hinda's Stanley left, Rhoda was shy to mention Leonard's name in front of her friend, as though his continuing presence were a guilty secret. Listening to the news one evening, Leonard announced, with the sober phrasing of an expert giving disturbing testimony, that the Navy was the most intelligently run branch of the service, and the next day he went down for the physical exam, never guessing the outcome: rheumatic fever in childhood disqualified him. When Rhoda heard the news, she was overcome with a deep and bride-like flush at the wonder of his maleness, the span of his chest and the hairs on his arm: the luck of having a man to live with. They did not celebrate but sat quiet over dinner, softly and companionably dismayed in their plenty, like tourists who feel themselves fat in a land of beggars.

The war did not change their lives so very much. Though among her friends she made weary references to "these grim days," Rhoda's own part was limited to the tasks of budgeting ration coupons and helping in scrap drives. Leonard did volunteer work for the Red Cross, measuring and labeling medicines.

He was very, very busy, working extra hours in the pharmacy now that the store was short-handed. The store, in which he had a sort of junior partnership, was doing well; the steadiest customers, the old and the sick, had been left behind, with the women who bought cosmetics. Kids with mothers at work came to hang out at the soda fountain, swilling down Morale Builder Malteds and Paratroops Sundaes (They Go Down Easy). By the winter of 1943 business had actually doubled from what it was before the war.

The stream of customers elated him. He liked the momentum of tasks done rapidly on demand. It was on such a day of capable exercise—sweat stains mottled his blue shirt and showed like highlights through his white coat—that Mrs. Leshko found him at her service across the glass counter. Mrs. Leshko had waited a good ten minutes while Leonard had helped a ten-year-old select a bottle of cologne for his mother and had prepared cough syrup for a woman who worked in a clothing factory and complained of fibres in her lungs. After her wait, the sudden beam of his attention turned on Mrs. Leshko caused her to melt and gush plaintive confession. "I shouldn't have come," she said. "I'm an old lady, the walk isn't so good for me."

"It just shows you can't keep a good woman down," Leonard said. He had learned a little from Rhoda about how to handle people. "I'm very flattered that you came all this way to see me. A pretty face on a busy day, it cheers me up."

Mrs. Leshko wheezed her breathy little fat-woman's laugh. She had walked extra, she said, because she didn't trust the other druggist in town. Last time she had counted the arthritis pills he'd given her, and they were four short. "I can measure them out right in front of you if it'll make you feel better," Leonard offered.

"You," Mrs. Leshko snorted. "You I wouldn't question. If the whole world was like you, there would be no wars."

Mrs. Leshko continued talking to him as he went behind the partition to fill her prescription. "I need some candy also. My nephew on a ship—it must be very boring, he writes to his old aunt even—he wants me to send him some sourballs. Five pounds."

Leonard walked to the candy counter and scooped out the little hard candies, dusty with their own sugar, into a paper bag and weighed them. "For you and the Navy, that's fifty cents. And two dollars for your medicine."

Mrs. Leshko was suddenly at a loss. The difficulty of getting this flimsy wrinkled bag into the mail and overseas hit her as an unexpected and bitter disappointment. She wanted a box, she needed some twine—"It's not so easy to tie a knot when you've got arthritis"—and she began to whimper.

"Mrs. Leshko," Leonard said, "if you give me the address, I'll pack it for you. It's all right."

The old woman was actually crying, thin short sniffs and gasps; tears leaked from her rheumy eyes. Leonard was appalled; he could not have been more uncomfortable if she had suddenly lifted her dress and revealed her grayed and withered private parts—for wasn't she, in flaunting her suffering, displaying all the quivering intensity of the most private part of all, the soul? Leonard was an agnostic, but he believed in the soul; this, too, he kept to himself.

He offered Mrs. Leshko his handkerchief, and she gripped his hand. "When he was little, his mother used to leave him with me when she went to work; he was such a sweet little boy. He called me Aunt Beffie, he couldn't say Bessie. You know how they are when they're learning to talk."

"I know," Leonard said.

"Oh, God," Mrs. Leshko wailed. "You have one of your own, I forgot. Be glad she's a girl. How old is she now?"

"Two and a half," Leonard said.

"They grow up so fast. What is she doing—walking, talking? What does she say?"

"Well, not much, actually. Mostly she just says 'dish' and 'dat' and points to what she wants. A woman of few words." He was trying to be very concrete, by way of shifting the subject.

"You're kidding. When Arthur was that age, he knew a whole nursery rhyme by heart. Even my Marion, not a genius, could say a full sentence." Mrs. Leshko was feeling better, braced by a glimpse of superiority, a vision as sustaining as any philosophy. "It's nothing to worry about. They all learn some time. When my Marion took so long to get toilet-trained, my husband used to say, Well, you never saw a bride under the *chupa* with a load in her pants."

"I'll remember that," Leonard said, and in the genuine pleasantness with which he said this, he showed himself to be, after all, truly different from Rhoda.

"She's just keeping things to herself," Leonard would reassure Rhoda. "In her mind she's composing *War and Peace.*" Suzanne's failure to advance into speech was not troubling to Leonard. She seemed to understand everything that was said to her, and in the quiet with which she absorbed the words of adults was a sort of composure which Leonard found appealing. She was a robust child, big for her age, with a square face and curly hair. She was slightly cross-eyed, which contributed to her brooding look; often she seemed to be watching something just over his shoulder when he spoke to her. She was not hard to satisfy, tolerating substitutions when a thing had to be taken from her, and when she played with her toys she chuckled to herself.

She had actually been noisier as an infant, when her crying had seemed to penetrate the walls of the house. For a while she

had jammered in high shrieking chirps, so that Leonard had
called her "our canary." Rhoda had expected her to talk early,
so she was especially piqued at having been made a fool of.
Recently, Rhoda had come upon her rolling from side to side in
her crib, as though rocking herself to sleep, and the sounds she
was murmuring, by way of lullaby, which Rhoda at first took
hopefully for words, were simply made-up noises, secret and
clearly satisfying without her sharing them.

Rhoda's own family all spoke loudly and quickly, vying for
each other's attention, so that the din at family gatherings was
often overwhelming. A clan of story-tellers, both of Rhoda's
brothers could imitate, do accents, stretch a joke until it burst
at the punch line—so that telling stories was for them what
singing together is supposed to be for some families. For
Leonard, speech had a different function; his words were
always "well-chosen"; he could argue current events like a
news analyst, debate religion, even pun with a soft playfulness,
but it was clear that the real issues of his life were kept safe
from the conversation at the dinner table, although it was
never apparent, perhaps not even to him, what these were.

Rhoda had been puzzling for years over the question of
whether there was any hidden scorn in his guardedness: there
didn't seem to be, but she wasn't sure. At the last Thanksgiving dinner he had been especially quiet. Her brother Frank (on
leave from an army base in Texas, where he had a desk job) was
horsing around with her brother Andy (Andy "commuted to
war" at Brewster Aeronautical in Newark). Frank was rather
childishly dropping roast potatoes onto Andy's plate, saying,
"Bombs over Tokyo!" while Andy put on his Jap accent and
hissed through his teeth, "Okay, you Yankee doodle dandy, do
your worst." He sucked back his lower lip to simulate an
overbite he considered oriental.

Leonard—who argued with great feeling against the Nisei
camps in California and hated to hear anyone even use the
word "Nip" in front of him—didn't seem annoyed; he seemed,
if anything, faintly amused. But then he was seldom really

frustrated when people didn't agree with him. Other people's fatuousness didn't ruffle or surprise him. He seemed regulated by an intense patience.

They had plenty of money now, although there wasn't much they wanted to buy from the range of goods available. Even the smallest things—lipstick in cardboard tubes instead of metal—seemed designed to last only for the Duration. At times Rhoda found herself mending and substituting, as though they were poorer than they were. She spent hours canning fruits and vegetables—wax beans, purple plums, things they never ate; rows of jars lined the shelves in the basement, which was where you were supposed to put things for safety in case of attack. The whole house had a feeling of plenty lying in wait. There was a spare bedroom ready for the next child, drawers filled with banquet-size tablecloths, never unfolded.

Rhoda felt completely secure in the house, although Leonard pointed out that it had too many doors—front, back, side—plus exposed windows to the cellar on the driveway side, so that it would be easy for burglars to enter. It was a large, substantial house, a bulky Dutch Colonial, and it had been a good buy, but it was old and full of hidden flaws—termites once—and the plumbing was faulty.

"You know how interested Suzanne is," Rhoda said one evening, as she and Leonard listened to the news on the radio, "in putting the little pail inside the bigger pail and finding the piece for her big wooden puzzle. With all that mechanical ability, do you think she could learn to fix the faucets by, say, maybe tomorrow?"

"The kitchen sink is on the blink again?" Leonard guessed.

"No hot water, that's all. Mr. Dinger is convinced it's not serious."

"Mr. Dinger's not so serious himself. Last time he fixed everything fine except that the cold water faucet was on the hot line and vice versa."

"You got used to it, didn't you? I admit—he's a lovely man but as a plumber he is not wonderful. Anyway, he's coming tomorrow to take the place apart—we'll be in New York at the play. Your mother's coming over to stay with Suzanne. Actually, he's crazy about children; he'll probably reassure her."

Leonard's mother, like many people who are not "good" with children, was slightly afraid of them. She preferred those directly related to her, but even they did not crow with glee at her arrival, and in time they grew bored and demanding in her presence, which alarmed her. Without charm or control on her part, there was no telling what they might do.

A play was generally something they went to see because it was in town, like a relative; Rhoda felt the beckon of cultural events as though they were shopping sales. In this case, the theater had mistakenly sent them tickets for a matinée instead of an evening performance, but because *The Three Sisters* was a play for which Leonard had a particular affection, he had chosen to take the day off from work. Rhoda was just as glad they were going in the day time; Broadway at night, with all its neon signs turned off to honor the dim-out, was not so cheerful, although you weren't supposed to admit that. Hinda was going with them, as she often did now, in need of escorts like a dowager or a younger sister. Rhoda's brother Andy had nicknamed her "the caboose," which tickled Rhoda.

Hinda was waiting for them at the bus stop, sitting on a bench knitting. She wore a blue wool suit with a sprig of fake cherries in the lapel. She had put on weight since Stanley's departure, but her appearance was hardly altered by it—she had always had a blurred and peachy attractiveness, the relaxed flesh of a pleasant person. "We'll have to report back to Stanley," Leonard said as they kissed hello, "that you really are stickin' to your knittin', kitten." Hinda laughed and put her needles and yarn away, modest as though she'd been caught reading a letter.

They were silent through most of the bus ride to the city. Leonard had brought a copy of the play with him so that he could review it before seeing it. He was odd about his books; he wrote his name formally in all of them—Leonard S. Taber—so that even the ones he'd never gotten to read became his in a way that led Rhoda to shun them, approaching them only to dust them once they acquired the gravity of his signature. She read actively herself, always before bed, but as a form of light refreshment, magazines and best-sellers. She could remember as a girl having wept over *The Mill on the Floss*, but that passion was merely comical to her now.

Hinda had the seat near the window; in profile her face was more imposing than Rhoda tended to think of it, and her unguarded expression was grave and inwardly absorbed. She had been "very good" about Stanley's being gone, although occasionally she did things Rhoda thought were silly, like sending him locks of the children's hair or saving menus for him from restaurants she went to. She was immensely fond of her husband, almost doting. He was a good-looking man, a sharp dresser, not too bright, often sour and sarcastic in his opinions, but never unkind to Hinda; his worst fault in marriage was that he spent money too freely.

Hinda never complained about managing without him, but she had fits of indecisiveness. She had taken to visiting Rhoda's mother (which didn't surprise Rhoda—Hinda's own mother was a notably useless person). Rhoda's mother, who believed any activity was good, had talked Hinda into being a bookkeeper for the temple's war-bond drive. Outwardly Hinda was still fresh and placid, only in her calm there was something a little dreamy and distracted, where a darkening knowledge had brought her into contact with larger forces, and marked her, even in Rhoda's eyes, with an altered stature.

Through the bus window, Rhoda looked out at the Jersey flatlands, muddy with melting snow; ahead, the city's buildings were coming into view from across the river. "Look how clear it is," Hinda said. "You can see the whole Manhattan skyline."

"It's always clearest in the cold," Rhoda said.

The bus went down into the dark of the tunnel and emerged suddenly into a daylight heady with noise and traffic. They walked east across Forty-second Street. Times Square was clogged with soldiers and sailors, slow-moving groups of boys with nowhere to go. Along the curb, at her own pace, a girl with a long, straining neck walked in the characteristic gait of the cerebral-palsied, one leg scissoring behind her as the other veered with the knee bent to bring her crookedly forward, bent wrists jerking in the air.

"Don't get lost," Rhoda said to Hinda. "Stay by us."

"I forget about the city when I'm not here," Leonard said. "We should come in more often. Everything is here. Everything. It's one of the great cities. Chekhov's Moscow must have been like this."

They had turned onto Forty-fourth Street from Broadway and were out of the congested area now. Near them a very elegant woman in a turban and an ocelot coat with wide sleeves was carrying, of all things, a bag of groceries. Rhoda was amazed that anyone lived around here, especially someone like that. Why live so close to raw, milling crowds when you could afford not to? Leonard could go on about the city's endless variety, its range of possibilities like a great playground for the enquiring mind. Rhoda liked coming into the city and she considered its proximity one of their advantages, but it did not draw her to it any more than a trip to a planetarium would have made her long to live on Venus.

They were early for the play—Leonard was rigorously prompt—and they sat in the theater, mouthing small talk to each other in respectful whispers as the seats filled with ticket-holders, women mostly, stepping gingerly in their high heels on the carpeted steps. Rhoda turned to say something to Leonard, and she saw he had picked up his book again. "Doesn't it hurt your eyes to read in this light?"

"Yes," he said, "it does."

"So put the book down, it's rude." He was about to give her a sharp answer when the theater went dark.

The play began. Three actresses in high-necked dresses were pacing back and forth or reclining in uncomfortable languor on a sofa, complaining of this and that, wistful and helpless. Their listlessness made Rhoda feel out of temper with them. Leonard was laughing—the army doctor had just stood up and declared, "You said just now, baron, that our age will be called great, but people are small all the same. Look how small I am." Rhoda smiled, won to a certain amusement by Leonard's enjoyment. But all that sighing: no wonder there had been a revolution in Russia. When one of the sisters asked, "But what are we to do?" Rhoda wanted to say, "Oh, go take a walk around the block." By the end of the second act, Rhoda knew they were never going to get to Moscow. Leonard said, "You're right," and it was odd to her that he found this thought satisfying.

He was awash in a rapturous melancholy, whose form Rhoda could recognize and follow, as one follows a tune—what she could not understand was how it was uplifting. She wanted dimly to partake of it. When the curtain went down, Leonard applauded for a long time; he seemed to want to stay in his seat, to retain the sensation produced in him by the play. Outside the theater, Rhoda said, with a deliberate brashness, "Well, that was a puzzler." Neither Hinda nor Leonard answered. "It just goes to show you," Rhoda went on, "what nothing lives they led then. It's a period piece."

"Some people still lead nothing lives," Hinda suggested lightly. She had been crying in the last act and now her face looked peasant-red in the wind. Rhoda didn't expect any elucidating analysis from Hinda, who was something of a simpleton.

But Leonard was irritated. "A period piece," he snorted. "Who taught you to spoil a great thing by giving it a name like that?"

"So what did I miss, so what's the message?" Rhoda said. Did they do anything, the characters, except walk around the stage complaining? Was it so crass of her to shrivel her nose at failure?

Leonard said if she didn't want to hear about failure, most of world literature was closed to her. "I know," he said, with an unusual and peevish bluntness, "you're not that dumb."

"Excuse *me*," she said, but kept quiet after that.

When they returned to the house, the kitchen was a mess of old, encrusted lengths of pipe, Mr. Dinger's smeared footprints, his toolbox surrounded by its issue of assorted wrenches, and the damp, mineral smell common to cellars. Neither Mr. Dinger nor Suzanne was anywhere in sight. Leonard's mother, who had been napping on the couch, explained that the plumber had gone to get more parts and had taken Suzanne with him, to give her the treat of riding in the truck. "She likes him," Mrs. Taber reported. "She was following him around, and he had her handing him his tools and everything. I stayed out of the kitchen most of the time."

Mr. Dinger arrived shortly after, carrying a cumbrous and undoubtedly very expensive stack of metal pipe; Suzanne was behind him, gripping a small paper bag which—she showed them—contained screws. "She's a good girl," Mr. Dinger said. "Very helpful. And she loves trucks. She was pointing them out all along the way on our little ride. But you better be careful what you tell her. She thinks you went to New York to pay your bills."

"We saw a play," Leonard said.

"That's it—play, not pay. I'm a dumbie for not knowing. Right, Suzy?" He winked at the little girl and made a clicking noise out of the side of his mouth.

Suzanne sat on the floor as the plumber crawled under the sink, twisting his body like a mechanic's under a car. She did not come forth with any bursts of conversation, but watched him with the same quiet absorption she usually showed in her playing. "So what is this great vocabulary you're keeping tucked under your belt?" Rhoda said, tickling the child under the chin, but Suzanne only wriggled.

That evening Rhoda tried her luck. "No more *dish* and *dat*,", she said, as Suzanne tried to grab a piece of cut-up banana from across the table, grunting her pronouns of request. "Say, *I want a banana, please.*" Suzanne said nothing; she was already eating the banana, and she gazed at her mother with a cross-eyed squint above the soft, smeared mouth.

But later, when Suzanne was dressed for bed and had been kissed by her father and was being led to her crib, she turned—just before being lifted and lowered into that nightly confinement which was no idea of hers—and said, "Wanna drinka wawter." "Say: *please*," Rhoda said. "Peese," Suzanne said.

"That's better," Rhoda said, and brought the little girl her own enameled metal cup filled with water; she wanted to call Leonard to come and hear, but she hesitated to make a fuss—Suzanne had, after all, only done what she was supposed to do.

"That kid could talk all along," Rhoda told Leonard, who chuckled appreciatively. "It makes me angry. How could she be so young and still keep secrets?"

By the next day Rhoda had tempered her response of mingled resentment and elation—the sting suffered by those who hate surprises and have just been pleasantly surprised—so that the incident was largely amusing. She told the story to friends with that style and relish for which she was well known, and with a touch of the aggravated admiration she usually reserved for her husband.

Rhoda now had a "girl" to help her out one day a week—and she liked to repeat Maisie's proverb, "The Lord gives them to you when you're young because that's the only time you can stand them." By such translations into the jokes of co-workers, Rhoda took Suzanne's developments; and like a clerk who waits for a promotion, she watched—with a level of interest and an eye out for the future—because they were planning, in a year or two, another one.

IV

"Everything goes faster the second time around," Rhoda's mother told her, in the eighth month of her second pregnancy. Still, Rhoda had no reason to expect that birth would take her by surprise; she was caught, as she later said, with her drawers down. Sixteen days before her due date, her water broke while she was trying to make the beds in the morning. It was all much too rapid and savage; she had no time to pack her suitcase for the hospital. Symptoms overtook her defiantly, by force, and she was in heavy labor by the time Leonard had her settled in the back seat of the car.

Once she cried out, "Drive faster," and she was noticing, like a movie shown at an oddly wrong time, delaying them foolishly, the familiar buildings on Lyons Avenue in Newark, when the head began to emerge. They were just outside the hospital gates when the incredible, bawling cry of an infant made Leonard turn around and gasp, "Oh, my God, it's over."

The baby kept yowling, urgent and continual as a burglar alarm. A very young intern came out to the car and cut the cord there where she lay. "Did it all yourself, I see," he said. "The baby looks fine. It's a girl."

Rhoda was beginning to be proud of herself. But when they lifted her onto a stretcher, she had the thought that she was being carried from a battlefield, on which, unfairly, she had been taken by ambush.

When she told the story afterwards, Leonard's helplessness at the time became charming, a measure of his concern, the routinely comic symptom of the nervous father. The baby was named Claire, after Leonard's mother, who had died from pleurisy the day after V-E Day, in the last month of Rhoda's pregnancy. The new baby was lighter and quicker than Suzanne had been, as though the rush of her birth was the first warning of a different, more volatile strain of energy. She had none of Suzanne's self-containment and comfort in amusing herself; she would scream for hours when lowered into her playpen. From the first, she was harder to control—she slid like a bar of soap when Rhoda tried to change and dress her, so that Rhoda's mother nicknamed her, more or less fondly, *vildeh hyeh*—wild animal.

Suzanne took the arrival of a sister with alternating disdain and interest. Big for her age at four, she did tend to hug the baby so hard that Claire, at first delighted, would scream and cry until a parent came to pry her from the squeeze; and yet she never shrank from Suzanne's touch.

This second child was eager to climb into anyone's lap, pouncing and ready with kisses, like a little dog. She had a shrill, piercing little voice, even before she knew how to form words. Rhoda, who was overwhelmed at how more than doubly burdensome it was having two at home, often shocked herself at her own impatience with both of them. They were too little to be anything but greedy—they would take and take, with no conscience or feeling of debt; it was their nature and she forgave them, but she would have wanted to be more "taken care of" herself. Leonard was too much her peer, and no better at managing than she was. She would have liked to feel bulwarked by his absolute protection; in lieu of this, she liked to watch him with the children.

He was much more patient with them than she was— listening to Suzanne's disjunct recitations, letting Claire kick at his knees in her stiff white kid shoes. He was hungry for them, he felt deprived if he arrived home from work after their bedtime, he liked the feel of them; there was something almost painful in the way he picked them up and smiled at them that slow smile broken by the lines around his eyes. She was touched by him at these moments, so that, watching him, she rested in the shade of his fatherliness, as though it were extended to her.

They were both very tired at this particular period in their lives, she from the children, he from the long hours at the drugstore. It sometimes made them companionably weary with each other. They sat reading in the living room in the evenings, and Leonard brought out plates of late-night snacks—odd, male combinations, tinned meats and sardines and toast—which she ate with a great show of praise.

Once, in bed at night, when he was dreaming fitfully— breathing unevenly and whimpering in his sleep—she put her hand out and laid it against the top of his head. His hair was soft and faintly moist at its thin spot. She felt a bit silly, solemnly pretending her touch could calm the waters, while he went on having whatever trouble he was having in his dream; all the same she felt a rush of tenderness. In the morning she realized, with a start of recognition, that she had been cradling the fontanel, the soft part of a baby's skull where the gap before the bones grew together always had to be protected. She must have been half-asleep herself. The whole shadowy remembrance of the gesture pleased and uplifted her. It made her feel like a simple, instinctively good person, capable of loving another adult in the unfiltered way one loved children.

Rhoda had rather hoped that Suzanne would help care for, or at least occupy, her sister. But as they grew older, the two children began to quarrel and fight actively. Suzanne was something of a bully, fond of closing her small hand into a fist and punching. Claire, being too much younger to fight back in any effective way, would scream before the blow was struck, so that any adult who rushed to the scene was faced with scolding Suzanne for something she hadn't done yet, a weak position which made Rhoda irritated with them both. The result was that they were largely left to their own devices; Claire spent a good deal of her life in a state of weepy outrage and resignation over the maintenance of her rights.

The one place where they never fought was at their grandmother's. Rhoda would leave them there for an afternoon and would return to find Suzanne quietly working at her coloring books while Claire scribbled in magazines, both kneeling on the floor and sharing crayons in the manner of serious draftsmen, workers in the same office. Rhoda was not surprised to find that her mother's house seemed to bathe them in mildness and calm, as though they partook of the benign order evident in the arrangement of its furniture and the cleanliness of its waxed floors. She admired her mother's deftness in dealing with them, the offhand way she relegated tasks to them without disrupting her own routine. But Rhoda was used to admiring her mother and hearing her admired; she regarded having such a mother as one of the ways she was superior to other people.

Rhoda did not remember, as a child, having quarreled much with her brothers in front of her mother. Her brothers had been so little (five and six years younger than Rhoda), almost another generation, hardly worth bullying. At home they had all been most occupied in keeping out of the way of their father, who shooed and swatted at them like dogs. Her brothers had never looked like her; they were both red-haired, with colorless lashes and soft features; their speckled ruddiness was completely different from Rhoda's own brunette clarity. They had grown into fairly nice adults, presentable men who kept house with wives and went to business. (Andy, bespectacled and hard-working, was an engineer, while Frank, the youngest—sly and handsome, his hair darkened to auburn with Brylcreem—flitted from job to job.) Even as married men, their visits to their mother were frequent. In her presence they were full of anecdotes, confidential, excited—so that Rhoda sometimes had to tell them to stop acting like jerks. She had grown especially proprietary about her mother in the past few years, during which—of all of them—Rhoda was the one who had gotten to spend the most time with her.

"This is the only house those rotten kids don't get crayon wax all over the floors," Rhoda said.

Rhoda sat in her mother's kitchen drinking tea while Suzanne and Claire, through a miracle of subtle directives on the part of their grandmother, acted as though it were their own idea to find and put away all the loose crayons. The tea was so hot it burned Rhoda's tongue, but her mother swallowed it without seeming to notice. She said, "Did you know that President Truman refuses to have a valet? I was just reading." Her mother was always telling her things like this. She was like the cosmic gossip with its eye on the sparrow; no item was too small or too broad to pass under her opinion.

"So who is he impressing that he knows how to dress himself?" Rhoda said.

"For a change he has some sense. With servants, I remember even when I was a little girl I thought so, there's no privacy."

Her mother's family in Europe had been a household of substance. She had the best traits of the urban Jews; she spoke five languages (although she'd forgotten how to read Russian and her Polish and German were weak now) and she was shrewd in domestic matters (Rhoda remembered her, in hard times, straining spoiled milk into cheese and turning their collars). She could recall visits to Bavarian spas and an aunt who only washed her face in almond-cream, but underneath the baroque luxury she seemed to have been trained and prepared for contact with harsher facts; it was a truly European life, conducted without naïveté.

She had bound herself to a man whose unusual physical height and habitual refusal to be ingratiating she had mistaken, in the flush of her youth, for stateliness or integrity. She had married unhappily, for love; she had lived forty years with a husband who read the rotogravure and the obituaries while she went to Workmen's Circle meetings; but she retained so much of her own will and shape and alertness in any situation, and she managed to infuse—partly through her socialism— whatever she did with wider life and radiant outlines, so that she seemed, of all women, the least constricted by necessity.

Rhoda had always assumed that in adulthood she would know how to do all the things her mother did; in her own house it sometimes surprised her that she did not. On visits, her mother's company wasn't always the most relaxing; at times she turned on Rhoda for having expressed an opinion which Rhoda had expected to be the same as hers, and had in fact formed in imitation of her (like this scorn of hers for servants—who could have anticipated that?). "She takes the wind right out of your sails," Rhoda told Leonard, but she almost liked being bested by her mother; it let her rest from the responsibility of always being right herself.

Rhoda was riding home with the two children in the car, when Suzanne said, "I'm very strong. I'm stronger than Grandma."

"A powerhouse you are," Rhoda said.

"No, really. I can almost lift Claire off her feet by myself. Grandma doesn't pick her up any more, she's afraid she'll drop her. She makes Grandpa come in and lift her up on the bed for her nap. I think Claire's getting to be a fatso."

Rhoda glanced at Claire, who looked very small and elfin strapped into her car seat and was certainly not getting to be a fatso. It occurred to Rhoda that her mother had been looking pinched, and wanting to go out less lately, and might not be feeling well.

In the evening she suggested to Leonard that he come with her to visit the next time—"You can look at her and see." There existed a superstition between them that Leonard, being a pharmacist, was almost a doctor. But when he arrived with her at her mother's on Saturday, he seemed to have forgotten the drift of their visit; he sat at the table, letting her mother keep getting up—to make tea, to warm the coffeecake, to find a block Claire lost under the sofa. "You should rest, you never rest, Ma," Rhoda said. When her mother replied, predictably, that you got to rest enough already when you were dead, Leonard nodded and said, "That's what I always think."

Under Rhoda's cross-examination, her mother admitted that she had taken off some weight lately, but she attributed her loss of appetite to the new people who lived next door; they were always burning cabbage ("either that or they're roasting rubber tires over there"). Leonard was willing to dismiss the topic of ill health; he was taking her mother's word for it. They were laughing together. Sometimes Leonard looked foolish when he dropped his jaw and laughed. Her mother was flirting with him; they were great fans of each other. Rhoda felt left out—for once she was the somber worrier, nurser of a secret sorrow, while Leonard was hearty and loose, and had the wisdom of the light in heart.

On the ride home Leonard talked about the World Series being televised for the first time this year. Rhoda answered in a slow trailing murmur that was a sign of depression in her; she cared less than nothing about the Yankees, and she realized she was angry with Leonard. He had told her he would see about her mother, and he had not. She was alone in her worry now; she felt herself exposed and cast out to the unknown, and she marveled that she had ever thought that marriage would be the one safe spot in the world, and that Leonard's sober good sense would interpret for her the muddle of human events and give it back to her as something clear and tolerable.

In the ensuing months Rhoda watched her mother closely. At first the evidence soothed her apprehensions; her mother could still answer the doorbell faster than Rhoda could get up; it was really very hard to think of her sick. When she started taking naps in the afternoon, she told Rhoda she was sixty-four and she was entitled. But in the winter Rhoda's father let it be known that she complained of pains at night.

It was hard for Rhoda not only to imagine her mother weak and ailing, but to imagine her own life taken up with this. Insofar as Rhoda had ever thought about the future—especially as a young girl unmarked by choices—she had seen her fate as regulated by the household formed by herself and her husband: who you married was what happened to you.

It was months later—almost a year—when they found that she really was sick and that the cancer would march slowly and incurably through her, predictably; it was a matter of time. Rhoda wanted to scream at Leonard that this was unbearable, that everything would be unbearable without her mother—but she knew this was unseemly—to say it would be to ignore, firstly, that she had Leonard there in her life, and also that he had lived through the loss of his own mother without finding it unbearable. But he had always been rather distant from his own parents; he seemed not to have known them very well, and had in fact shown much livelier feeling for Rhoda's mother. Rhoda could tell he was shocked and aggrieved now; at night they held each other in bed, mute. She was grateful for the bulk of him—she thought she could feel him shaking slightly, she wasn't sure—and then the contact of his embrace caused her to flood with feeling, which made her weaker. She felt, as keenly as she ever had, that they themselves were only children, stupid children.

Even Claire knew her grandmother was very sick, because they went to visit her every day, and she was usually in bed. In her bedroom the windows were always wide open, even in mid-winter, and she wore over her nightgown only a cotton batiste bed-jacket. Her breasts under the nightclothes were rounded against her body and discreet, like worn hills. Her gray hair, finger-waved in the front, was twisted and pinned behind. Kissing Claire, she called out, "There's no reason to shut the door, Rhoda. Let some air in. Is there anything wrong with air?"

"You're right, Ma," Rhoda said. "When you're right, you'r: right."

In the sunlight of the room Rhoda saw that the doctor was there, sitting in an armchair in the corner, and someone (Rhoda's father, most likely) had brought him a cup of tea and a piece of cake, which he balanced on his knee. The doctor's pants were loose, bagging in a crease under his belly and then smoothing over the swell of his paunch. He was faceless behind his black-framed glasses. He's a fuddy-duddy, Rhoda thought, watching him lick the crumbs from his mouth. We need a hero coming to the rescue and we get a character actor here.

It was useless to blame him, especially when he was so crazy about her mother, who amused herself telling him how handsome he was. "The best medicine," he said now, nodding at Claire. Claire was by the night table; she wanted to turn on the radio so she could "do ballet" to the music, swirling to show off her skirts. For reasons not clear to herself, Claire would swirl around and around in place, until the room swam and she made herself sickish. The doctor managed to leave during the performance.

Rhoda's mother made them hush for the news broadcast. "President Truman should go back to selling suits," she said. For years she had passed out leaflets, first in Eugene Debs's and then in Norman Thomas's reliably continuous campaigns, but during the war years she had warmed toward Roosevelt, so that now she considered herself betrayed by Truman's fiscal policies, outraged like any taxpayer. Rhoda refused to argue with her, even for practice.

"I got the recipes dittoed up for you," Rhoda said. "The

secretary at the temple was a little snotty but she did a nice job." One of Rhoda's tasks in visiting her mother was to run errands for the Golden Age Group which her mother "helped out." In her sixties Rhoda's mother considered it interesting, since her own family was grown, to extend herself toward the elderly, sending them on Mystery Bus Trips, museum visits with kosher box lunches, and picnic outings on Memorial Day. At home now she busied herself compiling the group's booklet, *Secrets from New Jersey Kitchens*. "Not for the bestseller list," Rhoda predicted, "but it'll pay for seconds on spongecake at their meetings."

"You have to help me think of a way to get more men to become members," her mother said. "You're laughing, very funny, but the women all complain."

"Have a jigsaw puzzle contest," Rhoda suggested. "That'll bring them in."

"Wrong," her mother said. "Free tickets to Minsky's Burlesque, that they'd like. We should only check to make sure they all have hats to keep on their laps."

Claire, who had been playing with her rubber doll on the floor, came up and rested her doll on the hump made by her grandmother's knees under the blankets. Her grandmother took the doll and made it hop over the bedcovers and bite Claire on the nose. She spoke in a high voice for the doll, pushing the rubber neck so the head bobbed. " 'Ello, Claire. I'm just a little baby doll. Doesn't anybody have a relief package of jellybeans for me?"

Claire hoisted herself up over the side of the bed and began to squirm toward her grandmother to get the doll back. "You're a worm," her grandmother said.

"Get down from there," Rhoda said. "What did I tell you?"

Claire, who was three now and constantly active, was always climbing and crawling to get burrowed close to people. It annoyed Rhoda now that she refused to understand that she wasn't allowed to move around on her grandmother's bed, where her sharp little knees might well hit a painful place. She wailed in a bratty, surprised way when Rhoda pulled her off, and Rhoda was angry at her for getting that hurt, glowering look on her face. Everything was hard enough, and now Claire was in a snit, pouting and tossing her shoulders over things being the way they had to be, as though she could shake them off. "The princess," Rhoda said.

"Claire, show the doll how you learned to salute like a soldier," Rhoda's mother said. And Claire brightened, shooting her hand up to the side of her forehead and giggling. I have to remember how she does this, Rhoda thought, how she gets the children to do anything. It was all going to slip away and be lost unless she remembered. She felt emptied and guideless at the possibility. Leonard will know, she thought. She wanted suddenly to get home to her own house, out of the sickroom and back into the warmth of her own kitchen, where there were preparations to be made for Leonard.

"Say goodbye," Rhoda said. "Time to go—Grandma's going to sleep, it's time."

Claire walked around the bed, hugged her grandmother, and took the doll from her hands. From the doorway she yelled back, "Good night! Sleep tight! Don't let the bedbugs bite!" and blew kisses—"M'm wah!"

"Sarah Heartburn," Rhoda groaned. "Always with the theatrical exits."

It irritated Rhoda that Claire would try, with her emotional showiness, to act "fake" with her grandmother, of all people. But Rhoda's mother seemed tickled; she waved them off, saluting.

At home much of the time between visits to her mother, Rhoda became obsessed with the look of the house, the placement of the lamps, and the way the shapes of the chairs and sofa went together. She had a sense that there was something too massive about the furniture, and that the wallpaper (a bottle green grass-weave) was too dark and had worn shiny in places, like an old suit. She was aware of changing tastes and the fact that the house had a murky-toned pre-war look (as well it might, since she hadn't bought anything for it since)—all the same, she thought that what she had once chosen as admirable should still be admirable. The entire subject made her restless; she would have liked to transform everything without changing anything. She bought blond-wood end tables for the sunroom and a squarish worsted chair, and had the downstairs rooms hung with sandy, nubbly textured drapes—pointing out, as she described or displayed them to friends, the good sense of refurbishing with washable fabrics and informal colors. Although she spent considerable time dwelling on it, her eye was not good and the logic of her choices was often sounder than the decoration schemes themselves. "The gold thread in the curtains picks up the rose-beige in the carpet," she would say, talking herself out of a niggling dissatisfaction. She did believe a thing once she said it, so that intercourse with friends served to ratify any uncertain bargains she made with herself.

She brought her mother swatches of fabric and they conferred about trends; her mother was even more watchful than she was to avoid what was passé. Her mother, with her natural interest in all things, would have considered it pitiable to be unable to form an opinion. Lately her absorption in material details had increased with her sickbed confinement. She had lost her taste for novels and for the socialist monthlies which piled up on her night table. Even her *Life* magazines, which Leonard brought from the store, were left unread.

Rhoda no longer brought Claire with her when she came to visit. The deterioration in her mother's appearance had been sharp and rapid, the damage sudden. Under her eyes were blackish smudges like thumbprints. Her skin had a bruised look, with splotches of broken capillaries in the cheeks, purplish with false health. She had lost a great deal of weight. The broad outlines of her jaw remained, supporting a damaged copy of her face.

The shock of the change still stung Rhoda to tears: she could keep them back, she learned, only by quelling a sense of protest. She would try to think *You can't look back,* or *This is just life,* and that served to calm her some.

This afternoon Rhoda had brought her mother a photograph of the completed downstairs rooms. Rhoda helped her rise to a more upright position on the pillows so she could see more easily; twice her mother cried out in sudden pain as she shifted her weight. Rhoda brushed her mother's hair, then held the mirror while her mother applied a light coating of lipstick, high over the cupid's bows as she had worn it for twenty years.

When she'd put the mirror away, Rhoda found her mother staring at her hands, and she thought, from her expression, that the gnarled, mottled look of them made her sad, or that she was looking down so as not to have to look directly at Rhoda when she was in pain. Instead she surprised Rhoda by asking her if she would give her a manicure the next day she had time. "You can be my beauty parlor. It wouldn't hurt to bring some lotion, too, if you don't mind."

Later in the week Rhoda brought with her a small bag filled with rattling bottles, and took from it the bottle of Revlon Plum Beautiful, with its long white applicator handle like the tail of a very elegant plastic bird. "See, Ma?"

Her mother, who was heavily narcotized under increased dosages now, opened her eyes slowly. "You don't have a lighter shade?"

Rhoda shook her head. While she dabbed at her mother's nails, her mother leaned back on the pillows, saying nothing, and held her hands perfectly still, splayed out stiff and patient, on the towel across her lap.

It was getting hard for Rhoda to be with Leonard in the evenings . He seemed unreal to her, and when he tried to be helpful she was often rude and scornful with him for acting as though anything could help. But at times he seemed to say the right thing, and she was sleepy and quiet as she leaned against him, and almost more grateful than she could stand. It was easiest to keep her bearings if she drew herself up and kept busy and took pride in her competence and the continuation of the routine under stress. Lately he had more or less chosen to take her at her word when she told him things should go on "as normal." She could, of course, only simulate normality; the normal was, for the time being, a paradise she had lapsed out of. She longed for it constantly.

This evening, after giving her mother her manicure, Rhoda arrived home in a state of desperate, slow sadness. Nor was she left for a minute even to the grim peace of her mood; the noise and disorder of the children was intolerable. She was up in Suzanne's room, yelling at her, when she heard the click of the door downstairs which meant that Leonard had arrived. She continued yelling, in a passion of irritation, which ended in her giving Suzanne a slap. "And more is coming," Rhoda said. Suzanne was crying loudly.

Leonard began mounting the creaking carpeted steps. Rhoda met him at the landing. "Your dinner's almost ready," she said. She turned back and shouted, "Start putting those things away."

They walked down the stairs together. "A nice greeting," Leonard said.

Rhoda sat down in the living room. "I'm too tired to talk about it."

"Well, listen," he said. "I had fairly good news today. Addie Shulman came by the store—he told me we're going to be able to rent the big auditorium at the temple for the Beta Omega party in June."

Beta Omega was Leonard's fraternity from pharmacy school. He had been president of his local alumni chapter for four years running—elected, Rhoda thought, because he was both well-liked and a cut above the other members. Addie Shulman was bright enough, an avid reader and an opera buff; Fred Meyers had a nervous tinge of leftist politics which, while it made him a volatile dinner companion, also gave him an undeniable air of weary integrity; but they were all, compared to Leonard, a bit coarse and off-base.

Rhoda didn't want to hear about their party, now of all

times, and she was disgusted with him for bringing it up; there was no stopping him with chilly replies. Leonard's enthusiasm for his fraternity was unqualified; the pathetic antics of the most puerile member evinced from him only a sheepish amusement. He was never freer, more expansive, more tickled with himself than at the annual Beta Omega parties. Rhoda went along in tow, enjoying herself well enough—it was easy for her to be hearty—but she had learned not to try to get more than his sporadic attention at these events.

"I thought you'd want to know it's going to be held on the synagogue premises," Leonard said, "in case you were planning to wear that risqué dress of yours with the see-through lace around the midriff." He was joking.

"It's not see-through," Rhoda said. "It has flesh-colored taffeta underneath."

"I don't know—I'll have to ask the rabbi about this. Of course, you see a lot of cleavage at Friday night services."

"Do you have to look?"

"I'm not so old," Leonard said, "that the cantor looks better to me." He was in high spirits.

Rhoda was sorry that she always told people what good care he took of her, how sensitive he was: they should see him now. She turned away to walk into the kitchen. Leonard followed.

He asked then, "How was your mother this afternoon?"

"Every day worse. She looks so old now."

"They're sure a hospital wouldn't be better for her?"

"She has the nurse at night," Rhoda said. "They give her that stuff for the pain and she sleeps. Pop's no help—he's not exactly cheerful for her to be around; why should he be any different now than he's ever been? When he comes into her room, he doesn't even talk, he just sits there and droops. I kick him out when I'm there."

"The only thing they can do now is cut down the pain," Leonard said. He made a tucking sound with his lips, the sound of resignation.

"Why can't they do anything else?" Rhoda said. "Why can't
they?"

Leonard winced, he raised his eyebrows in a pleading, sad
look, and then he turned away from her.

Rhoda stood at the stove. "Dinner," she said, forking pieces
of chicken onto the plates.

"We have to eat fast. The men are coming for pinochle at
eight. Did you forget?"

"Sort of," Rhoda said.

"But you wanted them to come. You told me to invite them;
it was your idea."

"I know," she said. "Don't tell me. I made cookies. I know."

The girls helped slide the bridge table out of the closet,
unfold its legs, and set it upright. It was an old table, lacquered
maroon to look like mahogany, and its padded oilcloth top
looked as if it had yellowed with use, although in fact it had
always been that parchment color. The table was too rickety to
stand firmly—Suzanne kicked at one leg to make it stop
bending inward. "You'll ruin it," Rhoda scolded. "That was a
very expensive table once." This was not true, but she
expected objects to be permanent, so that all her possessions,
upgraded by adoption, were treated like keepsakes.

The men arrived close together—first Addie Shulman, then
Hinda's Stanley and Richard Fern. The children were excited;
Claire, who had been allowed to stay up late, leaped at the men
and squealed their names. "Calm down," Rhoda said lightly,
mock-stern. "My goodness." When the men sat down to play
cards, Rhoda busied Suzanne with passing a plate of cookies
and bringing in glasses of rye on the rocks; Leonard alone
preferred Scotch. "A sophisticate," Addie teased. "Bidding is
open. Put your money where your mouth is."

Claire, who would not leave the room where the men were,
sat on a couch, coloring designs on paper napkins. Suzanne,
who was awkward at any precise handiwork like drawing,

admired them. This praise from her sister was so unusual that Claire decorated six or seven napkins, until Suzanne noticed from the uniformity of the results that Claire was copying the embossed floral pictures on the napkins. "But I thought you knew," Claire wailed. "Copying doesn't count," Suzanne snorted.

Rhoda had just finished settling the girls in bed when she heard the phone ring. "I'll get it," she yelled down. In her haste to get to the phone Rhoda switched off the light in Suzanne's room without thinking, so that she had to run back to turn it on again so Suzanne could read in bed. When she got to the phone, she was annoyed and flustered. Suzanne was still calling out that she didn't have the book she wanted. "Wait, I can't hear you," Rhoda complained into the phone, and then she called back to Suzanne, "Well, just get up and get it." Rhoda turned toward the wall so she could hear better; the men downstairs were making a great deal of noise. Suzanne had come into the hallway in her pajamas. She stared at Rhoda, who kept nodding gravely at the wall and wouldn't look at her. Suzanne went back to her room. Rhoda hung up and called down, "Leonard, come here. It's important."

He walked up the steps and met her in the hallway. "That was my brother Frank on the phone," she said.

"So why are you whispering?" Leonard wanted to know. Rhoda's mouth was set and hard, and at first he thought she had been quarreling with her brother, but her eyes weren't angry, they were soft and wet, almost romantic. Hurt. "Your mother," he said.

Rhoda was trying to think whether to say dead or passed away, and she was also clinging to the idea that if she said neither, if she kept everything to herself, the fact would perish on its own, become untrue. Too soon; she wasn't ready: she was trying to remember the terminology to explain to Leonard that her mother had succumbed to some secondary failure, some swelling complication, saving her, the doctor said, from the last agonized stages. She was thinking wildly *I don't have anything any more* and she was making herself dizzy with reckoning—she had Leonard, had Suzanne, had Claire—she was counting up all the ways she had and didn't have them. Leonard was dialing the phone, calling her brother to find out whether they should go to her father's house tonight or tomorrow.

Rhoda felt a seeping rage against her father, who was probably sitting in his chair right at this moment, staring dully ahead; he was as ready as he had ever been for a sudden shock. Rhoda had not thought to ask if the night nurse, coming upon her in bed, had heard her say anything. Rhoda did not much like the idea of last words; it seemed unfair to hold them against the witnessable totality of a person's life. Even Goethe's famous "More light"—hadn't they wondered whether he was hearkening to something celestial, or only asking that a lamp be brought or a window opened? The image of this made her think of her mother's room, with its windows always wide open, and a second painful shock came over her, a wave of homesickness for that room; in the worst of her mother's illness, it had never had the still atmosphere of a sickroom—it was too airy; any paper you put down in it was always getting stirred by the breeze. The blinds shaking, and the dresser scarves lifting at the ends—it had been almost too cold for Rhoda; she had always worn sweaters to visit.

Leonard was telling her that he was going downstairs to let the men know. She heard them murmuring and getting their coats out of the closet. Their voices were low, tender in a business-like way. They were very decent men; all the same she was annoyed that the news had overtaken Leonard in the midst of a pinochle game.

At her parents' house the next day, there was a din of voices, like the sounds of a party. To Rhoda, because she was the last of his offspring to arrive and the only daughter, was left the task of consoling her father. She tried distracting him. "Look, Pop," she said, "all these people have come to visit you."

"Talk, talk," he said. He turned his back and walked, with his shuffling gait, toward the bedroom.

Mrs. Leshko came out of the crowd to squeeze Rhoda's hand. "She was a wonderful woman, your mother. Bright, alert. Everything. They don't make them like that any more."

Across the room Rhoda's brother Andy, who had taken it hard, was being coaxed into a chair by his wife. His wife went to bring him a plate of food. On the way back from the buffet table, she made a detour to ask Rhoda, "Do you want anything?" As one of those directly bereaved, Rhoda was something of a guest of honor. She felt the attention of these people as something gratifying, and yet when she looked out at all of them she had a spiteful notion of their combined worthlessness. "She had more sense in her little finger," she started to say to Mrs. Leshko, but she was afraid the old lady was going to begin weeping.

"Hinda," she called out. "Look who's here." Hinda, a conversation away, turned around at once. "My friend Hinda," Rhoda explained, beginning to believe it as she said it, "always asks about you, Mrs. Leshko."

Hinda was among them, reaching out to grab Mrs. Leshko's freckled upper arm in a shortened embrace. "I hear your grandchild's a regular Einstein."

"You heard right," Mrs. Leshko wheezed.

Turning from them, Rhoda faced another older gentleman— the room seemed to be full of them, vaguely remembered— remote relatives, one-time trade unionists, kibitzers from the old neighborhood altered into seriousness for the occasion. The man was round-faced and heavy-jowled, wearing spectacles with black plastic frames—the doctor. He nodded at her and extended his hand; shaking his hand and saying his name, Rhoda felt herself smiling the stiff smile of a loser in a very long, grueling sports event. At least it's over, she was thinking (as though it had been something temporary), there's nothing left to happen.

V

As Leonard's pharmacy prospered in the post-war boom, he began to work shorter hours. Two extras were hired to work behind the counter—a somewhat silly older man and a housewife who wore noisy costume jewelry—while Leonard devoted himself to filling prescriptions and ordering the pharmaceutical stock, keeping abreast of advances by reading the medical journals.

As a schoolboy, Leonard had felt the desire to become a doctor. He was the middle child of three—his father had been a cobbler, a harsh, honorable man who beat his children with a strap when they were disobedient; his mother had been sweeter, mild and ineffectual (they were both dead now). Leonard had been a great student, the one groomed to be a professional. There was an older brother, small-boned and soft-spoken like himself (but not so quick), who had always been kind to Leonard. His younger sister Eppie had never been

quite right in the head. She was dull and dispirited, she seemed
to care for nothing; when you brought her things to play with,
she let them fall from her hands. She was all right in school;
she learned to read and write with her class, but she would
never play. At recess she sat by herself, unbuttoning and
buttoning her shoes or pulling up grass. Once she climbed up a
tree and would not come down. Before she entered high school,
Mrs. Taber took her to a store to buy a gym suit, but Eppie
would not try it on; she crossed her arms in front of her chest
and wrapped them about her sides, rocking up and down; when
they pleaded with her, she beat her elbows against the counter.
At home she took to lying in bed and feigning illness; one
morning she was found hiding crouched under the bed.

In her teens Eppie was put in a state institution. The family
went to visit her twice a month. Eppie never complained,
despite the horror of the place. Her father tipped the orderly to
make sure that she was kept clean, and she was, she said.
Leonard was the most loyal in his visits: for years he never
forgot her birthday. Once, to Leonard alone, his mother
confessed a lingering suspicion about Eppie's birth and delivery. The doctor, she said, had wrenched so hard with the
forceps that he had left, beneath the ordinary scabs, visible
dents in the infant's skull. "He meant well, I suppose,"
Leonard's mother said. "Who knows?"

Thereafter the whole notion of being a doctor sank in
Leonard's estimation, in the deep figurative sense of something
falling, slipping away: a sinking sensation. He had no fascina-
tion with the dreadful; the responsibility had become abhor-
rent to him.

He still loved the intricacies of medicines; at a time when
the influx of new drugs developed since the war was overwhelming, the quality and extent of his stock was unparalleled
in the neighborhood. He was known for being able to explain,
when asked, just what good a particular substance was going to
do for you. Physicians themselves often phoned him with
questions.

His partner Nat still handled the books; he was twenty years Leonard's senior, and he was now talking about selling his interest and retiring to Florida. Leonard was not ready to buy out the business: he was conservative in his ways of accruing money and he distrusted credit. Still, his stocks had done well, and he began to tease his partner about the luxuries of Miami sunshine.

In his expanded spare time, Leonard was active in volunteer work for the town's Community Chest. He was a regular at monthly meetings, and in the autumn he canvassed door-to-door collecting donations. His photograph appeared in the local paper for having pledged a continuing supply of medicines and bandages to the Ambulance Fund. Leonard watched the total of donations increase with the excitement with which he watched a baseball scoreboard; it was his hobby now.

This year he and Rhoda were invited to the annual kick-off fund-raising party at the home of a surgeon named McPhearson. To Leonard it was simply a meeting in evening dress; Rhoda was both excited and dubious. The McPhearsons' place was farther out in the suburbs, in swooping hilly country where the houses had manorial lawns and the streets had no sidewalks. "It's that one," Leonard said, "the one that looks like a castle." "Tudor," Rhoda said.

Mrs. McPhearson took their coats at the door; she was a plain woman in a black dress, wearing a pearl necklace that seemed bound by gravity to settle into the hollows of her collarbone. Rhoda surveyed the living room with vague disappointment; the room was large, but instead of the dark, spindly Chippendale and Hepplewhite reproductions which Rhoda and her friends all had, or the boxy sectional sofas they had recently come to prefer, there were squat Victorian hand-me-downs. There was even a maroon velvet chair similar to one at home that Rhoda had considered throwing out, but here it looked, not floridly overstuffed, but chilly and settled in its corner.

Rhoda sighted Richard Fern and his wife, Evvie, across the room; they were the only people there Rhoda really knew.

Leonard had persuaded Richard to take an interest in last year's projects, so he too had been rewarded with an invitation. Evvie made her way to them, brushing aside guests who parted before her rustling urgency. "Rhoda!" she squealed. "You look *elegant*." Rhoda was wearing black; she did have an air. Evvie looked jolly and tasteless in a flounced turquoise dress, but pretty: assured and innocent under all the makeup. Richard came up to join them and put his hands on both their shoulders. "Best-looking gals in the room," he said.

At dinner Rhoda was seated between Leonard and a gentleman whose card identified him as Dr. Findlay, a thick-necked, red-faced man with graying hair. "Do you practice locally?" Rhoda asked. "I'm a surgeon," he said. "I specialize in the biliary tract."

"Ah," Rhoda murmured, "so people come to you. From all over, I'll bet." He shrugged modestly, laying aside his grapefruit spoon.

Dr. Findlay waved away the maid who was attempting to put a plate of soup in front of him. "I can't stand soup," he explained to Rhoda. "Too messy. Only way to eat it is to lap it up like a dog. You can't do that in company. At home that's how I eat soup—my wife too—I taught her. Only way."

"Oh, Dr. Findlay." Rhoda laughed, getting the idea. "You're a character." Dr. Findlay stiffened.

"You could always tell people it was the French way," Rhoda suggested. "At home whenever I burn something I tell my little girls that's how the French do it. They're too little to know any better. I used to teach French, so they believe me."

Dr. Findlay showed no sign of being charmed by the cleverness of this. "Do you teach the girls to speak French?"

"Well, the oldest won't say a word, but the youngest knows a little. I ask her, *Quel âge as-tu?* and she says *J'ai SANK ans.*" Rhoda's voice squealed with stubborn perkiness as the sense that she was boring this man deepened.

"I know a doctor out your way," Dr. Findlay offered. "Good man. Dr. Hofferberg. An internist."

"We know them socially," Rhoda said.

"He's quite an interesting fellow. Bright, you know, witty. He has that younger wife with the remarkable figure. I was teasing him about her, I couldn't help it—how does an old dog like you keep up the pace? I asked him. He said to me—You know what they tell you when you're younger, that the best is yet to *come*. Ha, ha." Dr. Findlay, in his amusement, sputtered sauce on his chin.

Rhoda was mildly disgusted. But her instinct to hold the man's attention was stronger than her dismay at what impressed him. "One time," she said, warming to the occasion, "nine or ten years ago, we were staying downstairs from them at a hotel and we kept hearing this thumping noise from their room." She proceeded to tell at length the saga of Herb Hofferberg's prank. She had thought the episode tasteless at the time, but in the face of Dr. Findlay's amused snorts, she expanded the details, shaped a plot to it. At the tale's end he tapped her on the arm by way of appreciation. "Fooled you, didn't he?" Heads turned at the sound of Dr. Findlay's laughter. Rhoda smiled, as though easily masterful.

After dinner they listened to a long stretch of speeches by civic leaders. Dr. Findlay performed a mock pantomime of dozing off and snoring for Rhoda's benefit; she shook her head to feign laughing when he raised his head and winked at her. Leonard caught a glimpse of this and gave her a stern look.

When the speeches ended, they were free to rise, mingle, and prepare to leave. Rhoda turned to Leonard as though saving the last dance for him; she was ready for familiar company. Dr. Findlay reached from behind to shake Leonard's hand. "You have a charming wife," he said, putting his hand on Rhoda's shoulder. "I'm keeping her," Leonard said.

On the pathway across the lawn, amid the sound of goodbyes called out behind them, Evvie Fern sidled up to Rhoda and whispered, "Did you see the jewelry—did you see the *rocks* on some of those women?" Evvie's husband, on Rhoda's other side, said, "You know what I noticed—there was a lot of expensive bridgework there." Richard was a dentist. "Several thousand dollars was walking around in the mouths of some of those people."

Rhoda laughed. "That's a good one." Her high heels clattered against the flagstones as she shook off the Ferns and hastened down the walk. Leonard came up from behind her just as she reached the street; he was calling softly, "Why are you walking so fast?" in a tone of mild irritation.

"Oh," she said. She was unwilling to look at him—she felt caught. For a moment her resources failed her. In the pause of awkwardness she rallied, and turned upon him her stiff but nonetheless winning smile, the last look of interest left in her that night. She took his arm. Only when they were home and Leonard had gone to sleep and she lay in bed reading her book did her features once again arrange themselves into the taxed and helpless look, the released strain, particular to the loneliness of those who are natural with no one.

Rhoda was rather proud of the job she had done preparing Claire for the first day of kindergarten. Claire knew the alphabet, she could write her name, and she could spell cat, dog, and mother out loud, which was as much as Rhoda could teach her without poaching on the school's domain. The night before her first day Rhoda reviewed with Claire the names of children she had played with who would be in her class, but Claire, soaring with eagerness, was above such reassurances. "KINDAgarden," she screamed, running through the house, and would not go to bed until threatened that a shortage of sleep would make her sick and absent.

Walking with Claire down the school's hallway the next morning, Rhoda was startled by the din coming from the kindergarten classroom—a continuous wail of sound, like the roar of a crowd, marked by the claps of wooden blocks smacked together and occasional high shrieks—she had forgotten how noisy it always was in the primary grades; the walls were yellow tile, like a public restroom, and shouts echoed. Miss Stacey, the perennial-spinster teacher, stood at the door, looking girlishly eager, nudging the children inside. Every toy in the room had been dragged forth by five-year-olds reckless with guesses at what to do and frenzied by the sudden saturation of company. A boy shrieked as he held a flat wooden puzzle over his head and overturned it so the pieces rained like pellets. Two girls fought over a miniature tea kettle, while groups of children chased each other, gasping and giggling. The boy who had discovered the checkers kept yelling, "Bombs away!" as he scattered the box's contents. "Go on," Rhoda said. She dropped Claire's hand.

At one end of the room a wooden Junglegym loomed like a giant Tinkertoy; Claire climbed it to the top. When she hung by her knees, a boy screamed that he could see her underpants. "So what," she said, climbing down. "Bye-bye," Rhoda waved from across the floor, edging out the door.

Two weeks later Rhoda reported to Miss Stacey for a special consultation after school. When she returned home she took Claire aside for a serious talk, shooing Suzanne away. "This is private. Go play outside."

"I understand," she said, trying to look down at Claire gravely, "that the other children have been calling you a *schmatah.* Miss Stacey didn't even know what it was. It's an old rag."

"*I* know," Claire said.

"It's not even something you call a person. She said the children run around all day screaming *Schmatah Claire Taber* at you."

"They do not," Claire said. "They never do."

It had begun the first day, for no good reason, children she had never seen before were chanting her name as part of a phrase horrifically amusing. She had been stunned at the nightmarish senselessness of it, the opening of a door into the wrong room; on her face had been a look of wounded surprise.

"You're too shy. Miss Stacey says even when the other children ask you to play, you don't play along." (This was news to Claire.) " 'She's very unaggressive'—I heard all about it—

'doesn't assert herself.' You have to learn to be pushier. That's
all there is to it. Real tough."

Claire squirmed, skinny in her overalls. "I also heard that
Rita Shepp and Janey Littauer have been nasty to you. That
Rita made a fuss about not wanting to hold your hand for the
Mexican Hat Dance."

"She did not. Did not."

"All right," Rhoda said. "Talk's over. Go play outside."

Released, Claire ran out the door, past the front-yard shrubs,
over the lawn (she was not supposed to run on the grass) across
the street to where Judy lived. From the living room window
Rhoda could see her standing in the Finches' driveway,
knocking on the screen door. Judy Finch was three years older
and had been Claire's friend ever since her family had moved to
the neighborhood a year ago. Together the girls spent their
afternoons warding off the attempts of Judy's younger brother
to play with them. He was actually a year older than Claire,
but by Claire's alliance with Judy she considered him a baby.
Rotten kids, Rhoda thought. Remind me not to have them in
my next lifetime. She indulged momentarily in guessing, like a
shopper passing the time pleasantly, what else she might do.
Be a person in white slacks who sat under palm trees drinking
Bacardi cocktails.

For their honeymoon she and Lenny (she had called him
Lenny more often then) had stayed a week in Bermuda. She had
wanted the French Caribbean, which was beyond their budget.
In Bermuda the air was clean and mild and moderate, intensi-
fied in midafternoon when the famous pink beaches had a
hard, bright, holiday glare. Although neither of them drank as a
rule, in the early evenings they sat in a café on the harbor and
sipped exotic mixtures from pineapples, nursing them long
after darkness fell and the lights shone in store windows. They
admired the tactful manners of the waiters. "It's a tiny little
island," Rhoda said. She had been very keen then never to be
awed by anything.

She was amused, remembering. Certainly she had been

nervous and wary before the honeymoon. During their engage-
ment Lenny had presented her with a book called *A Manual for
Marriage*. He had underlined in pencil the sentence, "It is the
degree of affection between a married couple which truly
determines the success of their sexual life together," so that
she wouldn't think he was clinical simply because he was
modern. They discussed the desirability of waiting to have
children (she was glad not to have to argue about this), and he
had sent her to a doctor, a friend of his, to be fitted for a
diaphragm. Reading the book had excited her, but when she
felt the prod and spread of the metal instruments measuring
the mouth of her cervix, she was alarmed that it would be like
that, mechanical and violating. It was not. It was active and
orchestrated, with plotted falls and rises, and if she did not feel
completion, what she felt in aftermath was a tenderness—a
blurred sensation, like the faint swelling around the lips from
kissing—and a deepened admiration for Leonard.

She had a good memory, which she did not often exercise;
she could remember, for instance, the linen suit she had worn
on the ship, and the street where she had bought it in Newark;
also the unbecoming way she had worn her hair then, with
those awkward puffs over the ears. God, the lipstick they had
used in those days, like India ink: you had had to scrub with
Brillo to get it off a coffee cup. Of her physical self she
remembered chiefly that her waist had been trimmer and no
blue veins had shown in her legs when she wore shorts. At
thirty-six, Rhoda was aware that her small, long-nosed face had
grown stronger of feature and more important-looking, despite
certain textural losses in the skin. She was not poignantly
aware of aging because she had no special attachment to her
youth in any stage. Her childhood, admittedly better than
most, she saw as full of needless stupidities and privations.

Occasionally a sense of the past gripped her suddenly. This
morning she had been polishing the mahogany china cabinet in
the dining room. It was a favorite piece—a Baker copy of a
Sheraton sideboard—with seashell scrolls and narrow inlays of

lighter wood along the borders of the drawers. As she had been taught to do, she dipped a cotton swab in lemon oil to get at the crevices. What a good girl I am, she mused lightly, rubbing so the shadings of burl, well-matched on the lower drawers, showed richly. In the flush of accomplishment and the faintly dizzying odor of furniture polish, she felt a sharp lowering into melancholy. She had an absurd and painful urge to show her mother what she was doing. Intensely and desolately she missed her mother. The lack of her was terrible.

As a rule she kept her eyes on the present. She had a liberal's sense of the historical past as something you were always advancing from. In the waves of nostalgia which sometimes overtook Leonard, he had once or twice made her feel that she had neglected to notice things now gone. Her own opinion was that things (like Nipponware tea sets) or ideas (like Utopian Socialism) passed out of the everyday life around you because they died of natural causes, of revealed defects, and were replaced by better.

She knew, although they had never discussed it, that Leonard, since the early days of their marriage, had been disappointed by what he might have called her inadequate interior life. She saw it in the stiffening of his shoulders when, without thinking, she spoke to him when he was reading even a newspaper. The children, too, bristled at her voice breaking into their solitary games. This was unjust; she was more reflective than they knew. She was not so shallow or so careless as to take her own life for granted, for instance; but by this very knowledge, she clung fiercely to the surroundings she had made for herself, the objects of choice.

Rhoda watched the big horse-chestnut tree from the front porch. The tree was pretty in spring with its white blossoms; now the chestnuts were falling, their yellow innards squashing underfoot on the sidewalk. There was no use for them. The other day she had caught Claire trying to eat one, making a face at the bitterness.

She heard squalling from across the street where the children were playing. Suzanne had joined them. From the cries, Rhoda gathered that Suzanne had just hit Mikey Finch in the chest and pushed him into the bramble bushes. "You don't hit somebody else's brother," Judy was yelling. "You're a guest. Get off my property." She pushed Suzanne onto the sidewalk. Wordless as an ogre, Suzanne was butting her head into Judy's stomach. Judy shrieked for help, while Claire ineffectively pummeled her sister. "What is going on?" Mrs. Finch called out, slamming the screen door, and pulled the two children apart. "The sidewalk," Suzanne said, breathing heavily, "is public property."

"She hits everybody," Judy was saying. "Even when you come to visit at their house, she hits you when you're a guest. I would never do that. Nobody regular would."

"You are noble," Mrs. Finch said. "A saint." She turned to the others. "Go home, you two. It's suppertime."

Rhoda fed the two girls their supper, and they waited with her for Leonard to come home. At the sound of his entry—the dog always heard it first—there was a great scuffle across the living room to the front door. Claire's shrill voice was the loudest. There was no question that they preferred their father. It was natural, if painful.

Leonard was different with each of his children. With Suzanne he was discreetly companionable. Since turning nine she had been obsessively interested in bears ("Guess what my favorite animal is," she demanded of anyone who came to visit), and he took her to the Bronx Zoo, where they stopped respectfully before each cage in the bear section and read the signs out loud to each other. On warm nights like this one, they played catch out of doors after Leonard had his dinner, and Claire (who was too little to go out after dark) could hear the smacking sound of the ball passing from hand to hand in the driveway. When they came indoors Claire wailed complaints until he tickled her and swung her so that she could touch the ceiling, mimicking her squeals of excitement until she became too wild and he had to put her down. She tried to climb his leg.

"You're a tree," she said, shinnying. She grabbed hold of his sweater. "Stop that," he said.

Claire continued; she could hardly believe he minded—only once had he yelled at her hard enough to frighten her, when she had spilled her milk three times in a row. "Get down from there," Rhoda commanded. "You're a witch," Claire said.

"It's somebody's bedtime," Rhoda said. "School tomorrow, remember?"

In the emptied days with both children away at school, a new and pleasant concern arose. Nat Shrimpke, Leonard's partner, was finally about to enjoy his retirement to Miami: Leonard had bought out the older man's share and was now full owner of the pharmacy. There was to be no fanfare about the changing of hands; the name—Front Street Quality Drugs— was to stay the same. Rhoda suggested an opening day gala with some small cosmetic item given free to each customer, but Leonard brushed aside the idea; "It's not Macy's basement, you know." "All right," she said, "I know when to mind my own business," and she pulled her upper lip down like a flap, holding it stretched shut with her hand. "You look like Mortimer Snerd that way," he said. He was very happy.

Surprisingly, what he did care about was the décor; he planned a major revision. After hours, he showed Rhoda the rows of small, dark drawers behind the counter. "You never can find anything in them. In the front too—it looks like a poor student's garret with all this old brown wood around and the Latin labels. It needs lots of glass, I think—make it look airy and light. People always used to confuse learning with the antique; a little dustiness impressed them. Those days are gone gone."

"Gone with the wind," Rhoda said, casting her eyes up melodramatically. Still it troubled her faintly to think of Nat's aisles of cabinets stripped, gutted, and reconstructed. "What about the tradition of the folksy smalltown druggist? It means nothing to you, you moderne thing, you."

"It means superstition, that's what. Stupidity and stubbornness." He had these odd streaks of hardness in him. At Friday night discussions after services at the temple he was beginning to insist on the notion that you could be a Jew without believing in a revealed God. (The rabbi thanked him for raising the level of disputation.)

Now he threw himself into the project of remodeling the pharmacy. From the library he brought home books on the Bauhaus and Le Corbusier. Once she caught him looking at photographs of Gaudí's apartment house in Spain. "I trust that's not what you have in mind," she said. "Of course, it might help business by making people feel sick." He chuckled.

In the end he did less refurbishing than she expected. He settled for a larger display window, glass shelves and counters, fluorescent lights, and a floor of beige linoleum squares marbled with white. She called it his "ice palace"—half-alarmed that it might seem cold and unwelcoming—but once the goods were on the shelves, it looked very simply like what it was: a well-stocked store.

"It looks quite human," she said, by way of applause.

"Aha," Leonard answered. "You can see it's really true what they say—there's a very high human pleasure in the perception of order." She couldn't believe he was talking about a drugstore. He was not.

"My, my," she murmured. She was actually moved in some distant way by what he'd said. The rows of bottles, arranged in degrees of size, became interesting; her eye began to form patterns of the labels' colors. She settled for predicting, "I know it'll be a big hit."

There was, in fact, no way to tell whether it was a big hit or not. The same customers frequented the store, providing approximately the same amount of business. Leonard was not sure what he'd expected, but he felt a vague disappointment, so that eventually even the most rapturous compliments on the store's new look galled him. For perhaps not the first time in his life he became falsely modest as a symptom of faint bitterness. "*I* like it," he would say, shrugging.

Rhoda was so used to his working late hours that when she came home from shopping in the late afternoon and walked upstairs to change her shoes, she almost tripped on the threshold when she heard his voice saying, "Is that you?" He was lying in bed reading a newspaper. Her first thought was that something had gone wrong at the store so that he'd had to close early. The fluorescent lights—she'd always thought the electrician had been too offhand when he explained about the wiring. "I just got so tired all of a sudden," Leonard said.

"That's awfully sensible of you to come home when you're not feeling well," she said, sitting on the bed. "Not like you at all."

He seemed better later in the evening; he ate lightly, then he went back to the bedroom, although he kept the light on. There was nothing apparently wrong with him and she wondered if he were simply in low spirits now that the store was done, a post-holiday letdown. But it wasn't like him to choose to be sick.

The only person in the family who actually liked staying still was her father. "Not that my father wasn't an intelligent man in his day," Rhoda said, later in the night, as she straightened the pillow on her own bed and readied herself for sleep. She was lying under the covers while Leonard got up to close the window. She had been reading; a bestseller lay with its face down on the night table.

"You'll break the binding that way," Leonard said, coming over to the bedside and shutting the book properly. "But your father's not so old. How old is he? Sixty-five?"

"Sixty-eight. Look at the way he walks. He's been an old man probably since he first came to this country. Nothing was the way he'd imagined. What did they know when they came? None of them knew anything. My mother came a year after to join him and she found him sleeping on a park bench." This did not sound true as Rhoda said it—perhaps her father, who could fall asleep anywhere, had just been dozing over his paper—she had never thought about it before. "I think he never recovered from the humiliation. They were very well-off, his family. Very formal people, you should see them in the pictures, all sitting up straight like stuffed owls. He wasn't raised to take bad luck gracefully, if you know what I mean."

"You weren't even alive then."

"I know," Rhoda admitted. She had absorbed her mother's stories so totally that it surprised her that she hadn't been there. "But he looks very pompous and handsome in the old pictures. Completely different, very self-assured. But maybe he just had a good photographer and he was always the same."

Rhoda, who now took her father on occasional outings in an effort to maintain his interest in life, had brought him that morning to see Leonard's remodeled store. "Very beautiful. Clean," he had said. "Finish your business here. I'll wait outside in the car." Waiting outside in the car was a device he had developed years before, when his wife's visits had extended to hours of talk-talk-talk. He would wait, stiffly sitting behind the wheel of the old Hudson, sometimes leaning on the horn when he grew impatient. Now that Rhoda was his caretaker, he seemed to find comfort in the habit of waiting for her; today she had found him slumped asleep in the front seat.

"He gets on my nerves," she said. "And yet in his own way he likes company."

"I think," Leonard said, shutting off the lamp and getting into bed, "he's gotten worse in the past year, since your mother passed away. But he deserves respect. He's a dignified person."

Rhoda said, rolling to the edge of her bed that was nearest to Leonard's, "He has terrible table manners."

When Rhoda awoke, there was the sound of a mosquito in the room. She had been reading a historical novel about an heiress on a clove plantation in the West Indies and in her half-stirred waking she wanted to make some joke to Leonard about how they needed mosquito netting. He was the lighter sleeper; there was a good chance he'd been bothered by the noises. But, no, the sound was his snoring—short, whistling wheezes. Something was wrong: he was gasping for breath. He must be dreaming, as the dog did, that he was being chased.

"Wake up," she called, nudging him. "It's just a bad dream, it's all right."

A terrible choking hiss issued from his lips and his chest heaved as though thrust upward by some rudely brutal push. Again she nudged him: he would not wake up. She switched on the lamp. His face was contorted with the effort to breathe and the sounds of his rattling gasps became louder—frightening: they were nothing like Leonard; they were the animal noises of extremity. With one guttural push there appeared on his mouth a foam of blood-tinged sputum; it dripped down the corners of his lips onto his face; like a drunk or a baby, he did not feel the mess of it. "Oh, my God," Rhoda called out, shaking him. (Was it all right to shake him?)

She struggled with his jackknifing torso to prop him upright with the idea that this might help his breathing. I don't know what to do, she was moaning to herself. I don't know what this is. She went to the hall to phone for an ambulance, hearing, all the while she spoke, the whoops of his unearthly efforts for air.

Her voice was high and hoarse as she gave her address. "Tell them to send," she tried to say slowly, "whatever they send for a heart attack. I don't know what it is."

Having called for help, she gave up thinking what to do—leaving it to doctors, to hospitals—and surrendered to participation in the mounting horror. All the while she waited for the ambulance she called his name, a vain effort to share in the peril of his struggle, primitively to beat a drum for his heart. (It could not be his heart. He was forty-two years old.) She wanted to drown out the sound of his hideous gasping. She did not know when the sound stopped and she continued to call his name. (Now it's over, she thought. He can rest, he can recover.) He was livid and moist: pity poured from her like a flooding pool, which made her think of the children. I'm the only one awake, she thought wildly; it was newly terrifying. *Leonard.* She shook him once more.

She would not leave him until the doorbell downstairs sounded four times; before she ran to unlock the door for the emergency squad, she stood for a moment; then she touched

the corners of his mouth with her knuckles to wipe from them
the still-wet smear of spittle, tinged with blood.

The red light on the top of the ambulance was whirling—she
could see it through the low-hanging branches of the chestnut
tree in the front of the house. A policeman and two men in
white jackets with emblems on the pockets were standing in
the doorway. "He's in the bedroom straight at the top of the
stairs," she said.

"Mrs. Taber," the policeman said. "If you'll tell me where
your coat is." She was still in her nightgown.

"I'll get it," she said. "I'm all right."

She went to the hall closet.

"Are there children?" the policeman asked. "How old is the
oldest?"

"Nine."

"Think they'll be all right until we call someone from the
hospital?" Rhoda nodded. The two men were bringing Leonard
down on a stretcher. She watched them slide him into the back
of the ambulance; waiting in cold readiness was an array of
tubes, machines, a mask—they would not let her look. They
made her sit in the front seat, separated by white metal doors,
as the ambulance shrieked its way to the hospital.

She waited in the corridor, her nightgown flapping foolishly
about her ankles. The policeman, who had followed in his
patrol car, waited with her. He paced outside the phone booth,
looking in to check on her, as she called Sally Finch to come
stay with the children. An accident, she was saying; it was the
only word she could think of. Thank you. Yes. Thank you. We
hope so too. They were heavy sleepers, the girls, you could
move Claire from one room to another and she would sleep
right through. She thought of them, innocent and oblivious in
their beds.

The policeman gestured for her to sit in a chair while a clerk
asked her questions for the forms. The harsh, curative smell of
antiseptic was making Rhoda feel sick. The odor would be

familiar to Leonard when he came to. She was embarrassed before the policeman because her voice wavered. She was explaining that she didn't have her Blue Cross card with her when a doctor tapped her on the shoulder from behind.

He led her to a small square office which had been painted a bright, shocking, senseless yellow. He's going to ask me to sign a release for an operation, she thought; how fat he is, so young too, you'd think a doctor would know better; but he was saying, cardiac arrest, dead on arrival, know how you must feel. She was sobbing quietly, all the while thinking that she had lived for years under a misunderstanding about life, always missing the point that the core of it was tyrannically physical. "He was so intelligent," she heard herself whispering. She was going to say other things, truisms, to manufacture a eulogy on the spot, to *make conversation* with this man. The sound of her own voice jolted her.

She was sorry that at the moment the doctor had given her the news she'd been thinking of other things. She was trying to memorize what he'd said. She wanted to ask him to tell her again. "I have to go home," she said.

Afterwards Rhoda was to have no clear recollection of how the news was disseminated. The first days of mourning were confused and besmudged with social activity; masses of people swarmed the house. Someone else told Suzanne—she never knew who, her brother Andy perhaps—and she could vaguely remember telling Claire in her low, lecturing voice, something crazy about how people's hearts worked.

Rhoda preserved in herself a faint sense that she had perhaps heard wrong. A mistake: it was against all logic as well as against all decency. All around her in her own house she heard the voices of lesser people, still spitefully breathing, full-blooded, and distasteful in their familiarity. They were all more likely cases for fatal effects. Hinda's Stanley was six years older and had an ulcer. Her father, shuffling and stooping, inexplicably continued in the same middling health he had "enjoyed" for years. The fury she felt contemplating possibilities, permutations of disaster unrealized, made her want to jump out of her skin, to rend her clothes and tear her hair: the ancient mode, after all.

The children had no such sense of protest. Claire, in particular, was so little that the shock met no resistance in her; she was accustomed to being behindhand in understanding the way things were. It disturbed Rhoda when people inquired too closely after the children. The children were fine; currently Claire was at the Finches', Suzanne was staying with Andy; they were so fine that she could not be unwell, she had a sense of reserving herself for them, of resisting sleep so that she might be awake when they returned and continued in their relentless needs to be fed, provided for, talked to. They were blocking her from the luxury of mourning.

These things she thought when she could distinguish particular sentiments in her own will. At other moments she was at the mercy of something more simple and blurred. The fabled numbness of new widows had not set in. She felt instead a constant abstract panic, as though a room just behind her was on fire, and she had somehow to act as though it did not concern her, to pour coffee for guests amidst the roar and the flickering, to set her mouth in conversation: it was all for the good of some normal continuance she could barely remember; meanwhile bodies turned, screamed, and burned. People took her hand to soothe her.

Of the actual, specific, wrenching pain that Leonard was gone she could not think. She would think of it later; she had put it aside to save herself. It was all she could do now to speak in sentences; a syllable was constantly rising in her gorge— something wordless like the vague horror of flames outside her vision—she fought to keep it down, as one fights nausea. It was the natural translation of an anguish so acute that it ran rampant through the body. She felt as though she had been dragged through streets, not allowed to rest. All this served to distract her with a sense of unjust bodily discomfort, and dwelling on this, she bore it fretfully like a patient.

VI

In the days after the funeral, after the children had returned and masses of people still thronged the lower floors of the house, all her visitors arrived with boxes of candy in their hands. Chocolates mostly: dark 'n' light assortments, cherries with cordial centers, butter creams. A peculiar custom: she was too old to be pacified by sweets; for years (since her gall bladder operation, before her marriage) she'd been unable to swallow a piece of chocolate without feeling sickish—a fact known to most of her friends—and yet they arrived blindly bearing pound-packages. "People," she explained to Claire, who had been pointedly announcing her mother's dietary restrictions to guests, "don't think. They don't know what else to do. Stop opening another one. We're saving them—in the china closet drawer, that's right."

Sylvia Shepp was pinching Claire's cheek. "A face like a little doll." "That hurts," Claire complained. Sylvia crooned, "Oh, it does not, you big baby."

"She's not used to that," Rhoda said. She herself was expending a certain concentration in shrinking from the continual prod of visitors who kept patting her gingerly, as though testing her figure for stability.

No one seemed to know how to behave. They were simpering and childish; they cast their eyes up balefully to hers, seizing upon her look of glazed hurt as an invitation for sympathetic contact. She grew vague in conversation and apt to mumble, a symptom taken as fatigue, which was in fact an impotent sign of outrage at their presumption.

"Listen," Sylvia Shepp said, looking up from Claire, "if you want this one to stay with us, it's fine. There's Rita for her to play with."

"The young ones bounce back quickly," Philip Marantz was saying. "And you too. You're a tough cookie, I know it." He had his hand on Rhoda's shoulder.

"Later she can be a tough cookie," Annie Marantz said. "Now she should rest and sit down. Why aren't you sitting down?" Mr. Dinger, the plumber, stood up sharply to give his chair to Rhoda.

"Oh, Mr. Dinger," Bev Davis cooed. "I've never seen you in a suit before."

"Doesn't he look handsome?" Hinda said.

"Where's my Suzy?" Mr. Dinger asked.

"He loves children," Evvie Fern told her husband.

Liz and Herb Hofferberg were pressed into a corner, talking only to each other. Maisie, the maid, was the sole visitor dressed in all black; her eyes shone yellow and glassy under a pillbox hat with a veil. Leonard's brother broke away and began moving toward Rhoda; he looked awful—Rhoda had a great horror of hearing his soft voice.

"Why don't you go upstairs for a while?" Annie said. "You're allowed to be tired, you know." Rhoda moved toward the staircase, noticing as she did that the cube-shaped woman near the couch was Molly Gotham, her principal years ago when she'd taught at Rock Street (Rockbottom, they'd called it)

Junior High. "Isn't that nice of you to come?" Hinda was saying, as the woman accounted for herself.

Upstairs, with the pillows tucked into the chenille spreads, were the twin beds, with the night table between them. The one farthest from the wall was still hers. She lay flat on her back to avoid wrinkling her dress, and then, miraculously—as though her body were oblivious not just to pain and catastrophe but to day and night—she slept.

When she awoke the room was darkened; faint light showed around the edges of the window shades. She made her way downstairs where the living room, hushed and dimly lit with one lamp, was emptied of guests. Food remained, piled on the dining room and cocktail tables—a catered turkey half picked over, platters of cold cuts, and an untouched steamship basket of fruit in cellophane. Alone by the buffet was a tall, stoop-shouldered shape in a hideous shiny black suit. He nodded over his paper plate; he had waited for her: her father. "You're up now. Eat," he said. After all, he was a man who loved waiting. "Good," he said, pointing toward the turkey. He could not chew without smacking his lips. He was speaking again, reassuring her. He was going to stay overnight. Andy's wife had made up a bed for him in the sun parlor. Not to worry. Very comfortable.

"There's more blankets in the closet at the head of the stairs. I appreciate this," Rhoda said. "The girls are asleep, I suppose? Use your napkin, Pop."

She awoke with a deep, paralyzing wish to sleep herself back to another time. She thought—not of Leonard's face—that was blocked from her, as if she sought as she slept, with her hand over her eyes, to keep the light away—but of his body's outline, the particular barrel-shape of his ribs, and the chest, bifurcated and hard under the coating of light brown hairs. The absence of his form under the covers of the bed next to her engendered in her a sudden rage, as though she'd been robbed in the night. His bed was undisturbed, the chenille spread tucked properly around the pillow. She felt panicked and afraid—an actual physical shudder came over her, and then she had a dreadful urge to beat at the covers of his bed, to make him come out. She wanted to get up and look for him.

She was awake now with a restlessness of emergency; her head buzzed with plans, but in fact she had hardly moved; she lay back weakly against the headboard. She felt unequal to the task of stirring herself and dismounting from the bed without help, and she mourned again doubly that Leonard was not there to help her in her mourning.

She heard the children's voices from downstairs, and there was the smell of melting butter, which seemed alien and unfitting. She put on her robe and made her way down the steps. Downstairs in the kitchen she found that her father had made breakfast for both the girls. He had spattered a great deal of batter across the surface of the stove, but the girls were sitting peaceably at the dinette table, apparently content with their somewhat leaden-looking pancakes. Either Claire or Suzanne had made the request. Pancakes had been Leonard's specialty—a weekend treat—which Rhoda had not been "allowed" to make, because the children identified them as an exclusively male production.

Suzanne was rotating forkfuls of pancake in a pool of syrup on her plate—oafishly quiet, as always, but not troublesome. "They were very good, Grandpa," Claire was saying. "I'm just too full to finish." She patted her stomach. He touched his knuckles to the child's sticky cheek; the hand shook faintly. "Had enough?" he demanded. Claire nodded and gave him a forced, close-lipped smile. How can a five-year-old humor a grown man? Rhoda thought. The sight of it made her feel weakened and grateful at the same time.

How clever of the girls, with their child's rigid concern about these things, to think of a way not to pass a single Sunday without pancakes. They were already learning how to make substitutions. They were like ducklings ready to be brooded by any barnyard animal, fed with an eyedropper.

Her father's quivering pleasure was unnerving, a drain on everyone's generosity. After breakfast he settled himself in the sunroom and read a paper someone had left there the day before. He was still there in midafternoon, when Rhoda went upstairs to rest. She listened while he answered the front door when the bell rang, and she could hear Hinda, coming into the foyer, trying to ask him questions about himself (he was not at all hard of hearing, but people had a tendency to think that if they spoke more loudly to him, they would get more of a response). Then Hinda was asking, "Is she sleeping now?" and Rhoda, who had been about to get up, suddenly yielded to the temptation of letting them think she was alseep—she stiffened with the sensation of eavesdropping.

Hinda's husband Stanley was there with her; he was saying, "Let's go, doll, we'll come back later." He would be chewing gum, Rhoda thought, and wearing some floppy nylon sport-shirt that looked like a pajama top. He was probably edging Hinda out with his hand at the small of her back, genteelly guiding her through the doorway with a proprietary tender-ness; he was very nice to Hinda; but all the same there was something disgusting in this image of this—in all of it; Rhoda could hardly stand it from where she was.

The doorbell rang again; someone was answering it (probably Hinda). Rhoda could hear several voices—Andy's wife, Lainie, was calling down the walk, "Well, don't leave it there—bring it in from the car anyway."

When Rhoda finally came downstairs ("Look, sleeping beauty!" Andy said) both her brothers were in the living room with their wives, all of them still clustered around the entryway. Claire was showing Hinda how she'd learned to do a split, and Suzanne was kneeling and trying with her teeth to break the string on a large cardboard box someone had put on the floor.

"We just stopped by to bring you something that should be very handy," Andy said.

"I see the box," Rhoda said. "Thank you."

"It's a humidifier to keep in the bedroom. You were complaining that the heat in the house is so drying. You turn this on and it keeps the air moist all night; you sleep like a baby."

"This is not a noisy kind," Frank said. "It's the top-of-the-line model."

"Isn't that a nice idea?" Hinda said.

"You'll see—it'll give you such a feeling of breathing fresh air indoors," Frank said.

Rhoda thought this was a childishly peculiar present for them to have chosen for her. They were carrying it up the stairs, eager to install it at once (Frank's wife, Marsha, made them take a towel to put on the carpet under it); they were calling down to her—did she want it by the window or on the floor in front of the night table?

"They'll be futzing around with that for hours," Lainie said. The wives gazed fondly up the staircase. Rhoda sat across from her two sisters-in-law, who had settled themselves on the sofa. They were years younger than Rhoda—girls really, in their full skirts and wide belts—slender, good-natured, very proud of lending their husbands for the day.

Stanley wanted to get Rhoda a drink, it would be the best thing in the world for her. In his politeness he kept putting his hand behind the back of her chair, as though he had to support the upholstery. Hinda told him to go see if there was any soda in the house, if that was all Rhoda wanted. Alone with the wives, Rhoda listened to the sounds of other people's husbands doing favors for her in her house. They were arguing about an extension cord upstairs; Stanley was hacking at an ice tray in the kitchen sink.

The women let her be quiet for a while. Marsha pretended to be delighted when Claire pranced around with Marsha's scarf wrapped around her waist as a skirt, and Lainie and Hinda let Suzanne show them her card trick over and over, swearing they could never guess the secret. Stanley was in the sunroom, looking at the bookshelf (most of the books were Leonard's).

Rhoda sat holding her wet glass in her lap, until her brothers came down from upstairs; the women got up to join them, and stood waiting while the men brought them their coats, and then—all six of them kissing Rhoda's upturned face—they formed into couples again and they left, two by two, walking across the lawn to their own cars.

Her father stayed for another two days, managing to be something between a help and a hindrance—an eyesore always. She was, even in the fatigue of mourning, snappish with him; he shrugged and remained unalterable in his fixed private notion of duty—even after she sent him home, he returned for visits several times a week, and on weekends.

In the month after Leonard's death, she had more conversation with her father than she'd had in years. Now she welcomed having people around her. She was aware, all the time she spoke to them, of Leonard's image tugging at her mind, but the effort of double concentration made this bearable. In a blurred fashion she was glad to have him with her in this way, so that talking to anyone was a help to her at this time; it was a secret device for keeping his visitation with her.

Only at night she wept with an unspeakable bitterness. It seemed to her then that she had to school herself, to harden herself against his wounding image, in the way, as a young girl, she had always known to harden herself against a boyfriend who no longer came calling for her.

Her conversations with her father were rough and peculiar—from the gruffness of his personality, which she imitated in speaking to him—and because he spoke to her in Yiddish, which, as the language of her childhood, came handiest to her only in shaping certain thoughts. (It was not a language she associated with Leonard, although they had had jokes in it.) Her father liked to tell her things from the newspaper—Marines returning from Korea with bizarre injuries remedied by miraculous prostheses, mothers throwing their children from burning buildings, flood victims finding their family heirlooms floating intact downriver. Rhoda understood everything he said to her, but in the unfamiliarity of certain words for catastrophes, it struck her how much of her life had gone by without any need to refer to these things.

He liked to recount his news tidbits to her as she prepared supper. "Talk in English," Claire would squeal, climbing up her grandfather's knee. He sat on a red aluminum stepladder near the kitchen door, a hot spot (too near the radiator) which he had chosen for himself exactly the way a dog picks a quiet retreat under the table which is nonetheless in the way of everyone's feet.

In the ensuing weeks Rhoda realized that the rest of the family now viewed her and her father as being in each other's care; matched by default. Not one of his three children was fond of him, Rhoda least of all; ironically, her contemptuous refusal to fear him as a child had given her the reputation of being able to "handle" him.

To the extent of his capacities, he was interested in the grandchildren—especially Claire, who was the most affectionate—and on Sundays he brought them poppy-seed rolls from a bakery in Newark, and sometimes little gifts; once a toy harmonica for Claire, which she spent the afternoon bleating tunelessly. His visits did help fill the house, and Rhoda found herself expecting her father to be there often, his dry cough in the background of her housework like a radio half listened to.

She complained of his messy, depressing habits to her brothers, but in essence she succumbed to the mounting conclusion of his ever more frequent presence. So, almost by degrees, her father moved in with her, taking over Suzanne's room; Suzanne, who did not protest, was put in Rhoda's ample master bedroom. She was given the right-hand closet and the right-hand dresser for her own use. For a nine-year-old, she was neat in her habits.

Rhoda had moved Leonard's clothes up to the attic to make room for Suzanne, but she left his ties still on their rack on the door of his closet, and a few shirts of his hanging inside. Suzanne left them exactly as they were; she arranged her own belts next to the ties. She was remarkably self-contained for her age, not silly and restless like Claire, who would have been impossible to live with in the same room. She was husky and broad, slow-moving and clumsy; no wonder that she had once liked bears so much. She could be very stubborn at times, refusing to answer questions she didn't like—an unsmiling child. At night she breathed with the glottal thickness of heavy animals.

A re-shuffling: into the gaps, lesser shapes were pressed, makeshift but sufficient. The changes in her household lent to Rhoda a sense that she was doing something. It recalled to her the pride of wartime resourcefulness in ersatz, when they had poured steaming water over canned tuna and called it chicken. For the Duration. Her dreams were surreal, but in her waking life she continued to have a precise if distant notion of the personalities around her, as when in teaching the lower grades she had touched the tops of the children's heads to count the number present.

She had heard that widows sometimes, forgetting their husbands were dead, thought of things they must tell them later, or imagined themselves discussing everyday events with them. What happened to Rhoda was that her own thoughts began to rise up in Leonard's voice; she began to use his expressions for her own sensations, the way she might, after reading a book, find herself thinking in the syntax of the author. Idle, fugitive sentiments were tagged with his style: "Well-done, A-1," she would think, eating a piece of cake, or "No kidding, kiddo" (another expression of his) when she agreed with a commentator on the news. She could hear his *voice*, the familiar, barely rising inflections and low tones, not as though he were there keeping company with her, but as though his spirit had overtaken her mind. She was smothered beneath it, and she felt that a part of her was withering under the weight: certainly she was losing her concentration. It reminded her of her fear in the early days of their marriage when she had suddenly seen the terrible ultimacy of what it meant to live with someone: she could not get away from him.

Now he slept in her brain like a worm in an apple, and fed off her mental processes; this was what it meant to be eaten away by grief. Only this wasn't grief—she was past the pain of fresh mourning, wasn't she?—this was the slow erosion of personality by the habitation of some other. It was most like those mothers who died from toxemia carrying dead fetuses within them. She was sorry she had ever let her life be so linked, so ingrown, with that of another person. It was too late to escape now, but she was certainly sorry she'd ever had children; they were like the past, they clung and clung.

"You're in a good position, Rhode," Addie Shulman said, in the line of counsel as her accountant. "The business has no debts hanging on it. The store is fresh, neat, modern-looking. Since the war Americans love drugs. I should've been a doctor myself—they're cleaning up, the pill-pushers. But seriously— I'm serious now—one thing you should know: Sell now. Don't wait. You think I'm rushing you, but what you're selling also is a name, a reputation. Keep the place closed too long and it'll expire. A good name is beyond price; it happens to say so in the Talmud."

"And in the *Wall Street Journal,*" Rhoda said.

For three months Rhoda had applied herself, with Addie's guidance, to the store's accounts. It distressed her that over fifteen hundred dollars was owed in back charges by delinquent customers. She mailed out urgent bills, threatened the addressees with a collection agency; in a frenzy of aggravation she made personal phone calls. Mrs. Leshko, of all people, refused to pay her ninety-seven dollars and forty cents. "What are you bothering me, an old woman?" she wheezed into the phone. "You're well-off now, everybody knows he left you a bundle. What is my piddling bill to you? Crap, chicken feed."

Even Addie tried to persuade her not to get all worked up over accounts outstanding. "It's a write-off. Do yourself a favor, forget it. We're talking about a solid business of respectable size. Penny-wise and pound-foolish is you."

This meant that Rhoda had to relinquish her hold on the store. Briefly she weighed the possibility of taking it over herself, of acting as manager and hiring a young pharmacist fresh from school, but she was halted in her considerations by the memory of her sole sales experience. In high school she and Florence Pinskow had sold hats in the Five & Ten. On the heads of unwitting women they placed the world's ugliest caps, nodding as the ladies lowered their chins before mirrors, smirking as they left with reckless purchases in hand. It was all very funny then, but had left Rhoda with a correct image of the sales counter as a gate behind which you were held captive audience to a parade of the world's pettiness and short tempers: too old for that now.

Addie thought he had a buyer. The Sav-Mor Discount Drugs chain was showing interest; a fellow had shown up at Addie's office and had been given a tour of the premises. Rhoda balked at the price he offered. She sent word that he had mistaken her for a charitable institution. The man came to visit Rhoda privately, a balding, middle-aged Gentile in a wrinkled brown suit. He was not, he explained, the minion of a large, affluent corporation, but a poor slob trying to get a franchise. In southern California he had run a thriving drug and stationery center in a shopping mall, but his wife had left him for a blond beach bum with a tattoo, and he had come east to make a new start. He had a lovely new wife, a baby on the way, and he could go no higher in price.

Rhoda was not pleased to hear the sordid minutiae of his personal history, but she was persuaded that he was not a wily person, and the thought of further negotiations fatigued her. She relented: the man's sweaty, profuse joy was a pitiful and satisfying sight. Four months later he hired carpenters to knock through the stockroom partition and install a lavish fake-marble lunch counter with chrome and vinyl stools (not since the war had the place had anything so crass as a soda fountain). Rhoda was disgusted at the man's duplicity, his self-debasement in pleading false penury—she hated to go past the premises—but she kept, oddly, her original smugness in the transaction. Then and for all time she had formed the idea of her own financial competence.

Now that the store was sold, Rhoda found people asking if she planned to put the house on the market. Maisie in particular nursed a nagging fear on this point, despite reassurance. Sylvia Shepp wanted to know, in the midst of an otherwise impersonal conversation when they met in the library parking lot, "So are you thinking of getting out, Rhode?"

"Out of where?" Rhoda said. She could hardly imagine where people thought she might go. There seemed to be two suppositions on the subject. People like Sylvia thought she might want to hop off with the children to some place like California or Florida, out of a belief in the outside solution, the open opportunity. The very vagueness of the possibilities seemed to them thrilling and visionary. They were so tickled with themselves at having thought of this that it reminded Rhoda of a puzzle Suzanne made everyone try (she liked mathematical puzzles)—it was an insoluble maze, there was no way to reach the center without crossing a line or lifting your pencil, unless you made a great loop outside of it: the trick was to think of this.

Rhoda always heard, in examples like Sylvia's of a cousin who absolutely loved living in Denver, the underlying assumption that everyone really longed to go to such places. Rhoda had very few such desires; all her expectations had centered around her house—that settlement by slow choice invented, furnished, and populated, lit from within, the same house in which she was already living and in which she intended to continue to live.

People like Maisie, on the other hand, seemed to suppose that in the course of things Rhoda would have to sell the house because her widowed state represented reduced circumstances, a need for smaller quarters. This was actually the reverse of the truth; with Leonard's life insurance and the sale of the pharmacy, she had more unattached funds than she had ever had.

Rhoda was probably as good at money matters as most people; with the amount from the sale of the store, she bought—on different people's advice—stocks of varying performance. Even the "duds" she held onto, in small silly amounts, pushing them out of mind as she would edge a disliked piece of clothing to the back of a dresser drawer. It was the good, bullish market of the fifties and her smart purchases covered her mistakes. She did well, remarkably well, and she attributed her triumph to her own shrewdness, rather than to a fortunate investment period.

She had never considered the category of luck (a passive lower-class notion: every evening Maisie's husband gave the runner good money to play his lucky number and look what it got him). To show any respect for forces of fate outside your own will was, Rhoda felt deeply, to court disaster: to ask for trouble by giving it a name. Once, in the days after the funeral, Hinda had been helping her clean the house (keeping busy was good) and Rhoda, dusting a table, had knocked over a very pretty little glass candy dish, whose splintering pieces had scratched the table's finish. "Oh, Rhoda," Hinda had cried out, in a burst of whiny sympathy, "this sure isn't a lucky time for you." "You sound like your mother," Rhoda had said curtly.

That you make your own chances was a tenet she had been raised to believe; like everything from her youth, it had the quality of having been hard-won, as well as the radiant example of her mother to give it authority. She believed against all evidence—not the Depression, or the Holocaust, or her own witness of the fitful, senseless rebellions of the body had bent the dogged textures of her thought.

The money was a great satisfaction. Every month that she received a dividend check she had a sense of her own rightness about things. Addie Shulman congratulated her. "What you have," he said, "is security." The house was hers for good now. She indulged only in small luxuries—better cuts of meat, expensive shoes for the children. She was, she said, "not a shopper." Certainly the last thing she wanted was sweeping changes. For the house she bought, here and there, a fruit bowl or an antique umbrella stand, scattered objects in her own unsure taste.

Still, amidst the assurance of gradually increasing prosperity, the afternoons were long. She spent the mornings getting the house in order, working along with Maisie, on her days in, until the children came home to be fed; but by one o'clock she was weighed down by the sense of empty time that overtakes retired people. She sat in the kitchen eating her usual lunch, a mound of cottage cheese piled over lettuce (no eating from the container: like a colonist in an outpost, she was strict about keeping proprieties even when no one was looking); she heard from the next room the sounds of the TV set her father watched constantly now; and intruding on the mundane dairy textures, into her mouth came the watery taste of tears. She had slipped into a pool of self-pity; the blurry feel of it reminded her of the way she had "teared up" as a girl reading sad books. She thought of the scene in *Mill on the Floss* when Mr. Tulliver, his spirit broken at having his mill sold out from under him, mutters to his wife, "This world's been too many for me." In a glory of helplessness, she hugged the pain of this to her; twisting, she could remember Leonard's voice and the feel of his whiskers faintly moist with the oil of his skin.

The thing was to get a job. *Idle hands.* Anything to get out of the house. But not teaching. It had been eleven years since she had stood in front of a classroom, and she remembered with a shudder the freakish nastiness of certain students, now long since grown, no doubt, into foul-mouthed and law-breaking adults. She had lost her nerve. She pictured the rows of potentially mocking students, sitting in wait with their various versions of Suzanne's sour grimace, Claire's nittering laugh. *I've had enough of that at home, thank you.*

Through an old friend of Leonard's she heard of a part-time position as a doctor's receptionist. It was, as predicted, an easy job. She was good at it, keeping the appointment books organized in her clean Palmer script. She worked from ten to three, while her father or Maisie gave the girls lunch.

She was adept at managing restless patients in the waiting room: "Now here's a lovely magazine for a little boy with a runny nose." None of them was really sick, but they weren't well either, and the air of the office hung stale with nervous torpor. She swabbed the children's bottoms for injections—a shot of penicillin was considered the most effective remedy and mothers left disappointed if their offspring were considered unworthy; Rhoda's task was to expedite getting it done quickly before they knew what hit them. They always screamed a moment later and she mocked them for it—"It's all over now, you big noisemaker"—dispatched them with lollipops and sent them, betrayed and tearful, on their way.

Bev Davis appeared one afternoon in Dr. Aaronkrantz's office. Rhoda had seen the name on the appointment schedule with the word *gastritis?* pencilled beneath it. "Rhoda!" Bev called out. (Where did she think she was—a class reunion?) "You're working. I think that's wonderful." It had been eleven months since Leonard's death.

"How's Abe?" Rhoda asked.

"Fine, fine. I'm the only hypochondriac in the family. The kids are fine too. But you look marvelous. I have to tell you, it's fantastic the way you keep going on."

"Where else is there to go?"

"Rhoda!" Dr. Aaronkrantz bellowed from the examining room. He did not affect a genial bedside manner. "I'm waiting in here, you know."

"I hear ya, boss," Rhoda called, scurrying. She returned a few

minutes later, mildly embarrassed at having been caught in her
capacity as an underling.

"With that voice," Beverly said, "he could raise the dead. It's
a medical talent."

"You're next. Another minute."

"Let me ask you—if I invited you for dinner when Abe's
cousin was there—the one who never got married—would you
come? I mean, are you ready? I'm not one of those who would
push you."

Ready is as ready does, Rhoda thought wildly. "I wouldn't
miss one of your dinners for the world," she said, feeling, as she
shook her head in a vaguely contradictory gesture of assent, a
wave of abdominal tightness like stage fright.

Go and see had been her mother's dictum. In feeling herself
under the directive to act, to go meet this man, she thought not
of Leonard, but of her mother (she never thought about what
Leonard would have wanted her to do—rarely did she even
mouth the phrase—he wouldn't have cared: he no longer
cared).

On the upholstered bench in her bedroom Rhoda laid the
stockings next to her dress to see how the shade went. She slid
them up her leg and hooked them where the flesh escaped the
satin panels of her girdle. Dressing with care for the occasion
made her feel girlish: it was not a pleasant sensation—an
adolescent nervousness trapped in the body of a thirty-seven-
year-old. Claire scampered into the room out of intuitive
nosiness and stared at her mother stripped to the waist. "Get
over here," Rhoda said. "You can hook this for me." She had to
sit down for the child to reach the fastening on her bra. In the
drawer, buried beneath the slip she selected, were two foam
rubber cones stacked together—falsies; silly things—she
hadn't worn them for years, not since the styles had changed.
Once they had been standard, an expected artificiality like high
heels. "Bonus bazooms," Leonard called them. With no one to
share their irony they lay, bereft of humor, personal and

unsavory as clumps of used Kleenex. So much of physical life was raw and unseemly without him.

She dressed quickly, not stopping to look in the mirror until the effect was complete; the blue wool sheath was simple and stiff. Making-up was a business-like procedure for her; she rubbed rouge into her cheeks with the vigor of using an eraser. Though she considered herself good-looking enough, she was not in the habit of exploiting her looks as a way to please. Blotting her lipstick, she felt a stir of unwelcome excitement and a faint flutter of resentment toward the unknown, expectant male sitting in wait for her at Beverly's house.

He was too thin, or thin in the wrong places. His clothes fit him badly. Perhaps he'd lost a great deal of weight recently. (She thought fleetingly of the movie *Grand Hotel*, when the doctor says to Lionel Barrymore, "When a man's collar is three sizes too big for him, I don't have to ask the state of his health.") His gray sports jacket hung too long, like a zoot suit or a hand-me-down. He had thin lips and delicate eyebrows—a pale-skinned, dark-haired man—not bad-looking, but a bit shopworn.

He rose to shake hands. Decent manners. Eddie Lederbach. "I'm so glad to meet you," Rhoda said, stretching her mouth in that smile that showed her teeth to good advantage and made her look almost cruel.

Beverly brought them all highballs, forgetting that Rhoda did not drink; a ginger ale was brought for her instead. "Rhoda's just recently gone back to work," Bev explained. "She's working in a doctor's office." The man nodded, said nothing—was he shy?

"And what do you do?" Rhoda asked.

"I'm an accountant by trade. That's my training. C.P.A. Worked for the government for thirteen years. Bureau of Internal Revenue."

"Ooh, a tax man," Rhoda murmured, shaking her finger at him. "You greedy guys are always taking all my money away."

"Not me. No more. I'm in the private sector now." He exchanged glances with Bev's husband Abe.

Beverly began hustling them all toward the dining room. "Turn down the radio, Abe," she called out, as she slipped into the kitchen. "No, Rhoda, please, you don't have to help, really." On the radio a woman's voice was singing with perky gusto, *Enjoy yourself/ While you're still in the pink.*

"That's me," Eddie Lederbach said, as he held Rhoda's chair for her. "In the pink." He laughed silently. "A pinko in the pink. That's how come I don't work for Uncle Sam any more. Are you now or have you ever been." He leered at Rhoda grimly. "You're sitting next to a dirty Commie dupe of Moscow fellow-traveler spy traitor. Hope you don't mind. It's not catching."

"I'm not worried," Rhoda said. "What's your job now?"

"I'm a bookkeeper for a company that makes mercerized cotton socks. You need any socks?"

"Thank you, no," Rhoda said.

"I weave secret Communist messages into the toes of the socks. Ha, ha."

Beverly tried to introduce diverse topics; they discussed MacArthur's difficulties in Korea, Milton Berle's crazy costume on his last show, and the advantages of early orthodontia for buck-toothed children. But Eddie Lederbach managed to return all conversation to the awkward and depressing subject of his own blacklisting. He had, in fact, considerably less to complain of than some people: he had admittedly once belonged to the Youth Against War and Fascism, and he had attended a few cell meetings of the Party in the thirties. At least he'd actually done something; it seemed, Rhoda argued, that it would be considerably more frustrating to lose your job when the accusations were totally made up.

"Don't get me wrong, I think the whole thing stinks," Rhoda said. "McCarthy should be locked in a padded cell somewhere."

"Worse," Eddie Lederbach said. "What I would like to do to him. Draw and quarter the bastard, lower him into a vat of boiling oil an inch at a time."

"That's not funny," Rhoda said.

The worst of it was, aside from his overall aspect of being at loose ends, he was an attractive man. Mobile features, a good mime in his occasionally comic moments: he had probably once been charming. Before Leonard, who'd been broad-shouldered and short, she'd always been drawn to slim, boyish types. Eddie Lederbach's hands were long and graceful, with soft, sparse hairs growing tenderly about the knuckles. She was not prepared for a complexity of emotions. Either she would encourage him or she would not. Her chest rose with the increase of heat in contemplating the question: a quickening of breath as a sort of test. She looked at his eyes—small and maroon-brown—but she knew from teaching school that you couldn't tell anything from them—eyes were impersonal—the merest punk could have the mellowest eyes and be no better for it. His lips moved wetly in nervous speech.

"I couldn't defend myself," he was saying. "That's what sticks in my craw. When I get up in the morning now, the first thing I think of is, *it's not fair*. Sometimes I wake up shouting it in my sleep."

There was an awkward silence. Nobody wanted to know what he did in his sleep.

"What are you—a whiner?" Rhoda said suddenly. "Complain, complain." She made a clicking sound as though chiding a child. "The world is not such a fair place. Let's face it."

"You think there's another world?" He smiled wanly.

"I'm not religious," Rhoda said.

"Me neither," he said—sprightly all of a sudden, cheered by any opinion held in common. Good God, he was still trying to make contact with her.

"I mean," Rhoda went on, "anybody could drive himself into a frenzy just dwelling on his misfortunes. You could go bananas that way. We all could. You can't just lie back and kick your heels in the air like a cockroach." Bev tittered. "That ain't the way," Rhoda said, her voice low and goofy now. "You've got to remember the old Onward and Upward." She circled her fist in the air in mock-heroics.

"Buckle down, Winsockee," Eddie said sarcastically.

"Excelsior," Rhoda said jubilantly. "Give 'em the old one-two." She was pleased with herself as Beverly laughed and called out, "Oh, Rhoda, you could kid the absolute pants off anybody."

"I beg your pardon," Eddie said, laughing finally.

"Just a figure of speech," Abe Davis grumbled, winking.

"Don't take it literally," Rhoda gasped. She had a sudden vision of Eddie Lederbach standing up and his pants falling in one slapstick swoop down to a puddle at his ankles. In lewd, clownish despair—"the poor soul": he had neither the bulk nor the presence of mind to keep his trousers up. She was laughing.

"I'd like to take it literally," he whispered, leaning closer to her ear and touching her neck with his fingertips.

She shook her shoulders, laughing harder, and sloped back in her chair away from him.

"Jokes," Eddie Lederbach said. "This country has a wonderful sense of humor. Kick the underdog—that's funny."

"Oh, stop it already, for Pete's sake," Rhoda hissed. "We're all fed up." His face clouded—she had hit a bit too hard. Abe Davis had to contrive a string of compliments for the mashed potatoes in order to get them all talking again.

Later, when they were both leaving at the end of the evening (there was no need for him to see her home since she had come in her own car), he took her hand and said, "Well, it's been very nice."

"A pleasure," Rhoda said. She felt a twinge of triumph in his obvious disappointment at having failed to interest her: mostly she wanted very much to get home. She drove through the dull, darkened suburban streets, down the block where the yellow bug-light shone warmly over her own front porch. In the shadowy foyer she brushed against the new umbrella stand; she hung her good fur coat in the downstairs closet, and moved, with the great relief of homecoming, through her own living room, where the mahogany furniture glimmered in the half-dark like blocks of marble. In her bedroom she undressed and took from the drawer her long flannel nightgown, a matronly and yet childish style; her body seemed very small within its cottony folds. She buttoned the neck and settled into bed; she was very tired; it takes a lot out of you, this wild social life I have, she thought drily. She felt at once virginal, tremulous, and weary.

The idea Rhoda had was that you have to begin somewhere. Once she declared this, however, what began was a new and deeply distasteful stage in which the bleak dignity of her widowhood was exposed to careless mockery. She was subject to the suggestions of well-meaning friends regarding their unmarried brothers-in-law, their husbands' divorced business partners. The small claims they made for their offerings ("Gregory Peck he's not, okay?") struck Rhoda as callously disrespectful to her. At dinner parties she would find, invited on her behalf, men with bad teeth, loud ties, overdue bills—men who had not read a book in ten years—men who were so clearly out of her sphere of social compatibility that had they been women she would have behaved toward them with undisguised condescension. As it was, she laughed at their jokes, watched coldly but without protest as they slid their arms over the top of her chair. Occasionally she accompanied them to the movies, permitted her inert hand to be held in the moist unwelcome contact of their palms. She saw the need to make an effort. She felt like a fool. She began to spread the word among her friends: "Don't bring me any more leftovers."

Rhoda was beginning to hate her job—just when the children were getting used to her being away. At first Claire had sobbed, "You're *never* home"; now they both claimed they were much too big to care whether she was there for lunch.

She returned home from work one afternoon to find Suzanne playing with her chemistry set on the kitchen table, trying to impress Ina Mae Kaufman, the third most popular girl in the fifth grade, with the way the red liquid turned to green (Rhoda herself understood little of these experiments). "Big deal," Ina was saying. "I didn't think the litmus paper was so neat either." It was the fashion in the fifth grade to be negative.

Suzanne set the test-tubes in their rack and reached out to give Ina Mae a "feeny bird," a rap on the skull with flicked fingers, as Ina ducked away, screaming, "Get away from me!"

"How about," Rhoda suggested, "clearing off the kitchen table so you can have some good old peanut butter and jelly sandwiches?"

"Oh, boy," Suzanne groaned sarcastically. "Oh boy, oh boy, oh boy."

"*The boy,*" Rhoda intoned, beating time with a spoon at the kitchen sink, "*stood on the burning deck,/ His feet were full of blisters./ He tore his pants on a red-hot nail/ So now he wears his sister's.*" The girls, unfamiliar with the original poem (a staple of recitations in Rhoda's childhood) failed to find this wickedly amusing. "Oh, Mother," Suzanne grimaced. "Ina, for Christ's sake, would you please pass the jelly? I'm starving, you know."

"You poor old thing," Rhoda said. "You're so hungry you could dydee-dydee-dydee-die." Ina giggled. Rhoda poured a glass of milk for the guest. "Say when," she suggested.

"I *hate* milk," Ina yipped.

"Oh, we never serve milk in this house. This is cow juice. Don't be fooled by the carton." Rhoda smiled mysteriously.

"She thinks she's funny," Suzanne said.

"Four," Rhoda said to Claire, who was setting the table. Ina had agreed to stay for dinner, thus raising Suzanne's status in her class for at least a week. "Grandpa's not eating with us." Her father was now taking most of his meals by himself, which was better, really. "No, the knife goes with the blade facing in. You know that. It's all crooked, Claire, it looks like you just threw the silver on the table. Come here and do it again."

"I don't care," Claire said. "You *never* say I do it right."

"Nobody," Rhoda warned, "likes a whiner."

"Whiners have to go to bed early," Suzanne shouted, streaming into the kitchen. She slid on the waxed linoleum and stopped just behind Claire, whom she jabbed sharply in the ribs. Ina came from behind. They were keyed-up and noisy from having just spent an hour sitting absolutely still before the TV set. The dog circled and skidded around them, and then in a fit of old-dog excitement (he was twelve now), he lowered his head and barked a series of loud hoarse yips at Ina. "Don't get him going. Don't be so wild," Rhoda said. Timmy, who had stopped barking, wagged his tail slightly, walked to a corner, and lay down, sighing. "You can be seated now, ladies," Rhoda said. "Dinner is served."

She slid lamb chops from the broiler onto the girls' plates—all except Suzanne, who was served a dry little well-done hamburger, as always. A purist, she would eat almost nothing substantial but chopped meat, and no dessert that was not vanilla. Rhoda had lost interest in trying to force her. "I believe," she would say, defending her indulgence before other mothers, "that meal time should be a happy time." Claire, although more pliable, was also eccentric about food. She had confessed once that the thought of buttons (of all things) made her gag. Tonight she disdained cooked carrots for some secret reason. "Sensitive creatures," Rhoda sniffed. "How did I get stuck with two snobs? Some day you'll learn that the world is not your oyster."

"What's an oyster?" Claire wanted to know.

"Don't ask," Rhoda said. "That'll really make you choke."

"This is good," Ina said, gluttonously gnawing on a bone.

"Suzanne is a doodyhead," Claire whispered to Ina Mae, then smirked crookedly, just as Suzanne's hand reached out to whack her on the back of the head, hard enough so that Claire's chin hit the table. Claire shrieked.

"You were asking for it," Rhoda said, over the din of Claire's bawling. "I have no sympathy for you. Stop crying. Let me see—you're not hurt. You can stop crying now, do you hear me? No, don't try to scratch your sister—do you want a spanking? Is that what you want?"

"You're always hitting me," Claire screamed, turning on her mother suddenly. "Every day I get hit. Every single day."

Rhoda was taken aback: it was true—but just little smacks. Now Ina Mae would go home and tell her parents that Mrs. Taber was a child-beater. "Why can't you be good then?" Rhoda was shouting. "Go upstairs. Just go upstairs and get out of my sight. And you, young lady," she said, turning to Suzanne, "are just lucky that I won't say certain things to you in front of a guest. Consider yourself lucky."

Suzanne knew enough to say nothing in reply, and the three of them, after Claire's sobbing departure, ate their suppers in sober quiet.

Rhoda had trouble staying asleep that night; she kept waking up out of what seemed to be short fitful spells of rest. In her darkened bedroom she glanced hopefully at the windows, half-covered by blinds, for a sign that the night was beginning to break into respectable daylight. She had never been one to sleep late, even on weekends. "An old work horse," she would say of herself, pretending ruefulness, but she sneered at neighbors who spoke of languishing in bed past ten o'clock.

Lately, however, her pattern of early rising had grown excessive even to her judgment. She was awake at five-thirty, vainly adjusting her body to logically restful positions, until she resorted at last to sitting up and perusing, puffy-eyed, her latest book from the library. In the bed across from her Suzanne slept on, oblivious to the reading-light and the rustling of pages. Rhoda would take no sleeping pills, despite the packs of samples, sent to Leonard, piled at the back of the linen closet with other miscellany.

At seven o'clock Rhoda let the covers roll down her knees and stepped across the narrow aisle separating her bed from Suzanne's. Suzanne lay on her side, the blankets pulled about her tightly like a shawl. Only her nose and forehead showed above the turned-down sheet. Rhoda slipped into bed beside her, nuzzling against her back and stroking the child's springy hair, light-colored like Leonard's. Suzanne twisted slightly; Rhoda could tell by her breathing that she was awake now. She lifted the hair to kiss the back of her neck, which was pale and nacreous like the underbelly of a trout. Suzanne wore her favorite pajamas, old and almost-outgrown seersuckers with violets on them. She was ten, going on eleven now. Rhoda hugged the soft, handy, familiar shape. "Snuggleworm," she said. "I'm with you, Shooby Shoo." She began tickling Suzanne under the arms.

Suzanne squealed, but not with delight. "Mind your own business," she wailed.

"Look who's on her high horse," Rhoda said, and continued to tickle her.

In the fall of 1952 Rhoda quit her job with Dr. Aaronkrantz and occupied herself with occasional volunteer work for Adlai Stevenson's campaign. She had a great feeling, she said, for the *decency* of the man. (In a remote way Stevenson reminded her of her husband; they had the same build, for one thing.) She had no feeling at all for Dr. Aaronkrantz, who had been permanently insulted by her suggestion that he install an intercom system (he said, "With a voice like mine, who needs a gimmick?"); her brother Andy, with his penchant for nicknames, had dubbed the good doctor "the water buffalo." All very well to wisecrack about it, Rhoda said, quite another thing to daily shudder in her alcove and repeat very softly, "I'm not deaf, you know."

It was touch and go as to whether working for Dr. Aaronkrantz had been any worse than canvassing door-to-door in a Republican neighborhood; however, Rhoda's feelings about politics were not deep or passionate, and since her daytime visits were largely with women, the exchanges were polite if curt. "Next year I can sell Fuller brushes," she told Hinda. "I'm getting a good technique for getting my foot in the door."

On one occasion a woman actually did want to argue about

how many square miles of territory the Democrats had handed over to the Kremlin. Rhoda said, "Oh, we all know what an old tired issue that one is," and turned away, having, she thought, scored her point. The woman called after her as she walked off. She seemed grandiose and reckless, croaking her phrases from the Georgian portico of her house, and although Rhoda was the one campaigning, it surprised her how hotly real all of it was to this woman.

Since leaving her job Rhoda was home more often with her father. In good weather he sat for hours on the front porch, reading his newspaper or staring blankly before him with the idle gaze of a convalescent. He remembered closely what he read. Elizabeth Taylor, he announced, should never have married that bum Nicky Hilton, and he hoped her new husband wasn't running around on her either, she was still just a baby. "She's a personal friend of yours?" Rhoda said.

One damp fall afternoon he shuffled into the kitchen shaking his head dolefully. "So who did Rita Hayworth jilt this time?" Rhoda asked.

"The lady from across the street," her father said, "the one with the red hair that comes from a bottle?"

"Mrs. Finch," Rhoda supplied.

"Finch. She lets the delivery boy from the A & P put his hand up her skirt."

The thought of Sally Finch's tight wool skirt hiked up above her knees was not a pretty picture: maybe she couldn't help herself. "Is it your business?" Rhoda started to say, and then she saw her father smirking. "Your mind is going," she yelped. "With your bifocals, what do you know? You refuse to have your prescription checked. What are you saying—you can't even see straight."

"I know what I know," he said. "In the doorway he did it. Right up her dress between her legs he was putting his hand to feel."

It was a joke too dirty to be funny. Rhoda kept his vicious gossip to herself, where the burden of the secret made it gnaw at her thoughts. For a week she was distressed with visions of a pompadoured teenage boy reaching up to explore the moist helpless parts of Sally Finch; sometimes, too, she imagined her father's labored breathing and saw his palsied hand stroking the breast of a woman.

Sally Finch, under Rhoda's observation, seemed normal enough, a beak-nosed housewife who happened to dye her hair: not a crime in the state of New Jersey. This was not the last of her father's tale-bearing, despite Rhoda's announced scorn. Franny Moskowitz, a perfectly nice high-school girl who practiced her cheerleading routines in the driveway, he said wore no underwear. "Right outside for everyone on the street she does it—high kicks, splits."

"What are you—out there with a telescope?" Rhoda said. "At your age. It's pathetic. Read a good book for a change." She had little doubt by this time that his information was of his own diseased manufacture.

It was all too vivid—a pornographic movie thrust suddenly upon the orderly walls of her household. "Only the fact that you speak in Yiddish makes you fit to have in the house with children," she told her father. In a real way she had no use for these things. Two years ago she had been a natural wife in all respects, compliant and eager. Now the thought of sex had become foreign and outlandish to her, overheated, something multi-limbed creatures might do on the moon, or like the savage, invented games of childhood she half-remembered with mixed shame and wonder.

Still, it was her father who, with a clumsy effort at tact, first brought the news that Stevenson had lost the election. (Rhoda had watched some of the coverage on television the night before, but it tired her eyes to look through the set's domed magnifier with its greenish tinge, and the state-by-state count had bored her, until she'd fallen asleep.) Her father shook his head as he thrust the morning paper in front of her, with a rather handsome show of sympathy, since he himself felt little interest, and had had to be coaxed into letting himself be driven to the polls to vote.

"You know what he says? He gave a beautiful speech about losing," her father told her. "Beautiful."

"What could he say?" Rhoda snapped. She was feeling bitter that all her legwork had been for nothing. She bit at her toast testily.

"Go, read it yourself. Don't listen to me."

"I'm listening."

Her father cleared his throat. "He says—he was quoting Abraham Lincoln—he says he's not laughing or anything, he knows he lost—but he's too old to cry."

Annie Marantz came by in the afternoon to drive her over to the campaign headquarters, where they were already starting to clear out the office. "Who would've thunk it?" Annie said. "For nineteen years I've been a registered Democrat—all of a sudden I'm on the losing team again."

"So close, too, damn it," Rhoda said. "And I went and bought a new dress for the victory party they didn't have—isn't that always the way?"

"Don't tell me. And I had a fellow all picked out for you, a nice bachelor from my electoral district—I was going to stick my foot out in front of him at the party so he'd fall at your feet."

"I've got bunions—he wouldn't have been impressed."

"Well, he's in the car waiting for us now—I'm giving him a ride, too. Take a good look."

He was—Rhoda saw, as she slid into the front seat and swiveled around to nod at him—one of the fat, forty, and foolish variety. He lit up when he saw her, and crouched forward in the back seat to listen to her repeat his name. He was wearing a plaid golf cap. The car moved forward, Rhoda's shoulder lurched. She gave him as broad a smile as she could with her neck twisted.

VII

The Thanksgiving of 1952, by an overlapping lack of foresight from different branches of the family, Rhoda and the girls were left without an invitation for Thanksgiving dinner. They had a sour, quiet meal by themselves, clustered down at one end of the long dining room table. The children were not good sports about it, and they quarreled about who would do the dishes on a holiday. Claire spilled root beer on the sofa, which Rhoda had recently had recovered in a heavy, lichen-green damask, which, it turned out, spotted easily.

They were not enjoyable children in general. Claire, at seven, was still too volatile—apt to burst into long hyena giggles, and so skittish that when it rained she ran for blocks because worms on the sidewalk scared her. Often she stared blankly into space with a vague, wincing look. Suzanne, still a callous bully toward her sister, had occasional moments of mature conduct. She was eleven, a pale, too-tall girl with pink-framed glasses. Rhoda had coached her sketchily on the facts of life; Suzanne asked no questions and claimed that she'd learned about it already from the other kids at camp. She was indifferent to boys, hair-dos, lipstick, and the romantic intrigues plotted by some of her alarmingly precocious classmates. Her main interest this year was insects. She was full of facts about their brief, merciless lives: the efficient composite eyes of houseflies, the cruel mating habits of bees, the vicious internecine battles of wasps. Rhoda would not permit her to keep an anthill in a jar in their room, although twice she caught her trying to hide one under the bed.

The bad Thanksgiving proved to be an apt beginning for a bleak and unpromising new year. All that winter Rhoda did not feel much like going out. The weather was especially bitter and nasty, with hostile, icy winds. When she carried groceries from the car, her thin shoes minced through the crusty snow on the lawn. In the evenings she ventured out to play bridge with Annie or Hinda, or she let couples take her to the movies, but at dinner parties she had no patience for meeting new people; she had ceased, for the time being, to make an effort.

Her brief season of awful dates was long since over. Word had gotten out among her friends of certain sarcastic remarks she had made about the men they had generously supplied for her; they were as insulted as hostesses whose cooking has been impugned. *Nothing,* they said, or as much as said, *is good enough for you.*

It seemed to Rhoda that she was only resting, that chances she had passed up would re-emerge in more compelling form: there was plenty of time—it went slowly enough. Only the rapid growth of the children made her feel the passage of months, and she was sometimes alarmed by a certain spinsterish cold-comfort tingeing her habits.

In February she drove back to the house one late afternoon at twilight and saw a strange car parked outside. In the kitchen she found Maisie and Dr. Snyder, the internist with the black glasses who had tended her mother, standing over her father at the kitchen table. Her father had a nasty gash on his forehead. He looked as though he'd been in a fight (not possible, was it?). When he saw Rhoda, he rolled his head and raised his pale fish-eyes to her. "I made a mistake," he was saying. "I got confused."

"Oh, Mrs. Taber," Maisie said. "He fell on the stairs." It seemed that he had awakened from his nap in his room upstairs and had tried to make his way through the hallway to the bathroom, but the house had grown dark during his nap, and he had turned too soon, and fallen down the stairwell to the landing, where Maisie, hearing faint moans, had found him lying half-conscious in a pool of urine.

"Where were you going, hey, Jack?" the doctor said. Her father looked away from him.

After he had dressed the wound, the doctor called Rhoda aside and explained that it was not serious, but that a man his age could not be trusted near an open staircase. "Better make up a bed for him on the first floor from now on."

The next day Rhoda's brothers were there to express alarm, soothe the old man by teasing him, and offer solutions. Rhoda had a great desire to be rid of him for once, but he was so piteous and humble, with the white criss-crossed patch on his veinous forehead, like a bum or a patient in a battle ward. In the end her brother Andy suggested that Rhoda's screened-in back porch, which they never used anyway, could be walled up and made into a real room, insulated and made attractive with pine paneling.

"You can't change him, so change the house," Frank said.

Rhoda had a distinct memory of a bird's-eye view of the house; she was thinking of the blueprints, which she hadn't looked at since she and Leonard had bought the place—they had been quite confusing then, but she had looked at them with such excitement it seemed as if a stain of them must still lie pressed under layers in her mind—the twilight-blue with its ruled white lines showing the boundaries of the yard and

where the rooms were. The house-plans were still in the attic;
she could go get them. "It's not as if you're expanding," Andy
said. "You don't need them. Believe me. Where are you
running to?" She would only be closing in the drafty northwest
corner, mounting a protective bubble around the erratic
movements of her father, within the same space the house
already took up.

For weeks Rhoda interviewed contractors, getting estimates,
receiving the architectural recommendations of friends. In the
muddy days of early spring, a troop of masons and carpenters
came, messing the house and busying her days. By May her
father was installed in the new room, with a TV set of his own
(a hand-me-down from Andy), a studio bed, and a reclining
chair made of sticky vinyl. He kept more to himself this way;
he had long since chosen to take his meals alone—now he
ventured out only between TV programs.

Suzanne was given back her old bedroom, refurbished in pale
turquoise. She showed little enthusiasm for the move, aside
from picking a surprisingly garish pattern of wallpaper; but the
first day she tried (unsuccessfully) to barricade the room
against visitors by means of string and a bicycle lock.

In June Rhoda took a course in ceramic sculpture, where she
met a big, brisk-looking woman with short gray hair, named
Harriet Tuckler. What Rhoda admired about Harriet was her
attitude. At the beginning of each class she listened keenly to
the instruction, then pummeled the unrelenting clay until the
results produced in her a sighing bemusement. "Let's face it,"
she said one night, ready to drape a wet cloth over her
uncompleted effort to model a reclining dog. "It looks like a
turd."

"She has great joie de vivre," Rhoda told people. One week
Rhoda admired her tan, and discovered that Harriet often spent
her weekends at a resort in the mountains.

"Don't you put on weight there? I thought they did nothing
but eat in those places."

"This one's very low-key. It's not all full of har-de-har types and yukkaputzes, if you know what I mean. They get an older crowd, you should pardon the expression."

"Go with her some time, for Christ's sake," Annie Marantz said, when Rhoda mentioned it. "What the hell have you got to lose?"

Shadyside, on first being approached by car, presented a huge sign with its name spelled out in logs, then a farmhouse, flanked by rows of bungalows. They were all painted white, trimmed with a dark, foresty enamel whose color, Rhoda insisted, was WPA-project green. In the main building the desk clerk, a fat, overeager man, took their luggage and led them to the room they were to share. The place smelled like the summer camp where she sent Suzanne—steamy institutional cooking, fresh pine needles, and clothes left too long in the rain.

They arrived midmorning on a Saturday. Rhoda had bought a new swimsuit for the trip, black latex with a stiff boned-up bust. "Anybody leans on me," Rhoda said, tugging at the straps, "there's going to be a whoosh of air." She tapped at the bust to show it was hollow.

"An empty promise, I'd call that," Harriet said. Rhoda wriggled and shimmied to show that the suit didn't move with her. "Oh, you should see yourself," Harriet said. Harriet, in her red suit with its white cuff across the bust, looked dense and strong; she was barrel-chested, with very little flab on her anywhere. A tight ship: there was something so clean and matter of fact in her she was well into her forties, and had, Rhoda gathered from her stories, been married to a man much older than herself who had died early in their marriage. She seemed completely at her ease in being single. Once they had walked home from their class together and passed a shop window with a travel poster of an ancient, crumple-faced Italian peasant warmly urging them with a chip-toothed smile to come to Sardinia, and Harriet had said, "That's the kind that usually goes wild to take me out." It was a thing Rhoda never would have joked about—she had been quite startled. It had given her an odd, tense, cheerful feeling about her own future.

"Do these straps for me, will you?" Harriet asked her now,
holding them out to her. "They cross in the back." Harriet's
back was freckled and broad, damp and leathery to the touch.
In their beach shoes they walked along a path marked by
whitewashed rocks to the lake. Rhoda tested the edge of the
water with her toe. The lake, although crowded with people
fluttering in the water or sitting on rocks at the shoreline,
seemed oddly quiet, and Rhoda realized that she was accustomed to the shrieks of children in swimming areas. She
lowered herself into the water suddenly, fighting the cold, and
began swimming with furious energy; she was not a strong
swimmer, but she felt compelled to count laps, beating a vigor
into herself. When she stopped for breath, standing in shallow
water, a man on the shore crouched down to her and said,
"You're quite an athlete, aren't you?"

"I'm out of practice," Rhoda said hoarsely.

"Well, it's nice to see someone with spirit." He reached
down and they shook hands. From where she stood she saw the
loose edges of the man's trunks, the coarse bandage-like fabric
of his jock strap, and a glimpse of his testicles. They had
always seemed to her the least attractive parts of a man.
Suddenly she felt miserably discouraged; it was not his fault,
but he menaced her privacy. He shifted his weight, showing
even more of himself on one side; she tried to keep from
smirking.

"You look happy," the man said. To change her view, Rhoda
turned to watch the other side of the lake. A very tall,
long-legged man was approaching the edge; he was dark and
hairy, and he walked rocking one leg stiffly behind him.
"That's Moe," the man said. "He caught some shrapnel during
the war. But you should see him swim. Watch him now."

Rhoda could not see how well he swam, for all the splashing;
what she did see was that he kept it up. She watched for a
while, getting chilly as she bobbed, half-immersed. "Hey,
Moe," the man called out as he finished. "This lady admires
your stroke."

He dog-paddled over to where she stood. "Hello," he said. "Want to race?"

"Sure," she said. She felt the attention of the other guests on them. "You better rest first." He was breathing deeply, staring down at his stomach as it rose and fell.

"I'm okay," he said. The other man cried out, "On your mark, get set, go!"

Rhoda kicked off, laughing, which made her swallow gulps of water; she surfaced, sputtering. He was way ahead of her; suddenly he stopped, grabbed her shoulder, and pushed her— she was afraid he was drowning her, until he raised her arm high above the water and shouted, "The winner!"

"Well, it was very close," he said, "but I happen to be a pretty good loser. I'll buy you a drink later, how's that?"

Rhoda was blowing the water out of her nose. "It'll have to be a Coca-Cola for me. I don't drink."

"Too bad. If this was really a class joint, they would have some nice Perrier water for you."

"Two cents plain is the best they can manage here, I'm afraid. How do you know about Perrier?"

"I was in France during the war and I drank gallons of it. Great for a hangover."

"*Mademoiselle from Armentières,*" Rhoda began singing in a nasal, kidding voice.

"That was the other war. How old do I look?"

"*Est-ce que vous parlez français?*" Rhoda asked.

"Some," he said. "But I can't say anything clean in it."

Rhoda stopped rubbing the water out of her eyes. He was not as good-looking as she had thought at first—his chin was too long and his features were so rugged as to be almost homely— but he had a deep, boomy voice, and he was the first man she had met in three years who did not seem to be a fool.

On the other hand, she discovered when he sat across from her at dinner, he was not formally educated. They were seated at a long table of eight people; the waiter had just gotten

chicken grease on a lady's sleeve and someone asked him if he
was working his way through college and if he really thought
this was a better way than selling encyclopedias. "I often
wonder," the waiter said, dabbing at the stain with ice and a
napkin.

"Me, I never went to college," Moe said. "In fact, I never got
past the ninth grade."

When he was fourteen, he told her, his father—a dapper man
who had taught his sons to fish and to box like Gentiles—had
left one morning to take the subway from Flatbush Avenue
into Manhattan to look for work—"and that was it, nobody
ever heard from him again." Two weeks later Moe was kicked
out of school for picking a fight with an Irish kid and winning.
His mother, a timid, ignorant woman who to this day spoke
almost no English, found him a job in, of all places, a ladies'
specialty store, on the argument that his unusual height would
be an asset in reaching the higher shelves. There he spent his
days folding and unfolding the merchandise of silk stockings,
corsets, and lace-trimmed teddies. ("You can imagine, I almost
went crazy—it was like heaven being in there with all that
underwear.") His first girl was a typist who spent all her pin
money on blue satin garters; he got her attention by stealing
them for her. For this he was fired, but he was then hired by a
wholesaler named Rifkin who needed a boy with good muscles. A month later Moe discovered the man was homosexual;
he repelled his advances but to Rifkin's great relief he kept his
secret, as he would have guarded the reputation of an adulter-
ous wife who had offered herself to him, and they became
friends. Rifkin was making a big splash with a line made from a
sleazy artificial silk called rayon. The stuff could not be ironed
without melting and came out of the wash looking as though a
cat had chewed it, but Moe—promoted to salesman—knew his
territory: Brooklyn would go for anything modern. He talked
Rifkin into buying up more of the new man-made fabrics; all
through the Depression Rifkin Intimate Apparel survived
when other businesses went under, because they had a cheaper

line of goods. At twenty-one Moe was a full partner. They worked a twelve-hour day; Rifkin spent his weekends in sad waterfront bars, while Moe went to the gym or to the park; he had given up boxing but in summer he liked baseball. Rifkin was "artistic"; under his tutelage Moe got to know good music, and, having always read the newspapers, found that he liked history; he worked his way through Gibbon and Macaulay and finally Spengler.

For years he argued with Rifkin that war was inevitable in Europe. After Pearl Harbor he enlisted in the army; he was then twenty-eight, in perfect physical health, a bachelor with a weakness for baby-voiced blondes. Nothing even in Gibbon prepared him for Anzio.

While he was away, Rifkin (not for the first time) was badly beaten by a sailor he brought home one night. He lost his nerve and at the age of fifty moved in with his mother. In a last act of sense before his spirit broke altogether, he sold the business and put half the proceeds into a bank account for Moe. When Moe returned to the States he bought into a plastics factory; he was now the chief national supplier of the protective bags used by dry cleaners. He still worked a sixty-hour week; he read less nowadays, prone to headaches from a residue of chemical fumes.

"Now you know all about me," he said. "More than you wanted to know, I'll bet." The dining room had emptied out now except for a small group at another table. Some sort of lively Latin music could be heard coming through the windows from across the lake. "They're starting the entertainment at the barn," Rhoda said. "We should go in."

They walked through the moist and breezy night air around the lake to the barn which had been set up as a rustic nightclub. Inside, people were sitting at round tables before a stage, where a couple—available for instruction in the daytime—were demonstrating dance steps. The woman was twirling her skirts, showing her legs; they paused on the beat and struck stiff, dramatic poses. They demonstrated the samba, the rhumba, the mambo, and the tango. "The tango," Moe whispered, "is a very sexy dance. You lead with your stomach."

"They taught you that at the gym?" Rhoda winked.

Then a comedian came on and told them all the funny things that had happened to him on the way to work that night, most of which Rhoda had heard before, but she opened her mouth to laugh anyway. A boy singer came out, first attempting perkily to ask how much was that doggie in the window, then softening to a croon as he sang of a love from here to eternity, begged do not forsake me, oh, my darling, and then whispered that most of all he wished them love. He ended with good night, ladies.

When they got up to leave, the night had grown black and chilly. "Look at the stars," Moe said. "Watch out—you lean back like that, you'll fall." The lake made faint lapping sounds in the wind, and there was a constant din of crickets. Fresh, mossy odors were around them. There was something painfully young in all this, and Rhoda felt in her a stirring that was not happiness.

She yawned, and excused herself. "It's been a long day," he said. They were in front of the main house. He put his hand on her shoulder, fatherly. "You go up and rest now. I'll see you tomorrow, yes?"

She passed through the pillared doorway. He was walking away; the tall manly shape of his shoulders loped into the half-darkness. She turned down the hall and went up the staircase to her room. She felt vapid and tired: probably she wasn't used to swimming all those laps, she had overdone it. *I've met someone,* she thought, turning the key in her lock, but the prospect didn't make her feel glad or light. Nothing did: what would? Her strongest desire was for a good night's sleep. And, really, she had been resting too long.

At breakfast he was sitting across from a black-haired woman in red toreador pants, and there were no seats left at his table. He waved and shrugged as she went by. "Who the hell is she?" Harriet said, pulling herself into a chair. "She looks like a hairdresser from Canarsie."

"Maybe that's the kind he likes," Rhoda said. "Probably what he's used to." Through breakfast she was distracted by a sense of the two of them leaning forward to speak to each other, but it was worse when she looked back quickly and saw they had left.

She and Harriet spent the morning on the hotel's hilly nine-hole golf course. On the fifth hole they rounded a bend behind an oak tree and came upon Moe Seidman and the woman in toreador pants; three people were with them. Moe had the club high over his shoulder, and the others were watching his ball amble its way across the grass. "Bravo," Rhoda said heartily from behind him. He saw her and touched his brow in salute.

"I'm not really playing," he said. "I'm just showing."

"It's all right," Rhoda said. "We'll wait until you people get through."

The group was already moving on. "Come on, Moe," the black-haired woman was calling from behind a tree.

"It's okay," he said. "Go ahead without me for a minute."

"It's yours, Rhoda," Harriet murmured. Moe was still standing, watching. "I'm just a beginner," Rhoda said. She chopped at the ball fast to get it over with, and missed. "As you can see."

He asked if she minded his showing her, and she consented. Behind where she stood, he put his arms around her and guided her hands over the club. "Relax," he said. She could feel his belt buckle pressing into her light cotton shirt. She was laughing foolishly, excited by the feel of him, behind her where she couldn't see. "No giggling," he whispered into her ear.

He braced himself and, increasing his grip over her hands so that he pinched her knuckles, bore down, drew her arms back, and pushed her into a powerful arc, cracking against the ball, and ending in a sort of pas-de-deux with their arms upraised together. The force of it dazzled her for a minute. "Gawd, you're strong," she said, as he let go of her. She shook her hands to show he'd been squeezing them hard.

Harriet was applauding. "Look how far it went."

"You okay?" he said.

"That was fun," she said. "Whooh."

He stayed with them through the rest of the course, letting Harriet trail behind them, until he remembered her and turned to ask her questions. Rhoda did not care about hurting Harriet's feelings—she cared for very little now except the continuing elation produced by his company, a buoyancy like a sudden flood of relief. She liked him, really liked him. She was remembering what it felt like.

At lunch the Sunday papers had arrived, and after the meal they sat on the lawn in deck chairs reading, littering sections of the grass. Moe did different voices for the characters in the funnies. Brenda Starr he did in a wispy falsetto, the gangsters in a growling bass. "That's my younger daughter's favorite," she said, when he came to Blondie. "Is she blonde?" he asked.

"No," Rhoda said. "Sort of medium brunette like me. The other one's fairer."

"Pretty, like their mother, I bet."

Rhoda stiffened—she was something, but she wasn't pretty. "Oh, they're gorgeous creatures," she said. Actually, she had forgotten them, which was a measure of her interest in him.

All the next week she was in a state of constant physical excitement, a revved-up restlessness that ate into her concentration; she was like the children before the first day of school. When, on Tuesday, he finally called, her voice on the telephone was simpering and nervous, so cloyingly pleasant that when she hung up she thought, God, how nauseating of me. Already she was homesick for her old ordinary life.

On Saturday she saw Suzanne off to camp early in the morning. All day she felt rushed and expectant. They met for dinner in an odd sort of restaurant he suggested in midtown Manhattan, elegant but Chinese. The red-and-gold decor startled her, hard-edged in its notion of sophistication. He was seated at a table when she arrived; he was wearing a well-cut brown suit, and he looked bony-faced, with a five-o'clock shadow. His expression lifted with pleasure when he saw her, but she had remembered him somewhat differently: less coarse.

He made a point of calling the waiter by name, and he tried to get her to order the most expensive things on the menu. Seeing the strain of his efforts, she felt a touch of pity for him that was not altogether affectionate. "Know who that is over there?" He nudged her. There was a dark-haired, chinless woman at the next table. "It's Dorothy Kilgallen."

"I see she's having the almond chicken, too," Rhoda said coolly. He seemed disappointed. "Wait till I tell Suzanne," she added. "She always listens to *Dorothy and Dick* on the radio." They could not quite overhear what Miss Kilgallen was laughing at, but a group in a booth caught Rhoda's attention—two shiny-haired and straight-nosed college girls with their dates, Ivy League types. They were laughing about a practical joke one of the boys had pulled on the maid who cleaned his room at Yale—he had filled his pillow with shaving cream on sheet-changing day.

"Rich kids," Moe murmured darkly.

Conversation in the room lowered when a silk-clad hostess announced a phone call for Dorcas Feldspar; one of the girls they had been watching got up, smoothing her dress and tossing her head, and followed the hostess.

"Some name," Rhoda said. "Good poise, though."

"Kids like that drive me crazy," Moe said. "They know nothing about the world. Never will. Don't have to."

"It doesn't bother *me*," Rhoda said. In truth they both felt shabby and envious; the heedlessness of these young people was somehow depressing. Why was that? Years ago, Rhoda told Moe, she and her girlfriend Ellie had saved their money and taken a trip to Europe. On the boat they met and befriended a really nice girl named Alicia Peacock—she happened to come from a very prominent family but you wouldn't have known it. "We never felt any different," Rhoda said. This was a mild exaggeration, but certainly they had not been jealous—of what? They were all equally young, with an abundance of possibilities that could be turned down, like dates; the thought that certain chances never recur had been beyond them then.

Rhoda's dress, which had seemed very winning when she had chosen it to wear that evening, now struck her as being too short in the hem. Across from them Dorcas Feldspar, with a great deal of rustling and giggling, was resettling herself into her seat. "Move, Tommy, will you?" she said, bumping her friend's date playfully.

"Nothing will ever happen to these people," Moe said. "It makes me hate them."

She thought that Moe was a little too pointedly proud of having been through much, having had things "happen" to him: his war limp, his poor-boy background. Her own true and constant feeling, even with Moe, was that nothing had ever happened to anyone but her.

Leonard's death had given her—in a reversed and twisted but permanent way—the same sense of superiority to ordinary people that having him for a husband had given her when he was alive. How could she not be susceptible to the feeling that there was something elevating in being a widow? Even the children thought they knew something that put them above their heedless contemporaries—especially Claire. Rhoda had found, in the jewelry box where Claire kept her treasures, a poem written on lined paper in her third-grade printing:

> When at night I go to sleep,
> I think of thoughts that are very deep.
> My thoughts from others I save,
> I think of loved ones beyond the grave.

Moe was lighting a cigarette. He had stopped hating the young people in the booth, and he was talking about how well this year was looking in the plastics business. It was actually becoming cheaper to manufacture all sorts of containers, the technology had progressed at such a rate. In the faint boredom with which she followed his enthusiasm over certain chemical processes, she was reminded of how Leonard had gone on about the future of medicine; but Leonard hadn't cared at all about the money in it, whereas Moe was interested in the money and the power in these things; she liked this about him.

She saw his hands, as he fingered his cigarette; they were very large and long-fingered, but what was remarkable was the nails—they were wonderfully rosy and healthy, with just a line of immaculate white showing above the quick—a miracle of grooming: they were the most well-mannered hands she had ever seen on a man.

"I wish my girls could see your fingernails," she said. "It might inspire them in the right direction."

"Oh," he said. "I get them buffed and all where they cut my hair. They asked me once if I wanted it, and it seemed like a good idea."

This did not seem effeminate to Rhoda; it seemed to her part of a luxury and a solidity beyond these considerations. For her the one attraction of wealth had always been its thorough and exquisite tending to detail. The satisfaction of this made her want to rest against him. When he reached forward to light her cigarette, his hands smelled pleasantly of lemony soap. He hadn't done these things just for her, he did them all the time—there was a mastery in it, an acquirement of perfections—and she thought of all the attentions he must pay himself with such unquestioned ease.

At the end of the evening he walked her to the parking lot where she had left her car, and while they waited for the attendant, they embraced. She felt the warm slip of his tongue in her mouth, and she was thrilled, moved by the way he held her fast. "See you soon," he said, and she repeated it, edging away from him. She was waiting for the clear sense that this was one of life's high moments, and it did not come. He would never be Leonard. At first she felt unspeakably sorry and bitter, but then, as her car was brought and she slid behind the wheel, desire and a pride in him returned—he was waving to her—and she felt, after all, able to like him.

The next week she spent much time on the phone describing him to friends, embellishing his "points" as though shouting down her vague disappointments; she talked of him so repeatedly she violated her normal sense of privacy, so that when she put down the phone she felt shamed and incontinent. Her friends were excited for her, almost too excited; they were frankly impressed by his money (which she of course had brought up) but when they squealed back over her good luck, it sounded vulgar to her.

Still, to tell them about him was to publicly confirm (otherwise it would have been nobody's business) that she was part of a couple again, which made her feel full of hard, ordinary strength in a way she had not in years—the enjoyment of long-denied rights. That weekend he took her to the movies; in the dark of their seats she watched his profile next to her in silent satisfaction.

They saw *Roman Holiday* with Audrey Hepburn—Audrey Hepburn was a princess who thought that the only way to have a good time was to pass herself off as a commoner. Afterwards, walking toward a steak house he thought she might like, they talked about the spots where the movie had been filmed, and he told her gritty stories about Rome after the surrender, bands of children stealing clothes off drunken soldiers, socks and all. He seemed full of information, an interesting person. There was nothing very difficult about leaning on his arm while walking, asking questions and smiling during the pauses in conversation. She had not forgotten how after all.

The streets were hot and crowded; an old man on the corner tried to talk Moe into getting his shoes shined; Moe steered her past him deftly. When they crossed the street, he switched to keep to her outer side. He seemed very well-versed in this. His height and his physical tactfulness made her feel, in her light summer dress, like another version of herself, smaller and sweeter. His favorite movies, he told her, were *The Lavender Hill Mob* and *Henry V.*

They had reached the restaurant; after the fetid smells of the street, the aroma of broiling meat seemed rich and homey. "I hope you're starving-hungry," he said, and when she cocked her head and patted her stomach to show that she was, he laughed happily.

They agreed that the next weekend he was to come visit her in New Jersey. By mid-week it occurred to her that it might be best to warn her father that there was a gentleman coming to visit on Sunday. "So when's the wedding?" he said.

"Don't get your suit pressed yet." The girls had just finished supper, and Rhoda was clearing the dishes.

"You're not getting any younger," he pointed out. "What I want to know is—is it Mr. Right or Mr. Wrong?"

"Just be friendly when he's around, okay? Say hello or something."

"When Mr. Right comes, I'll say hello," he said, and shuffled back to his room. Claire was at this moment engaged in dumping into the dog's bowl a sizable piece of perfectly good meat which she would not eat because she said it was all full of fat and stringy parts. I'm surrounded by purists, Rhoda thought.

She met him at the bus stop with Claire in the front seat. "What a little doll," he said. Claire had buck teeth and looked more like a mouse than a doll. She rubbed against him in homely sweetness. Rhoda ruffled the child's hair. "*Qui est jolie?*" she said. "*Claire est jolie.*"

"Know what?" Claire was saying to him, as Rhoda drove. "I got my Junior Swimmer's license." She held out her arm to show him the red rubber band on her wrist, a badge from day camp. "Isn't that something?" he said, as she played with his cuffs and then held his hand. He was beaming, as adults did who were not used to the easy attentions of children.

"After lunch we can take a Sunday drive," Rhoda said when

they pulled up in front of the house. Claire got out of the car and ran ahead, waiting at the front door until Rhoda unlocked it.

In her living room he circled, exploring. "You have so much room here," he said. She thought Moe himself looked very large and outsized, hedging around the arrangement of her furniture, and when he settled into the cushions of her couch his knees rose above the level of the coffee table. The rose-veined marble table and the green damask sofa, with its woven pattern of curling scrolls and flowers, looked suddenly feminine as he sat at them eating sandwiches, a dog on its haunches in a garden.

Claire, who had been playing in the backyard, joined them for the promised drive. Moe seemed to think he was in the country, despite the presence of supermarkets, branches of New York department stores, and moderate to heavy traffic. He admired the way the tree branches in full leaf met overhead from opposite sides of the street. She showed him the houses in the wealthy section and the reservoir. "You've never thought of moving?" he asked.

Rhoda had the same attitude toward the town as toward her possessions; any choice, once made, fixed in her a sense of superiority to those who didn't have the same. Fifteen years ago she and Leonard had selected the town for its attractive streets and its excellent school system; it seemed to her, as it had seemed then, the most sensible of places.

Moe amused her with dead-end-kid stories of growing up in Brooklyn. She teased him about his accent. They began talking in mock-Brooklynese. "Holey moley," Rhoda said. "Whatsa matter wid me? I missed the toin over dere."

"Over dere, over dere," he began singing. Then he called out, "Watch out, it's muddy." Paved blacktop had given way to a dirt side road; rains had softened the rutted surface. "It's a treat to beat your feet in the Mississippi mud," he began singing. He switched to a Yiddish version—it had been a great parody years ago. Rhoda chimed in on the key words—she was laughing so hard she was afraid the car was going to go off the road. In his deep voice, Moe kept lowing like a bull their Bing Crosby pickaninny ditty in Yiddish. He was singing "fees in der Mississippi schmutz."

Claire, in the back seat, went wild. She was clinging to the top of the front seat and squealing, "What are you singing? What does it mean?" She had never seen her mother like this. "Teach me the song." They tried to explain it, but she couldn't see the funny part. "Oh, you're just silly," Claire said, and they laughed harder.

They had stopped in front of her house, by the horse-chestnut tree, whose dropped leaves crackled under the wheels. Claire thrust open the car door and ran to the back of the house, where the dog barked from his run. In the front seat Rhoda arranged her hair in the rear-view mirror; her face had a blurred, wild look, as though she had been crying or kissing. Moe leaned toward her, touched her neck, and whispered, "I love you."

A thrill of shock went through her—she was sure that was what he'd said—but it was too soon, too easily said, too sloppy. Still, it was nice of him. She squeezed his hand, looking down, demure suddenly. The only thing she could think of to say was thank you.

He was not pushy about physical contact, for which she was grateful. After supper, when Claire went out-of-doors to play, they sat in the sun parlor, smoking cigarettes and letting a hesitation grow between them. For a while he held her in a great comfortable crush and then they necked like teenagers, letting their mouths move slowly over each other's faces like cats lapping milk. His big hands were not intrusive; when she opened her eyes, he saw and stopped.

When she talked to Harriet the next day, Rhoda described the visit as having been a "great success."

"I think it's exciting," Harriet said. "One trip to the mountains and look what you come home with. It shows the spirit of romance is not dead in this world." Rhoda had been

somewhat loath to dwell on her current triumph in front of
Harriet, but Harriet's enthusiasm seemed genuine. At present
she was sitting in Rhoda's kitchen, patting the dog under the
table; she had just come from a morning golf class—she was
wearing a white blouse and a knee-length white piqué wrap-
skirt, and with her cropped silver hair and her deep tan, she
looked, Rhoda told her, "extremely sporting."

"He loved the house," Rhoda said, "especially the backyard."

"Well, coming from the city," Harriet said.

"I thought I'd take him for a walk around the reservoir the
next time."

"He may be uncomfortable walking too long in damp areas,"
Harriet pointed out. "I think his leg might bother him
sometimes. It's three miles around the lake and awfully
marshy all through there."

Rhoda had very happily planned this as their next expedi-
tion; she felt a little irked at Harriet.

"So you carry him. A new experience." Harriet winked.

Rhoda did not want this sort of experience; she wanted her
old experience back. Leonard had once hiked ten miles on a
trip to Canada.

"Maybe you'll bring the dog along with a keg of brandy,"
Harriet said.

The dog gave one of his groaning yawns as he stretched to
stand up. Timmy was getting gray around his muzzle. Harriet
scratched him behind his floppy ears. His cocker spaniel breed
had gone somewhat out of style. TV shows used collies and
German Shepherds, more heroic types. He had been primarily
Leonard's dog, although he hadn't acted especially depressed or
confused after Leonard died. Rhoda remembered, with a touch
of disgust at the dog's lack of constancy, how he had jumped
and fawned over Moe on Saturday.

After Moe's visit to the house they alternated, week by
week, meeting in his city or her suburb. Rhoda had never been

to his home, a two-and-a-half-room apartment in Brooklyn Heights; he suggested it once, but he did not pursue the topic when she demurred. They saw movies together, he took her to *Lili* and *Moulin Rouge*; and one steamy night they went to an Italian street festival where they ate ices, he gambled and lost on the Wheel of Fortune, and she brought back a doll on a long stick for Claire.

Suzanne met him when she returned home from camp; as expected, she was polite but not forthcoming. He liked to spend money on all of them; he bought Suzanne a large coffee-table sort of book on butterflies—as insects went, they were not her favorites, being too commonly appreciated, but she warmed to him a bit more after that. Both children insisted on calling him Mr. Seidman and could not be coaxed into using his first name.

In the fall they went for drives into the surrounding countryside. He had found a roadhouse off the highway—a dark, cavernous place with neon signs in the window; Rhoda never would have picked it. He drank cocktails while the kids ate hamburgers. It was called The Embers, in an attempt at urban wickedness; sometimes the two of them returned alone at night for steaks.

His tastes were not exactly her tastes. He wore, for instance, a diamond pinky ring and heavy gold cuff links. Though he could well afford to, he never traveled—not since the war, if you counted that. He showed sometimes, in speaking of irritations in business, a crudity of language and a raw anger that dismayed her.

He had the long lantern jaw of a gangster. She watched him in restaurants; when he chewed his meal, quietly enough, he worked his back teeth like an animal. She wondered what she had told people about him. She was afraid she had exaggerated herself out of belief. A stiffness, as though she'd been caught in a lie, sometimes stole over her—she was in the wrong time and the wrong place—but it didn't matter because she had to be there anyway. After dinner they held hands.

That he could speak of loving her so cheaply and so easily
struck her as a lapse in judgment, a sign of insufficient depth in
his character. He was, as the English would say, "a bit too
free." Still, the words had been said; they existed, as the past
did, in sublime finality. In private moments they did come
back to her, and she was awash in awe; it was as though she'd
awakened one morning to find that she had already slept with
him. She could not have been more shaken or more haunted
with impression; she was, truly, so startled as to be reduced to
girlish gratitude, yielding to self-congratulations and pitiable
confusions.

In November she brought Moe to a large party at the
Marantzes'. He was surprisingly quiet and shy, a nodding
presence at her side. "A good-looker." Annie winked behind
his back. "Nice work, Rhode." In general her friends were
blindly encouraging in this way; he was presentable; it wasn't
up to them to look more closely. What if this is as good as it
gets at my age? Rhoda thought. Millions of women had
remarried on less. But they were small-minded people.

They left the party at midnight, and as she drove Moe to
meet his bus (the trains had stopped running at that hour), he
said, "Your friends think highly of you. I could tell that." The
streets were empty; the car's motor seemed quite loud and
disruptive making its way through them.

"I've known most of them for years," Rhoda said.

"What do they think about the idea of your marrying again?"

"Some of them think of nothing else," Rhoda said, laughing.

"Good," Moe said. "Very good. I've got them on my side
then."

Rhoda realized that in a manner of speaking—a trivial and
somewhat corny manner—he was proposing to her; she was
making a turn at that moment and she couldn't look at him.
When she did catch his glance, he gave her a slow, meaningful
smile. He went on about how pleasant all her friends had been
to him; he had only meant to present the question, to

disseminate it as information, and not to demand an answer.

The bus was coming—he reached for her and after they kissed he held her in a long treasuring hug which was much more suave and tender than his passing speeches. On the dark ride home, she was painfully lonesome for Leonard, with his natural stateliness and his sense of occasion. It made her slightly hysterical to think in this way. She could go neither backward nor forward. She couldn't think of any man she knew, including her friends' husbands, whom she really liked better than Moe.

Once she caught herself telling Suzanne, "Wait till Mr. Seidman gets here. He'll fix the rung on that chair," and she knew that she was getting used to expecting him. Suzanne said, "I think we should just throw the chair out," but Rhoda took this—not as a slur against Moe or his abilities—but as another sign of Suzanne's attitude lately. She had fallen into an early-adolescent scorn for the décor, the neighborhood, Rhoda's cooking. But she had too much of a sense of privacy to be rude when Moe was around, which was another reason to welcome his visits. In December, with the weather nasty again, Rhoda suggested over the phone that he spend the whole weekend this next time. "There's a sofa downstairs big enough for your big feet," she said.

She had no fixed idea of what she meant him to think. She knew perfectly well what possibilities the arrangement suggested. After all she was "a grown woman" (as she sometimes described herself to Maisie)—direct in her judgments and not squeamish about sex; still, she was, in her own mental conversations with herself, discreet about her own desires. She was not capable of celebrating raw sexual feeling. Moe had, at certain times, evoked sensations long since gone to sleep in her—she was glad to know them again, but when the stirrings rose, they always came up against the limit of her feelings for him and settled back down again. The whole process made her restless and jumpy and desperate. She would have liked to have been hypnotized—sent into a swoon—by the intensity of his affection. She did trust his feeling for her. How could he not be devoted to her, when she was so much more than he was?

He arrived bearing a little leather overnight case like a doctor's bag, and a gift for her, a book of cartoons he thought would amuse her. *Fractured French* it was called—*"Femme de ménage"* pictured a fortyish woman with deep cleavage and the definition, "a woman of any age," and so on. "Clever," she said. She was far too weak to dislike anything.

It snowed in the afternoon—which was very pretty and romantic, seen from the windows in the living room—but which kept them indoors. Claire talked them into making fudge with her, but she grew bored when it took too long to reach the soft-ball stage and she ran outside to build a snowman and left them to finish. They stood at the stove, taking turns stirring, sweating slightly over the sugary vapors. They brushed past each other, changing places, and Moe put his arm around her aproned waist. Rhoda felt sticky and drowsy. "What work!" Moe said. He took off his sweater in the heat, lifting it over his arms, there were deep, wet stains on his shirt. He pushed his shirt into his pants quickly, like a child tucking himself up before anyone yelled at him for his loose shirt-tails.

He apologized so profusely for letting the candy burn at the bottom of the saucepan that she began to think he was slightly afraid of her. All day he was full of foolishly fond, melting looks. "I love the way your mind works," he told her when they were discussing Eisenhower's foreign policy, while they played honeymoon bridge. And at dinner he said, oddly, "You have copper-colored eyes." They were simple brown. She had nothing to say back. She murmured at him coyly. At the end of the night she gave him a pile of sheets and an extra pillow and went up to bed by herself.

But lying in her twin bed with the light off, she was surrounded on all sides by the fresh image of the humility of his passion, until the poignance of it pressed on her and drew out her own hungers. In the middle of the night she went to him. It was quite dark in the living room. "Is that you?" he said. They tumbled about, hearing each other breathing hoarse, impersonal gasps. She had expected to think of Leonard, so that when the direct physical memory came upon her, it was not so awful, and pain commingled with arousal: she was heartsick in a way that made her helpless and deeply moved. But across the heated exchange of sensation, as his hands reached to ready her, she had a sudden vision of what sex really was—the blunt crudity of its positioned grappling, the spreading intimacy of its secretions and exposures—so that it became unthinkable with this man, and in the end she stopped him just short of the act itself. They lay perfectly quiet, still bent and folded around each other in a form which was somewhat silly now because it had no purpose. "It's all right," he said. She felt like a crazy woman.

Her first thought—when she woke from a shallow sleep— was that she had to get rid of him as evidence of the terrible muddle she had made of everything. She began to slip away from him to return to her own bed, but when she stirred he reached out in his sleep and drew her to him with such resolute need that she was moved once again to melting confusion. She experienced an overwhelming temptation not to think about anything.

It persisted to the next day, and made her sleepy; she had difficulty following conversation, but Moe, who stuck to her side like a puppy, was full of amiable recitation and easily satisfied by smiles and nods. They were sitting having lunch in the dinette—the girls were outside—when she heard him say, "I don't ever want you to have the idea that I would push you into anything," and she thought, oh, no, he's going to talk about it. But he was saying that he supposed she knew he wanted to marry her and what did she think about all that? She thought he must know better, from his business, than to begin a request by apologizing (he had dropped all the devices from his own world in coming to her, so that he approached her unarmed, awkward as a civilian). He had taken her hand, in courtly fashion, and in her embarrassment she looked down at the fingers covering hers—his nails, with their sanded elegance, so different from the hard rawness of the rest of his body, with its forest of hair and the pale shiny scar on his thigh. He seemed so painfully well-intentioned. She wondered if he was reassuring her because he thought she'd had eleventh-hour hesitations about her honor, whereas in fact she cared less and less about these things as she grew older. She gave him the answer he had provided her with. "It's too soon to tell," she said. It was the exact opposite of the truth.

He was the most compliant person. In the matter of sex their relationship was to stay at the same stopping-point for the indefinite future. Moe never complained; they developed a slow way of lying together, sweetly comradely, as though a shared fatigue kept them from the edge. The muddle of their truncated contact became completely normal. At times they were even playful with each other, romping.

It did seem to surprise him to find himself in this situation, a grown man. He would get up and hop about, kicking down the cuffs of his trousers, and moaning, "It only hurts when I walk, for instance. Who needs to walk?" He clutched himself in mockery of his own discomfort. It became a sort of family joke between them.

She actually liked him best when he was not around. She felt attached to him by reason of their nebulous but nonetheless factual physical intimacy. She allowed herself to think that she was *used to* his faults—everyone had faults, didn't they?—his jokestering, his bad taste, his lack of serious purpose. He was just Moe (Moe-your-beau: one of his lines); and in the guise of fond acceptance she enjoyed, with the perfect languor of an auto-induced delight, the preening of her own generosity.

Just before Christmas they arranged to meet in the city so that they could walk up Fifth Avenue and see all the displays in stores, go window-shopping. At Lord & Taylor there was a wonderful diorama of little mechanical elves busy at their workshop. At Saks there were cool garlands of icicles and blue lights, piles of sweaters in luxurious, nonchalant heaps, and a scene of elegant girl-mannequins standing around a Christmas tree in their jaunty, vacant poses, arms stiff, wearing the most amazing loungewear.

"Look at that one," Rhoda pointed. It was a dressing gown with an outer layer made entirely of lace, tiers of white over white chiffon. "Now that's a gorgeous item. It must cost a fortune."

"It's Alençon lace," he said. "You'd look pretty splendid in it. Quite the lady. I wouldn't be at all surprised if they had one in your size. What are you—a ten?" He took her by the hand; he was about to lead her into the store—he wanted to buy it for her; Rhoda could not believe it. She drew back, dismayed. She had never worn a thing like that in her life.

"Where would I go in it?" she asked.

"It doesn't matter. Even if you only wore it around the house. Even if you just looked at it in the closet."

"What's the point?"

They walked on without speaking. "Are you sure?" he said. She nodded. He was always wanting to spend money on her, bringing her gifts. There was something infantilizing about having to clap your hands over a boxed set of earrings, and his own puppyish pleasure in pleasing her was not an uplifting sight. But the dreamy beauty of the gown had gotten to her—it was a perfect thing—and he meant well, even in his vulgar and irritating way of always flashing his ready cash, and she took his hand as they walked, attached to him with the faint stirring of regret.

That evening they went to a Greek night club and watched a belly dancer. She was a young, broad-featured woman who ended her act by leaning into a full backbend, her upraised stomach still rippling; men slipped dollar bills under her costume or stuck them to her sweating flesh. Rhoda, smiling, clapped in time.

Moe saw her to the station (she was taking the train home

this time) and kissed her before she boarded, like a war bride going home. In her sense of people watching them she forgot to kiss back; she was feeling both besmirched and flattered.

The night was bitterly cold, and her coat was inadequate. She hugged herself in her seat like a waif. It was too dark to see much out of the windows, she might be going anywhere; there was only one person at the other end of the car, an old man wearing earmuffs, falling asleep against his seat. She was overcome by the melancholy and the sense of being unlucky which overtakes travelers alone at night. But she'd had a good time, hadn't she? Their times together were like candy, cheaply sweet and insubstantial. She was less than she might be. She thought again of Leonard, a more serious person. Lord Graveairs, she had called him once, after a character in a play. "Laugh," he would say, "everything is a joke to you." The train passed noisily out of one station; she saw the street lights reflected in the windows and then she saw herself, with her makeup paled and her lips dry, and she felt shallow and lost and not suited for better things.

Moe's overnight visits were apparently exciting some interest among the neighbors, but since they'd spread rumors long before he'd ever spent the night and Rhoda had been righteously miffed then, she declined to get nervous now. Her father had spoken to Moe only once; since then he had retired to his room out of shyness. He who was normally so seedy-minded never questioned his daughter's virtue; occasionally he teased her about her suitor. The children said nothing. Claire was glad of the company; Suzanne slept late and kept to her room till noon; still she had a tendency to know things. My kids, Rhoda thought, don't ask questions.

Moe still slept on the couch when he stayed at the house. Rhoda, who was a light sleeper, could hear him in the night, padding back and forth to the bathroom. Once, on a windy night in February, she woke suddenly, hearing something at the front door. A train went by, clattering on its track a quarter of a mile away, and then she heard from downstairs a long, low moan, like a ghost in gothic tales. She thought she heard it again, a moaning.

She went down to the living room to find Moe crawling on his belly in the foyer, hitting his shoulder against the front door and rattling it. When she leaned over him, he clutched her with such sudden muscular force his fingers dug viciously into her ribs. She called to him to wake him, and he stared at her stonily until his eyes cleared and his grip loosened. "What was it?" she whispered. She was badly shaken, trying to remember how to calm someone safely. He shook his head. "Sometimes the war repeats on me like onions," he said.

G.I. humor. *He crawled on his belly through enemy fire*, she remembered. Apparently it was the sound of the train that had set him off. He sat on the sofa with the blanket wrapped around his shoulders. "I'm fine," he said. "Go back to sleep."

Rhoda said, "I wonder if they just changed the train schedule." In fact she was fairly sure the train went by at the same time every night. It was one of those usual noises in the suburbs, like radiator pipes or rain on the roof; sometimes it woke her. There was no place they could put him where he wouldn't hear it. She'd often seen the scar on his leg, a pale pink crater with a whitish line trailing off from it like a worm. She had not much cared, except from curiosity, but now he seemed abnormally disfigured, and she resented his taking her with him into disturbance. I need this like a hole in the head, she was thinking.

But the next day he was charming with the children, the night was gone, and it seemed overhasty and unnecessary to act on the basis of freak accidents, things done in sleep.

She was relieved when he asked her to meet him in town the next weekend, at his office in rooms above the factory. Following his directions, she went to an address in Manhattan's grimy warehouse district at the close of the day, riding up in a rickety freight elevator manned by a leering young Spanish fellow chewing gum. The second floor was one huge room with a high tinned ceiling and walls showing heating pipes. People worked at makeshift cubicles partitioned by filing cabinets. At one end a row of women sat typing; behind them was a door with a sign saying THE BOSS; beneath it another sign said, NOBODY, BUT NOBODY, KNOWS DE TROUBLE I SEEN.

Rhoda gave her name to one of the secretaries. "What?" The girl grimaced. It was hard to speak politely amid the typing and the rhythmic chug of the machines from below. "Taber," Rhoda said.

"Oh, go on in. He's on the phone but it's okay."

He had his back to her when she entered, and he stood gripping the phone receiver and crouching forward as though he were about to pounce at the wall. He was yelling into the phone. "Forget Farber. Farber can go shove it up his ass as far as I'm concerned. You don't keep your word, you don't get your orders." He turned as he heard her—his face was wrenched and hard; when he saw her he put his arm up with the palm raised: the sign to wait. "What are you saying to me? You will not. Not to me you won't. Farber is a cheap scumbag. He thinks he's so smart, next time he walks in here I'm going to break his arm and beat him over the head with the bloody stump." His voice wavered into a high, hysterical note—"I don't need him and I don't need you"—and he slammed down the phone.

He kicked the desk. "Punks. I deal with punks." Rhoda stared at him: he was out of control. Suddenly he reached forward and touched her hand. "Sorry about that. Bad day here."

"So I see," Rhoda said, smiling tightly and raising her eyebrows.

"Sorry," he said again, shrugging. He began pulling papers out of a pile of invoices on his desk; he really was not the least bit sorry.

"It's all right." She was still bristling with horror at the violence of the language. She was also a bit frightened, afraid to say anything to him. Her instinct was to stay put and keep quiet, as though she had walked into a bad neighborhood with no protection. What if she'd had children with her? He actually thought it was *all right* to be like that. Probably it was normal in his world.

A low, pig-like way to behave. She could not stop thinking about it long enough to make conversation with him. He looked up from his desk. "Ready to go?"

"Whenever you are," she said.

He put on his jacket and they left the office, walking east across town to a small Italian restaurant he knew. It was an unseasonably warm night—the crest of a brief mid-winter thaw—and the air was softly breezy with a foretaste of spring. She was reminded of the summer before when they had met; so it had been—what?—seven months.

They ordered veal and pasta for dinner and the waiter was very jolly because they both knew a few words in Italian. Moe's accent was surprisingly passable. She did not, at that moment, dislike him; she had already reached the stage of forgiveness, pressed by the knowledge that it was over between them. She couldn't see what there had ever been; she looked back, as through a tunnel, and saw nothing. She felt inestimably cheapened by the fact that she had permitted herself to hope.

"You liked that little restaurant on Prince Street, didn't you?" he asked her the next time.

"Oh, I had a really terrific time," she said. She felt comfortable lying to him now because she was decently sure he didn't merit the effort it would have taken to tell the truth. He, on the other hand, grew edgier, always touching her hair and telling her how happy she made him, disturbing her in private with tight, tooth-scraping kisses. She would toss her head and laugh. In conversations she took to rubbing his hand reassuringly.

By spring she still saw Moe occasionally but he no longer came for more than a day's visit. She developed new interests. In April, when the tulips came up in the front yard, she noticed they'd gotten smaller and smaller every year since Leonard had died, because she neglected to dig up the bulbs and store them over the winter. She began to work in the garden herself, putting in roses and begonias around the back, and hosing down the peony bushes to rid them of ants. When she dug in the earth she wore an old, ratty, red flannel shirt of Leonard's, which hung loose and eccentric-looking over her dress and amused the children enormously. She wiped the sweat off her face so that the soil from her hands smeared her upper lip like a mustache, and she did not care. Not caring had a calming, luxurious effect.

On Moe's last visit he brought with him a wooden pull-toy for Claire that was much too young for her. She thanked him with such mature resignation that Rhoda mused about what sort of man he was, so weak even children knew they had to lie to him.

They sat on chairs in the backyard to get some sun; a breeze came up late in the afternoon, and Rhoda drew her cardigan around her like a shawl. "I saw Annie Marantz the other day," Rhoda said, "and she asked for you. She's crazy about you."

"Too bad for me you're not under her influence," Moe said. "Tell her I'd marry her except she's already married. I can't marry you any more, can I?"

She tried to explain tactfully about how she couldn't, really, as though forces beyond her will kept her from wanting to. He stiffened and said, "Well, I hope I haven't wasted your time," and she shook her head emphatically, although that was exactly what she thought.

"Well, that's good," he said. He was standing in her garden, a crook-necked, defeated man with a prominent Adam's apple, wearing a sports shirt whose short sleeves his laundry had pressed too crisply, so they flapped at his arms like creased wings. "My heart," Rhoda told Hinda later, "went out to him," expressing, in that generous common phrase, her pity, her contempt.

VIII

In July she left for Europe with Harriet Tuckler. On the French ship they lay in deck chairs and Rhoda grew tanned and handsome, congratulating herself at getting away from the children, away from the trailing attachment to Moe, who had persisted in calling her long after it was officially over between them, bothering her with late night calls, coaxing her into tense lunch-time meetings. It had been more than twenty years since she'd been to Europe with Ellie—it surprised her now that she hadn't gone back before this. The time with Moe had left her feeling, by contrast with his commonness, refined and keen-minded, delicately tuned; she would have taken up needlepoint had that had any appeal for her—instead she was drawn back to the one sophistication she had, which was an acquaintance with the everyday culture of Europeans. She was so used to making reference to the way they did things in Europe that by now she expected to impress even the

Continentals with her knowledge of their ways. And in fact on
the French ship the stewards applauded her accent and her
spirit; she explained menus to Harriet, told her French people
never wore white shoes in the city in summer.

In Le Havre a *petit fonctionnaire* misdirected their luggage
and they had to wait for an hour at Customs in the wet chilly
night until Harriet's valise was found. But when they were
taken finally to their small, quiet hotel, the room, with its iron
bedsteads, its Empire-striped wallpaper, and the balcony doors
overlooking the street, was poignantly recognizable. Nothing
had changed: the furnishings were like clichés no one had the
sense to retire, the trappings of a thousand modest hotel
rooms. "This stuff must have been here since the year one,"
Rhoda said happily.

She remembered telling Leonard about a hotel room much
like this in Paris, where she and Ellie had stayed. He had been
so taken with her descriptions. The more bemused she had
been in recalling the ancient clawed feet on the bathtub off the
hall and the dark splintery *chiffonnier* whose drawers had
stuck, the more worldly and intellectually evocative they had
seemed to him.

Harriet went to sleep directly; Rhoda sat up in bed, alert
with sudden contentment, listening to the occasional sounds
of footsteps and male voices calling to each other in blurred
French from the alley below; she was jolted into an excitement
close to panic. She went to the window. They were only on the
third floor but she had the feeling of expansion which sometimes overtook her on great heights, a desire—quite the
opposite of a fear—to leap down and out into the space below.
She could hardly stand the feeling of hope. Only the sense that
it was attached to the pre-measured limits of her vacation
made her calm enough to sleep.

In Paris she found that she remembered the names of the
streets, and the names of people came back to her at unexpected moments. Harriet repeated the information after her, with a
delight that surprised Rhoda. The Parisians on the street had

changed—colder, as everyone said—they had been through a war, after all, and they'd grown tighter, more money-constricted than ever. Of course, she was older, young men did not ogle her or try to paw her girdled rump as she went past. She had great gaps in her vocabulary; when she wanted breast of chicken in a restaurant, she had to pantomime with her hands the outline of a great bosom before her. The waiter laughed at her, imitated the gesture, and brought her the correct portion; she pointed and made the gesture again when he had put the dish down. Being a foreigner made you clownish by necessity. She felt free and gay, making bold childish motions with comic skill. The waiter told her she should go audition for Marcel Marceau. Harriet applauded; Rhoda took a small bow. It was exactly the sort of joking Suzanne and Claire found so annoying.

She did not try to locate any of the people she'd once known there—for one thing, she was afraid to find out about them (many of them had been Jews). And Moe had once told her a story of an army buddy of his who'd gone back to Paris and found the hotel where he'd once had a rather sweet affair with the girl who brought coffee in the mornings. The fat, slack-jawed proprietor was still there, and when the American introduced himself, the old man began to weep. Moe's friend had thought it was because the man was so glad to see him, but it turned out it was mostly from shock at how old the soldier had gotten. "*Mais vous avez changé,*" the hotelkeeper kept saying, and raising his hands as if he were under arrest.

She wasn't the sort of person, she told Harriet, to go dredging up the past; and in fact she didn't seem like that sort of person now. They walked for hours in all sorts of neighborhoods, scoffing at the timidity of other Americans. In a restaurant a family with two young children—hearing her speak to the waiter in French—asked if she could find out if the milk was safe to drink. Rhoda tried to ask the waiter if the milk had been treated "*dans le moyen de Pasteur.*" "He says he never heard of Pasteur," Rhoda said, "but everyone drinks the milk." She thought it was an insulting question to ask in a civilized country.

As Harriet said, they were rubes, these other tourists; Rhoda, whatever her failings, was not a rube. She had never enjoyed more fully the rich, slightly cynical heartiness of her own personality. At Les Halles they bought peaches from an old woman who tried to raise the price after she had taken their money. For ten minutes she and Rhoda remonstrated into each other's faces, repeating the terms of the bargain. "*Voleuse!*" Rhoda began to shout in an ecstasy of vocabulary; she was practically spitting, in an imitation of Gallic nerve. She lost the argument, but back at the hotel she and Harriet thrilled themselves retelling the incident to each other. "Thief! Thief!" Harriet squealed. "You were something."

An old sense of herself as formidable came back to Rhoda. She hadn't realized how far she'd come from that, how much Leonard's death had broken her confidence.

In Rome she got a postcard from Claire at camp. "—Last night we had a pajama party with Bunk 12 and we all traded beds. Bunk 11 slept in Bunk 12's beds and vice versa—get it? I got a letter from Mr. Seidman with 2 DOLLARS in it!!! I bought a giant Hershey Bar with Almonds when our bunk hiked to town, but I am saving the rest. I didn't know you could send money through the mail."

She spoke of her children often, but it occurred to her that she remembered them differently from the way they actually were. She had lost hold of the squirming intricacy of their characters, reduced them to something manageable in the mind. Her life at home seemed pale and languid to her now—the town and her own social milieu seemed stale and provincial. It depressed her even to think about eating the fruits and vegetables at home.

In Rome Harriet was amazed when Rhoda knew how to ask for a double room in Italian. "You've pulled another language out of your hat," she said. In truth Rhoda knew only a few Italian phrases, but she delivered them in a fluid accent and she could understand a lot through cognates, so that she almost believed she spoke Italian; she regretted that she normally had so little chance to use it. She remembered that one of Chekhov's Three Sisters had complained of what a waste it was to know three languages in a town like theirs.

In Florence they went to the Uffizi, walked through the long crowded halls of the gallery, wearying their feet before paintings of simpering Virgins, sinewy Old Testament patriarchs shouting into lightning-filled skies, and limp St. Sebastians mutely bleeding from arrows piercing the flesh. To Rhoda's amusement a young Italian in absurdly tight pants tried to pick her up; he blocked a huge panorama of a Biblical battle scene, turned round, and breathed into her ear, "You like this painting? Beauteeful or not beauteeful?" She was mildly insulted that he could imagine she might be interested in him; she and Harriet had just been saying that single and widowed people weren't regarded as so unfortunate here. "Oh, go away, I'm too old for this nonsense," Rhoda said, and walked away herself.

The presence of beautiful objects was not uplifting to her; she found these things magnificent but macabre in their religiosity. She was impressed by the artist's attention to detail—she would stand in front of one piece and satisfy herself noticing things—until through this she worked herself into sharing the swooning intensity of feeling. She was not moved by the viewing but she was filled in some way.

In Vienna, Harriet (who had once studied the cello) indulged herself in five straight nights of concert-going. Rhoda (who could hum the better-known classical themes from the 78's they'd had in her childhood, and who'd been musical enough in school to be given a part in *Iolanthe* where she'd sung "Tripping hither, tripping thither" in a fast, comic tempo) sat in a velvet-draped hall and listened to Mozart with growing interest. The light sweet rhythms, the circling repetitions, the fulsome jubilant phrases, were warming and pleasurable. By the third concert her attention wavered; in her faint sleepiness she mused on the gilt garlands over the stage and she felt the pulse of the music rather than heard it—another sort of civilized pleasure.

She returned home with wooden shoes and costume dolls for Claire; for Suzanne a cuckoo clock, a music box in the form of a chalet that raised its roof, and a book in German with exquisitely reproduced color photos of reptiles, Suzanne's new enthusiasm. At the pier she could see them on the other side of Customs, bobbing at her; Claire was brown from the sun like a little rabbit, and Suzanne wore a sailor's cap with the brim pulled down. Her brother Andy and his wife were with them; they waved and waved, drawing her back. When they saw her wave to them, they began to point and gesture like cops beckoning her into another traffic lane.

She was wearing a green, tightly fitted suit she had bought in Rome; pinned to the lapel was a carnation that had been given to all the ladies at the ship's farewell breakfast. She was so used to feeling faint vibrations under her feet on shipboard that the stillness on land was nauseating, like a stifling room. She kept taking the commands on Custom Bureau signs for words in French or German; had she read them aloud, she would have mispronounced them.

Claire was leaping on her, and the others waited in turn to kiss her, ignoring Harriet, who stood apart. "The best trip ever," Rhoda was saying. "Did you know I was all the way up on one of the highest mountains in Switzerland, Claire?" She gave Claire a croissant she had saved from breakfast. "It's not sweet," Claire said, biting into it and giving it back.

"Wait till you see the things I bought," Rhoda said, getting into the car. "See this wallet? That's the fleur-de-lis, the national flower of France." The children were not much interested; Suzanne said nothing, and all the ride home Claire chattered about color war at camp and a girl named Marcy. Andy kept turning toward her, letting his eyes drift from the road, to tell about some plumbing problems that had developed in her house over the summer. Already she missed Harriet, who had been met by her sister. Rhoda could see that her own rushed excitement—the traveler's breathlessness—made her strange to them.

Suzanne kept tapping at the front seat with her foot. "Try to stop that," Rhoda said. The change in Suzanne was startling; in the rapid way of teenagers she'd grown suddenly older over the summer. She was acne-ridden, and she had lost all the soft sweetness of her face; it was now filled with unseemly expressions, crooked smirks, and sudden closures.

"The house might still be something of a mess," Andy said, as they turned into Rhoda's block. "Maisie's been cleaning up all morning." Rhoda had hardly thought of the house all summer; she had gone from one hotel room to another and found it quite satisfying, looking forward to the variety and regional touches.

The furniture in the living room, sheathed under plastic coverings once given to her by Moe, waited for her like ghostly infants to be changed and tended. Maisie, who was in the dining room, turned off the vacuum cleaner as they came in. "Everything was all so dirty," she said, with great sadness. She was standing in front of the mahogany china cabinet with its burl inlays on the drawers, and she had hung, somewhat crookedly, the beige drapes made extra long to "break" over the carpet. "One of the teacups got broke when I was polishing the cabinet," Maisie said. She obviously had to say this right away to get it over with.

"Don't worry about it now, Rhode," Andy said. Rhoda opened the cabinet and found the teacup with its handle lying next to it. "It can be glued," she said, glaring at Maisie. It was cream-colored glazed parian, plain except for a sculpted pattern, the most translucent and fragile of her china pieces; of course the crack would show. A pretty little cup: she felt a sting of shame at her own disloyalty—her foolhardiness—in thinking she ever could have lived without these things.

In a flurry of settling in again, Rhoda was warned by her brother Andy that she might notice drastic changes in their father. "He's showing signs of a marked decline," Andy said. "He's not clean about his person. He forgets to put his teeth in. He asks about cousins who died thirty years ago and he can't remember what he did the day before. He has prostate trouble; he wets the bed sometimes." Andy's wife, who had tended him all summer, said, "He tries, he really tries."

By the end of a week Rhoda had decided that he did not try hard enough. He was nasty with the children, who fortunately went back to school after the first weekend. He could not eat a bowl of soup and keep his hands from shaking; he refused to wait for his food to cool and he burned himself constantly. At night he complained of the children's shouting.

He was right about that. It was horrible—they were like howling domestic harpies. It was mostly Suzanne's fault now; she had grown cruder and more fixed in her bullying tactics; she had developed a set of malicious fingernails and a truly unattractive side to her personality.

Suzanne had never been as pretty as Claire, but she had once been a robust child with a round jaw and fat knees. Now she was ill-dressed and unfortunate-looking; her blouse was always hanging out of her skirt, and she had odd whims for garish colors and clashed pairings. When she walked to school she clutched her books to her chest as though she were cold or afraid of thieves. She was in junior high now.

Her teachers reported that although she was bright she failed to hand in assignments, except in science class. In her room were two large, glossy zoo posters—a hawksbill tortoise, with fatty, soft feet splayed out from beneath an impressive shell, and an alligator with its eyes bulging above the water line. Suzanne asked if she might keep a tank of tropical fish by the window; Rhoda first said yes, but then she had to rescind when she found out how expensive the equipment was. She offered goldfish instead but Suzanne snorted in contempt. "They've got a real piranha in the pet store, I saw it yesterday," Suzanne said. "That's lovely," Rhoda said. "Yes," Suzanne said, "I'm going to buy it and slip it into the bathtub some time when you're in the water."

She grew mushrooms in the basement for her project in the Science Fair. They did well in the cool concrete room, surrounded by boxes of the girls' discarded games; Rhoda's only request was that Suzanne keep the dirt away from the Ping-Pong table, which Maisie used for stacking the laundry. "Do they really grow from your watching them so much?" Rhoda asked. Every day after school Suzanne spent hours in the cellar. "It's an obsession," Rhoda said, and shuddered.

Rhoda was eating her usual cottage cheese on lettuce for lunch when Maisie came up from the basement suddenly, clattering on the stairs, and slammed the door. She was usually quiet and orderly in her movements; Rhoda looked up from her magazine ready to comment about the noise. Maisie was leaning against the cellar door panting and she called out as though she were afraid to move. "Mrs. Taber," she said, in that voice that was always so high and light for her squat frame, "there is a SNAKE down there."

"Ugh," Rhoda said. "It must be a garter snake that got in from the garden. Have you been leaving the side door open?"

"Not a garden snake, I don't think so," Maisie said. "It's in the closet under the stairs. I went to get some bleach out of there for the wash, I opened the door and I see this thing coiled up on one of the shelves. That thick around, it's got light and dark markings on it. I shut that door and latched it. I saw it move; it's alive."

Rhoda called the junior high school at once and got them to get Suzanne out of gym class. "All right," she said, when Suzanne's voice came over the phone. "What kind of snake is it?"

"Did you kill it?" Suzanne shrieked. "If you killed it, I'll kill you. It's my snake, I paid for it, you had no right to go near it."

"No one has done anything," Rhoda said. "What sort of person do you think I am? Do you think I go around killing things? You went and bought it at that pet shop, didn't

you?—I'm going to have a talk with that man. They have no
business selling things like that to children."

"It's a king snake," Suzanne wailed. "It's harmless. It
wouldn't hurt anybody. It's better than you are. A lot better."

"That's enough," Rhoda said. "I'm going to call the pet shop
and have the man come and take it away. When you come
home it will be gone—do you understand? Do you think it
likes being locked up in that closet? How long have you had it?
Answer me."

"None of your business," Suzanne said. "Two weeks."

"Oh, Lord. What did you feed it? No, don't tell me."

"He's perfectly tame. They're not slimy or anything. I was
taking perfectly good care of him. I had him so he liked to come
rest in my lap."

"That's enough. You knew you couldn't keep it, Suzanne,
you knew and yet you defiantly went out and bought it. Why
did you do that? Answer me."

"You're a stupid, ignorant bitch," Suzanne said. "You'll be
sorry. Good and sorry."

Thirteen years old and she talks this way to me, Rhoda
thought. What's next? What's next? Rhoda found the number
for Green Pastures Pets and Exotic Animals: Mr. Werner was
out to lunch, back in an hour. "I hope you closed that closet
door so it stays shut tight," Rhoda said to Maisie. It had
suddenly occurred to her that they were alone in the house
with a snake until someone could be persuaded to remove it.
She was not unduly afraid of reptiles, but she had a normal
disgust; you couldn't control them by yelling at them as you
could with a dog. Of course if it was *that* thick it couldn't slide
under doors; the real horror of snakes was their motion, the
muscular swaying and menacing ripple forward. How staunch
Maisie was; she looked ashen but she continued with the
vacuuming, humming to herself. "Some boy who helps in the
store couldn't come get it, could he?" Maisie called out over
the sound of the motor.

"We need someone who really knows what he's doing,"

Rhoda called back. "Otherwise we're liable to have a *mess* on our hands." She always said *mess* in that sibilant way when she was referring to the disasters of the earth (the Korean War had been a mess to her, for instance); it was better to approach these things with jeering nicknames—enlisted men in the army had the same theory—than to confront their melodrama head-on.

To make matters worse, Claire arrived home from school before Mr. Werner arrived (he was late; he had promised two-thirty)—Claire, who could not stand the sight of worms or caterpillars or anything crawling, who had set up a crying wail when Mr. Dinger the plumber said he was going to send a snake down the drain, because she had thought he meant a real snake. Rhoda had been planning to make everyone agree not to tell Claire.

She coached Claire in her low, calm, teaching voice, appealing to her maturity, just as Werner's truck was pulling into the driveway. "Now we're going to stand outside in front of the house," Rhoda said, "and you don't have to look or see anything." Claire was absolutely silent; really, she was a good child; she posted herself on the flagstone walk while Rhoda told the man—a crag-toothed old coot he was, but he had been nice on the phone—the location of the closet. Mr. Werner went in carrying a rope looped into a noose at one end and a gray sack like a laundry bag; he emerged in about ten minutes with the bag draped over his shoulder; beneath its folds something stirred slightly. "It's probably more scared than we are," Rhoda said.

"*Mother,*" Claire whined, "don't *say* anything."

"Listen, don't have any nightmares," Rhoda said. "Do me a favor, okay?"

Whether Claire had nightmares or not, Rhoda never knew (she didn't complain and there was no need to ask), but Rhoda herself suffered from bad dreams. She dreamed that in her living room a large serpent nestled on the carpet before the mantel; it was brown like a leaf and it lay motionless in a coil. "Well, it's not bothering anyone," she thought in the dream and began to move toward it cautiously, but suddenly she saw that beneath the thick coils swarms of tiny wriggling infant snakes were issuing forth. They glowed with a white, crusted heat, and their numbers increased, moving forward in a pale, quivering mass like the grooves of a brain. As they poured into the room they began to burn or eat through the furnishings, cutting dark holes in the carpet; they made their way up the curtains, shredding the satin and filling the room with their peculiar scabrous glow, like the phosphorous given off by decaying objects. Rhoda began to run from the room but she was seized with outrage when she saw the creatures start to mount and consume the velvet covering of a chair that had belonged to her mother. She wanted to save her household and she began to shout for Maisie.

When she woke, she was angry with Suzanne for having brought into the house the thing that caused this natural horror; then she felt ashamed for the fantastical extremes of her dream, and faintly amused that in her sleep she had been so worried about her furniture.

For six weeks Suzanne was denied her allowance as punishment, and the money the pet store man had refunded was held for her in a special envelope which might or might not be returned to her, Rhoda said, depending on her behavior. Suzanne was no more tractable or sweet-tempered during that time—if anything, she was worse—but after a month and a half Rhoda decided to bury the hatchet (really, it might be best not to make too much of these things), and she used the money to buy Suzanne a gift, an orange mohair sweater with a cowl collar; the sweater was on sale and orange had been her favorite color as a child.

"Only jerks wear that style," Suzanne said. "I'm allergic to wool. You know I'm allergic to wool."

"Whatever I do for you, it's wrong," Rhoda said.

"That's right," Suzanne said.

"I'll take it," Claire said. "I like my sweaters real big."

"It's not for you," Rhoda said. "Suzanne'll wear it. You're not allergic, that's a lot of crap. It's about time you stopped walking around like a ragpicker. I'm going to throw out that snotty corduroy jacket of yours; I'm sick of looking at it. You know you walk like a hunchback, a pathetic old goon who chews her nails? Very nourishing, fingernails are. You know what that looks like? This is what it looks like, Suzanne." Rhoda shuffled forward with her fingers thrust into her mouth up to the knuckle, and let her mouth drop like a mongoloid's. Claire laughed and laughed.

In December Rhoda gave her name to the Superintendent of Schools to be put on the list of teachers available to work per diem as substitutes. Within three days she received a call in the morning to report to a grammar school several towns away. When she saw the roomful of fourth graders milling about, she had a great desire to either bolt from the room or throw a blanket over all of them to still the motion and the noise, but when she wrote her name on the blackboard they took their seats and sat squinting up at her attentively, like little mice. They were a well-trained lot, eager to show her where books and materials were kept; they read aloud from their assignments in sweet, straining voices, so that at the end of the day Rhoda felt less weary than when she started and she had a new, disembodied sense of refreshment and calm.

Within weeks Rhoda was in great demand; she could work every day if she wanted to. Principals were full of praise for her maturity, her experience. Once she had a group for ten days while their teacher went to Kentucky for his mother's funeral; at the end of the time the class made farewell cards for her with crayoned drawings of figures waving goodbye.

In the mornings her own children fought over the phone when it rang, shrieking and wrenching the receiver from each other's grip, barking into the mouthpiece and then handing it to their mother, annoyed that it was for her. The school secretaries were too polite and formal to comment, but Rhoda knew what they must think: in her own home she had no respect. Her children seemed to see through everything she did and attribute to it an ugliness of motive. She who was so *effective* with other people's children faced, every evening, two countenances ready with disbelief. They acted as if they knew something no one else knew.

In the evenings there were often dreadful fights about TV programs. Suzanne saw no need to let Claire take a turn at choosing; the older girl was like the terrible swift sword of self-appointed justice; she lifted her hand ready to strike and Claire, whimpering, yielded. The real trouble came when Suzanne left the room during commercials and Claire switched the channel.

But on Valentine's Day, all three of them peaceably watched together a ninety-minute special of singing and dancing about Romance in these United States. When the chorus line, giving a history of American dances, got through with the Castle Walk and started the Charleston, Rhoda got up and began doing the Charleston, kicking her heels and singing, "Made in Carolina, some dance, some prance." Claire was laughing— opening her mouth and letting her pointy face crinkle; she could show pure joy at times and the sight of Rhoda breaking into any physical hoopla always struck her as hilarious. Rhoda slapped her hips, turning in place, and pantomimed licking her palms—she was working very hard at amusing them, and enjoying herself. She began doing the Bee's Knees, crossing her wrists back and forth in front of her knees so that her legs seemed to slide through each other. Claire kept laughing, while Suzanne tried to figure out how it was done. The only emotion she ever seemed to extend to her mother was a kind of grim admiration. She acted as though knowing how to do the Bee's Knees (which was simple and which everyone had learned when Rhoda was in school) was as impressive and technically difficult as *faire des pointes*. With a grave expression she watched Rhoda demonstrate the moves. Then Suzanne tried herself—she could do it slow but not fast—breaking into a smirk in the unaccustomed foolery of performance.

"Very good," Rhoda called out, loud over her own gasping. They were strangers to each other in this mode, which increased their elation and made it wilder but also short-lived. When the music stopped they went back to their chairs like recalled puppets.

It reminded Rhoda of things she used to do with them when they were little. She hadn't been one of those mothers who got down on the floor and rolled and played with her toddlers, but she had sung to them (made-up lullabies, and later, jingles about animals), and at birthday parties she had led them in "Farmer in the Dell." She had expected them to be rather jolly children; as infants they had shown the usual liveliness, grabbing at dangling objects and crowing when bounced on knees. Insofar as she'd thought about it, she'd foreseen them as outdoorsy and rollicking (and in fact considered herself unusually tolerant of high energies in children). The backyard, where she could hear them, had seemed such a convenient arena for their anticipated bursts of simple animal spirits; she was always trying to get them to play in the backyard; she'd assumed they would be more aggressive and athletic. Bright healthy units of pure life they had seemed—her notion of "life" had been rather primitive, hadn't it?—as though health only grew in one direction. The backyard was now the province of the dog, the wash, and a shrubby garden.

In the late spring Harriet Tuckler went back to Shadyside for a weekend. She asked Rhoda to join her but Rhoda said she didn't have the strength for it; that place was exhausting with all its healthy activities. Harriet came back with the news that the lake had been washed out in last year's floods and had been re-dug and newly landscaped and was quite attractive now, and that Moe Seidman had gotten married. So soon, Rhoda thought, but he was capable of acting quickly and decisively when not obstructed by a strong, recalcitrant personality like herself, and probably some woman had considered him a very good catch. He had been looking to get married all along, she saw that now; that explained why he had talked himself into falling for her so hard and so prematurely in their relationship, and why he had put up with her hesitations in hopes of holding out for the final gain. He had married a coarse sort of person, according to Harriet, a divorcée with a bad reputation. She would most likely suit him better as a mate than Rhoda would have; it was odd that he had not known that himself a year ago. A wife is an abstract idea to some men, especially men who have lived to the age of forty-two without having had one. It seemed to Rhoda that at some time before meeting her, Moe must have made up his mind to get married, and in the course of things she had been a preparation, a *thoroughfare* en route to that goal. The word was in her mind because the sixth graders in one school sang, O beautiful for pilgrim feet/ Whose stern impassioned stress/ A thoroughfare for freedom beat/ Across the wilderness.

It was the second or third verse to "America the Beautiful." Her mind was full of lines from poems she'd learned years ago, advertising slogans, snatches of lyrics from songs that had never even been catchy; they rose to the surface at odd moments as though seeking some use and sank back in defeat. They bubbled out in her speech and the children shrugged at them. Only she herself always got some sort of kick out of saying them. They didn't need to have meaning, only the authority of long and vivid usage triggered into remembrance by some literal association. "Loose lips sink ships, isn't that right, Suzanne?" she would say playfully. "Mairzy doats and doazy doats and liddle lamzey divey—eh, Clairsie?" Neither Suzanne nor Claire was amused. Moe had been amused, and Leonard had been amused; both of them had been ready with either chuckling acknowledgments or snappy comebacks.

Perhaps there was a kind of jocular mimicry only members of a couple enjoyed, satirizing the life of their times and humoring each other's raucous traits. She was lonely for Moe's appreciations; nowadays her life at home was very poor in enthusiastic responses. She was suddenly very sorry she had had to lose his company so totally. She hoped he would be fortunate in his marriage, she told Harriet.

In June, Rhoda's father underwent surgery to remove a blood clot in his leg. The operation, a fairly simple one, was successful, but because of his age he did not heal quickly and the doctor suggested that unless Rhoda planned to nurse him full-time he might be better off in a convalescent home. Andy found a highly rated, astonishingly expensive place on the grounds of an old estate in hilly country. (Rhoda and her two brothers had agreed to share the fees.) "It looks," Andy said, "like an Ivy League college. You're going to like it, Pop. I only worry that the nurses are too good-looking—might get you too excited at your age. What do you say to that, huh?"

Rhoda's father was not saying anything to anything. He had already said that he didn't want to go, and he had been told that he did. "Make a list," Rhoda told him a few days before he was scheduled to leave. "Write down everything you want me to pack for you." "Diapers," he said. "Ha, ha," Rhoda said. "No, really." "Whatever fits in a suitcase," he said.

On weekends Rhoda, Frank, Andy, and the wives alternated their visits; the children were all off at camp. It was a long drive, into the rural part of the state. The place was impressive, with croquet grounds and a dining hall painted pale green with white molding, like a Wedgwood plate. In an effort to get their father to form social relationships while he was there, they took to conversing with the other residents, who were often lively, intelligent people—dapper gentlemen who read up on current events, hearty, flirtatious old ladies. It was considerably more gratifying to chat with the other patients, since their father was often silent and uncommunicative, but when on the next visit they asked where that nice Mrs. Appleby or Mr. Crewes was this week, their father never knew. They had not died: that was one thing. People were not allowed to die at the Sarah Stinson Finn Home; terminally ill patients were not admitted, or were sent elsewhere.

When the children returned from camp in August, Rhoda insisted that they come with her to the home. Suzanne, surprisingly, did not balk and in fact explained to Claire that she had to go with them even if she had already told Janey Littauer that they were going to the movies together. Suzanne might have a sour disposition but she was highly principled in the way Leonard had been. She was always catching Rhoda in slight discrepancies, howling over her most innocent white lies as examples of hideous hypocrisy. "You can't get away with *any*thing with her," Rhoda told friends, with some admiration. Moe had once said, "It's the function of teenagers and muckraking journalists to point out the inconsistencies of the world."

At the home Rhoda's father let pass onto his face a slow, shaky smile when he saw Claire, who was his favorite, and he reached up to her with trembling arms. "I had the lead in *Alice in Wonderland* at camp," she said. "Did you know that, Grandpa? I was Alice." Suzanne let herself be hugged and then disappeared; she was seen later examining the hydrangeas and the rows of red salvia before the administration building.

Rhoda sat with her father on the terrace. Mr. Dotson came by—a dog-faced, garrulous old man who was about to be transferred because his melanoma was worsening. He drew up a chair next to them. "See you've got another pretty girl come to visit, Jack." He winked at Rhoda's father, patting Claire. "Lots of kids here today. I just had a long chat with a young lady who says she might want to be a doctor some day. What a wonderful bedside manner she'll have, very affable and pleasant. Yes, you've got that part down, I told her. Got the personality for it. She looks very smart—she wears those harlequin glasses you see girls wearing now. She says she wants to be a doctor or a marine biologist. You've got the bedside manner, I told her."

With a shock Rhoda realized that he was talking about Suzanne. Suzanne did not want to be a doctor—he had that wrong—she wanted to be a medical researcher (or, as he said, a marine biologist). Rhoda would hardly have recognized her from the description—affable indeed—but she'd had indications that the children (and Suzanne in particular) presented different characters to the rest of the world. Suzanne was nice to small children—she let cousins come into her room to look at her microscope; they sat rigidly still with the fear of breaking anything, but they stayed, seemingly rapt, for hours while she explained the different slides to them.

It was Rhoda who had to endure from her the raw, unseemly eruptions, the lapses into primitive behavior. Home life brought out the worst in all of them; once she had smacked Suzanne so hard she'd sent her glasses flying across the room. It had frightened Rhoda herself at the time, and she had felt, in the midst of her rage, the most profound embarrassment. Whatever she'd been saying at the time had been puerile, unintelligent, and foolish. It occurred to her that anger made fools of people the way love was supposed to. She had gathered the spectacles from the sofa and handed them to Suzanne; they had landed safely on the green brocade sofa and sunk into a crevice between the cushions. They were thick, loose cushions; the heavy elegance of the sofa, with its ball-and-claw feet, was painful to her at that moment—genteel scenery for scenes of mess and turmoil, stagey eighteenth-century lines of order where there was no order.

On the ride back from the convalescent home Rhoda felt a swelling ache in her gut just below her breastbone; at first she thought it was from aggravation—she had just gotten lost, as she generally did, by missing one poorly marked exit on the highway, and she was angry with the children for having distracted her at the crucial moment. They passed a settlement of factories, an industrial eyesore that smelled of burning oil, and the fumes made her nauseous; the nausea stayed with her all the way back to the house and through the evening. When she undressed for bed she saw that her midriff bulged slightly and hurt to the touch, just as it had in the years before her marriage when her gall bladder had given her trouble, except now she had no gall bladder.

For two days she could keep no food down; on the third day she peed dark brown, and she wondered why disaster was never over in her life but continued to open and unfold like a package with a hideous message at its center. For once she felt herself going under without even outrage to sustain her; tears formed in her eyes; everything hurt, she burned a low fever. "Something with your liver," the doctor said.

"Something wrong, you mean," Rhoda laughed. She had the bitter taste in her mouth of rising bile. Apparently the cure was to stay still and take drugs. "Rest," the doctor said, "is absolutely essential. I know you—you'll want to be up and around. Don't, don't, don't get up before I tell you."

"Don't worry," Rhoda said, and closed her eyes.

The fever kept her weak while a vague internal ache made her sleep fitful. In the continual drowsy state of illness she did not want to leave her bed; the mattress seemed dear and enveloping, and when Maisie turned the pillow so that the cool side lay against her cheek she felt a childish pleasure in the clean-smelling percale. She did not ask why she was sick, she did not think about getting well, she had ceased to argue the matter mentally. She was bedridden for three weeks, and in the succession of days and nights filled with trailing naps and desultory reading, she floated—in the afternoons especially— toward a dim, still realm of resignation. She had hardly allowed herself entrance into this sensation before, and although afterwards she was to feel some shame for it, in this brief period she permitted herself to succumb to the pale, calm rapture of defeat.

At the end of the second week she began to take some notice

of the movement of the household around her. Her brothers came and wearied her with talk. One evening Suzanne, on her own initiative, carried the television set into Rhoda's room. Suzanne swayed under the weight of the big steel chassis; she was strong but she was clumsy—she made a suspicious scraping noise lowering the set down onto the night table. "Kerplunk!" Rhoda said, not cheerfully. "Lift it up—I can see—you certainly took a slice out of the varnish there, didn't you?"

At three in the afternoons she watched Bess Myerson swirl in her mink coat on *The Big Payoff*, and she saw pitiable women compete in parading their misfortunes in hopes of being selected Queen for a Day. She knew when Suzanne was home from school by the sounds of records being played in her room, the same tunes over and over.

Suzanne asked serious questions about the symptoms and advised her against getting up too soon, but she was neglectful in a grim, distant way, and kept out of the sickroom. Either Maisie or Claire brought the trays with her meals on them; Claire was almost eleven now and could cook most simple things—she went in for artistic touches (she was hurt if Rhoda failed to notice)—a dollop of jelly in a cut glass dish, a marigold in a water tumbler, an invented blend of fruit juices for variety. Rhoda smacked her lips in appreciation, as if she cared about these things.

Difficulty in digestion robbed her of any pleasure she might have had in eating, and she was confined to the spiceless, bland-textured diet of invalids. What was it her mother used to call it? ABC food—Already Been Chewed; she used to say it was like what mother dogs fed their litters when they were weaning them.

She thought of her mother's small, square-shouldered body, subjected for a year to the humiliation of dying slowly in bed. To the last she had "kept herself up," kept her joking and her concern with the presentation of her person—hadn't she had her nails done the day she died? A lesson, Rhoda thought. She perceived with a sudden shock that it was too soon—she was too young—to begin emulating her mother's behavior in her final days.

But in her confused and slow recovery, the constant napping in the daytime, repetition seemed natural and everything seemed familiar; nothing new or fresh could permeate the sickroom. There was an internal pattern in her life she was coming to know, as a woman with too many children might know the signs of unwanted pregnancy. In her most dispirited musings she kept returning to the fact of Leonard's death, which seemed to catch like a hook at whatever fabric of events flowed past it.

But it was only in the low fevers that she let dread bleed into resignation and indulged herself in such visions; as she began to recover her old strength she hardened again into simple irritability. At breakfast she snapped at Claire for bringing a half-filled cup of tea and sent her back down again to return with a properly full cup. She was restless; she ventured downstairs to supervise Maisie and suggest that she vacuum behind the sofa. She stayed downstairs too long and she was suddenly burdened by a sinking fatigue; when she rested, her heart raced defiantly within the weakened frame. Falling asleep in her bed, she had those waves of soft childish peacefulness that came with being sick; she felt sentimental after her nap. When Claire brought up the afternoon tea— staring at it with her lips pursed, trying to balance the tray so the hot water didn't all seep into the saucer—Rhoda's eyes filled with tenderness and she said, "Oh, that looks lovely, let me take it." She sucked the tea up noisily as a sort of joke to show her gratitude. "Ah, that's good." She lowered her voice. "I love 'oo, Clairsie Coo."

"Me too, Moo," Claire said, clearing the juice glass from the table and trying to look efficient. Rhoda wondered for a moment if she were being mocked, but it was only that sticky excesses of affection sounded more mannered and facetious from other people's lips than from your own.

Claire was all right; only she was nearing puberty, growing very modest about her body and very stingy with her caresses. She wouldn't snuggle in bed any more; she said she was too old. Everything was tinged with sex at that age; there was nothing more prudish than a pre-pubescent girl. It occurred to Rhoda that the real deprivation of widowhood wasn't the frustration of desire, which waned of its own accord, but the fact that the only times she was ever held was when relatives hugged her at family gatherings. She missed Leonard physically—which was not at all the same as merely missing him sexually—it had to do with the remembered feel of him as a discrete bodily shape, the lost habits.

Hinda and Annie came to visit; she had neglected them of late, but they were loyal and refrained from mentioning it. She sent Claire to bring an extra chair into the bedroom. She felt a flush of resentment that they might sit fully clothed on chairs, while she could only prop herself against the headboard and draw her robe around her shoulders.

"The President has a heart attack and she doesn't want to be upstaged so she gets sick too," Annie said. "Isn't that just like her though? We're onto you, Rhode."

Suzanne came home from school with a book from the library for her, a murder mystery that Mrs. Salt the librarian, a woman with surprisingly lurid tastes, had recommended—Mickey Spillane, of all things. "Who wants to read that crap?" Rhoda said. "Get it off the bed—watch out, you're going to knock over the juice."

"You must be getting better," Suzanne said. "You're getting nasty again."

"Smart kid," Annie said.

"You'd never know it from her school work," Rhoda said.

No one would ever know anything from Suzanne's school work (Rhoda explained as Suzanne stood there) because she failed to do it, except for science. She stood a good chance of flunking ninth-grade English if she didn't hand in the term project, which was to write your own autobiography. Suzanne said it was absurd for fourteen-year-olds to recollect their life stories and anyway it was nobody's business. Rhoda said it was meant to be an exercise in composition and not in confession. "Don't be such a smart aleck," she said. "Just do it."

"Take it easy. When you get better you can aggravate yourself about these things," Annie said.

"A prophet," Rhoda said.

Into the sickroom occasionally came the sound of Suzanne practicing her clarinet for the school band. She had played the instrument for years, always producing the same reedy, tuneless wavering. Now she rehearsed shrill marches and pounding football songs, annoying in new ways.

Her one friend in school was one of the few other females in the woodwinds section, a bug-eyed, freckled girl named Natalie, whose father was the vice-president of some company. The family lived in a large house surrounded by vast acreage, on which, in their permissive Gentile way, they allowed their daughter to keep a variety of pets. She had a goat (until the neighbors cited a violation of the zoning ordinance and made her get rid of it), an enormous green macaw that whistled like a train and could draw blood if it bit you, and an aquarium (Suzanne reported) with neon gobies, angelfish, and some spined monstrosity called a hogfish; for a while she had kept rabbits until the Russian wolfhound had gotten into the garage and eaten them.

Suzanne was supposed to be confined to the house after school so that she'd be compelled to do her homework, but she ignored this dictum and still spent most of her time at Natalie's house. The amazing thing was that she would never lie about it, never bother to invent alibis about research at the library or band practice. Suzanne never told lies because the last thing she wanted to do was to placate anybody. She was quite high and mighty about it. Not so with Claire—Claire was a squirmer. She read her English compositions aloud at night and they were full of nauseating cuteness—"Boy! Was my face red!" or "What fun they had—never would Judy and Marcy forget their day in the country"—smarmy with the desire to please; she was a good student.

"Very nice," Rhoda would say. "Lively." Claire would dash around the house, whipping the pages in front of the dog's face. The dog flicked his ears, confused. "He's going to throw up on the carpet if he gets wind of what's on those pages," Suzanne said.

Rhoda received a phone call from the school giving warning that Suzanne would be forced to repeat ninth-grade English if she didn't hand in her term paper within the next month. Rhoda didn't understand how a child couldn't be made to do a simple thing like that—she had been too lenient with Suzanne. The school suggested that she might be driven to the task by having her confidence bolstered at home. "A person with your I.Q. could knock this paper out in no time," Rhoda said. "I feel sorry for the others when yours is in there as a standard of comparison. A person with your reading background. Think about it."

This was so unlike anything that usually transpired between them that Suzanne stared at her. "Do you think you're talking to one of your friends?" she said. "That's what you always sound like with them. That cooing condescending crap."

"My friends have not complained," Rhoda said.

"Some of them are as far gone as you are," Suzanne said. "You probably can't talk straight any more."

"I don't need to hear this," Rhoda said. "You do this sort of thing in school too, don't you?"

Suzanne had taken to heckling and correcting her teachers. The slightest narrowing of fact, the merest shading into opinion, made her wild. She was, according to her own notion of the truth, a pathological truth-teller in the way that people were pathological liars. In the dullest, blandest classes—history, geography, French—she fought with an odd, savage insistence on the harshness of the real nature of things.

There followed an almost nightly series of increasingly severe confrontations. Suzanne would be discovered after dinner standing by the closet, pulling on her jacket. Rhoda would try to keep her temper as she quizzed her as to where she thought she was going. Rhoda almost admired the austerity of her responses; in her awkward way she had a surly dignity. She was stony and sullen but she was not hysterical in the manner of most teenagers. Her rare fits of temper were low-pitched and terrible; she roared, as Rhoda said, like a wounded bear. Her language was violent and ugly; never were obscenities more piercing than when they issued from her taut mouth; shit became, not just a figure of speech, but genuine excrement, so immediate was the revulsion with which she hissed the words.

"You don't talk like that in this house," Rhoda said. She had to dam the torrent of abuse before it despoiled the surfaces of her one safe zone. She was frightened of Suzanne. She reached out to smack her in the face, to stop her in her tracks (that was the phrase for it in her mind), and she was right, at the impact of the slap Suzanne's face melted and she became once again a normal, girlish figure, dissolved in tears. "I'm sorry," Rhoda said, "but I had to do that." Suzanne made no protest, she hid her face in her hands and waved Rhoda away when she tried to come closer, edging back from her. "What are you afraid of?" Rhoda said. She had been ready to comfort her. "Don't worry. No one's bothering you now."

Suzanne lifted her face for a moment—it was red and contorted like an infant's face, raw with the strain of crying; suddenly she shouted, "I'm going out of here and you can't stop me. You're so sick. No one can stand to listen to you. It's disgusting. You think if I write this paper I'll be such a wonderful person. You don't know what you think. Every time you open your mouth a lie comes out." Rhoda was slapping her again. Suzanne's skin was wet as Rhoda's hand came across it; this time Suzanne did not hide her head but stood there squinting; her nose was running. "And more is coming,"

Rhoda said darkly. She had no idea what she meant by the threat—what more was there? more hitting?—but she wanted Suzanne to know that some punishment would always lie ahead of her defiance. Rhoda herself felt sick and dizzy, tingling with the internal vibrations of rage. When she lifted her hand to hit she felt that she was doing it as part of a struggle to keep her balance. "Have you had enough?" she called out. "Haven't you had enough?" It was half a threat and half a plea.

There was no answer but Suzanne bolted finally—so much for her taking a bold stand—and ran like a rabbit, shamefaced and skittish, up the stairs; they could hear her slamming the door to her room.

Claire, who had watched the whole thing from the kitchen, skulked through the living room with her eyes down as though avoiding the scene of a crime, and went into the den. She seated herself before the TV and turned on what must have been a Western—a harmonica was playing "Down in the Valley, the Valley So Low." "Suzanne has a really bad mouth, doesn't she?" Claire called back to her mother.

"Don't start up," Rhoda said. "I'm fit to be tied as it is." Whenever one girl was punished, the other one always got arrogant through pride of having escaped. On the TV a man's twangy voice was singing, "Hang your head over, hear the wind blow." It made Rhoda think of what Maisie said; Maisie played the organ for her Baptist choir—she was devout and conservative and she thought the bus boycotts in the South were making a lot of trouble for nothing because the world, she said, was supposed to be just what it was, a Vale of Tears and a Valley of Humiliation. The phrases, heavy and cloying with flowery tragedy, were commonplace to her, and she did not look particularly inspired as she said them. "They teach you that in church, don't they?" Rhoda had said, but now she had a sudden vision of the valley, the vale of tears Maisie spoke of—it was a sighing, rain-misted place, sweetly desolate and windblown, exactly like what the man's voice sounded like when he sang, hear the wind blow, and held the notes in the chorus. A place of slow melancholy and decent mourning, much nicer than the moil and toil of earth. Claire was singing along; she knew the words from school. "Maria Callas you're not," Rhoda said. She was thinking what humiliation really meant, something ugly and spitting. "Who's she?" Claire said, and kept on singing.

As soon as she felt well enough, Rhoda went back to teaching school. She was driving home one afternoon from a particularly successful, steady day with a group of smart sixth-graders, and she passed through Front Street just as the junior high was letting out. Kids were pouring out of the building in a chaotic gush which, over the course of a block, broke into smaller clusters. The girls looked carefully cute, with their streaks of bright coral lipstick and the smooth ironed bodices of their man-tailored shirts. The boys carried their books on their hips while the girls all carried them buttressed under their breasts; they bobbed behind them, occasionally calling out to each other or breaking out into a teasing chase. Amid the stream, which thinned out into different streets, Rhoda caught sight of two girls who walked with a drooping, listless gait, and were continually passed by the others. They stopped, annoyed, when a boy elbowed past them roughly, but they did not quicken their steps and they continued, absorbed in conversation with each other. Rhoda saw that they were Suzanne and Natalie.

Surrounded by their bouncing, monkeyish contemporaries, with their slow, sodden walk they were like nuns in a playground or spinsters at a prom. It was apparent to Rhoda that all the others were somehow animated by sex; Suzanne, although she was their physical equal (not that she would ever have the startlingly large bust Rhoda was amused to see on some of these young girls), was untouched by sex. She was stranger than that. Rhoda almost would have preferred—if there had to be problems—that she had been too fast instead of too slow. Of all things not to care about.

So Rhoda was genuinely surprised when Suzanne brought home Francine Scazzi. Francine was a small, pretty, cheap-looking girl who wore too much makeup and rolled her skirts up at the waist to make them shorter. She did not seem very bright, but she was quiet and well-mannered—humble even; she shook Rhoda's hand formally when they met (which was unusual for a girl that age) and at dinner she turned down steak because it was Friday. She rolled her dark-lined eyes when she spoke of how strict her father was. She laughed at Rhoda's jokes, faintly embarrassed at their boldness. *"Plato caldo,"* Rhoda said, passing a hot serving-dish of broccoli to her, to let her know that she knew a few words in Italian, and Francine looked up, startled, and smiled uncertainly; she was a sweet, simple creature.

"Mother," Suzanne said, "don't show off."

Rhoda could not fathom what the two girls could possibly have in common; it turned out that Suzanne was tutoring Francine in English. The week before exams Francine was at the house every day after school; they retreated to Suzanne's room, from which Rhoda could occasionally hear Suzanne's flat voice explaining and Francine's high, breathy answers.

The Sunday before exam week was Father's Day. It was a fixed custom, by this time, to visit the cemetery on Father's Day, to plant geraniums and weed the grass away from the footstone. A few hours, Rhoda told Suzanne, couldn't make that much difference in anyone's studying.

The wind, as they walked from the parking lot, was quite strong; the cemetery was as large as most parks, and its treeless acreage acted, Suzanne said, like the moors in England, which also attracted winds. They followed the concrete paths, which forked here and there around a large ostentatious monument.

Claire dug holes where Rhoda pointed, on either side of the wide, slightly glittery rose-brown headstone with Leonard's name and dates on it, and Suzanne carefully loosened the plants from their pots and patted them into the earth. For once the girls worked nicely together, although only Claire really liked coming here—Suzanne had once pointed out that the geraniums always died by the next year before anyone but the caretaker saw them.

The actual putting-in of the plants was more like work than like a ceremony, and had no inherent dignity. Nonetheless the occasion (even when Rhoda had done the work herself and worn her gardening gloves) had always had great solemnity for her.

Suzanne was walking back to the caretaker's lodge to get some water to soak the plants with. Both girls had always been very quiet here. They had certainly never complained about being cheated out of a national holiday, they didn't seem envious of other families, they didn't—nowadays—seem to like the idea of families altogether. Claire had already announced that she didn't think she wanted to have any children, and Suzanne, who was so surly about having to go to relatives' houses for dinner, wouldn't even watch TV shows that involved members of a common household who weren't criminals. Rhoda, not a sentimental person, had at least had rosier notions on the subject at their ages, a sweeter eagerness. But it was quite obvious—they had made it evident many times—that they thought her idea of happiness was inadequate.

Traffic was thick on the ride home, they got back later than expected, and Suzanne immediately biked over to Francine's house. Rhoda thought this was a good sign, and might portend improvements. When the grades came out, Francine had passed with a C while Suzanne, who got an A-minus on the exam, had flunked nonetheless because she'd never handed in her autobiography. (She had incidentally also failed Sewing because she'd never finished making a sleeveless blouse.)

"You did this on purpose," Rhoda said bitterly, signing Suzanne's report card. "Do you know what this means?" It meant her college record was permanently stained with an F. It meant that she had abdicated the only thing of obvious merit in her person, which was her intelligence.

"I give up," Suzanne said. "What does it mean?" It was sheer, stubborn, stupid rebellion, intransigence of the most useless order. For days Rhoda followed Suzanne about the house, hissing at her; she would not let her be. Even Hinda, hearing Rhoda's long, agonized rants over the phone, urged her to let the subject rest and give herself some peace. Suzanne said nothing; she sat in front of the TV set for hours and did not turn around when she was addressed.

Rhoda had lengthy conferences at the school where, by agreeing with their harsh appraisals of Suzanne's conduct, she got them to consent to let her make up the credits in summer school. Suzanne did not balk at having to go.

That summer she continued her loose friendship with Francine Scazzi, who was evidently of some genuine interest because her father was a landscape gardener, so she knew about plants. Francine obviously found Suzanne strange and remarkable. Natalie still came to the house, but never at the same time as Francine. Natalie dismissed Francine as bubble-headed, while Francine said Natalie was "faggy," which— Rhoda was relieved to discover—did not imply homosexuality (she had once had suspicions about the girls' intense attachment), but meant that she lacked the proper flair and wore the wrong things.

One afternoon a car pulled up at the house—a hotrod of some sort with a design of flames stencilled on the sides; in it were Suzanne and an older boy with greased hair who turned out to be Richie Scazzi, one of Francine's brothers. He had given Suzanne a ride home, which was innocent enough, but on the way Suzanne had unfortunately discovered that he worked as an exercise boy at the racetrack. When she came into the house she was all excited that he had offered to let her come visit the stables.

Rhoda was powerless to forbid her, since out-and-out orders always solidified her defiance. Rhoda also doubted that his motives were base: a boy like that could do better for himself than succumb to the negligible attractions of a fifteen-year-old with pitted skin and glasses and a square, childish build.

After one visit to the track Suzanne's coat smelled like a barnyard and there was no getting the smell out; it was ineradicable, like garlic or grease smoke. She described with great seriousness how Richie had let her help brush some concoction of cornstarch onto a horse's ankles to make them look whiter. Rhoda did not think of horses as beautiful—they had skinny legs totally out of proportion to their chesty bodies: no one ever seemed to mention this. Suzanne didn't know how to ride, herself; she was interested in horses in a technical way—she was already learning the victories and the running records of champions the way small boys memorized baseball statistics.

Suzanne made repeated visits to the track—Rhoda was not sure how often—but once, at dinner, she told them that Richie had been kicked and suffered a bruised rib from grooming a colt who was ticklish under the barrel. "He's okay, though," she said. "He says that sort of thing happens all the time; they get used to it around the track."

"Very brave," Rhoda snorted. "He sounds like a horse's ass himself, if you ask me."

"Most of the horses are tame," Suzanne said. "You can pet their muzzles and they sort of gum your hand, checking to see if you have any food. They have very soft loose lips, but their teeth are enormous." It struck Rhoda as odd that Suzanne, who was so meticulous about some things and went into paroxysms of disgust if a line of fat showed up on her own plate of meat, should especially like the moist flappy chops of an animal otherwise admired for its muscular tautness. "I hope you're not sticking your hands into any horse's mouth," she said.

"Oh, Mother," Suzanne said. "You don't know anything really, do you?"

The flavor of the racetrack seemed innocent and old-fashioned—like a Jackie Coogan movie, after all. Suzanne came back with words like "cross-tie" and "dandy brush," and explanations of how putting oil around a horse's eyes made him look "typey." It was classy and low-class at the same time—no doubt there were unsavory characters around the track, but Suzanne really had nothing to do with the gambling part—it was all so anachronistic in a time of hotrods as to make it seem eccentric rather than dangerous: only Suzanne could have come up with such an interest. It was Richie that Rhoda worried about.

His car stopped before their house with the brakes squealing, and peeled out of the driveway at highway speed. He belonged to the only jacket gang in town, a sort of bikeless motorcycle club whose rites Rhoda could only hear hints of; they seemed to be bad only in a loafing, sullen way. They confined themselves to verbally terrorizing anyone who walked past a certain candy store where they stood outside, and drag-racing on a particular strip of the parkway. Last Halloween one of them had stuck a lit cherry bomb up a cat's ass and thrown it out a car window so the animal exploded on a policeman's lawn. Rhoda could not believe Suzanne condoned anything like this—she who was so tender toward animals and in her own way so proper, who always reacted negatively to mindless, boisterous behavior.

Still, Richie Scazzi had an influence on her. She spent hours in her room listening to radio stations that played what Rhoda called jungle-bunny music. She never adopted makeup but she took to wearing a black head-scarf like Francine's, draped around the neck and tied from behind. It made her face paler, which may well have been its goal, because she did look older in that guise. For a while her appearance was an odd amalgam—her hair forced into a bouffant ruffled with cowlicks where her rollers had failed to catch the end-hairs, her collars turned up at the back of the neck to look tough, and her old plaid Bermuda shorts, pleated skirts, and decidedly unsexy baggy socks. Then she had her hair cut short and straight with bangs, the sort of cut small children had before they went to camp; on Suzanne it was adamantly plain, but it gave her looks a more coherent aspect; she had obviously decided to look intimidating by looking masculine.

That summer Suzanne took to staying in her room all day. Rhoda, who read much of the night, longed for morning and woke in a blind, cheerful relief. When she made the beds she beat the pillows until the feathers re-gathered into plumped and regular shapes; she wanted everything to stand up, smooth its edges, and take shape; her own severe vigor filled the household like the workings of a bellows, just as Maisie's pounding at the ironing board could make a collar stand up without starch.

Tasks had to be done in the morning so that the household didn't linger, sagging under its own slovenliness, and corrupt the day. In the midst of her motions from room to room she was stopped before the closed doors of her daughters' bedrooms; Claire could be roused by repeated knocking at around ten, but Suzanne's quarters were like a tomb in which she slept, in defiance of all noise, with the blinds drawn against the daylight. "She's like those ghouls that sleep in their coffins all day," Rhoda told Maisie. It did seem to her that Suzanne's clinging to sleep was a shameful simulation of death, and, like everything she did, a deliberate abdication of her own advantages: fresh air, late summer, youth. In a real sense she was wasting away, despite the fact that she was strong, healthy, and well-fleshed. When Rhoda reached down to shake her awake, she noticed that Suzanne's face didn't, like most people's, go slack and childlike in sleep; her features were tightened and hard, she seemed to be squinting with her eyes closed. She wore, oddly, flannel pajamas even in summer.

Andy had said recently that Suzanne was getting to look more like Leonard every day, and it was true: she had his straight-cut, slanting eyebrows and his square jaw; she would be solid and handsome when her cheekbones came out a little more. Rhoda still kept a picture of Leonard on her dresser; she had recently been startled to notice that his face was now younger than hers. Claire liked to take down the photograph and look at it; she had once, from reading those Victorian children's books they always stocked in school libraries, asked to have a miniature copy of the portrait to keep in her locket. Rhoda, surprised and touched, had gone to the camera store and had them make up a little postage-stamp-sized print. Within a month the picture in the locket developed white spots on it like a mold—from Claire's habit of wearing the locket when she bathed, Rhoda discovered; in time the surface of the portrait had dissolved into pulp.

Unlike Claire, Suzanne never asked questions about her father, but she occasionally showed remarkable turns of memory (she remembered, for instance, that Leonard had always carried a penknife, which Rhoda herself had forgotten). The constant presence of the particular photograph on her dresser had permanently shaped Rhoda's remembrance of him; you could guess the date it had been taken by the high, broad collar on his shirt and the width of his tie. Sometimes she saw him in dreams as he'd actually been, and his expression was different. He stroked his nose, as though rubbing it to a shine, and sniffed. He seemed quite foreign to her—she was shocked at how much she'd left out in her habitual image—the vividness of him was terrible, and yet she was flooded with gratitude at the gift of his presence again.

What she hated most about these dreams of Leonard was that they brought to her, like a headache, the notion that she had never come to rest in any feeling. She had to forget this again until the next dream came. Suzanne's face was like Leonard's faults—his disapproval and his stiff virtues—come back to haunt her.

"What's the matter with you?" Rhoda asked, shaking Suzanne until she opened her eyes. "You're not sick. Get up. Do you hear me? I'm talking to you. I'm pulling the covers off—it's time already. Stop holding on, it won't do you any good." Suzanne was still too weakened with sleep to grip powerfully; Rhoda pried her fingers from the top of the seersucker coverlet and in one fierce jerk stripped the covers from the bed, exposing Suzanne in her faded, none-too-clean pajamas; the sheet caught at the end on one of her toenails— Suzanne yelped and the fabric ripped. "Now get up," Rhoda said. "Have you had enough? Get up."

Suzanne rose from the bed, saying nothing; she walked to the bathroom, where she spent an hour in the tub. Nothing could make her move quickly. Reading magazines in her bathrobe, she lingered over breakfast until three. "I can't stand it," Rhoda said. "What are you, a vegetable? Stink in the house all day. Go ahead, see if I care."

At the end of August Rhoda received a letter in the mail announcing that Suzanne had not succeeded in fulfilling the requirements of her summer school courses and the school was currently reviewing her case and considering whether it was appropriate to take the drastic measure of having her "left back."

"So you'll forget about college for her," Annie Marantz said. "She'll get married, or she'll go to work for a veterinarian somewhere. She likes animals better than people anyway."

"What are you saying?" Rhoda said. "That girl has an I.Q. higher than both of ours put together. And you think she has a future shoveling shit. That's very nice, thank you very much." She felt tears actually rise to her eyes; she had marshalled all her energies being furious with Suzanne—Annie's useless advice suddenly formed a gap through which the real pain seeped. For spite, it was all for spite: why should her own children thrash out against her? No matter what you did. Like babies spitting up on you the good milk you gave them. An innate defiance seemed to form in them with the hardening of their bones. But Rhoda felt that she could've put up with anything predictably awful. What she couldn't stand was the especial freakishness of her own situation—a condition which had leaked into her life despite her never, through any extravagance of her own nature, having done anything to tempt catastrophe.

No matter what you did. She remembered that man Bev
Davis had tried to foist off on her—Eddie Lederbach the
blacklist martyr—how he kept whining *It's not fair* and how
childish she had thought that. Recalling him was exactly like
remembering a sentimental song you had gagged over but
which stuck with you, so that eventually you came to
participate in its meaning. She no longer hated Eddie
Lederbach, it was normal people she hated. Annie, thinking
she knew anything: she had married, much too young, that
slug of a husband, and she had borne him two boys and a girl.
They were not sweet, simple children—she doubted that
Jewish kids ever were—they were full of hypocritical enthusiasms and sly jocularity; but they were almost mawkishly
attached to their parents. She considered Annie unremarkable
and her husband cowardly; she herself was remarkable, brave.
How was it that in the face of all that had happened to her, she
hadn't learned anything that was of any use to her? She was
full of old sores; everything galled, hurt, chafed, and nothing
healed.

"Don't get so excited," her brother Frank said. "You take
everything too much to heart. Einstein flunked math in school,
did you know that? Is she a juvenile delinquent, does she go
around stabbing people or stealing cars or getting pregnant?
She doesn't even cut school, there's nothing wrong with her
attendance record. You could really have things to worry
about—think of some other parents—but you don't."

"Please," Rhoda said. "I have enough aggravation already
without having to be grateful about it, too." Really, she was
starting to sound like Job talking to his comforters.

Suzanne returned to school as half a repeating freshman and
half a sophomore (under the cajoling conditions that if she did
well she might be a regular tenth-grader by the second
semester). In her social life—such as it was—she also seemed
to occupy some nether-world. Natalie still came to visit, but
she was obviously put off by Suzanne's tougher style. Francine,
puzzled but admiring, came by occasionally; Rhoda guessed

that Suzanne still had some contact with Francine's brother but he was no longer allowed in the house—Rhoda had put her foot down; "Richie Scuzzy" she called him, over Suzanne's whines to "stop *saying* that." Suzanne smoked now; at first it had been furtive (Rhoda could smell smoke in the house when Suzanne was in her bedroom thinking she was being so sly); now she openly sat out on the front porch after dinner with a lit cigarette, dragging on it in a vague, distracted way.

She sat out on the porch as Rhoda's father had done (no one else would tolerate those unstable, dented aluminum chairs, but neither of them seemed to notice), and Rhoda thought that he was perhaps the one person in the family whom Suzanne most deeply resembled. She had never expected to see her father in her own house again (and had in fact begun using his old room for storage), but he was doing surprisingly well at the Sarah Stinson Finn Home—apparently the care was good: it cost enough—and there was an excellent chance that he would, as the administrators said, soon be returned to the comfort of his family.

While Suzanne idled on the front porch and Claire sat at the kitchen table doing homework, Rhoda sorted through coats in the hall closet, seeing which ones she would drop off at the cleaners the next day. She had bought Suzanne a new plaid wool topcoat for fall, but Suzanne persisted in wearing that loathsome corduroy jacket from four years ago (she had shot up all at once at the onset of puberty, but she'd grown very little since then—it fit her as well as it ever had, shapeless garment that it was). A cleaning wouldn't hurt it, although the lining looked as though it would dissolve into shreds if you blew on it. She felt in the pockets to make sure no change or Kleenex was there, and she came upon a long object, plastic and metal, shaped like a very narrow folding comb. When she withdrew it she saw that it was a penknife, white mother-of-pearl with palm trees painted crudely on it. She ran her thumb across the handle and when she touched a dot like the top of a screw, a blade flashed out suddenly. She was so startled she almost dropped it on herself; it was like an animal baring its teeth with no warning. A switchblade: a gift from Richie Scazzi? Something to impress Richie Scazzi? She pressed the button again to get the lethal spurt of metal out of sight; and then she pressed it again, this time just to see the gadgetry of it once more. It made a hissing, snapping sound; she felt her adrenaline rising, she was excited with the horror of it, and then she was suddenly amused at the picture of herself, a housewife in a closet, sheathing and unsheathing a weapon and threatening the coats like Don Quixote.

It was not funny. Suzanne really carried this thing, which was not designed for innocent whittling or breaking string. She felt it every time she put her hand in her pocket, left it nonchalantly in her school locker every day, and at night smuggled it back into their house, the Taber house. Rhoda did not think, past the first minute of alarm, that Suzanne would ever use it on purpose; she was sometimes a bully but she was not a sadist; the sight of blood made her woozy—she had once thrown up at the dentist's office after seeing her own tooth on a piece of cotton. It was an extended version of carrying a rabbit's foot, symbolic armature merely: except that she might brag about it to the wrong person and find herself in real trouble. Even if she only played mumbletypeg in private—what *did* she do with it?—that blade was sharp and treacherous-looking, and could lead to nasty accidents, self-mutilations.

That motif of palm trees on the handle: in the forties anything tropical stood for luxury—here it was meant to appeal to some hideous Latino pride of origin—and what did Suzanne have to do with that? It was a knife for some Pachuco hood with greased hair and tattoos to carry.

Rhoda stood in the doorway and called out to Suzanne on the porch, "You'd better come in here. I want to talk to you."

"Later," Suzanne said. "When I'm finished with this cigarette."

"I have something to speak to you about, and I'm not going to discuss it in front of the whole neighborhood. You'd better come inside."

"I'm almost finished," Suzanne said. "Just leave me alone for a second instead of bothering me."

"Leave you alone?" Rhoda said. "You're not making sense, Suzanne. No one comes near you. You don't have throngs of people around that I can see. No one except that droopy Natalie. Who is bothering you all the time, I would like to know. Not me, I've got better things to do." Rhoda approached Suzanne in the shadow of the yellow bug-light under the mansard; she opened her palm to show her the knife. "I found it in your pocket," she whispered.

Once in the house Rhoda let her voice rise. "Who gave it to you? That's what I want to know first. How did you get this?"

Suzanne shrugged. "What were you doing going through my pockets?"

"What possible reason could you have for carrying this? Do you go to some ghetto school where your life is menaced under every stairway? Does every other girl in the school walk around carrying a thing like this?"

"I doubt it," Suzanne said.

"What is the matter with you? That's really the point, isn't it? That you have to equip yourself like some moral defective."

"You better give it back," Suzanne said. "It's mine, you know."

"You must think I'm crazy. You think I would let you bring this in the house and keep it?"

"All right then, suppose I go destroy some object that belongs to you. That would be fair, wouldn't it? You had no business putting your goddamned hands in my pockets."

Rhoda was shouting, and Suzanne was barking back her senseless replies thick with obscenities. They were shouting for a long time, repeating, it was tedious and it was useless. In the end Suzanne stormed up to her room. In an hour she was downstairs and had the TV on.

Having the knife was the worst thing Suzanne had done, and yet the fight had the form of every fight; nothing mattered. Rhoda felt that she was being smothered in repetition and that all disasters in her life were coming to have the same meaning.

The thing about Suzanne, Rhoda thought later, was that her outer behavior was flat but her imagination was macabre. She was like one of those prim nineteenth-century clerks with a drawerful of secret fetishes—yellowed newspaper clips of freak murders, knotted riding crops. Adolescents did, of course, have distorted self-images, which led to reckless experiment. Patsy Jawitz had just dyed a white streak in her hair out of thinking she was a femme fatale; the chemical stress of trying to re-dye it dark again (at her mother's insistence) had made it turn greenish; Mrs. Jawitz was inconsolable. Rhoda's advice to her had been not to take these things too seriously: kids took themselves too seriously, it was up to adults to laugh at them.

But Patsy had at least made a misguided attempt at glamor. What disturbed Rhoda about Suzanne's transgression was not just that she had the knife, but that she had wanted it in the first place. On whom did she imagine herself using it? She probably didn't really know: what did she know? It was the not knowing that was dangerous.

The next evening Rhoda went out to walk the dog just before supper. It was a chilly autumn night; the air smelled of frost and of smoke; someone on the block had been burning leaves. It was a poignant smell—sweetly nostalgic although not specific to any memory. The windows of her own house glowed yellow and when she went inside the heat felt wonderful: the comforts of home. Claire was setting the table and wanting to know why they couldn't turn the thermostat up, she was freezing. "You have thin blood," Rhoda told her. "Go get a sweater from upstairs."

Suzanne came into the kitchen as Rhoda was peering into the oven; she dropped her schoolbooks on the counter, and one of them hit the floor and thundered. "You did that on purpose to annoy me," Rhoda said. "I almost burned myself here." Then she looked up and saw Suzanne's face—compressed and stiff and furious.

"I found out what you did," Suzanne said. "You went to the

racetrack and told them not to let me hang around there." She was bellowing. "Don't try to deny it. Don't lie the way you always do. You deliberately humiliated me. You went behind my back."

"I should have done it long ago. And they agreed with me. They always wondered what you were doing there in the first place. They knew you didn't belong there."

"You think this was such a triumph for you—telling them I had a genius I.Q. but I was ruining my future with them. I don't know how you thought you could threaten them with the police—they thought that was pretty bizarre. You think people are insects, you can insult them and they won't notice. You don't know anything about what really goes on in the world and you never will because you do the same things over and over. You should lock yourself in a closet and rot, that's where *you* belong."

Suzanne was almost spitting as she spoke; she squinted and hissed and flared her lips wetly. Rhoda raised her arm to stop her the only way she knew how; she had not hit Suzanne for some time but now she was asking for it; Rhoda smacked her smartly across the cheek. Suddenly something lashed painfully into Rhoda's face; Suzanne had swung out with the back of her hand and swiped her flattened knuckles across the bridge of Rhoda's nose. Rhoda heard herself roaring in terror and outrage. Her first instinct was to feel her nose to see if it had been broken—it hadn't been hit hard enough to break, but it was soft and swollen.

"This is horrible," she said—her voice was low and darkly fierce, but her hand was still over her nose. Suzanne wouldn't look at her, she was gazing at the floor. Quickly she turned and ran.

Rhoda went to the bathroom to splash her skin with cold water; she couldn't tell then if she'd been crying because her whole face was wet. Her eyes felt hot. When she saw herself in the mirror she gasped in disgust and pity; her features were bleary and reddened, her mouth was like a drunkard's. She sighed and dried herself.

She turned off the oven and all the burners on the stove and she went upstairs to her own bedroom. The Sunday papers were still piled at the foot of the bed. Her strongest urge was to hide and rest and sleep, to crawl back into animal misery as though the disasters of life were simple and physical. She pulled back the bedspread and lay under the blanket, not bothering to remove the ruffled sham-cover from the pillow, thinking *I might as well live in the slums*. She wondered if there was screaming and violence at Maisie's house. Maisie kept her secrets. *A Vale of Tears and a Valley of Humiliation*. At least she thought she had some place to go from here.

She was lying in the dark when Claire yelled up to ask if they were eating soon and should she start fixing the salad. She was calling out as she mounted the steps and stood at the entrance to Rhoda's room, "It's six o'clock already."

"Can't you see I'm not feeling well?" Rhoda answered; she could see Claire's outline in the doorway. "Just heat up all the stuff and eat it yourself. Suzanne probably isn't coming in for supper."

"Yes, she is. She's right downstairs now watching TV. We're both starving."

Rhoda rose slightly and then lay her head against the pillow again. "Go ahead and eat," she said. "See if I care. Eat, who's stopping you?"

Claire began to move away and then she called back, "What should I make for a cooked vegetable?"

"Horse manure," Rhoda said. "Don't ask." There was no dignity in anything. She heard the sound of their voices below and then she heard the vexing noise of pots being rattled in the cupboard. When the odors of the meal began traveling up to her—melting butter and the meat re-heated—she felt stirrings of something like an appetite for food. She heard the radio in the dinette turned on to the news and she knew that they were sitting down to supper. She felt suddenly left out, like a child put to bed without dinner, as though another sort of family sat, impossibly bright and glowing with tremulous life and health, gathered in the warm kitchen below.

IX

Suzanne's behavior was often subdued after a severe outburst, as though she'd scared herself. She was notably "good" for several weeks after the slapping incident, weeks during which Rhoda did not feel at all well. She lay in bed and brooded bitterly over Suzanne's calling her dishonest; it was the last thing Rhoda would have guessed as her failing, she who had always been known as forthright, perhaps even too outspoken. She was honest enough for most people and most situations, but not for Suzanne. That was the curse of her life, Rhoda thought—her virtues were more than plenty good enough for the conditions she would have reasonably expected, but not for the unfair exception her life had become.

In late October of that year the dog died. He was over sixteen and his indoor life had long been confined to the kitchen, where, in the helpless incontinence of old age, he had stained all the corners of the linoleum. Arthritic but still excitable, he had died in a fit of doggish bravado, growling at a cat who had perched outside the dinette window. Outraged at the cat's insolence, he had hurled himself against the window and, in a paroxysm of hoarse barking, had gagged on his own voice and expired. Rhoda was the only one in the house at the time; she had been quite shaken, and after the vet came and removed the body, she had lain in her room all afternoon, feeling afraid and nauseous. The girls had taken it surprisingly well. "He was an old dog," Claire kept saying.

They did not speak much about the dog afterwards; it was hard to know what either of them thought about anything nowadays. They were each busy in their own corners of the house; they had, as they said, their own interests.

Suzanne's latest hobby was photography, and one evening she set up floodlights in the living room and posed Rhoda for a portrait. She muttered about shadows and angles, and she made Rhoda change her clothing twice. Rhoda was well pleased at the attention, but when she saw the printed pictures she felt that they were the cruelest ever taken of her. The fevers and her fatless diet had sapped the elasticity from her skin and left it grainy. Her features, which had always been small, no longer held the structure of her face together; she looked shrunken instead of delicate. I look like a bird, she thought, the ruin of a bird. In some ways she was reconciled to the loss: where was she going, anyway, Miss America?—as her father used to say.

Neither of her girls was as vividly appealing as she remembered having been at their ages. She had always assumed that the girls looked like her—now she was surprised by their differences. Where had they gotten them: their darker hair, shorter waists, bowed legs? How had that happened? They told her it had always been that way.

Claire was the prettier of the two, but in public she still had that scared-rabbit look, stiff and wincing. Suzanne refused to take her picture. "When I'm a famous actress, you'll have to pay me to take my photograph," Claire said. She was all keyed

up about her part in the Thespian Society play; she was the
only seventh-grader who'd been given a major role. They were
doing *The Barretts of Wimpole Street*, and she was playing a
younger sister, Henrietta.

Dreamy and intense, Claire was the one who read secret
books under the covers at night with a flashlight. She had none
of Suzanne's stoicism or her insistence on the truth—she
would have lied in the service of any strong emotion. Already
she was taking bus trips into New York with friends, "just
walking around looking" (not for trouble, Rhoda hoped). She
came back rapturous, complaining that their own town was
"incredibly sterile" and "limited." "You woman of the world,
you," Rhoda said. But she was vaguely glad that Claire felt the
need to venture out: she saw under her affectation the
burgeoning marks of a natural sophistication.

Rhoda had received a note from the school drama coach
explaining that mothers were expected to sew or "contrive
from hand-me-downs" a convincing nineteenth-century costume. "How old do they think I am?" Rhoda said. "I don't have
any hand-me-downs from the nineteenth century." But she
had assured Claire that they would find something wonderfully suitable hidden in the recesses of the attic, and in the
evening after supper she led Claire up the stairs to the third
story.

The attic had always been something of a mystery room to
the children; the flooring was only tarpaper under the eaves
and they had not been allowed there alone when they were
little. Now it was filled with discarded furniture; there had
been trouble with squirrels at one time and a baited humane-
trap still stood in one corner. "Yuk," Claire said, as Rhoda
unzipped garment bags. "Everything smells of mothballs.
What's that?"

It was a tiered black taffeta evening skirt which Rhoda had
worn in the late forties—worn, in fact, to the dinner party for
that charity Leonard had been so fired up about. The skirt had
been very New Look, the black gone rusty now—they could

bunch it at the waist with a sash and it would fit Claire. Claire swished around, holding it to her hips. Rhoda found a dotted-Swiss blouse with puffed sleeves that she had worn to teach in. "That'll go with it," Rhoda said. "That's it. Looks very old-fashioned."

Rhoda was ready to go downstairs but Claire began picking through cartons. She wanted the uses of things explained to her. She sat in Leonard's rowing-machine—a cumbrous steel contraption with springs and pulleys and foot-stirrups. "It might develop your bust," Rhoda said, but Claire found it too hard to pull back the oars.

"He was strong," Claire said. In a carton of income tax records from 1941 Claire found a photograph with the words *I left my heart in Atlantic City* printed on the mounting. The picture showed Rhoda and Leonard and the Hofferbergs with their heads stuck through a painting of flowers and bumble-bees. They were all laughing, like fools in a pillory. Rhoda had always thought she'd been prettiest at that stage, but she'd never been good with her hair—in the picture it was too tightly crimped, and parted in the middle, which made her nose look bigger. "Is that Daddy?" Claire said, pointing.

She still referred to him as Daddy, since she had never know him at an age old enough to call him anything else and she couldn't, to Rhoda, call him "my father." She had always asked about him in that low, embarrassed voice children used for religious inquiries. They really did not speak about him very often. Leonard's eyes, half-closed in laughter, looked kind, as Rhoda remembered them, but his mouth was clownish and slack. "It's not a very good picture," Rhoda said.

There was a carton of books; Claire was going through the top layers. "Did he read this?" It was *The Most-Loved Poems of the American People.* "Oh, look at his handwriting." Claire had found his signature on the flyleaf—Leonard S. Taber. There was a moment of shared gravity as they both contemplated his Palmer script. Claire turned the pages to see if he had written any notes in the margins. "Oh, look at this one. I used to know this from another book I had. 'The night will never stay,/ The night will still go by.' " She read with slightly British inflections. " 'Though with a million stars/ You pin it to the sky.' "

Rhoda pantomimed playing a violin. "Da-da-da-dee-dah," she sang, soap-opera background.

"It's not funny," Claire said. "It's one of the most-loved poems of the American people." Claire took the book downstairs with her, and reported later with great disappointment that there had been no notes in the margins.

On the evening of Claire's play, the junior high school was lit from the outside like a monument. The auditorium, filled with several hundred parents dutifully rustling their playbills, banged with noise; schools were always loud, with their bare floors and curtainless windows—harsher and simpler than the regular world. Suzanne sat silent next to Rhoda. She wore a gray flannel suit that made her look like a prison matron.

Claire appeared onstage about ten minutes after the play had begun. She was supposed to be the sprightly gay sister whose spirit was not broken by the tyrannical father—her voice was bouncy with expressiveness so that it squeaked, and she moved her hands Semitically when she talked. The girl who was playing Elizabeth Barrett was really very good—there was always one like that.

Rhoda thought it was too mature a play for them. The claustrophobia of poor Elizabeth's sickroom—all that theatrical languor and the complaints about staleness—won Rhoda's sympathy with an intensity which surprised her. She was still weakish herself and she had come tonight glad to relieve the tedium of her own recent role as a stay-at-home.

Claire was doing a bit of flirtatious business buckling a sword around the waist of her soldier suitor. The gesture made her seem suddenly older, a sexual being—of course, she was costumed and made up to be a "lady"—but the sly pertness of her tones was all hers. Rhoda had noticed it before and had chosen to be amused: all those giggling phone conversations with girlfriends, where they used code names for their crushes of the month. But the coy eroticism with which she was pawing this boy actor startled Rhoda; Claire was sneaky, she was romantic and quiveringly responsive to praise, and for all her timidity she had a reckless streak: she would have to be watched.

After the show they waited in the hall for Claire to emerge from backstage. Rhoda heard her laughing down the corridor; they could see her waving goodbye as she turned, and for a moment Rhoda caught a glimpse of a male figure, too tall for one of Claire's classmates, tapping his forehead in parting salute. It might have been a teacher, except that teachers didn't wear leather jackets—it looked distinctly like Richie Scazzi. But of course he knew Claire from having seen her at the house, it was more or less natural that he should speak to her in a friendly way if he came upon her in public; he was probably there with one of his innumerable younger brothers or sisters.

Claire walked to them, holding her rustling skirt as though she were about to curtsey; her makeup was still on—clown-white with coral circles rubbed on the cheeks, her braces gleaming under the lipstick. "Here's the star," Rhoda said, hugging her. "What an actress! You were great. Tomorrow night try not to say your lines so fast with your words in bunches." But Claire had left them; she was hugging a girl who had been one of her sisters in the play.

The next morning Rhoda was dismayed to find that she had tired herself badly from staying out late. She stayed in bed, feverish again, with no energy to move and no appetite for anything but sleep and dry toast. "Too much excitement for me," she told Hinda, who came by after supper to drive Claire to the school. "I'm really getting to be an old biddy when watching a school play wears me out."

The frequency of her bouts with illness was beginning to

alarm Rhoda. She had, it seemed, a bad liver, in the same way that people had bad hearts or spots on their lungs. "It's faulty plumbing," she told Hinda, and it did feel like pipes backing up in her system, sending undrained bile out to muddy the waters. "Mr. Dinger must have put in this set of valves and left a wrench in the works."

"It should only be so simple," Hinda said. "But you can always kid about everything. Where's the princess?"

Claire came into the room, wearing her camel's-hair coat over the long skirt. She looked like a country girl going to a prom. "Break a leg," Rhoda said.

Claire was scheduled to get a ride home from Janey Littauer's parents. Some time well after midnight Rhoda heard a screech of brakes outside the house; she could hear Claire's voice and a man's voice, and then the roar of an engine with no muffler zooming down the block. The lock clicked as Claire came in the front door. She walked through the living room; from the kitchen Rhoda could hear her opening and shutting the refrigerator. Violent scenes had come to Rhoda's mind with the violent sound of the motor—Claire with her skirt up, under the steering wheel; Claire in a ditch, raped and abandoned— but the banal noise of the refrigerator door made this seem silly. Claire was downstairs eating a piece of Jane Parker Fudge Iced Yellow Cake, she wore cotton underpants and a double-A bra: she was too young. But Richie Scazzi was not too young.

At eight in the morning Rhoda pushed open the door to Claire's room and slipped into bed with her daughter. Claire always slept to one side of the bed, hugging the wall in a semi-fetal position. Rhoda slid next to her back and Claire stirred slightly. "What time is it?" Claire murmured.

"It's early," Rhoda said. "You can go back to sleep. What time did you get in last night?"

"I don't know. Late."

"And who drove you? I heard some hotrod outside when it was close to one o'clock."

Claire squirmed toward the corner so that her forehead pressed against the wallpaper. "Why don't you let me sleep? Why can't I ever sleep late if I want to?"

"I want to know who you were with."

"I don't remember."

"Try to remember. You're awake now, Claire."

"I got a lift from Richie Scazzi. He had his car with him."

"You know he's not allowed around here," Rhoda said. "You know what I think of him. I don't want him anywhere near the house."

"Well, the streets are public property," Claire said.

"This is the last time I want to hear about your being in company with him. Is that understood?" Claire said nothing. "Don't be like that, Clairsie. Don't be defiant." Rhoda curved her arm around Claire's waist—how tiny and light-boned she still was. Claire lay motionless, and the two of them fell asleep again.

Rhoda woke when she felt Claire clambering over her to get out of the bed, but she was gone down to breakfast before Rhoda had a chance to speak with her further. Rhoda returned to her bedroom and slept fitfully through the early afternoon. When she heard Suzanne shuffling back from her bath in her slapping leatherette slippers, she called out to her. "Come in here a minute." Even after a bath Suzanne's eyes were still sleepy and her hair was tousled and spikey. "First of all, I'd like it if you could find time to fix me a soft-boiled egg. And I want to know—what is Claire doing getting rides from your friend Richie Scazzi?"

"Even if I knew anything I wouldn't tell you," Suzanne said. "You would be the last person I would tell."

"I thought she hated hoody types. She doesn't go for motorcycle jackets and hair tonic, she's not that sort of kid."

"That was last week. She goes for anything or anybody that's the least bit nice to her. She has no character at all. Anything for attention."

"I see," Rhoda said.

"She's trying to reform him. She reads poetry to him."

"I suppose he's developed a sudden fondness for Edna St. Vincent Millay? Keeps a copy in his back pocket next to his switchblade?"

"If you know all about it already, you don't have to ask me," Suzanne said.

Claire was definitely missing from the house more often; she no longer came home directly from school or called from a girlfriend's house to give her whereabouts. Once, when she had no appetite for supper, she confessed to having stopped after school for a hot fudge sundae at Skeeter's on the highway. There was no way she could have walked there. "Richie Scazzi drove you there, didn't he?" Rhoda said. "And then you went and stuffed yourself with cheap sweets and forgot everything. You forgot that we'd be eating in an hour or two, you forgot that you should be home helping me. I've been seriously ill, the doctor doesn't even want me moving around, and you're off having sundaes, that's nice."

"Why can't I go to Skeeter's?" Claire whined. "Everybody else goes. They have home-made fudge sauce. Why can't Maisie stay later and help you? You can pay her. You have enough money."

"When are you going to turn into a human being?" Rhoda said. "All these years I've been waiting, for both of you. I'm not against your having a social life, Claire, but you have no pride. Look at how you're sitting, with your shoulders hunched, slumped into your plate."

Claire was crying. "I didn't say I went any place with anybody," she sobbed.

"Don't you think that's enough?" Suzanne asked Rhoda. Claire looked up, surprised. It was so rare for Suzanne to defend her sister, especially when she acted "emotional," that they all sat silent, and Rhoda let Suzanne put the radio on.

Rhoda planned to telephone Richie Scazzi (he still lived at home, she'd learned—he wasn't as old as she'd thought, only seventeen) and either give him a piece of her mind or request him, as a gentleman, not to take Claire for any more rides. She was framing in her mind a way to cleverly appeal to his maturity, when Hinda phoned after dinner. "As far as the Scazzi kid goes," Hinda said, "I always felt sorry for him because he was so short. It backfired the last time you tried to interfere."

"He's not so short," Rhoda said.

"He used to be. I don't know the family or anything, but he was in Danny's class. He couldn't have been more than five feet tall when he dropped out of school to become a jockey, but *then* he shot up to normal height, which is terrible for a jockey. He's lucky now if they let him be an exercise boy. I suppose he cleans the stables and empties the slops and I hate to think what-all."

Rhoda remembered that she had never been able to actually connect Richie with Suzanne's possession of the knife—and later she had even come to suspect Natalie, who'd traveled with her family in Mexico the summer before, and who might have tried to win back Suzanne's favor with a gift that showed how daring she could be. Rhoda had always thought of Richie Scazzi as a thing to be gotten out of the way or jeered at. Hinda, with her benign bit of gossip, had let it be known that Richie's outer appearance, while it probably did not hide anything Rhoda would admire, was at least the crust over a complete human existence. It brought Rhoda up short, as passages from certain books sometimes had.

"His sister Francine was always very polite," Rhoda said. She had already decided not to call, and was feeling pleased at this.

Rhoda had little time to congratulate herself over her own tact, because the next afternoon Claire was not there when she needed her. Rhoda awoke from her afternoon nap with a violent pain under her rib cage. She twisted in her bed in an attempt to get away from it. She felt that she was being attacked: who was it that had his liver eaten out by eagles? She thought that if she lay still this thing would roll off of her, and in fact when she forced herself to lie flat, with her arms stiff at her sides—the corpse position—the pain ceased, quieted to something bearable, as though the attacker had left her for dead, or, like a snake, preferred only live food. But when she rose to reach for the phone, a second spasm passed over her. Her strongest thought was that the doctor must come at once to fix it.

She propped herself on the pillows very slowly and gingerly and began to dial Information for the doctor's number. Her voice sounded so startlingly normal she was afraid the doctor would fail to believe her; perhaps, after all, it was over now. But the after-image, a dent of pain in her upper abdomen, remained in urgency.

The doctor was not in his office, but the nurse would try to reach him. How bad was it? Did she want an ambulance? "Don't bother," Rhoda said, "I'm sure there's nothing they can do," and she settled back into her pain like a diver re-descending; there was some relief in not having to try to speak. She was already so tired from resisting that she abandoned herself to writhing and moaning softly—but when the pain increased, she opened her eyes and tried to straighten her body once again.

It had ebbed by the time Dr. Snyder arrived. She was running a raging temperature (something she had hardly noticed before) and she was wet and shivering. Suzanne, who was home by this time, showed the doctor upstairs; she assumed it was one of his routine visits, and was faintly surprised by his gravity when he asked her to leave the room. He put his hands on Rhoda's tender spots, pressing and testing, and Rhoda submitted to the calming effect of the cool, deliberate feel of his palms.

As she had suspected, there was very little he could do. The fever indicated infection—her bile ducts had learned on their own how to clog and infect themselves; he prescribed antibiotics. She would probably feel as she did now for several days, perhaps as long as a week, but the attack itself (he, too, called it an attack) was over. "Eat lightly, lots of little meals throughout the day," he said. "Get the kids to wait on you."

By the end of the week Rhoda could get about by herself, but she tired quickly and her general recovery was slow. She kept to her bed a good part of the time, and she began to establish a pattern of receiving afternoon visits from friends.

"I've taken a detour on the road to recovery," she told Annie Marantz, who came by one day after lunch.

"The road to recovery," Annie said. "Wasn't that a movie starring Bing Crosby and Bob Hope?"

"Tell me something cheerful," Rhoda said. Callers had a tendency to tell her gruesome stories—descriptions of other people's operations; Hinda's mother was a notable offender in this.

"I happen to have good news," Annie said. "Don't fall over or anything—obviously you can't fall over, you're already lying down—my oldest is getting married."

"Victor?" Rhoda said. "He's only twenty, I thought. He's still in college. What is he, a sophomore?"

"A junior. He says he figures they've got housing for married students, he might as well go live in it. He's got a point."

Rhoda turned her face to the wall. Sometimes Annie's willful heartiness was a bit hard to take; it was a form of detachment—it was also a form of stupidity. As though marriage were some sort of simple task, and either you could or you couldn't. For herself, Rhoda felt she couldn't any more. It had become beyond her ken—unfamiliar: a common privilege whose denial she was resigned to, like her restrictions in diet.

The realization that her health would never fully return made marriage even more remote to Rhoda. She was ineligible. It called to mind some sort of peasant fable, the prospective husband appraising a girl's constitution, checking her teeth for soundness like a horse's. You could expect a man to stand by in sickness and in health after a marriage, but not to willingly contract for a faulty helpmate. A patient cannot be a bride,

Rhoda thought, Elizabeth Barrett Browning notwithstanding.

"You don't like the idea, don't send a wedding present," Annie said. "I'm not sensitive. But they're serious about it."

"I should think so," Rhoda said. "Marriage is serious. Even for fully grown adults." It seemed perfectly clear to Rhoda, even as she said this, that most people went on being shallow and clownish regardless of how serious their circumstances.

"I'll send a present, don't worry," Rhoda said. "Who am I to be a killjoy?"

Annie stayed another hour at least, prattling on about what a sweet girl Victor's girl was. She was there later when Hinda arrived. Hinda let herself in, walking through the open front door and calling up, "Yoo hoo, is anybody home?" It was a few minutes before Hinda joined them upstairs, and when she walked into the bedroom she was carrying a teapot, holding it cautiously by the handle with a potholder. "Hot stuff," she said. "The tea, not me." Behind her Claire walked, bearing a tray with the rest of the tea things on it. Claire was very careful to offer refreshment when there were guests.

"If I had visitors all the time, I'd get fed non-stop," Rhoda said. "Set it down over here on the bench."

"But she's a good girl," Hinda said. "Look at how she cut the pound cake in little slices on the plates."

"She's very good, a good nurse," Rhoda said. "When I get better, she'll disappear again."

Rhoda's strength built again slowly as spring approached, and, true to Rhoda's prediction, Claire went back to spending time away from the house. Once, from the living room window, Rhoda saw Richie Scazzi's car stop in front of the house, and Claire got out; Rhoda was surprised to see Suzanne get out after her. The two girls waved as the car pulled out, and then walked silently up the path together.

So that was it: they had been arriving home at the same time lately. What an odd trio they made—Rhoda could hardly believe Suzanne voluntarily kept company with her younger sister. She *had* been slightly nicer to Claire around the house lately. It was funny Suzanne wasn't jealous—but then Suzanne never really was jealous. She was possessive about her belongings, but she wasn't greedy for people's affections.

Probably Suzanne had decided Richie Scazzi wasn't all that great. She had been making slighting remarks lately about how he'd changed. Rhoda could see, even from her window, that Richie had in fact changed his style. He had gotten his hair trimmed—nothing so regular as a crewcut, but at least it was brushed back without the pompadour—and he wore a suit, cut tight in the trousers, with a narrow silver belt.

"What happened to his greasy leather jacket?" Rhoda asked Claire, when the girls were in the house.

Claire looked up, startled to have been seen with him. "He's trying to improve himself," she said.

Claire, who was not good at keeping back information, admitted that Richie had decided there was no future at the racetrack and had set about looking for another job. Probably he was going to be a junior trainee at the Prudential Company.

As the weather grew warmer in the springtime, Claire sat out in the backyard reading, and on weekends Richie Scazzi came and sat with her. Claire had chosen to interpret Rhoda's dictum that he wasn't allowed in the house to mean, legalistically, that he wasn't barred from the grounds. They read verse aloud to each other in thoughtful voices (Suzanne had been right about that). Perhaps, having left school, he was hungry for the written word now, or freer to find it uplifting. "Very pastoral," Rhoda said, when Claire came in to get lemonade. "You're a wood-nymph in a bower reciting poetry *en plein air.*"

"Oh, Mother," Claire said.

Later, when Rhoda was in the kitchen ironing, she heard Claire squealing, "No. Stop that. Give that back to me. It's none of your business." Rhoda went to the screen door to look. Richie was trying to pull back Claire's fingers to wrest her notebook away, and she was struggling to keep her hand over the cover of it.

"I just want to see what's in the heart," Richie was saying. Like all the girls in her class, Claire had defaced her looseleaf binder with ball-point drawings of hearts filled with love declarations—C.T. L. P.C. referred to Peter Crimshaw, who was everybody's crush this season. "Just tell me who he is, the little turd," Richie said.

"Oh, just a boy."

"A little jerk-off, I bet."

"He gets straight A's and he's six and a half feet tall."

They were sitting in the grass with their backs to Rhoda. Suddenly Richie pinned Claire to the ground, pressing down her shoulders like a wrestler; he was leaning over her. "Stop it," she shouted. "I told you. I don't want you to kiss me, I don't want you to." She was tossing her head, trying to keep her jaw away from him. "What's the matter with you? I *told* you. I'm not *int*erested, not *int*erested. Stop breathing on me like that. Get away. I'm telling you nicely!"

Richie Scazzi got up, kicked slightly with each leg to shake his pants-creases down, and walked out of the yard. He did not leave by the driveway, which was the normal route to the street; instead he walked straight back into the thicket of trees which bordered on the neighbor's yard behind theirs. He had to squeeze his way through the bushes and stoop to avoid an overhanging branch, so that the last sight of him was of a figure skulking off into the brush like an animal.

Rhoda felt slightly sorry for him. Well, she had been wrong about Claire's wildness. No matter what you calculated about the behavior of your own children, they always caught you off the mark. They were always different than you could imagine. It eroded one's confidence; she hadn't been fully content with herself since the children were babies. Leonard had once accused her of having a very narrow imagination, so that all surprises were nasty to her.

Rhoda's next surprise was a slight relapse; for weeks she lingered in that annoying state in which she was neither well nor sick. The visits of her friends had thinned some, and she often felt lonely and depressed, waking from her naps. She was glad, one afternoon, to hear footsteps coming up the steps, and she smiled when she saw Liz Hofferberg.

"But I'm disturbing you," Liz said, as Maisie showed her into the bedroom. "I'll come back later, Rhode."

"I'm up, I'm up," Rhoda said. "Wide awake and ready for trouble. Sit here by the bed. You're looking good these days."

Liz Hofferberg was still a trim, darkly pretty woman. She wore her straight shiny hair in the same Buster Brown cut she'd had for years, and she radiated a level-headed sweetness. This was particularly remarkable in light of the fact that her husband had just left her for a much younger woman—his receptionist, as it turned out, a woman who held the same job Rhoda had had with Dr. Aaronkrantz years ago. (The suggestion that Dr. Aaronkrantz might have made advances in those days made Rhoda snort in contempt.)

Liz had taken the whole matter of her husband's desertion as well as one could take these things. Rhoda rather wondered just how much of a surprise it had been—Herb had always been a caddish sort. Liz let the children visit with him on weekends. She let people invite her to dinner and she took courses in night school. She had just met a man, a very interesting person, in her Current Affairs seminar. "I think you might know him, Rhode. Bev Davis said you knew him. Eddie Lederbach."

"Him?" Rhoda said. "I think I met him at Bev's once."

"He's so well-read," Liz said. "I find him very worthwhile to talk to."

Rhoda was about to tell what a pathetic jerk she'd thought he was, but instead she held her tongue. If Liz thought he was fine, she was entitled: it was none of Rhoda's business. Am I too critical? Rhoda thought. For twenty-odd years Liz had lived with her boor of a husband and never said a word against him; to all appearances, she had been a great fan of his puerile humor, an admirer of his narrow opinions. Now she was going to latch onto a new one and perhaps they would suit each other; he was a sensitive, gentle man probably. I'm too critical, Rhoda thought, I'm not like other people. Indeed, most of her friends' husbands had always seemed like oafs to her. She looked at Liz, who was not a stupid woman, and for the first time she envied her bitterly.

Outside Suzanne was hammering stakes into the ground for the tomato plants; they could hear her through the bedroom window. "Sounds like she's constructing the Eiffel Tower," Liz said.

"It's the one sort of work she does around the house," Rhoda said, "gardening. Lately some half-cocked guidance counselor's been sending her home with pamphlets on careers in Forestry and Landscape Design from a community college. Those aren't careers for her."

"What does Suzanne say?"

"Nothing. Same as always." Suzanne didn't care, but Rhoda knew what they were going to have to do. They were going to have to send her to one of those fancy junior colleges for young dumb ladies, a place that would take anyone whose parents paid. Suzanne's response to all this was a shrug. Rhoda hoped she wasn't planning any last-minute rebellions.

All that autumn Suzanne tended the garden, which bore squash until the frost. Rhoda stayed indoors, took naps, and grew better. Claire continued to grow breasts, at a rate much too slow for her own satisfaction, but whose peaked appearance under her clothing startled and amused Rhoda. Her bras always wrinkled under her blouses because she convinced herself she wore a larger size. Still, her figure would not be taken for a child's even from a distance. "You know what you're going to need next, don't you, to hold up your bust?" Rhoda said. "Basketball nets."

"Everything is a joke to you," Claire said. She often lashed out just when Rhoda was feeling she had said something friendly and inoffensive. "You just don't like it when I outgrow anything and then you have to buy me something new. If it was up to you I'd be wearing stuff I wore in the sixth grade."

"Well, that was only two years ago." Rhoda smiled. "I wear outfits that are from ten years ago. Some styles are classics."

"Ten years ago I was three and a half years old," Claire snorted.

That afternoon Rhoda was in the supermarket when she ran into Sylvia Shepp, whose daughter Rita was in Claire's class. Rita had always seemed to Rhoda an unpleasantly self-assured child; but then Sylvia was a smoothly coarse woman—always smartly dressed—who spoke in a powerful, throaty voice. Rita, who already looked a good deal like her, slipped up behind them to put a bottle of shampoo in the shopping cart. "Look at how big these kids are getting nowadays," Sylvia said, crushing the child to her in a hug. "Yours too, I know. Real young ladies."

"In time," Rhoda said.

"This one is going steady," Sylvia said. "Can you imagine? At her age. A junior sophisticate." Rita fiddled with the chain around her neck, on which some boy's signet ring hung. "So how's your own love life these days?" Sylvia said.

"Very wild and swinging," Rhoda said, rolling her eyes and rocking her head like Eddie Cantor.

"I know a fellow, if you ever want a blind date."

Rhoda laughed. "Is he blind in both eyes or just one?"

A week later Rhoda received a phone call from a man who said he had been given her phone number by Sylvia Shepp. He did not sound charming—he sounded too old and a bit simple—but Rhoda found herself saying yes to him for lack of a way to say no. He wanted to see her in the daytime on a weekend, which seemed odd to Rhoda (perhaps he retired at eight with a cup of hot milk). Would she like to go ice skating? (How old does he think *I* am? Rhoda thought. Eleven?) Skating sounded a bit strenuous—she was about to suggest they meet for lunch like civilized adults, when he proposed they take a drive into the countryside—had she ever been up to Lookout Mountain? Maybe her children would like to come too. Ah, Rhoda thought, he's a gentleman, he thinks I might feel the need for a chaperone.

Claire begged off going, but Suzanne—surprisingly—agreed; there was a rock formation on the north side of the peak whose topsoil created some sort of interesting response in pine trees. Suzanne asked nothing either about the man or the idea of taking such an outing in the dead of winter. My kids, Rhoda thought, don't ask questions. Nor did Suzanne register any expression other than her usual flat, squinting look when, on Sunday afternoon, the man arrived and he was exactly as Rhoda had feared.

A short, squat man, he stood in their front doorway stamping his feet: to no purpose—all the walks had been cleared and there was very little snow on the ground any more. He wore glasses with clip-on sun-shields, he had on a hound's-tooth overcoat, and he was sweating slightly. He was close to sixty. "Hello, hello," he said. "Ready to go for a Sunday drive?"

"I'll just get my coat," Rhoda said. Better to be on the road with this one and get it over with. "This is my daughter Suzanne." He was surprised when Suzanne shook his hand.

"Hope my beat-up old jalopy makes it up the mountain," he said, as they walked toward the street. "Sometimes it gives up when the going gets rough."

"Maybe we should take my car," Rhoda said.

He looked at the car in the driveway. "Could we? I'll do the driving, if you don't mind. You can just relax. Sit back like a lady."

"Fine," Rhoda said. Suzanne got in the back seat behind them.

"They said it was going to be a nice day," Rhoda said. It was in fact a nice day, bright, clear, not too cold.

"I notice there are clouds," he said. "You see the clouds? When the Weather Bureau tells you it's going to be a nice day, that's when you have to worry. I think they tell us wrong on purpose. You think so?"

"I don't see why they would," Rhoda said.

"They're very clever people, very. But why should I make you worry? Nobody wants to be with someone who makes them worry, right?" Suzanne coughed. "You want a Kleenex back there?"

"I have one, thank you," Suzanne said.

"What are your interests?" he asked Rhoda. "You have any hobbies? You must have hobbies."

"I have a family," Rhoda said. "I don't really have time for that sort of thing."

"I like to watch sports. And I like nature. I have a lot of respect for nature. Respect and love. Some animals, of course, I'm afraid of. Certain unique animals. If I thought there were snakes on that mountain I wouldn't get out of this car."

"You wouldn't see them in the cold anyway," Suzanne said.

"We might see a deer or a raccoon," Rhoda said. "We had a raccoon that used to come eat our garbage. He was enormous, wasn't he, Suzanne?"

"You saw him. I didn't."

The man said, "I got people in my office that are like snakes. They'll attack you without reason."

"Snakes don't do that," Suzanne said.

"Without reason. Behind your back. When they think no one sees. Sudden attack. You know what I do? I don't turn my back. You don't believe me." The two-lane blacktop changed into unpaved dirt road; it was the same route Rhoda used to take on her drives with Moe. "Look at that sign," the man said. "We have to slow down here in open country when there are no other cars around? Does it make sense? I bet this car could really take the turns. A new car like this. It's a wonderful car, by the way. I bet it could really do it."

"It's a Chevy," Rhoda said. "It's not a hotrod." They were heading near the turn-off road that led up the side of the mountain, and Rhoda was regretting that she had let this stranger take the wheel.

"Better take it slow on these hair-pin turns," she said. "They're murder."

"Don't be so nervous," he said, patting her knee. "You should relax and don't be a back-seat driver. You're in the front seat, huh? I hate a back-seat driver. But I'll listen. A gentleman always listens to a lady. Is this slow enough for you?"

"It is," Rhoda said, "thank you."

Halfway up the mountain they parked the car and got out. There was a clearing with picnic tables and an open-sided shelter, like a rough-hewn bus stop, from whose log pillars they could lean out in one direction and see the view. "There's our house," Rhoda said. "No, it's somewhere over there." Behind them they could look up at the further reaches of the mountain, snowy and dotted with stripped birches and dark firs.

"This is where we get to go exploring," the man said. "I'm glad to see you both wore boots, very nice boots."

"Ah, no, it's too cold for my old bones," Rhoda said, drawing her coat around her. "I'm just going to stay here under the shelter where it's out of the wind."

Suzanne had enough sense to stick by them and did not go off to examine her pine trees. She was quite talkative, offering information, in her dry way, about glacial movements and the Appalachian chain. "Quite a reader you are, I can see," the man said. "I can see your whole family is highly intelligent. Look at the hawks circling up there. They might be eagles, bald-headed eagles."

"They're not eagles," Suzanne said. "Not around here."

"Well, this is it, this is our excursion. Take a good look," the man said. Rhoda turned in place obediently. The only sound was the wind in the branches. There's not a soul up here on this damned mountain, Rhoda thought; who would be fool enough to come out here in the cold? At least Claire knew they were out here.

"You sure you don't want to take a walk?" the man said.

"Not me."

"I don't blame you. Spoil your boots."

"We should leave before it starts to get dark," Rhoda said.

"So, we came, we saw, we conquered, it's time to go. After you, ladies."

On the way down the mountain the sky began to change and they watched the sunset, losing it and catching it again as the road bent and swerved back. "To a person like myself," the man said, "nature is the only thing that doesn't cost money."

"Look at the colors," Rhoda said. She watched the pinks and reds streaking the sky, and then they all grew silent as the dusk fell.

"I'm not such an interesting person for you to take a ride with," the man said. "It improves me to spend time with people like you. I can see you think I'm not so interesting."

"Don't talk against yourself," Rhoda said. "I always tell my girls not to."

"I'm not so interesting but I'm unique. I can see you're unique too. That's why I like you." Rhoda felt that she had been riding in the car for days. When she cast her eyes back at Suzanne, Suzanne's face had a blank, strained look; when she caught Rhoda's glance it changed to something milder, a supportive embarrassment.

The car finally made the turn onto Rhoda's street and stopped by the chestnut tree in front of the house. By the street light Rhoda could see the man's face again; he was spitting slightly as he spoke. "Well, it wasn't so bad, was it?" he said. "I'm sorry I didn't take you to a fancy restaurant. Fancy restaurants and me, we should go together, but we don't. You have to understand that I'm controlled by forces against my will. There are people—powerful people, much more powerful than myself—who don't give me an inch. Not an inch." He grimaced, almost baring his teeth.

Rhoda, turning in her seat to face Suzanne, raised her eyebrows and whispered, "*Il est fou.*" She had to say something, to mark herself off from participation in his craziness. Suzanne nodded. The man couldn't hear anyway; he was outside the car, opening the door for them.

Rhoda wondered whether Sylvia Shepp had ever actually met the man. Probably not. This is the last one, Rhoda thought, the last time. As they walked toward the house together, she said to Suzanne, "I thought you behaved very well today."

"That guy was gone," Suzanne said. "He could have been dangerous. It was just typically oblivious of someone like Mrs. Shepp to sic him on you." Rhoda was surprised at how bitter her voice was.

Once inside the house, Suzanne, who kept her coat on because she said she'd been chilled, stood at the gas range and put up hot water. She made tea for Rhoda and black coffee for herself, and the two of them sat at the dinette table, warming up.

"Why do you hang out with women like Mrs. Shepp?" Suzanne said. "I'm asking seriously."

Rhoda had already finished one cup of tea; Suzanne had just unearthed some week-old pound cake from the refrigerator and Rhoda was indulging in the slightly boorish luxury of dipping a slice in her second cup. "I've known her for so long," Rhoda said. "You can't cut yourself off from people."

Suzanne was plucking her piece of cake from the toaster. "They're oblivious on purpose," Suzanne said. "And they're always at it, they never stop."

"It's true, those women could drive you nuts," Rhoda said. Suzanne had been referring to what she considered their habitual treachery, but what Rhoda really minded was the way they besieged her with trivia: some of them could go on for hours about what articles they'd had dry-cleaned. (There were of course exceptions—Harriet and Hinda and others—people even the girls liked.)

It was the first indication she'd had that Suzanne differentiated her from the horde of middle-aged matrons she spoke of so scornfully, and thought of her as suited for higher company. It drove Rhoda to a kind of frenzy trying to think who else she might have peopled her life with; but no nobler figures rose to her mind; nor could she fully imagine, when pressed, what else exactly they might talk about. It drew her to a muddled, non-specific despair. You could lose your grip altogether trying to feel for what it was, this other shore that was more deeply real. All the same she was glad Suzanne regarded her as wasted on her surroundings.

For a while after this incident, Rhoda began to think (as she did whenever Suzanne behaved well) that Suzanne was finally going to leave behind the disagreeable personality she had assumed since the onset of puberty, and emerge as an admirable and worthy adult. She had the stuff, as Annie would say: she was straightforward, rational—formidable in her own way; she could well become the sort of woman who was highly respected, if only she would make herself more affable.

But she still lashed out in occasional venomous attacks on Rhoda—calling her a hypocrite and a nag—and she was going to be allowed to graduate in June largely because the school couldn't think what else to do with her. In April she was accepted at a women's junior college in Florida, and Rhoda had hopes that she might begin to mature properly once she was away from home. Suzanne said very little about the whole thing. She was not excited—but then nobody thought she should be; it was a crummy little school—full of sappy Southern girls dressed to the nines—Suzanne had made fun of the place when they'd visited.

In June Suzanne announced that she was not going to her own commencement, she thought the whole thing was a farce. "Don't be so idealistic," Rhoda said. "I waited a long time for this. Of course you're going." And the next day Suzanne came home with the white robe that she was to wear; Rhoda pinned up the hem for her. "Turn," Rhoda said, fierce because she was gritting her teeth to keep the pins between her lips. Claire helped judge the length as Suzanne held out her arms and pivoted in place.

Later, when her mouth was pinless and more benign again, Rhoda said, "I can't wait to see our Suzy on the stage Thursday night."

"Balderdash and poppycock," Suzanne said, but she sounded jolly enough.

———

On Thursday night Rhoda sat with Claire and the other parents and waited while some hundred-odd students whose names began before. *T* walked, one by one, from the football field to the jerry-built podium to receive their diplomas, until Suzanne was called. Rhoda, who had expected to feel primarily a rush of relief, was surprised at the wave of sentimentality which came over her. Suzanne was shaking hands with the president of the Board of Education, then she was walking back across the grass to her place. Rhoda was touched, caught off guard at the poignant normality of it all. *Suzanne H. Taber* was a quantitative phrase in a list, not substantially different from anyone else's name, and Suzanne, back in line, was indistinguishable from the other figures in white.

Afterwards Rhoda mingled with the other parents, and beamed congratulations at those she recognized. Even after her illnesses, she was still in better shape, handsomer and more well-turned-out, than some of the mothers (non-Jewish women didn't age well, Rhoda thought). When she saw Natalie's mother she said, "Well, they got through it all right, didn't they?," and then she was surprised when the woman took her hand and held it with great feeling.

The next day Suzanne was gone from the house all day— Rhoda assumed she was off celebrating with Natalie or someone, which was only fitting—and when she didn't show up for dinner, Rhoda was annoyed but not worried. At eleven in the evening the phone rang and it was Suzanne. "Hello there, girl graduate," Rhoda said.

"I'm not coming home," Suzanne said.

At first Rhoda thought she meant she was staying overnight at a girlfriend's house—and then the fear flashed through her that Suzanne was spending the night with a boy and was for some reason calling home to announce it. "Where are you?" she said.

Suzanne said that she was somewhere "down the shore," she was not about to tell where, she would rather not say when she was coming home, maybe never. She didn't sound drunk, she sounded dry and cryptic.

Rhoda was speaking in a low tone full of menace—she was trying not to say things that would make her sound like a nag or a hypocrite—over and over in various ways she was saying, "You'll be sorry," and "There's something wrong with you," and "Haven't I had enough?" and "This is crazy." She mentioned the police.

"They'll laugh at you," Suzanne said. "I'm hanging up now."

Through the night Rhoda lay awake forming angry speeches to Suzanne. She wondered if Suzanne was sleeping on the beach. She would get through the night with nothing worse than a few sand-fly bites, as long as she stayed away from the penny arcades, which could get rough at night. Suzanne was natively wary, and as long as Rhoda stayed angry with her, it was hard to think of her as a victim. She would have to come home, that was one thing: at heart she was a nervous, dumbstruck creature, not brash enough to go it alone.

The next day when Suzanne did not return, Rhoda first called all the other mothers who might know of Suzanne's whereabouts—none of them knew, and most were alarmed in a scornful way—and then she called the police. The police were sympathetic but not helpful; Suzanne was over age, and it was too early to file a Missing Persons report. "Lots of times they get all worked up after graduation," the officer said. "Mostly they come back right away. You sure you don't know the boyfriend's name?" It dawned on Rhoda what the officer meant by "all worked up." Rhoda knew that he was wrong because you were never right about Suzanne if you supposed explicable common behavior.

All afternoon Rhoda raged over the phone with friends (which gave a counter-irritating relief), until Claire "remembered" with a phony faltering uncertainty that one of the older Scazzi sisters was married to somebody who lived near Asbury Park. Claire didn't know the married name and nobody was home at the Scazzis' house in town.

At nightfall, Suzanne walked through the front door and into the living room; she said, *"Hello,"* smiling in a foolish, guilty way, and began walking up the stairs. Rhoda called after her, but she would not say what she had done or how she had gotten home, whether by bus or by car. Her face was red from the sun. "I'm going to sleep now," she said.

Rhoda stood outside her door and said loudly, "I feel like giving you what-for, but you're too big to hit."

"You wouldn't dare," Suzanne said. "I'm asleep now, I can't hear you."

"Our mighty wanderer has returned," Rhoda told Hinda over the phone. "Back home with her tail between her legs. Who invented the idea of teenagers anyway?"

"But you were so frightened," Hinda said. "You do bounce back quickly."

"Life's too short for this aggravation," Rhoda said. "I'm ready to give her back to the Indians at this point."

She could hear the childish bravado in this, but she assumed that if she yielded now to any milder feelings, she would become someone pathetic and she would slip into dreadful wallflowerish longings for the privileges of everybody else's life.

All that summer Suzanne moped sullenly around the house, sleeping through the days. In September she permitted herself to be packed off to college, and Rhoda saw her actually board the plane. She wrote them one note, telling about her classes. She seemed to be all right, but it was hard to tell. Rhoda took to phoning every week; by November, she had thinned it to twice a month, on Suzanne's request. "You could call yourself once in a while to find out how I am," Rhoda said.

"How are you?" Suzanne said.

"Better," Rhoda said.

She actually was finding herself progressively weaker. At times she felt like a nineteenth-century consumptive, resting, always resting, in her room. She had her vials of pills, antibiotics, painkillers, fat-digesters, to be taken before meals, after meals, 2x daily, 3x daily, in case of nausea, as needed. The pills didn't seem to help, but she was afraid not to take them. She told Suzanne, "Not that it matters to you, but I have the doctors to thank for keeping me alive."

Claire helped some. She would stay home with Rhoda in the evenings, when asked. Boys sometimes came to visit her while she sat vigil. From her bedroom upstairs Rhoda could hear them talking and giggling in the living room below. When the silences got too long, Rhoda would call downstairs to have something brought to her.

Claire would come up the stairs then, red in the cheeks and not wanting to look Rhoda in the eye. It made Rhoda remember the summer just after Leonard's death, when she had walked the boardwalk, seeing people, thinking, Why is the whole world in couples? It had seemed to her at the time an obtuseness on the part of the world. Everyone cared for the person at hand, the person handy, and her sorrow was an eyesore, an exception to the rules, in which they were not much interested (you could hardly blame them), an example of a higher reality of which they would rather not think. She wanted Claire to think.

Of course it behooved her, as the mother, to be vigilant of her daughter, to shoo the boys out before midnight in a good-natured way. She saw no reason to trust to Claire's judgment in these matters. She was too apt to be "easy" for someone else to control. Rhoda heard her laughing like a hyena at boys' witless jokes, she heard her voice bobbing for their attention.

Sometimes she thought, Suzanne doesn't care about pleasing anyone, and Claire wants to please everybody. Still, Claire was all right. Around Easter time she brought home a bag of jellybeans and scattered them around the house in little glass dishes. "They're for you," she said. "They don't have any fat in them, they're mostly just sugar. I thought you might like them as a treat."

"They're not bad," Rhoda said. "Except for the black ones. I haven't had them in years." She was growing gluttonous about small pleasures.

Claire had bought the candies on one of her many trips to New York, and the potted hyacinth she brought home with them reminded Rhoda that it was spring, and had been for a while, and as long as she was feeling stronger she might go out for an airing. She put on a light jacket and walked down the block a bit, feeling slightly weak-kneed; the ground seemed to be spongy and soft-edged. In the years that Rhoda had lived on the block, the street had changed only slightly; someone had built a ranch-style split-level on the corner lot, and aluminum screen doors had become popular, tinny and flimsy in the arched or pillared doorways. Rhoda waved to Sally Finch, who was on her hands and knees digging around the azaleas in her front yard. "Look who's out," Sally said. "Come on over and sit on the porch awhile."

Sally's looks didn't change from year to year, Rhoda thought, crossing the street. It was because she dyed her hair such a violent red color that you could never remember her other features well enough to judge if they'd aged. Her hands were freckled; Rhoda couldn't decide whether this made them look girlish or old. "Don't look at my fingernails," Sally said. "They're all full of dirt. That's the better chair, the nylon web one. You look a lot better, Rhoda. How's everyone else? How's your father? He was always such a nice old gentleman."

"I haven't been well enough to visit him lately," Rhoda said. "I send him packages sometimes. He's in a different home now, not a country club like the last one, I'm sorry to say. His health is really not too bad, all things considered, but his memory's going. He thinks FDR's still President."

"I wish he was," Sally said.

"He says the same things he always said, only they're not connected to anything. He says, *Go without me, I'll wait,* and *You think you know everything, Gittel.* Gittel was my mother's name."

"At least, even when nothing's happening, he still has the same opinions," Sally smiled.

"Consistency is a strong point in our family, it's true," Rhoda said. "But it gets grotesque at this stage—he just insists on giving the same answer no matter what you ask him. My sister-in-law thinks it's very brave of him."

"They don't get better in those homes," Sally said.

"Sometimes I come in and he tells me how wonderful it is there, the food is wonderful, the attendants are wonderful. Then if I agree he argues with me."

"You want some lemonade?" Sally said.

"No, thanks, don't bother," Rhoda said. "I'm about to head for home any minute." Then, as she crossed the street, it occurred to her that she had really wanted that glass of lemonade, that cold drinks were nice, taken outside, and that Sally was a good neighbor; but what she wanted most intensely was to lie down.

The next day Rhoda woke with pain. She made her way downstairs for breakfast; it was Saturday and Claire still sat at the table, eating Rice Krispies and reading *Life* magazine. Rhoda was walking stooped over. "Are you all right?" Claire said.

"I think I ate too many jellybeans," Rhoda said.

Rhoda was sidling into the chair, arranging her body-weight with great care; when she looked up across the table she realized Claire was laughing. She was on the inward breath, then she let the air out and burst into giggles. "Jellybeans," Claire said, gasping. "Wasn't that immature of you—hee hee—to let yourself go wild over jellybeans?"

"Oh, it isn't all that funny," Rhoda said. Claire always found it humorous when her mother did anything the slightest bit off the usual or out of character. She had laughed herself silly once when Rhoda had come from the store having bought herself (admittedly a mistake) a pair of black toreador pants and a leopardskin print pullover. Even afterwards Rhoda could never wear that outfit without Claire's going off into fits of laughter.

"Control your hilarity," Rhoda said, "enough to make me a cup of tea without scalding yourself. It's an effort for me just to sit here. Everything hurts me."

Later, sitting up in bed, listening to a talk show on the radio,

Rhoda felt freshly vexed at the relentlessness of her troubles. Moe Seidman used to have a sign in his office: THEY TOLD ME, CHEER UP THINGS COULD BE WORSE—SO I CHEERED UP, AND SURE ENOUGH, THINGS GOT WORSE. The recollection of this amused her. She could remember his office very clearly. What was odd about looking back was that she seemed to have been very young and robust then, whereas at the time she had seen herself as seasoned and weary.

Old Soldiers, she and Moe used to call themselves, in a loose jaunty way (it was not long after MacArthur's famous farewell speech and everybody was full of various witty paraphrases about how old whatevers didn't die, they just did something-or-other). Moe had hated MacArthur, come to think of it. "A real jackass," he had said. "I had a buddy in the army who had a theory about generals like him. They always stuck to their mistakes because they got to be generals from being such stiff-necks. The last thing they ever wanted to do was to change their minds on account of a little thing like facts. Heroes," he had snorted.

"Facing facts" had been a favorite phrase of Moe's. Moe had always implied that a fact was a thing you could stare down, get a grip on, and wrestle to the floor, like an adversary or a demon. Suzanne had often accused Rhoda of being deliberately obtuse—"blind to the realities," something like that—and Rhoda had been shocked, having always considered herself remarkably down-to-earth: but it occurred to her now that facts might well be something you'd let slip through your fingers, from a natural fastidiousness at touching them.

She was beginning to feel about her own body that it was something she would not have touched had it not belonged to her. It was scarred from her gall bladder operation years ago, pale and dimpled, with a paunch in the midriff. She was not a vain woman but the sight saddened her. To the best of her ability, she had taken care of herself, cleansed daily, gone for walks, and eaten sensibly, but her body had not kept its part of the bargain, had violated all rules and turned against her as an enemy.

There was something particularly wrong with her middle section; lying in bed, she folded her hands across it as though they could smooth it or give calm; the bulge puffed out in an aberrant way; the distortion of it made her shudder.

Dr. Snyder was not pleased either. Rhoda wished that doctors would learn to veil their dismay, to muffle their self-important murmurs of alarm. Of course she knew the healthy human body wasn't supposed to look like this, anybody knew that, she hadn't been shut up so long as to forget.

Rhoda was shrugging at him for making such a fuss about things once he was called into the act, when she heard him say the word hospital. Rhoda remembered, from his care of her mother, how he chose to avoid hospitals (he had let them keep her mother at home, in the old way). "For tests," he was saying.

"Tests for what?" Rhoda said.

He was so discreet in his answer that Rhoda realized her ailment had become too sophisticated for him and he only hoped someone else could figure it out. He spoke of the wonderful scientific care she was going to get, until Rhoda began to picture the hospital as a place where she could close her eyes and rest, as she rested here, only there she would be surrounded by such competence, such accuracy of diagnosis and prescription, that she would wake up well and refreshed. Instead of always half-well: she wondered, in fact, if idling with Dr. Snyder had kept her from a cure up till now.

"We look like a family convocation," Rhoda said, gesturing around her to the group that was walking with her through the halls of the hospital. Her brother Frank walked ahead, carrying her overnight bag, while she leaned against Andy, and Claire and the two sisters-in-law fluttered about her, trying to be helpful.

They settled Rhoda into her room, putting things in closets and beating at the bed-pillows and drawing the curtain that separated her from the sleeping old lady who was Rhoda's "semi-private" roommate. They flustered the young nurse with bantering pleasantries while she fastened a plastic name-bracelet on Rhoda's wrist. "If found, drop in the nearest mailbox," Rhoda said. The nurse shook her head, and smiled uncertainly.

"Isn't she a beauty, though?" Frank said. "A strawberry-blonde beauty."

"It's her own natural color, I'll bet," Rhoda said, as the girl fled with her clipboard.

"You'll get good service here, I know," Andy said.

"Better than at the Ritz," Rhoda said, waving them off with the flapping gesture one used to wave bye-bye to babies. Only Claire remained to help her change into her nightgown. Claire was flattered at having been singled out to give help, but she wasn't much good at it, and Rhoda had to swing herself into the sleeves while leaning on Claire's shoulder, which was, however, a handy height.

When she was changed and lying in bed, Rhoda closed her eyes and said, "I'm so weary."

"Do you want me to do anything else?" Claire asked.

"No, you can go," Rhoda said, with her eyes still closed. "Tomorrow I'll show you how to crank up the bed." She heard Claire banging the Venetian blinds as she fussed with the pulley, and then she fell into the drifting sleep of the hospital.

Five days later Rhoda lay in the same bed and watched, with grim outrage, the nurse draw blood from her finger. "Twice a day they wake me up to do this," she said. "What are they, vampires down there in that lab?"

She saw Andy and his wife Lainie standing hesitantly in the doorway and she waved to them with her free hand, and called out "Hi-dee-hi. You can come in, the ghoul is just leaving now."

"Well, you look so much better," Lainie said, drawing up a chair. "How are you doing?"

"Everything's copacetic," Rhoda said—an expression she hadn't used since the forties, but which seemed to fit the sickroom.

"So what do they know about you that they didn't know before?" Andy asked.

"Some of these tests are real zingers," Rhoda said. "They shoot you full of air, they shoot you full of barium. You got to have guts to have any guts left after this business."

"It sounds awful," Lainie said gently.

"You'll be happy to know that we're arranging," Andy said, "to pack up all your troubles and send them directly to Gamal Abdel Nasser, where they'll do some good."

"That's a very efficient idea," Rhoda said. "There's a man who deserves a good shot in the *kishkes.*"

They were working out an elaborate system of smuggling her problems into Egypt by a relay of disguised couriers, when a very old, old man shuffled through the doorway. He was wearing street clothes but he looked as though someone might roll him into a hospital gown at any moment; he nodded slowly at them, and made his way to the other side of the room. "He visits his wife," Rhoda said.

"He's the healthy one in the family?" Andy whispered. "Oooh, they've got problems."

"One of the nurses was saying they shouldn't allow very old people as visitors the same way they don't allow very young children," Rhoda said. But in truth she was sometimes jealous of the old man's visits, which consisted of his sitting and reading a tabloid newspaper and listening as his wife, from time to time, complained softly to him, while Rhoda lay on her side of the partition and watched the TV, dateless.

Claire came to visit around noon. Her school had recessed for Easter vacation, and she had found a way to come by herself by bus; she always arrived a bit breathless from walking up the hill from the bus stop to the hospital. "I'm not better," Rhoda said, picking at the lunch tray in her lap, as she talked with Claire, "but I've been mapped and graphed and plumbed like a piece of valuable real estate. They know things about me even the rabbi doesn't know." (This was mostly a joke—Rhoda was not on confidential terms with any rabbi, and had in fact shooed one away from her bed when he'd shown up to pray with her.) "One thing I would like to know about hospitals— what is it with them that they think Jell-O is a fit dessert for grownups? You want some of this?"

"I didn't even like it when I was little," Claire said. "I'll eat some of the peas you left, though." Rhoda liked it when Claire shared her lunch; it made the routine seem more human and social.

Rhoda was beginning to get fretful at how slow the tests were to show conclusions—although she felt vaguely proud that her ailment was serious and subtle enough to elude easy classification. Her one fear was that they were going to send her home uncured, having suffered the tests for no reason. When Claire left, the nurse whispered that a surgeon was coming to talk with her. Rhoda was so startled that her first thought was that she wanted time to tell somebody about it. Nasser should only go have some operation, she and Andy could say.

Two men were already walking toward her bed. The first was the most innocuous-looking surgeon Rhoda had ever seen, a bland, thin-lipped man with rimless spectacles like the ones Woodrow Wilson had worn. He's like the quiet young man no one ever thinks will commit a murder, Rhoda thought. With him he had another doctor, tall, very red in the face, with iron-gray hair. Rhoda had the immediate impression that he was blustering and eccentric, and she wondered if he resembled an actor who played character parts. "I know you," she said suddenly. "I sat next to you at a dinner for the Community Chest about ten years ago. You're Dr. Finney."

"Findlay," the man said. "Did you, now? You see, you never know—little did you think then you'd be sitting in bed having a conversation with me in your nightgown. You weren't wearing that nightgown then, were you?"

"I was wearing a black skirt. My husband was very active in the fund-raising."

"Well, he must be a more patient man than I am, then. God, they had awful food at those dinners. My wife used to drag me. You didn't know my wife, did you?"

"I don't think so."

"She passed away two years ago. They still having those dinners?"

"I wouldn't know," Rhoda said. "I guess so."

"Oh, they were boring. I hope I behaved well, since you remember me. I told you, Ken, I know all the pretty girls in the hospital."

"You're still a character," Rhoda said.

"We're making Ken jealous here," Dr. Findlay said.

The other doctor took this as his cue to lead them back to the purpose of their visit. He squinted when he spoke and he was hard to follow; he seemed to be explaining in schematic detail the workings of the human liver and digestive system. Rhoda wasn't listening—he was so much like a high-school math teacher. "You can understand that under these conditions," he said, "we have no choice but to go ahead with exploratory surgery."

There was a pause, and Rhoda realized that he expected her to nod, which she did. Dr. Findlay explained that he would be acting as a consultant, and if they found that her system had really managed to clog itself with its own scar tissue—at this point he became hearty in his description—like tailors, they would re-route her innards, making a permanent detour out of some bypass out of the liver. Suddenly Rhoda saw, in a wave of horror, that these alterations would be permanent. "My own intestine, that I've had since I was a little girl," she said, parrotting an old line.

"That's a good one," Dr. Findlay said. "I have to remember that." It was when he was reassuring her about the danger of the operation that she stiffened with panic, and she realized that for some time she had been afraid to move or blink, although she was sitting up at an uncomfortable angle. "Everyone has a natural fear of major surgery, but you know that Dr. Weintraub here takes especially good care of my old girlfriends."

She felt the need to ask serious, intelligent questions, but instead she said, "I'm sure that both of you will do the best job possible. I have every faith in you," and surprised herself at how perfectly all right that sounded.

"The important thing is to get your beauty sleep," Dr. Findlay said. "And no martinis on the sly."

"You're still a big kidder," Rhoda said.

"We'll whoop it up with iced tea afterwards," the doctor said, winking as he left.

The wisest course, Rhoda advised herself when they were both gone, was not to dwell on this, especially not to dwell on the morbid aspects. She made the nurse's aide put the television on, and throughout the afternoon she refused to let anyone turn the volume down, no matter how the patient in the other bed complained. It made no difference, of course; she might as well have been watching a blank screen; but neither was she able to think in a focused way. Dreadful images from horror movies came to her, coffins opening. Dark as the grave, As I lay dying, When I am dead, my dearest, sing no sad songs for me. Her head rang with phrases, all of them useless. For many a time I have been half in love with easeful Death. Death, be not proud, though some have called thee Mighty and something. She thought naturally of Leonard, who was so absolutely gone from her, and then she recalled, of all things, a line from General MacArthur: In war there can be no substitute for victory.

She couldn't think!—she had a sense of time racing, and her thoughts running skittishly in circles—she kept seeing a door closing against her, she was trying to get out of a room, where she was shut up alone. And then a shudder passed over her of pure loneliness and terror; and she saw that the only thing to do was to hold onto her mind and wait.

———

When the nurse brought her dinner tray and then clucked over its contents left uneaten, Rhoda made a face. She was musing over whether it was worth it to frame a sarcastic reply, when she heard footsteps halting outside her doorway. Everyone in the family had already been to visit once that day, and it was almost at the end of visiting hours. She saw a short man, too stocky for the old lady's husband. I might have known, Rhoda thought: it was the rabbi, come to visit her again.

In Rhoda's own congregation the rabbi was a smooth-faced liberal, but this was one of the old school: hairs grew from his nose, he had red wet lips, and he breathed heavily when he spoke. "I thought you might want company," he said. Rhoda greeted him in Yiddish, she asked him what a handsome young fellow like himself was doing hanging around a hospital full of old sick people. "I only come visit the beautiful young girls like you," he said. Listen to him, Rhoda thought. My, my, there's life in the old boy yet, and then she flinched at the phrase. The life that lives in the spirit when the body dies, was he going to talk about that? If he did she would turn away and shrug, roll her eyes rudely. She was loyal in her religion, but without thought, as she would have been loyal to a somewhat simple relative. She believed in God, of course, but not personally, and she certainly regarded Him as a Being with the decency not to force an intimacy. Everything in her went against the idea of a life continuing without an attachment to normal daily occupations. She had never seen the need to bother with what Leonard, in one of his melioristic philosophical phases, had called "developing spiritual muscles," and the last thing she wanted now was any scarifying arguments, any intimations of mumbo-jumbo.

The rabbi touched her shoulder. He was talking about the history of the Jewish people, what tragic and difficult times they'd had, and how brave they were. "Even in the camps," he said. Why do they let him in here? Rhoda thought. She considered ringing for one of the nurses, but she couldn't think of an excuse that wouldn't backfire. She let him go on about the Warsaw Ghetto uprising ("Through the sewers they escaped, like rats") until a nurse finally did come to brush visitors away. She brought with her a sleeping pill, which Rhoda took without complaining, for once.

Rhoda lay awake in the hospital room in a flat anguish, blocked from speculation. She was just drowsy enough to feel that she was in horror of something dreadful, but not to think clearly what it was. She had a great desire to get up and *do something* in the ward, to go to the little sink in the corner and wash out one of her nightgowns, to write out her car payment check, which was due this week, to make a list of the things she wanted Claire to bring if she was going to be here longer—but she hesitated, because she knew that if she started anything one of the nurses would come in and stop her from finishing. She would have to argue with some snippy supervisor, *But I'm not done.* And then she remembered what she was afraid of was not being able to finish anything.

That made her so violently anxious that she actually rose up, but the drug had made her groggy so that her own weight was hard to support, and she slid back on the pillow with her arms at her sides. At this point she cried out. A nurse came at once, a young mousey thing—they must put the students on at night—she hardly looked older than Suzanne. She stared at Rhoda in the half-light without saying anything, timid to ask and perhaps waiting for Rhoda to volunteer her complaint; between them there passed a moment of deep embarrassment. "Was it you?" the nurse said. "Is there a problem?"

"They gave me a sleeping pill that wasn't any good," Rhoda said.

"I don't think I can give you another one but I'll check the chart at the station," the nurse said, and she left the room.

You could wait till Labor Day till she figures out the chart, Rhoda thought. She lay awake, listening, but the nurse never came back, and she lapsed finally into a twilight sleep.

———

In the morning, when they woke her for breakfast (although she wasn't to be given any breakfast), the glaring dailiness of the hospital made Rhoda feel that she'd been foolish to let herself get carried away with sick fancies the night before. Andy phoned at eight to wish her well in the operation, and they had a fairly intricate conversation about the logistics of exporting surgical misery to Nasser.

Presently Claire arrived. She was more dressed-up than usual, wearing a pink spring coat; her face was very pale. "This is the day I get to be chopped liver," Rhoda said.

"At least they're getting on with it so you can be out of here sooner," Claire said.

"My sentiments exactly," Rhoda said.

A male orderly came in the room, wheeling before him a white metal gurney with a sheet hung over it like a tablecloth. "You're Mrs. Taber?" he said.

"It's too late to deny it now," Rhoda said.

Pulling and banging, the orderly extended the two end-panels so the cart lengthened into a cot. "I can get onto it myself," Rhoda said, as he reached his arms under her. "Please don't lift me." She had already been changed into a hospital gown and when she swung herself onto the cot she tried to keep it over the back of her with some modesty. She slid down and lay back, Claire standing by one side.

Rhoda reached out and took Claire's hand, and immediately Claire's grip closed around hers—she would never rebuff you physically, that was one thing about Claire. The man was still fussing with the brake release, and there was a long minute during which Rhoda felt the flow of sweetness from Claire's hand and the panic of her own grip. She could tell how frightened she must seem from the look on Claire's face. Claire held the look, and then her features wavered, she was having trouble being this serious. Of all the family she should have been the most prepared for it, with her taste for poetry and her quick tears in movies; but her expression faded to an artificial stiffness, except for the open-eyed gaze which still held a shimmer of pity. The man was backing Rhoda's cart out of the room, and in order to keep Claire in view, Rhoda had to raise her head as best she could, rolling her eyes to one side, as he wheeled her out of the room.

When Rhoda came out of the anesthetic she found, first, that something was burning, in a blurred way, under her rib-cage, and then that they had put tubes up her nose. Her *nose*—of all things—one up each nostril—of all the hideous, unnatural practices—there was nothing wrong with her nasal passages. She reached up to pull the things out, but a nurse stopped her, stood over her and said, "No, no, we mustn't do that yet." Rhoda whimpered and fell back to sleep.

When Rhoda woke again she knew that she was still drugged because she was in pain but she didn't mind; her body felt fuzzy and indistinct; it felt, in fact, like the cotton around a wound. She fell in and out of sleep—for days and nights, it must have been—at times she would lift her head and try to ask the nurses questions, but no matter how many times she repeated herself they couldn't manage to understand; they shook their heads, puzzled and polite, and blinked sympathetically.

Finally one of them seemed to be answering her. She pointed to her wrist and held up four fingers and mouthed, "It's four o'clock." Rhoda realized that she must have asked her what time it was, but that wasn't what she'd meant. She wanted to know how long she had been there, but she couldn't think of the phrase for that.

Once she woke and the room seemed crowded with visitors—people she hadn't seen for years—Addie Shulman, Mrs. Leshko, the man who'd bought Leonard's drugstore, children she'd taught at Rock Street school before the girls were born. The room was much too full—she knew perfectly well the hospital had rules about how many were allowed in the room, and she announced that some of them would have to leave, but they only backed away and made themselves smaller. She saw the couple who'd run the hotel in Paris and she didn't understand how they could have paid their way from Europe; she had an argument with them about it in French.

"This is ridiculous. I'm getting batty," she said to one of the nurses. She was talking much better now.

"You'll feel much better once you're on solid food," the nurse said. "You've had infection. Thirteen days on an I.V. makes anyone restless."

Thirteen days—that was the most disheartening piece of information she'd received so far. In the afternoon they brought her a dish of Cream of Wheat with no butter. Rhoda ate with her free hand. "Cream of wallpaper paste," she said, mushing it with her spoon. "Glug." Claire was there; she held out a glass of watered-down juice and tilted the straw to Rhoda, who sipped at it greedily. After lunch they made her walk back and forth to the window, just to be moving; the nurse helped her drag the pole behind. When the nurse was gone, Rhoda adjusted the clamp on the I.V. tube so the fluid flowed more rapidly, thinking they might come take it away sooner that way.

In the evening an intern did come and slip the needle out without putting a new one in. He was gone before Rhoda had a chance to thank him, but she walked up and down the halls to celebrate.

Just before lights out, another of the interns edged into the room, wheeling before him the I.V. tank on its pole. "That's not for me," Rhoda said.

"Just for a few hours," the man said. "Hold your arm still." He was having trouble finding the vein. "There."

"I'm supposed to be through with all this," Rhoda said. "It's depressing."

What do they think I am? Rhoda thought, lying in bed after the intern had left. She ripped off the adhesive which held the needle in place and slid the needle out from under skin. Her arm was sore and bruised. She got up out of bed and began searching on the floor for her slippers.

They were not under her bed and she went to the closet. When she put them on she felt how long her toenails had grown, like the nails of the dead growing underground. Then she put her coat on over her nightgown; she had trouble with the buttons and she had to start over again a few times until she got them lined up properly. She went out into the hall.

Who do they think I am? she thought again. Obviously they had no idea. For weeks they had hardly understood a word she said. *All my life I've been talking to idiots.* Lying like a stone day and night in that ghostly ward, with its weird milky light, she'd gone way, way beyond them.

She passed the mousey little nurse who had come to her in the night before her operation. She really looks scared now, scared out of her wits; maybe she thinks I'm a zombie, Rhoda thought, and smiled to herself. Harry Belafonte sang a calypso song about the zombie jamboree, all the zombies dancing in the graveyard. Maybe I'll do a dance, Rhoda thought. She kept walking down the corridor.

The bounce of her own motion was painful—but she felt all hot and glowing, rapturous with escape. She shuffled, but she could still walk a brisk step, like a sensible person. A person like her didn't belong in a place like this. It seemed to her that she was finally acting on something she'd known for years.

A big black nurse was walking alongside her. "Going on a trip?" she said.

"It's depressing being in the hospital all the time," Rhoda said. "It's very depressing here. I think I would do much better if I just got out."

"Well, there's a good bit of logical truth in that," the nurse said. "Only you have to think about whether you're ready or not. I think you're probably not ready yet."

"I've been here for weeks," Rhoda said. "I've got bedsores." But she let the nurse take her arm and lead her back to the room.

"Another day," the nurse said, unbuttoning Rhoda's coat and hanging it up.

"I know you understand," Rhoda said, "because you know all about voodoo." The nurse laughed softly and tucked the covers around Rhoda's shoulders.

———

When Rhoda came awake again, she found that she couldn't raise either of her arms; it felt as though her sleeves were caught on something, perhaps the bed-frame. They've put the sheet in too tight, she thought, but why isn't it giving when I push against it? She began crying out for the nurse, since there was no way to push the buzzer. When no nurse came, Rhoda was suddenly afraid that she had been tied in a gunny sack and left in a back room of the hospital, as a punishment for walking around when she wasn't supposed to.

But it seemed to be her same room, with her bottle of Dierkiss talcum powder and her blue-handled hairbrush on the table next to her. It looked like Claire sitting on a chair near the bed, Claire and another person Rhoda thought might be Suzanne, but then she saw it was one of the boys who came to the house to visit Claire. "Nesser," Rhoda was saying. That wasn't the right word, no wonder no one was coming. "Nurch," she tried again. She knew how to say the word but on the way to saying it she forgot.

The boy ran out of the room and when he came back he had the red-haired nurse with him. "This is awful," Rhoda said. She said it perfectly clearly. "I'm strapped to the bed! It's like a strait-jacket."

"No, no, stop pulling at it," the nurse said. "It's only for a little while. They have to do it. Try to just lie back and rest."

Rhoda struggled and kicked at the sheets, but in the effort she saw that she was really very, very tired, and in a moment she lay back. "Claire," she said. "Are you cigrit?"

"Am I what?" Claire said. "Try to speak a little more slowly. It's hard to understand you."

"*Are—you—cigrit*?" Rhoda said. She was getting annoyed. "Moking a cigrit."

"I think she wants to know if you're smoking a cigarette," the boy said.

"It smells," Rhoda said. "It smells in here."

"You can't smoke in the rooms, nobody can," Claire said. "They don't allow it."

"It stinks," Rhoda said. "Farkel. Farkel dreck. Fumpfen in farfel."

"Is she speaking Yiddish?" the boy asked.

Claire said, "I don't think so."

"Soap and wincher. Wincher," Rhoda said, and then she began to laugh to herself because she knew that wasn't right. "Winchik. Pinchik. Itzik." She was giggling to hear how it came out. Then she remembered that she had been trying to tell them something and they weren't listening. "Please!" She shouted. "Soap and wincher!"

"I can't understand you," Claire said. She was crying.

"*Ope—and—wincher*," Rhoda said. "Where's air?"

"I'm right here," Claire said sniffling. "And Suzanne is at college. She'll come later some time."

"Air," Rhoda said. "Air I want."

The boy said, "I'm going to try opening a window."

"Hooray, hooray. A brain," Rhoda said. She heard the boy pushing open the sash. "Better."

Claire was sniveling. "Don't you have a Kleenex?" Rhoda said. "Blow your nose. Really blow it and stop all the sniffing. I could never teach you to blow your nose right."

"All right," Claire said, dabbing at her face.

"It's disgusting," Rhoda said.

"She's right," the boy said. "Don't you have any more tissues?"

"They're all in shreds," Claire said. "I can't help it."

"Winchik," Rhoda said, and laughed till she was breathless. There was a long and terribly difficult discussion with either Claire or some other people, during which she kept trying to correct something they were getting wrong. She knew she was being noisy but she had to be. She cried, "Stop that snot!" over and over. Then she moaned because talking made her so tired, and she went to sleep again.

When she came to, there was no one in the room but a nurse. She wanted to get up, the bed under her felt damp, but she was still strapped in. "This is awful," she said. "I can't get up to do anything or anything."

"They'll probably come and undo it soon," the nurse said. "Feeling better, are we?"

"I was out there, off into a little trance like one of those voodoo people," Rhoda said, when Frank came to visit the next day.

Frank shook his head. "It's the drugs," Rhoda said. "They know what they do by themselves but they don't know what happens when they combine in your system."

"The human body is a mystery," Frank said.

Rhoda still felt stunned and exhausted. She dimly remembered having been abusive to Claire, and she felt a flush of shame. One of the nurses had told her about her attempt to leave the night before, and her determination rather amused her now. Walking around like Ophelia in her nightgown.

"It's a shocker," she said. "Of all things I expected to happen, this was never one of them."

"Who knew?" Frank said. "Who could foresee something like that?"

"Beyond the pale," Rhoda said, and shuddered. "But what do I ever know. The trouble with me is that I'm too much of an optimist."

"But you're feeling better now, that's the main thing," Frank said.

"Up and at 'em. Full of the devil and fit to be tied. Every day in every way I'm getting better and better."

"That's good," Frank said.

"I think it's their fault," Claire said, when Andy brought her by in the evening. "The hospital."

"I must have been pretty far gone. Did you know they had me strapped to the bed?" Rhoda said.

"Of course," Claire said.

"It's a good thing Suzanne wasn't here to see it," Rhoda said.

"She was always the sensitive one. With all her biology experiments, she was still the one who always got queasy at the sight of blood."

"I didn't know that."

"Where is Suzanne?" Rhoda said. "I got one get-well card and one phone call before the operation."

"That was a cute card, with the picture of the old lady in longjohns."

"She could be here. It's not so hard to take the plane from Florida."

Claire said nothing. "It's too much for her," Rhoda said. "She can't take it, it would be too emotional for her."

"Hospitals depress a lot of people," Claire said. "It's because she cares for you, it's too much for her."

"Don't give me that crap," Rhoda said. "If she cared so much, she would be here."

Several days later a resident told Rhoda that her surgeon was coming in to talk to her about the question of further surgery. "They must be kidding," Rhoda said. "Let him talk, I'll laugh." But she was frightened.

After lunch the little colorless doctor who looked like a math teacher showed up at her bedside. He explained to Rhoda that in a week she was going home "on probation" and they were suspending decisions about another operation according to what they saw when she came back for periodic check-ups. Rhoda said, "I'd love it if I never walked into this hospital again."

"They all say that. It must be the cooking here."

Rhoda sighed and closed her eyes. When she opened them, the doctor was making his way out of the room. She started to ask, "So when is Dr. Findlay coming to have an iced-tea orgy with me?" but he was already gone from the room before she had a chance to finish.

It seemed to Rhoda, as she made plans to return to the house, that someone should have fetched Suzanne before this; Florida wasn't on the other side of the world. Rhoda had the feeling they were all slightly afraid of Suzanne—or they had thought it pointless to summon her because they despaired of her cooperating. Rhoda saw that she would have to take matters in hand—her life at home, at least for a while, was going to be severely limited and she would need help. Suzanne would have to be made to understand this.

"We can't find her," Andy said.

"What do you mean?" Rhoda said. She was sitting up in bed, instructing Lainie which things to take home early to wash. "They have to sign out and say where they're going before they can leave the campus. The school has rules."

"Something funny has been going on," Andy said. "First we tried calling, and her roommate kept telling us she was out—she was obviously covering up for her. I finally called the Dean of Students. She tells me Suzanne sent them a note three weeks ago saying she was dropping out and suggesting that they refund any remaining part of the tuition to you. I haven't noticed them rushing to send you any checks, incidentally."

"I knew it," Rhoda said. "I was afraid of this."

"So I started calling the roommate again. I finally got her to admit that Suzanne tried to volunteer for the WACS—that was her first idea, apparently—but they turned her down because her vision wasn't good enough. So now she's living in a rented room in the town and she found a job working in a school for retarded children. But we can't get the address. The roommate keeps saying she doesn't know but of course that's baloney. My feeling is that when the summer is over she'll get fed up and go back to school."

"She only had a month more till the end of the semester," Rhoda said. "What makes you think the school would take her back now? They probably don't want to have any more to do with her. I don't blame them. Why didn't you tell me this before?"

It was very irritating—Andy's businesslike way of reporting this as though it were something commonplace and expected. When she raised her voice at him, he blinked—an old habit from childhood—he still had the same thick, pale lashes (he had been a rosy, pretty child)—and she saw, in his nervousness, that he was only trying to keep from humiliating her with the real shock of the news; he was no more liberal or calm about Suzanne's behavior than she was. Probably more appalled, in fact: her brothers were very loyal to her.

"We sent a registered letter in care of her roommate—the girl signed for it, but Suzanne never bothered to answer it."

"That's stinking," Rhoda said. "I never knew she was so rotten."

"What can I say?" Andy sighed. "When's she ready, you'll hear from her. She has her own way."

"I have to wait for her to be ready, while I'm lying here? That stinks to high heaven." Andy and Lainie were both silent.

When Rhoda arrived home, there was a pile of mail waiting for her, and she went through it at once, thinking there might be some word from Suzanne. From her father (who had not been told about her illness and had been given some hokum story about how she'd gone to the mountains for a vacation) there was a Mother's Day card—gold-stamped forget-me-nots and a rhymed verse inside—which was signed, Love, J. Spansky (POP). There were get-well cards (some, through clerical error, forwarded weeks ago from the hospital) from Bev Davis, Mrs. Leshko, Hinda, Annie, Liz Hofferberg, Dr. Aaronkrantz, Natalie's mother, Addie Shulman, and Leonard's brother. Harriet had sent a copy of *Kon-Tiki* with a note that said, "Read up. This is how we're going to Europe the next time."

Lainie wanted to arrange all the cards on the dresser, the way people did with Christmas cards, but Rhoda scotched the idea. "It's bad enough I have to pretend to use all the toilet water and powder they bring me. Gawd, we've got boxes of the stuff. There must be a general belief that sick people smell."

Sally Finch and Hinda were there to visit that afternoon, bearing (with an almost touching, naïve faith in their originality) their wrapped boxes of Bluegrass and Evening in Paris. Throughout the evening the doorbell continued to ring, bringing visitors, and Rhoda grew vivacious, warming to the company, telling hospital stories, until Lainie had to guide them all out and remind Rhoda that she wasn't up to round-the-clock reveling.

The heavy flow of callers continued through the following days; between Maisie's shifts (she had agreed to "give" a few more days a week) and Claire's tending to her when she came home from school, Rhoda found that she was rarely alone. In fact she was by herself far less than she'd been in years.

"It's like Macy's basement or Grand Central Station here," Hinda said, on a day when no fewer than six people had overlapped their visits and extra chairs had had to be carried up to Rhoda's bedroom from downstairs. "See what a star you are, Rhode."

"She holds court, that's what she does," Annie said. Annie, who had gotten even skinnier and more ropy-necked with age, had developed a cackle.

"Like Miss America with her entourage," Rhoda said, casting her eyes upwards. "Let's lay it on real thick while we're at it."

"Claire's getting to be quite a looker," Evvie Fern said, "speaking of beauty queens."

"You hear that, gorgeous creature?" Rhoda said. Claire was unfolding a bridge chair; it was from the same rickety set Leonard had played pinochle on, and the joints were too loose for it to stand upright easily. "It's since her braces came off," Rhoda said.

"So how old are you now, a sophomore?" Evvie asked. Rhoda hadn't seen Evvie for some time, and she was, as always, garishly dressed and somehow brightly attractive. "My Sary's a junior. Getting the college catalogues already. Mostly she's not a scholar, she's primarily interested in boys."

"That's very normal," Annie said.

"So how is Suzanne liking college these days? What's the word from Florida?" Evvie said.

Hinda said, "I think junior colleges are really a good idea for a certain kind of kids. That way they can transfer after two years if they want to and if they don't they still have something."

"Stop talking like a guidance counselor. I want to hear about Suzanne," Sylvia Shepp said. "What do you hear? Does she have a boyfriend, you think? She was always an unusual sort of kid."

"I haven't heard from her for a while," Rhoda said. "When she needs money, I'll hear."

"Well, she knows you're all right now, she figures you don't need her," Hinda said. "Young people are like that—they think everything gets fixed fast."

"I'd like to give her a good belt where it would do some good," Rhoda said, "only I can't do it through the mail."

"Ha, ha," Annie said, "a belt in the mail."

"If it were my kid, she would be on the phone to me every night," Sylvia said. "I don't know how you stand it. You're making jokes because that's your way, but no one is fooled by your cheerful demeanor. We all know it must be a heartbreak for you, Rhody. Look at your face. I think it's shocking, I really do."

Sybil Jawitz, who had been sitting in the corner saying nothing, got up to leave. She wanted to know if Rhoda could eat spongecake; she would bring some next time, home-made. Some of the others rose to leave with her. "I'm sorry I can't see you out," Rhoda said.

"Don't be silly," Sylvia said.

Why do the mediocre prosper? Rhoda thought, after all the women had left. I should have asked the rabbi at the hospital. Something for the old boy to chew on. What would he have said? *It only looks that way.* He gets away with murder as it is, the rabbi, nobody ever asks him anything serious. The Sylvia Shepps of this world, what do they get? Swimming pools in their backyards, husbands with suntans, children who think everything they do is great.

Rhoda was weeping softly to herself. Sylvia had been wearing a suède suit, a little warm for May, but a wonderful deep green color, beautifully cut. She's a fairly bright woman, really, Rhoda thought. We started off with the same ideas. Why do I have to know things she doesn't know?

Suzanne, in her scornful tirades, always used to make scathing references to Rhoda's friends; "fat and phony" was one of her favorite descriptions, Rhoda remembered. (Sylvia, actually, was very lean and svelte.) "So what is wrong with not looking for trouble and wanting a comfortable life?" Rhoda used to ask her. "Anybody would have it that way if they could."

"That sort of life," Suzanne had said, "is just always a lie."

"Only young people want to think that," Rhoda had said. "They're very big on experience." Her kids always complained that she deprived them of their natural right to suffering; Claire with those soulful-woeful poems she copied out and stuck to the bulletin board in her bedroom.

Rhoda made her way out of the bed and into the hallway. Someone had given her a new bathrobe, a yellow cotton duster with eyelet trim, a little cheap, but pretty in a breezy way. Rhoda sat at the phone table and dialed the number of what had once been Suzanne's room in her dormitory. The room-mate answered and said she had no idea where Suzanne was, but she sometimes called in, did Rhoda want to leave a message? "I know what you're doing," Rhoda said. "I'm not dumb, you know. You can stop talking to me in that sweet voice. You can tell Suzanne that she better get in touch with me if she knows what's good for her."

Three days later the phone rang at ten in the evening. "Hello, it's Suzanne," she said, in that flat voice of hers.

"I can still tell your voice," Rhoda said. "I suppose you've been testing to see how long it takes me to forget and that's why you haven't called."

Suzanne asked politely about Rhoda's operation. (She sounded firm and distant; Rhoda didn't remember her speaking so slowly before.) She was methodical in her questions; she was the first person Rhoda had explained the thing to who knew the difference between the jejunum and the duodenum. "That must have been quite an ordeal," she said. "That's very complex surgery."

"You could have called," Rhoda said. "I suppose you were too busy ruining your life at the time. Why didn't you answer Uncle Andy's letter when he wrote to you?"

"I was going to," Suzanne said.

Rhoda said, "You don't care at all, do you?"

" 'At all' is putting it too strongly," Suzanne said.

There was no pushing her; she was always so careful not to hide the ugly truth with lies. (No wonder she was so tight with her words: if you were afraid to lie and you didn't want to be frank and confidential, you didn't have much choice but to clam up.)

"When are you going back to school? You have a whole quarter to make up—you know what that costs?"

Suzanne sighed. Rhoda said, "When are you coming home? It's time already."

"I have to fill in for the cottage parents on some weekends. It's hard to know when I can get away."

"That's a completely grisly job you have. I don't even like to think about it—a state institution filled with retarded kids."

Suzanne said she was trying to remember whether it was this weekend or the next that she had to sleep in Cottage D while the resident couple took a break. "Stop being ridiculous," Rhoda said. "You know you have to come home some time. You can get someone else to take your shift for you."

Suzanne finally consented to name the next weekend as feasible. "I'll put the money in your account for the ticket. I can't wait," Rhoda said. "I can't wait to see your face around here again." She suddenly felt happy. "Suzanne?" she said.

"What now?"

"I don't want you backing out at the last minute, do you understand?"

"You never change, do you?" Suzanne said, and hung up.

———

Rhoda woke the next morning at the sound of a woman's voice in the doorway. "Maisie?" Rhoda said. "I can't hear you. You always speak so softly." Even with the door open, Maisie would never cross the threshold of the bedroom unless asked. Rhoda was vexed at having to call across to her.

"Are you all right, Mrs. Taber?" Maisie said. "It's ten o'clock already."

"I don't care whether I get up or not," Rhoda said, turning her face to the pillow. "Where's Claire?"

"She went to the park to swim."

"She went to meet Ronnie Saaterfield, I'll bet you anything." Rhoda sat up in bed. "What is going on that she always has to meet him outside the house? Bring me my hairbrush, will you? It's on the dresser."

"Your hair looks very nice since Claire set it for you," Maisie said. "Almost like the beauty parlor."

Rhoda had gotten the idea of asking Claire to do it from watching her roll her own hair on mesh cylinders with little brushes inside; through some act of teenage resolve, she slept every night with the inner bristles jabbing her scalp like a yogi's bed of nails. For whom? For anyone. "She must think I'm deaf, dumb, and blind that I don't know what's going on," Rhoda said, brushing her own hair hard till the waves got too flat. "You can start breakfast, I'll be down in a minute."

Rhoda was in low spirits this morning, and it struck her as particularly depressing that Claire really did not like Ronnie Saaterfield personally. She would go and meet him because he had asked. Claire was not popular with the kids in her class, but from nearby towns she had found a group with kindred enthusiasms—ban-the-bomb slogans, black turtlenecks, old labor-movement songs: that sort of thing—and anyone who knew the key phrases was all right with Claire.

The park was not very large, but it had its thickets and heavy shrubbery; even benches under trees afforded privacy now that the foliage was thick with summer growth. Claire would do whatever she did for the adventure of it; it would be an abstract idea to her, gratifying her more or less insatiable notion of herself rather than in response to a particular affection.

Rhoda was not sure how mature Claire was in her sexual feelings, how "developed" (as they used to say when girls started growing busts) in her desires. She avoided bringing boys to the house, so Rhoda didn't often get to see her with them, but there had been one she'd really liked—not the one who'd come to the hospital (that was Charlie—a decent sort—and she'd gotten rid of him soon enough), and not this Ronnie, but a tall, narrow-shouldered blond named Lonny or Lanny. He used to come watch TV in the sun room with Claire; he was fond of the Three Stooges and he had a theory about why they represented the best of American humor. Claire would bring him elaborate snacks, laughing too hard at the Stooges' moronic stunts, fawning over him; Rhoda overheard him telling her not to kiss him on the neck while Curly was talking.

"I don't want to see you doing that again," Rhoda told her after the boy left. "Begging for crumbs of his affection like that. That's a very unwise way to behave." Claire responded by shouting that Rhoda didn't know anything about anything, it was none of her business, and she'd better shut up about it. "You're gone," Rhoda said. "There's no talking to you. You're like a wild animal."

Rhoda often had dreams about animals invading the house, and it was no wonder. Squirrels had, in fact, gotten into the attic again; remnants of Suzanne's nature projects sat up in her room—a snake's skin on the dresser, and a row of grayish cactus plants Rhoda had sworn to tend. Her father kept writing splotched, shaky letters wanting to come home to visit; and Rhoda's own body had become a thing uncontrollable, the worst sort of irrepressible animal life.

And now Claire: it never did occur to Claire to try to control either herself or other people. She of course saw her sly, acne-faced beaux as great conquests, triumphs to her charm. Rhoda heard Maisie calling now from the kitchen, and she managed, with considerable effort and pain in motion, to put on her bathrobe and descend the stairs. "You've made me an egg," she said. "Why did you do that?"

"I thought you'd like some variety," Maisie said.

"I can't eat them," Rhoda said. "You know that. I don't think I'll ever be able to eat an egg again." She sat at the dinette table and bit into a piece of dry toast with jam on it.

"Oh, no," Maisie said. She was almost whining. "You don't mean never ever."

"It's a very unpleasant subject to me," Rhoda said.

"You're just saying that on a day you feel discouraged. You had that whole operation so you would be better."

"Eggs are not very important to me," Rhoda said.

Claire must have foregone any trysts she'd arranged with Ronnie Saaterfield, because the next Saturday she stayed home and waited with Rhoda for Suzanne's visit. Rhoda sent her out to the garden to bring in marigolds and snapdragons from the beds Suzanne had cultivated the year before. Claire came back through the kitchen door bearing an armload, the torn stems green-smelling and darkened with soil. She had put a blossom in her hair. "That looks very festive," Rhoda said. "Very Hawaiian."

"Welcome to our island," Claire sang, giggling. She was waving her arms around Rhoda's face and doing a mock hula. She put a bachelor's button in Rhoda's hair, just over the ear. Rhoda touched it and left it there, patting her hair-do. She'd gone to the beauty parlor this week (having felt well enough for an outing), and by way of making a great fuss over her return, the girl had set her hair in elaborate rows of small tight waves close to the head. At home afterwards Rhoda had felt a little formal and foolish with her hair done-up while she went around the house in her bathrobe, but today she seemed to herself attractive and well-groomed; she wore a pair of earrings Moe had given her.

She felt more pleased with everything than she had in months. She was looking forward—really—to seeing Suzanne's face again, the round contours and the intelligent squinting gaze. All morning she had the lover-like distraction of dwelling on the removed pleasures of earlier times in their relationship. She remembered Suzanne as a small child, how quiet and good she was, sitting in your lap when you took her places, how intently she concentrated in her playing, and how she and Leonard used to play catch together in the driveway in the evenings.

Rhoda expected her to arrive by lunchtime; of course there was no telling whether she would call from the airport or arrive unannounced. When she was not there by three, Claire ate half of the fried chicken Maisie had made and talked about maybe going to the library. "You might as well go," Rhoda said. "It's bad enough I have to sit and wait like an idiot." Rhoda sat in the sofa before the TV set; she grew drowsy and dozed off; occasionally she thought she heard the door, but when she opened her eyes, the noise was from the program on the screen.

At twilight, the sound of the front door opening woke her, and she sat up with a start; it was Claire, home from the library or the park. "Why don't you turn on some lights?" Claire said. "It's like a tomb in here. A tomb with the seven o'clock news on. Where's Suzanne?"

"Do I know?" Rhoda said, stirring under the blanket she had put over herself.

"Maybe she forgot."

"Forgot, my foot."

"Did you call?"

"She doesn't have a phone in her place, or so she says. There's no way to reach her. I'm not going to talk to that roommate again."

"Maybe she's on her way."

"Her way, my foot." Rhoda went upstairs to bed. Her back hurt from having lain on the sofa, and she was very angry with herself for having felt cheerful at the beginning of the day. The day had been nothing but awful, and she wanted to get away from it by going to sleep for the night. Before she lay down on the pillow, she remembered to wrap a hairnet around her head, tying it at the forehead and slipping a Kleenex around the ears and the nape to protect the set, the way she would have wrapped and stored in the pantry a remainder of food for which she had no appetite any longer.

The next Saturday at around eleven in the morning Rhoda saw a taxi stop in front of the house, and Suzanne got out, carrying a suitcase. She walked up the flagstone path, banging the suitcase against the slate. When Rhoda opened the door, Suzanne, looking pale from the journey, was wiping the sweat from her upper lip, which made it dirtier. "Everything was ready for you last week," Rhoda said.

"I *told* you either next week *or* the week after," Suzanne said, permitting Rhoda to hug her. "Sometimes you only hear what you want to hear."

Rhoda had her sit in the kitchen, and she tried to ask her questions about her "summer" job, while Claire fixed lunch. They all sat down to eat. Rhoda waved a napkin gaily and said "well done" when Suzanne finished all the food on her plate; she thought how familiar and yet strangely thrilling it was to hear Suzanne's voice at the table again, but the pleasure had gone out of it for her, she no longer cared. Claire, who was normally more polite to her mother, was eager to impress Suzanne since she'd been away, and made fun of the way Rhoda had put out butter knives and two kinds of forks for them; Suzanne smiled at her sarcasms. They were getting on well; Rhoda was glad to see it. Claire was in high spirits, squealing with amusement at Suzanne's new faint, wry remarks about how "not very *b-r-i-g-h-t*" the children at the school were.

Rhoda felt warmed watching them—they were so harsh and active—but she wasn't interested, her interest had been broken. What did I bother for? she thought. She went into the living room, leaving them still talking at the table. They were awfully lively—Claire was showing Suzanne how she could touch her forehead to her ankles (she had been taking a modern dance class). There was some sort of scuffling on the floor and comic groaning as Suzanne tried it. Rhoda was sick of them;

she didn't want to be in the same room with them. But the house sounded full and cheerful with them in it. Sometimes it did. An old longing came over her, a longing with a bitterness to it.

The girls came into the living room. "You look tired," Suzanne said.

"She looks better than she usually looks," Claire said.

Rhoda smiled faintly, as though she had a secret. "Ah, flattery," she said, "I'm used to it."

Two weeks later school was out, and Claire went off to work as a junior counselor at camp; Rhoda was left alone in the house. Friends still came to visit, but their ranks had thinned, as she observed to Maisie. Hinda was the most loyal in her visits, stopping by two or three times a week. Mostly Rhoda talked with Maisie. Sometimes she forgot what she had said to Maisie and what she had said to Hinda. She would stop in the midst of recounting a long incident to Hinda and realize she had told her all that before. Or she made references to people Hinda insisted she'd never met or heard of. At first Hinda called this to her attention ("Give me a break, Rhoda. Who's Arnold?"), but in time she simply nodded and smiled; Rhoda accused her of not listening.

"There's something almost bovine about Hinda," she told Maisie. "That means cow-like."

"She's always such a *nice* woman," Maisie said. Maisie's drawl was like a whine at times. She was also getting clumsy—she had knocked a chip off a vase the other day while dusting under it. But she had a good, brusque touch when she plumped the pillows under Rhoda's head—the fawn-colored palms and the dark leathery knuckles always smelled of soap—and she was discreet, almost strict in her propriety. She giggled like a schoolgirl when Rhoda made jokes the least bit colorful.

"I look like someone with a load in his pants, only I'm carrying it up front," Rhoda said, referring to the puffed appearance her pendulous middle gave to even loose-waisted dresses.

Maisie said nothing when Rhoda began returning to her bed in the afternoons, falling asleep on top of the covers with her dress unbuttoned at the belt. But she wouldn't leave in the evenings until Rhoda stirred again. Rhoda would wake to the sound of Maisie's voice calling softly from the doorway, "Are you awake, Mrs. Taber?"

Rhoda was once again burning a low fever in the evenings. She kept this disheartening fact to herself; she had grown more self-contained since Claire was gone. When the infection raged more fiercely, reducing her to shivering sweats so that she writhed in the bedclothes in the night, she took cold baths to lower her temperature, and in the mornings she had Maisie bring washcloths with ice-cubes folded in them to place on her forehead. But when she had trouble keeping her food down, she became alarmed, because she was also losing the mealtime doses of pills which were supposed to be making her get better. She had Maisie call the doctor.

"You've had another attack," he said, running his hands flatly up and down her torso as though frisking her interior for weapons. "Look at you, you're yellow. What are we going to do with you?"

"Bottle me as mustard," Rhoda said.

"You ought to think about going back to the hospital if there's no improvement."

"You think about it," Rhoda said. "I'm already nauseous."

As an interim solution, a practical nurse was hired to stay in the house on weekends and on Maisie's days off. She was a round, gray-haired lady, breathless and somewhat simple. To Rhoda's surprise, Claire arranged to get a ride home from camp to visit with her on her "day off." She arrived late in the evening, shiny with tan and long-legged in her Bermuda shorts. "Sleep now, we'll talk in the morning," Rhoda said. Later she could hear her rummaging in the kitchen.

In the daytime she sat on the side of Rhoda's bed, ate with

her, and talked. She wore her hair in a messy Bohemian topknot, bristling with bobby pins and loose tendrils. She moved her hands when she spoke, a habit Rhoda had tried to break her of because it seemed too Jewish, but when Rhoda let her go on without stopping her, Claire tossed her head and spread her palms, her voice rose and fell as she spoke quickly, and she brought to the sickroom a rush of animation and charm, a quality of life.

Leonard had once said, in the early days, long before the girls were born, that he liked all small children, even the worst of them, because they were such units of pure energy. "Energy is eternal delight," he had said (he was reading Blake and Swedenborg around then). At the time she had dismissed this as the sort of soaring naïveté men were given to. But she leaned back on the pillows now and watched Claire—Rhoda was following the form of her rapid trilling speech more than she was actually listening to her (something about a friend's attempts to teach her tennis: she was making it funny for Rhoda, pantomiming her mistakes with the racket)—and Rhoda sensed what Leonard must have felt in anticipation, a gratitude for the vibrancy quickening the air around her. Rhoda nodded, moving toward it out of her own torpor, and then she leaned back again and let the rippling monologue play out before her.

Claire had a way of pinching her face in mimicry that reminded Rhoda of her mother, who had always thrown herself into telling a story. Claire was "political" now—she had a button on her shoulderbag which said SAY NO TO NUCLEAR TESTS (no, she was not backing Kennedy in the campaign; he was just a liberal)—and she had asked about her grandmother's socialism: had she been a strict Marxist, or a reformist Social Democrat, or a Trotskyite? (Rhoda had no idea.) Claire wanted details, she wanted to find resemblances, traces of a spirit of advancement which, she implied quite strongly, had skipped a generation.

Rhoda did find herself vaguely tickled at the thought of Claire's taking up her grandmother's "causes" (although it was odd, because of all things about her mother these seemed to Rhoda the most outdated). Of course it was not exactly flattering to have Claire think of her as the blank spot in the family lineage. Rhoda reminded Claire that her grandmother— intensely patriotic, like most immigrants—would not have been impressed that Claire no longer spoke the Pledge of Allegiance in school (although she stood when the other kids did). Still, Clair's answer had actually sounded like something from one of Rhoda's mother's pamphlets. "I consider myself," she said, "a citizen of the world."

Rhoda sometimes felt that she personally considered her own self just a citizen of 32 Chestnut Drive, which was of course not a bad place to locate yourself. Claire wanted to get away from all that—she had already made that very clear—she would go to almost any lengths to get out of where she came from; she regarded the trappings of her background as trivial embarrassments, she would have preferred not to be attached to any decade or period, she would have liked to be something abstract and romantic. She was fixing a stray lock of her hair, which was piled in a bun actually quite like the way her grandmother had worn hers, and in this gesture, with her arms raised, by the light of the half-shaded window, Rhoda saw her as she wanted to be seen, a figure outside of time, radiant and transcendent.

She was fixing her hair because it was time to leave. She pulled her purse over her shoulder and leaned over to kiss Rhoda. The girl's cheek was smooth and cool. Rhoda kissed her and said, as she used to when Claire was little, "*Qui est jolie? Claire est jolie.*"

"*Au revoir,*" Claire said, saluting, as she left.

"Well, I certainly know that was your daughter," the nurse said, coming into the room afterwards. "Anybody can see that. She looks just like you, doesn't she?"

"Oh, boy," Rhoda said, "don't let her hear you say that," and she cast her eyes up to the ceiling balefully, which did not hide the fact that she was pleased.

———

Hinda must have sent out word, because the large-scale visits of friends began again. Rhoda could tell by their narrowed glances how God-awful she must look—she was losing weight, and her hair, which had thinned from the fevers, was pulled back with a ribbon (a childish, slightly demeaning style). Her voice was cracked and weak and she was too weary to follow conversations well, so that her remarks (intelligent enough in themselves) sometimes confused her listeners.

She wrote to Claire at camp—"Sounds like you're having a ball. Lotsa luck, with your ten-year-old terrors. Mobs of callers in and out here—I have to give them the bum's rush or it gets to be too much for me. They are trying a new medication on me. Right now I look like death warmed-over, but I hope to be a medical wonder by the time you get home. Your ever-lovin' MOM."

She had trouble focusing her eyes while she wrote. Twice in the next week she dozed off while people were sitting by her bed talking to her. A teacup fell out of her hand because she had to clench too hard to hold it; fortunately the tea was only tepid, but Maisie had to change the sheets, and while Rhoda waited in a chair, she fell asleep again. She was not asleep so much as in a netherworld which was less painful than keeping alert; she could hear her own labored breathing; Maisie was trying to guide her back to the bed, with great difficulty, and it occurred to Rhoda that she wanted to buzz for the nurse.

The next day Rhoda could not get up at all, and when the doctor came, she listened to him suggesting admission to a different, fancier hospital outside the state, and she nodded. Specialists, he was referring her to specialists. A wonderful clinic in Boston, she would have to be flown there; a member of her family would of course accompany her.

"My younger daughter can take me," Rhoda said.

She postponed trying to reach Claire at camp, thinking that by some fortunate coincidence Claire might call home herself (she did sometimes). Rhoda phoned twice the next day—once Claire was on a hike and once she was at the boys' camp—but at dinnertime they fetched her from the mess hall. Claire was breathless when she got to the phone. "The doctors in Boston want to look at me," Rhoda said. "My liver is so gorgeous the big guys want to ogle me."

"I thought you were better," Claire said. "I thought you were through being sick all the time. I think someone else is going to have to take you. I have the lead in a play, and it's this weekend. We're doing *Of Thee I Sing*; it's a musical about running for president."

"So you'll be a movie star some other time."

"It's hard to hear you," Claire said. "Do you have laryngitis? Also there's something else—Lonny Frankel has the part opposite me."

"Which means?"

"You remember him, he used to come to the house and watch TV with me. We were going together again for the first part of the summer but then we broke up again. And if I can't be in the play, people in this camp will think it's because I'm still upset and I can't handle it."

"Really, Claire, this is very petty. Tell Lonny to explain to people if you're so worried. He'll do it if he's decent."

"I can't *do* that." Claire was beginning to cry. "You *never* liked him. You were always mean to him when he came to the house. You're glad we broke up. I came home once already. It's a four-hour trip. Nobody else has to go home all the time. Can't Maisie take you? Why can't Maisie take you?"

"*Maisie*," Rhoda said. "I wouldn't be calling you if I wanted Maisie to take me. What is the matter with you? It's an emergency. Don't make me ask you this way."

"It's all right. I'll do it," Claire said. "I'm coming home, it's all right, I'm coming."

Claire arrived home a day later, and in person she was quite contrite and gentle. She sat at the edge of Rhoda's bed and told stories about camp. She gave a long funny description of how a new girl had to be rehearsed for the part and how she kept muffing her cues and speaking her lines out of turn. "I felt like Pavlova trying to coax an underling into shaping up," Claire said, stretching her arms out dramatically. "I was like an old pro retiring from the boards."

"You're a good girl," Rhoda said, and she saw Claire's eyes suddenly shine with tears. Rhoda's own eyes felt as though they were burning in their sockets, and she closed them for a minute, which gave some relief from a certain pressure of heat behind them, but she wanted to stay awake a while longer while Claire was there. She asked Claire to bring her a drink of water. "Your hands feel so cool," she said, as Claire handed her the cup.

Claire touched Rhoda's forehead with the back of her hand. "I'm laying my soothing hands upon your feverish brow," she said.

"Well, it feels delicious, keep doing it," Rhoda said. "Only in a minute, get me another nightgown. This one's all wet and sweaty."

When Rhoda lifted her arms to slip off the old nightgown, she saw Claire staring at the protrusion from her middle. Rhoda had forgotten how pendulous and distorted it must look; because they had cut through muscle wall in the last operation, the swelling was free to sag like a pouch. "Pretty bad, isn't it?" Rhoda said. Claire's face was truly frightened.

"Here's one sleeve coming over," Claire said. "Don't make a fist, it won't fit. Who designs your nightgowns, Little Bo-Peep's dressmaker?"

"It's the goose, it's Mother Goose I look like," Rhoda said, buttoning the front, "with my scrawny neck and this little ruff. I do itch all the time, maybe I have feather mites."

"Get you some Hartz Mountain powder in the morning," Claire said.

"Cheep, cheep. Thank you," Rhoda said.

"Good night," Claire said. "Sleep tight, don't let the bedbugs bite."

For much of the airplane ride Rhoda slept with her mouth open, so that the rattle of her own uvular breathing broke into her sleep, until she woke, finally, under the gaze of a very scared stewardess who was whispering to Claire, "Is she awake. Can we get her up now?" They slid her into a wheelchair—Claire had been very worried that the wheelchair wouldn't be there to meet them, and Rhoda said, "See, I told you," but it was too tiring to turn her neck to speak and she slumped against the leather padding, letting her head loll, while Claire steered her jerkily through the airport.

She slept through the taxi ride, but at the end she pretended to be interested in the modern façade of the hospital. Very Bauhaus, Leonard would have liked it; she tried to explain this to Claire, but Claire nodded vacantly. It was a perfectly nice hospital, as far as Rhoda could tell. Her room was pink and green and streamlined. The sheets were still the cheap, scratchy kind. "I just want to sleep," Rhoda said, but a nurse made her change out of her street clothes.

"How long have you been this way?" the nurse wanted to know, as the blouse rose away from Rhoda's distorted middle.

"Don't ask me now," Rhoda said. She was tired of everyone's panic at the sight of her. It was bad enough looking that way alone—now she had no decent privacy. She still felt—she always felt—that she was a normal woman with an attractive fate who was trapped in a mistake. She was waiting for the mistake to lift. "Can't they draw the blinds?" she said, closing her eyes.

When she opened them, a different woman stood before her. It was the dietician, who had been sent to interrogate her about food preferences before they would let her sleep.

"She doesn't like Jell-O," Claire was saying. Claire was still there.

"The odor from that woman's mouth, did you notice?" Rhoda said. The dietician was going out the door.

Claire frowned. "She can hear you."

"Of course, it's not her fault, poor thing. Remember how in Italy they used to come right up to you and talk into your face? We got used to that all right, didn't we? The Latin way."

"Well, it's sort of a matter of opinion," Claire said.

"You weren't with me in Italy, were you?" Rhoda said. "I forgot."

When Rhoda woke again, a spoon was being jabbed in front of her face. "Lean forward," the nurse was saying.

"I ate already," Rhoda said. "I ate this morning. Everything hurts me. I'm not hungry." She shook her head to get away from the spoon, and a sticky, bad-smelling liquid splashed onto the sheets.

"It's medicine," the nurse said. "It'll all be over soon."

"What will?" Rhoda said.

"Just open up."

Rhoda's back ached, and the effort to fit her mouth around the spoon seemed more than what should fairly be required of her. "Ugh," she said. "It tastes awful." She let her head sink back on the pillows. She was irritated that they hadn't let her stay asleep. She hated waking up, now that she kept waking up worse.

"I'll get you a drink of water to take the taste away," the nurse said. She was wiping Rhoda's mouth.

When she held out a paper cup with a straw for Rhoda to sip at, Rhoda found that it hurt her to swallow. "This is awful," she said. "How did I get to be so sick?" She felt so disappointed. "No more water," she said, turning her head.

When she woke again, she was in a different room. It was a large, open room, slightly darkened, and near her was a hissing sound, like a fan or water boiling. Andy and Lainie were standing at the foot of her bed. "Why is everyone whispering?" Rhoda said.

"You're in intensive care," Andy said. "You are getting the best possible care in the entire hospital."

She couldn't move one arm, which was attached to the I.V., but she got the other out from under the covers and placed it in its natural spot over the pain in her middle. They had put a white tag on her wrist, and against it her hand was discolored, especially around the knuckles and veins, which looked smudged and bruised. The skin was the color of shadows under the eyes. "How did I get to be so *black*?" she said. She looked at her brother and his wife; she could see they didn't know anything. "Where's Claire?" she said.

"They only let in two at a time," Andy said. "I sent Claire down to go get some lunch. We can't stay too long."

Rhoda asked if there was a mirror anywhere. "In the chest by the bed, sometimes they put one there."

"There isn't one," Lainie said.

"I don't want to look anyway," she said. "I'm all black, aren't I?" She was remembering how her mother had looked in her illness. "I can't hear you. You're mumbling."

"How are you feeling now?" Andy said.

"I feel like I'm never going to get up again."

She could feel their shocked silence. She shouldn't have said this—Andy seemed to be telling her so. She was whining—she had never been so physically miserable before and she wanted them to know it.

She didn't want to answer Andy. She was thinking of the way the kitchen in her house had looked with its original wallpaper; she had a strong memory of the smell of beef cooking; Leonard trying to chew the roast she had overcooked one night, and the both of them laughing. Bright-faced, sturdy, lucky people. And not fools. Cognizant of the small failures between them, the demands of the world they strained against; "realistic" people, willing to bear what was within the realm of the bearable. She had been waiting—with great forbearance, she had always thought—for the form of this life to return.

She had done whatever there was to be done, she had always felt that quite clearly: she had known what to do, that was one thing. Now she saw that she had not known. She had made mistakes, especially with the children, precisely for whose sake she had guarded against the luxury of finding herself in error. It was all a muddle of misery now: she struggled to think what she might have done; she racked her brains and she was dizzy in her fevers, she whimpered.

"I'm so tired and disgusted," she said. She licked her lips, stretched her mouth, and winced with her whole face—it was a terrible flinching, a grimace of disgust at her own anguish.

"It's not like you to be discouraged," Andy said. She sighed and closed her eyes so that she wouldn't have to talk to them.

Andy was offering her some cracked ice; she moved her mouth away from him. She had to work to shift her head. She felt so heavy all the time now. Falling into naps, she sometimes felt herself sinking into the soft mattress and dreamed of being stifled in its creviced curves under the mound of sheets. She had become something denser, like a mineral, pulled down.

Like a stone: she had awakened in the night and known what it was—it was the weight of her own stubbornness, her own unchanging shape. Resistant, almost crystalline in its fixity—events had worn her but they hadn't altered her, so that she had had the hardest of lives, boring her way obdurately through circumstance.

She kept dreaming about food. Foods she hadn't been able to eat in years: chocolate truffles—of all things—she and Hinda had once finished a box between them. Totally heedless, they couldn't have been more than fifteen at the time. She could remember very clearly biting into the centers and the lines your teeth made in them. Angelic foods. In Paris she and Ellie had bought for dessert a cheese that was like churned whipped cream. The craving was like a mystery in her sleep. Lying there, she had a sad, pleasant longing for these things, and the thought of them calmed her.

When they came back later in the day, she had begun to pick at herself. With her eyes closed, she was plucking at her nightgown and at the blanket. She was squinting fretfully, pursing her lips and making smacking noises, as though she were alone, but she was aware that they were by her bedside, and she spoke as Claire leaned toward her. "What did you have to eat for lunch?" she said hoarsely.

"A ham sandwich," Claire said.

"That's not kosher," Rhoda whispered.

"Always with the jokes," Andy said. "Keep it up. I'm going out for a few minutes now so someone else can come in. You have a surprise visitor waiting out here."

Rhoda opened her eyes and she saw, making his way toward her with his slow, shuffling gait, her father. How had they gotten him here on the plane? She raised her hand slightly to wave to him. By the time he reached her she had closed her eyes again but she could hear his labored wheezing mingling with the murmurous hissing of the machines in the room, as he brought his bristled face against hers to kiss her. His kiss felt dry, which startled her; she remembered his mouth as always being unpleasantly wet.

"Rest is what you need," he was saying. "It's good you're resting."

Rhoda said, "I am not"—as soon as she said it, it struck her that obviously she was resting, what else was she doing lying flat on her back?—and she started to laugh.

"Look, she's laughing," her father said to Claire.

"Are you cold?" Claire said. "You're shaking. I'm putting the blanket over you." Claire was at the side of the bed; in a deft motion she must have copied from the nurses she was unfolding the blanket while reaching over Rhoda so that it furled out in its own breeze and settled around her. Rhoda lay under the waffle-like fabric, designed to trap warmth in its empty thermal pockets. She did not feel warm from it, but she felt lighter: a sudden airy lightness in her own body.

She shook then—violently—her shoulders rose in a suddenly strong, involuntary fit, trying to shake off, once and for all, all the long series of conditions she couldn't stand and wouldn't stand for. The great buckling of her body subsided, but she continued shivering, in a sort of outrage. Her fingers pulled at the neck of her nightgown—it wasn't her own ruffled flannel, it was the laundered muslin of the hospital—and she was fretful at not having her own things around her, until she remembered that the hospital gown would, by her use, take on her own scent, and from her dampness get some vaporous essence of her in its fibers, as things did.

It made her quite happy to think of her personality rubbing off into the objects around her. Her own unremitting force of character—her one unmistakable attribute—seemed splendid to her then. Her body shook once more, sank down again, and then she saw a rectangle of glistening dark. She was seeing her kitchen again, the window over the dinette table. It was night outside and against the pane of glass she could see both the outlines of bushes in the backyard and the reflections of the yellow light-fixture overhead and of people eating. Inside it was very bright. They were eating with the cutlery they used to have, cheap stainless with red plastic handles, and when they lifted it, the strong light came through the translucent handles and left thin rosy shadows on their palms, as though the living heat of their hands had changed the material to something purer and barely visible.

Claire was talking to her father, or to Andy, who seemed to be in the room now. Rhoda was breathing with a heavy rattle. "I'm noisy," she said. She couldn't hear what they were saying, she was making too much noise. Under their voices she thought she heard Leonard—he always insisted on speaking so softly—his tones were so level and even that when her breathing rose and crackled she drowned him out entirely. "Stop mumbling," she said. There was a blur of sound inside her own head—at the end of each breath she could almost hear what she wanted to hear—she tried to hold down the hissing in her throat in an effort to still the wrong noises, but the trailing murmur seemed attached to the whistling rush of air and faded when it faded, until she could no longer hear even that.